IN THE HEAT OF PASSION

"If you don't need me, why the pout?" he asked.

Her gaze was full of daggers. "I supposed it would be much more convenient should you kill Glayer Felsteppe for me."

"Like it was convenient for you to marry him after your father died?"

"Rather more like it was convenient for you to run away to the Holy Land rather than be humiliated by Patrice's infidelity."

Constantine raised his hand and Dori stepped toward him. "It's painful, isn't it? The truth? Especially when you're not using it to self-deprecate like some . . . some *martyr*."

"Shut up, Theodora," he warned.

"*You left* your family, your home; *you left* the friends who helped save your life. All to serve your own agenda. When all I ever wanted was to *keep what I had*."

"Shut up," he repeated.

"And now I'm to wait on you as well, until it's absolutely convenient for you to *keep your word*!"

Constantine thought that he only kissed her to ensure her silence, but in that moment after he dropped his mouth to hers, the only thing he could think of was tasting those lips that had condemned him so thoroughly . . .

Books by Heather Grothaus

THE WARRIOR

THE CHAMPION

THE HIGHLANDER

TAMING THE BEAST

NEVER KISS A STRANGER

NEVER SEDUCE A SCOUNDREL

NEVER LOVE A LORD

VALENTINE

ADRIAN

ROMAN

CONSTANTINE

HIGHLAND BEAST
(with Hannah Howell and Victoria Dahl)

Published by Kensington Publishing Corporation

Constantine

Heather Grothaus

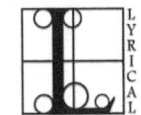

LYRICAL PRESS
Kensington Publishing Corp.
www.kensingtonbooks.com

LYRICAL PRESS BOOKS are published by

Kensington Publishing Corp.
119 West 40th Street
New York, NY 10018

All Kensington titles, imprints, and distributed lines are available at special quantity discounts for bulk purchases for sales promotion, premiums, fund-raising, educational, or institutional use.

Special book excerpts or customized printings can also be created to fit specific needs. For details, write or phone the office of the Kensington Sales Manager: Kensington Publishing Corp., 119 West 40th Street, New York, NY 10018. Attn. Sales Department. Phone: 1-800-221-2647.

Lyrical Press and Lyrical Press logo Reg. U.S. Pat. & TM Off.

First Electronic Edition: February 2017
eISBN-13: 978-1-60183-402-7
eISBN-10: 1-60183-402-0

First Print Edition: February 2017
ISBN-13: 978-1-60183-403-4
ISBN-10: 1-60183-403-9

Printed in the United States of America

For EKG

Prologue

July 1179
Chastellet

Glayer Felsteppe swaggered into the king's antechamber, his heeled boots—so vain and out of place here in this land of sand—clicking conspicuously on the red floor tiles striped black with cool shadows. None of the Templar soldiers in retreat from the heat of the day paid the thin man's entrance any heed, and Constantine kept to his own vantage point in the shadows behind where the king sat. He had waited a long time for this moment.

Felsteppe came to a stop before Baldwin and sank to one knee, spreading his arms and dropping his head of flaming hair in a grandiose display. "You called for me, my liege?"

The king flicked his bandaged hand, releasing the man from his show of homage, but Felsteppe was too entrenched in his performance to notice. "Lord Felsteppe, it has been alleged that you have once again taken to fraternizing with Saladin's envoys," Baldwin said, his tone sounding more tired than irritated. "More than fraternizing."

Felsteppe's head snapped up and he rose, his gaze going to the darker area behind Baldwin's chair as if by instinct.

Like a cockroach that senses the raised boot above it and skitters away before it can be stomped, Constantine thought as he emerged from the gloom. He left the evidence of the charges he had leveled still hidden on the table behind him. There would be no skittering this time.

When Felsteppe saw Constantine, his already beady eyes narrowed further before they looked back to the king of Jerusalem. "My liege, General Gerard constantly seeks to besmirch my good name with his outrageous claims. The man is clearly obsessed with me."

Constantine said nothing, refusing to be baited.

The king's sparse eyebrows rose. "Do you then deny that you were fraternizing with the Saracen legates?"

"I spoke with them, certainly," Felsteppe scoffed, drawing his coiffed head back as if shocked at the absurdity of the question. "It was my duty to chaperone the men of lesser rank while you met with Saladin's general. Unlike some"—here Felsteppe leveled a haughty look at Constantine—"I feel it would not further our cause to be overly combative. After all, Saladin sent his men seeking peace."

"He's seeking an end to Chastellet!" Baldwin barked and slapped his hand on the arm of his chair, causing many of the soldiers lounging about the quiet, shadowed room to glance toward the king. Adrian Hailsworth, architect of Chastellet and the only man Constantine could reliably call his friend, did not look up, absorbed as he typically was in the sheets of plans spread out before him at his table in a far corner of the room.

Baldwin ignored the looks of the soldiers. "Saladin knows that while our mighty fortress stands, there is no chance of him seizing control over the crossing at Jacob's Ford. It's imperative we remain, no matter the cost to us, and no matter how many dinars he offers in bribes."

"Your communications with the Saracens were far from mere courtesy," Constantine added, unwilling to let Felsteppe attempt to turn the charges against him into a pointless political debate. "You're a liar. And a traitor."

"General," Baldwin warned in a low voice, turning his head only slightly toward Constantine. "The man shall have his say."

"A traitor as well now, am I?" Felsteppe sneered. "And what fantasy, pray tell, have you concocted in your mind this time that I am to be held liable for?"

"Selling Templar weaponry to the Saracens. In the very bailey belonging to the men it was crafted to defend."

At these allegations, the soldiers who had before only glanced in the direction of the king now turned toward the trio of men fully, prompting many of the rest to do the same. The quiet murmurs of conversation ceased, and an air of expectation swelled against the stone walls.

Felsteppe's laughter cut through the silence and seemed to echo. His smile was wide as he threw up his hands. "That's preposterous."

Baldwin spoke. "You deny General Gerard's accusation?"

"Of *course* I deny it!" Felsteppe scoffed. Constantine turned back to the table behind him while Felsteppe continued. "Surely you must see that the general's claims become more and more outrageous? I would never—"

His words were cut off as Constantine turned, his arms laden, and tossed the evidence to the floor between Baldwin and Felsteppe. If any in the room hadn't been paying attention before, the echoing crash and clatter of weaponry ensured that all eyes were on the three men at the head of the tense room.

Even Adrian looked up from his plans.

Felsteppe stared at Constantine for a moment, but then blinked and shrugged. "Am I supposed to be moved by this rather noisy display?"

"The weapons you sold the Saracens," Constantine clarified through gritted teeth.

Again Felsteppe laughed. "Oh, really? Then why are they in *your* possession rather than the Saracens I supposedly sold them to?" He rolled his eyes.

"I bought them all back," Constantine said. "From General Abdal himself."

Felsteppe looked to the king with an air of exasperation. "Ridiculous, my liege. It is Gerard's word against mine. Perhaps a Saracen's, as well, if even his scheme went so far."

Baldwin was staring at Felsteppe, but when he spoke, his words were directed at Constantine.

"How much did Abdal claim he paid?"

"Three hundred dinars, my liege," Constantine said.

"That is a paltry amount for such steel." Baldwin looked away for a moment, as if collecting his thoughts. "Judd," he called out, and his summons was answered at once by a lanky soldier who levered himself aright from a woven mat beneath a far window, shuttered against the baking heat.

Judd bowed before the king. "My liege."

"Take possession of Lord Felsteppe's purse, there on his belt," Baldwin commanded. "Empty it before us all, and let it be counted and the nature of the contents noted."

Constantine's jaw clenched as he saw the panic enter Felsteppe's eyes and the man's hand twitch toward the bulging leather packet hanging upon his side.

Judd turned to Felsteppe, his palm out. "If you please."

Now Felsteppe's hand did cover the purse, as if trying to protect it. He looked up at Baldwin. "My liege, I am greatly disappointed that you would think I—"

Baldwin interrupted. "Take it off, Lord Felsteppe. Or I shall have Judd do it for you."

Felsteppe's bony throat convulsed. He hesitated only a moment more before loosening the purse strap from his belt, his voice trembling noticeably when next he spoke.

"I cannot see how the contents of my purse could possibly incriminate me. It is common knowledge that all men in this country must trade in many currencies. I-I—" He struggled with the knot for a moment, and Constantine thought his fingers must be shaking. He at last worked the strap free and handed the weighty purse to Judd before looking once more to Baldwin, his pointed chin lifted. "I have done nothing wrong."

Judd turned slightly and dropped to one knee, so that his actions could be seen by both Felsteppe and the king. As he opened the purse, a handful of Templar soldiers rose and drew nearer, not daring to encroach on the scene outright but clearly interested in the outcome of Judd's accounting.

The tinkling wash of coins on the tile floor was like sudden rain on a roof, and even before Judd began to sort the coins near the pile of weaponry, Constantine knew. He knew from the raises and shadows of the coin faces; the color of the metal; the number of stacks equal in height.

"Three hundred dinars, my liege," Judd said without emotion. "Two pieces of Chastellet gold; one penny."

The men gathered outside the circle raised their voices in sudden outrage, and Felsteppe seemed to shrink away from the crowd, turning to face them, backing closer to the wall.

"It's not as you think!" he cried. He looked to Baldwin, his eyes wild. "My liege, I—"

Baldwin stood. "Clear the chamber!" he shouted, and then looked around at the angry group of soldiers. "*Clear the chamber!*" The king waited, his chest visibly rising and falling as the Templars streamed through the far door, leaving Felsteppe and Constantine—and the once more oblivious Adrian Hailsworth—alone with Baldwin.

"It's not as you think," Felsteppe repeated, then licked his lips, advancing a step toward Baldwin. "These pieces are clearly broken, useless; surely Gerard retrieved them from a refuse heap. I-I—"

"The pieces *were* discarded. For *repair*," Constantine growled. "Regardless of any excuse you might concoct for your thievery, you cannot deny the coin in your purse."

"Constantine," the king warned. He looked back to the accused man. "You understand that every allegation General Gerard has levied against you now has many times more weight."

"He is a danger to Chastellet, my liege," Constantine insisted, the words out of his mouth before he could stop himself.

Baldwin looked between the two men with a sigh. "I was to leave for Tiberias on the morrow and I'll be damned if the pair of you will cause me to shirk my duties." His eyes pinned Felsteppe. "*You* were to be left in charge of the hold during my absence, but it could mean danger to the fortress or yourself should I leave you unattended—with or without my authority. You shall accompany me to Tiberias."

Felsteppe's jaw flexed, his sneer just below the surface of his skin. "As you wish, of course. My liege."

Then Baldwin turned to Constantine. "Which means that *you*, General Gerard, must continue to attend your duties at Chastellet until my return."

No; no, no, no.

"Bal—*my liege*, surely you have forgotten that I was to depart for my home within the fortnight. Am I to be punished for bringing the actions of a thief and a traitor to light?"

"I have not forgotten. Nor do I mean to punish you, Constantine," Baldwin said, and although he had twice used Constantine's given name, the king's tone was still stern. "But what did you think would happen if your accusations were found true? Would you now leave Chastellet in his care?"

Felsteppe's face reddened further, but he was wise enough not to comment. It was Constantine who felt the fool now.

"What of Hailsworth?" Constantine said, pointing toward the man still hunched over his plans in the corner. "He's been in residence as long as I. And he's titled. Surely he could—"

"No." Adrian Hailsworth did not so much as look up as he called out. "Not a soldier. Don't care about the lot of you."

When Constantine looked back at Baldwin, the king had one eyebrow raised. "It's a short journey. You will be free of my tyranny forever upon my return."

It was not in Constantine's nature to beg, but he could not help expressing the yearning pain in his heart. "I want to go home, Baldwin. My son was only four when I last saw him—little more than a baby; Christian's nearly seven now. He needs me. Have I not served you faithfully for two years?"

"You have, and I am grateful. But you'll stay until my return or risk besmirching an otherwise exceptional career." Baldwin paused and then pressed, "Your answer, General?"

Constantine's anger simmered. "As you wish, my liege."

Baldwin turned to Felsteppe. "I've not passed judgment on you before the men as of yet and so you will probably be safe. All the same, it is best if you do not encroach on the soldiers' common areas this eventide." He glanced at the piles of coin and weaponry still on the floor. "You may, however, see the return of your purse and your *penny*."

The king turned and, as he limped toward the doors that led to his private chambers, called out, "And do pick up the mess on the floor before you're off." He slung the door closed with a crash behind him.

Constantine looked back at Glayer Felsteppe, whose reddened, watery eyes and curled lip gave evidence to his rage.

"You son of a bitch," Felsteppe snarled. "You just couldn't stomach the idea of me being in charge of Chastellet, could you?"

"I couldn't care less who Baldwin retains to fill my appointment after I am gone," Constantine replied, turning his back on the loathsome man to walk to the large cask mounted on its side against the wall. He watched the liquid flow into his cup and wished it was wine. "But while I am responsible for the welfare of this hold, I will report anything I feel the king needs be aware of. Especially if it is of a traitorous nature."

"You're only trying to further your rank," Felsteppe continued behind him as Constantine raised his cup to his lips and let the cool water flood his mouth. "Lazy, entitled bastard! You deserve not even the tiniest fraction of the power you claim at Chastellet."

Constantine swallowed and then sighed, his eyes trained on the smooth stone above the cask. He called to mind the verdant landscape stretching out around Benningsgate, the wet greenness of the very air in her forests. He imagined sitting in his own hall of an even, drinking from his own casks and speaking of things such as crops and flocks and servants. Hearing the gossip about the town. He thought of the moment—delayed now, true, but only by weeks—he would approach Benningsgate and see the blond little boy running for him, leaping into Constantine's arms. . . .

He felt slightly calmer. "Any power I have here has come hand in hand with my duties, and both were given to me after I proved myself worthy."

Felsteppe sputtered. "Did you earn your title? Benningsgate Castle? Did you work your way into your earldom? Your wife's bed? I've heard the latter at least can be done with little effort."

Constantine ran his tongue along his teeth and closed his eyes for a moment before turning to face the man, who seemed so distraught that Constantine wouldn't have been surprised to see him collapse to the floor to pound his fists and boots against the tile.

"You can't keep blaming others for your failures, Felsteppe. Eventually, you will have to claim responsibility for your life and the choices you make."

"Choices?" Felsteppe said on a false laugh. "You mean like the choice Baldwin has made? You know it's only a matter of time before Saladin orders the attack on Chastellet now that our *king* has turned him away yet again. The fortress isn't even properly completed!"

"It's almost done," Adrian Hailsworth muttered from his corner, his head still down. "Only the glacis to complete. Strong enough now."

"The foundation is exposed!" Felsteppe cried out to the architect. When Adrian failed to respond, Felsteppe faced Constantine once more. "You're all fools! Baldwin has guaranteed your deaths."

Constantine's eyes narrowed. "It is our duty to defend this stronghold and the river crossing below. That's what you swore to do when you accepted your charge."

"I came here to make my fortune, same as all the others."

"Perhaps you should have sought assignment in one of the ports, then. Promise of riches is not why men come to Chastellet."

Felsteppe stared at Constantine and then sniffed a half laugh, his thin lips quirking in some semblance of a grin. "Oh, yes. That's not why *you're* here, is it, Gerard?"

Constantine's back stiffened, but he kept his expression neutral as he gestured to the pile of armaments still littering the floor. "Do as the king commands and retreat to your cell before the sun sets. Some may lie in wait for you." He turned and started to cross the floor, heading toward the double doors and his own chamber in order to grieve the delay of his departure.

Perhaps many men's futures—indeed, the future of the world—would have been quite different had Glayer Felsteppe held his tongue and allowed Constantine to leave without further comment.

But, alas.

"*You're here* because your wife is a very rich whore with a constant itch and everyone doubts the son she bore is yours!"

Constantine halted, still facing the door.

Baiting you again. That's all.

He started forward once more, and this time he saw that Adrian had raised his head and was now watching Constantine with a wary expression.

"That's right—I know. *Everyone* knows," Felsteppe taunted. "Who can predict how many children you'll have to your name upon your return? Perhaps even now, little Christian is on some other man's lap, sitting in your chair at supper, calling him papa."

Constantine stopped again, his feet sticking so firmly that he swayed in his stance.

"You'll never outstay *that* rumor, Gerard," Felsteppe chuckled. "It will live with you—and the boy—for the rest of your lives. Christian will never *really* know if you're his father or not. Rather sad, isn't it? I feel sorry for the lad, truly. Whore for a mother and a coward—"

Felsteppe continued to talk as Constantine turned and stalked back toward him, but he had no idea what the man said; the blood was roaring in his ears so loudly that it drowned out all other sound. Felsteppe, however, must have realized he had finally hit his mark for now he drew his sword and sank into a defensive posture with a satisfied smirk.

Constantine, too, swept his weapon from its sheath as he continued to rush forward. When he was nearly close enough to strike, Felsteppe changed tactics and charged. But Constantine was ready, and in two swings, Felsteppe's weapon went sliding and clanging across the floor. Constantine was upon him, then, and rammed the butt of his hilt into Felsteppe's nose once, twice, sending blood spraying from the man's face like a fountain.

Felsteppe staggered back with a cry, his hands covering his dripping face while Constantine sheathed his weapon—if he didn't, he was certain he would kill the man outright. But even though he was no longer readily armed, he wasn't yet finished with Glayer Felsteppe.

And neither was Felsteppe finished. Once he saw the weapon was sent home, he charged at Constantine with his bloody fists clenched, a scream of rage coming from his sticky mouth. Constantine met his fury with his own, ducking Felsteppe's swing and coming up with a fist under his chin and then two swift blows to the man's abdomen. When the redhead doubled over, Constantine grabbed him by the back of his leather hauberk and slung him around in an arc.

Felsteppe flew through the air toward Adrian Hailsworth's corner table and landed across the end of it, sliding through the piles of parchment as his hands scrabbled for purchase. Adrian pushed his chair back with a screech and stood.

Constantine stomped after Felsteppe, seizing him and flipping him over on his back, a shower of crumpled ivory pages raining down around them. Felsteppe swung with a weak yell, his fist clenched around a wad of parchment, and Constantine took the blow on his chin. He hardly felt it, though, as he drew back and hit Felsteppe in his already battered face, his knuckles making sick, splashing sounds by the third blow.

Before the sixth could land, Adrian hooked his arm around Constantine's and pulled him backward with a mighty heave, allowing Glayer Felsteppe to slide to the floor in a crumpled, gasping heap.

"Killing him won't make Baldwin change his mind," Adrian said near his ear as he pushed between Constantine and the bleeding, wheezing man on the floor. "You've made your point."

As much as Constantine appreciated the friend he had found in the brusque, scholarly Hailsworth, he was not quite satisfied that he had indeed made his point. He swept Adrian aside and after two strides sank to one knee over Felsteppe, seizing the front of his sodden tunic and pulling the limp rag of the man close to his face.

"Dare not speak my son's name again. Verily, never be in my sight after this day, Glayer Felsteppe," Constantine said as calmly as his still seething rage would allow. "Whether Baldwin allows your return from Tiberias or nay. Perhaps I could not prove them before today, but I have not forgotten—nor will I—your many, many misdeeds at Chastellet. The rapes of the merchants' slaves; the thefts; the traitorous discords with which you sought to infect the men. You are *scum*, and you deserved to be wiped from the land. The next time I see you, I *will* kill you."

"You think everyone is afraid of you, Gerard," Felsteppe rasped, bloody spittle flying from his split lips. "I'm not. You're not *holy*; you're not *superior*. You're a pampered house cat who's been made to believe he's above covering over his own shit."

"I do believe this particular house cat has shown you his claws," Hailsworth muttered as he returned to his chair, his eyes for naught but his precious scrolls as he straightened his exploded stacks.

"Fuck you, scribe," Felsteppe snapped, and then he glared back into Constantine's face. "You'll pay for what you've done today. Today and every day since you came here and tried to ruin me." Felsteppe pushed at Constantine, and he stepped back and allowed the beaten man to stagger to his feet at last.

Felsteppe pointed a bony, stained, trembling finger toward Constantine, his other hand still curled around the ruined parchment he'd dragged from the tabletop. "I will see everything you love burn. Everything."

"You couldn't come within a score of miles of anything I love, Felsteppe. You're fortunate the king didn't dismiss you outright. I believe he still might. Then where will you go? Back to Land's End to herd sheep?" It was a low blow, but his fury seemed to let the words flow like the water from yonder cask.

Felsteppe's face matched his bright hair, between the blood in and on his cheeks. "Everything you love," he repeated. "No matter what I must do."

"Get from my sight," Constantine demanded and then turned away from the man before he was tempted to fall upon him again.

He heard the door open, and Adrian Hailsworth called out in a sardonic tone, "Oh, no, please—do keep those parchments. They weren't quite right and rather covered in your blood any matter."

The door slammed shut.

"Maggot," Adrian muttered.

The air in the room seemed to tingle with the altercation that hadn't fully absolved Constantine of his anger. And when his gaze fell upon the pile of contraband Felsteppe had failed to collect and return, as commanded by the king, Constantine sighed. Even though his muscles still burned and his breaths left a metallic scent in his nostrils, he crossed the floor and began gathering the broken swords, the cracked shields, the worn pads himself, his hands still wet with Glayer Felsteppe's blood.

It was his duty, after all.

Glayer Felsteppe staggered through the narrow, dark interior corridors of Chastellet, his humiliation unrelieved by the fact that he passed no one. It mattered not—by now, Glayer knew every warrior monk, every base laborer, even the meanest slave had been appraised of the goings-on in Baldwin's antechamber. No one at Chastellet would ever let him forget what had happened. Perhaps it was best that he left.

He swiped at his dripping face with the wad of soft paper in his hand, then paused near a tall, wide tapestry to press a finger to one nostril and blow the contents of the other into the seam of floor and wall. His breath hitched in his chest as he coughed and spat; he thought perhaps at least one of his ribs was cracked. He stood there a moment, looking at the tapestry while he tried to regulate his searing breaths. The symbols of the Templars seemed to mock him as they hid among the trees and rivers woven into a rich, fantastical battle landscape: a dragon flying from a castle perched on a craggy peak; giants treading through a surf littered with wreckage; a figure with flowing red hair hovering above it all, seeming to stare down the corridor in the direction from which Glayer had just come.

Baldwin would never elevate Glayer to a senior officer of any kind now. Bastard leper, prancing about as if he were fit to command battalions when he was barely out of nappies.

Glayer reached up suddenly, flinching at the stabbing pain in his side as he grasped the heavy tapestry and wrenched it from the wall. He spat again upon it, then strode across it and down the corridor, his pace quickening as his mind urged him on.

Bastard Gerard, behaving as though he owned the world, with his title and his estate and his heir. His pious standards and pharisaical morals.

Glayer had been sincere in his desire to destroy Constantine Gerard, but in truth, there was nothing for him to go back to if he was turned away from the Holy Land. He'd come here to make a name for himself—to earn lands, riches, perhaps even a fief of his own. He would not become Baldwin's servant in Tiberias, traded to some Frankish baron as if he were little more than a page. To be laughed at here, then forced back to his mother's poor cottage on the westernmost point of England with nothing to show for his years away than a nose more crooked than when he'd left.

His vision blurred as he came into the blinding light of the bailey, and the shimmers of heat floated up from the baked earth. Glayer threw up a forearm and ducked his head as he struck out into the center of the space, to shield his eyes from the sun and from the sight of whomever might be watching him, laughing at him. He walked quickly.

He hated Gerard. And Baldwin. And his mother. Hated this damned oven of a fortress; hated the men it sheltered. He glanced up and saw the light-colored robes of Saracens still gathered near the wide gates, obviously readying to depart. In their midst was General Abdal himself, the soldiers around him protecting both the messenger and the coin Felsteppe knew he still carried. An ambitious man, Abdal, who knew how to wield the power he had been given in this land of enemies and thieves.

Unlike weak, sick, stupid Baldwin. Glayer wondered if anyone else but he knew how many thousands of dinars Saladin had offered in exchange for the razing of this godforsaken place. For Christ's sake, the foundation wasn't even . . .

Felsteppe stopped suddenly in the blinding, hot bailey, his heart pounding, and looked down at the crumpled rendering of Chastellet's most private parts. His skin went icy, clammy, as he raised his head, and the tall General Abdal turned toward him as if Felsteppe had called his name. The two men stared at each other for a long moment.

And Glayer Felsteppe realized his time had come at last.

Chapter 1

March 1182
England

Dori came awake with a gasp and then gave a weak cry as the side of her head banged into a hard surface. Her neck was too weak to hold herself erect in time to avoid the next rocking blow and she tried to throw out her hands in the churning darkness as her lungs struggled to draw sufficient breath. Oh, God, she must be in hell—a cold, damp, black hell that was trying to shake her bones from her body and deafen her with its roar.

She spun her fear into strength and lunged forward, praying she wouldn't launch herself into an eternal descent. "Help me," she croaked, her arms flailing in the darkness.

But someone caught her. "There now," a stern voice cautioned, taking firm grasp of her left forearm and right shoulder, pushing her backward once more but so that she sat aright. "You must come to your senses, Lady Theodora. Light the lamp, boy; perhaps if she can see, she will not be in such a fright."

Dori's lips felt half numb, blubbery, so that the words she struggled to speak were little more than humming mumbles. Panic wrapped around her heart like an icy fist. Where was she? Why was she so frightened of this dark place? And why did she feel as though she had been dunked in the frigid spring river running past Thurston Hold? Cold, so cold . . .

A searing, yellow-white flash blinded her; she hadn't known for certain her eyes had been open. Now she squeezed them shut and tried to turn her head away from the explosion of brightness, rewarding herself with another blow to the side of her face as the seat beneath her lurched and sent her into what was possibly a wooden panel.

Then the roaring sound filtered through her panic: wheels on a road. The rocking, jostling—she must be in a carriage. It was night. But why was she wet? And what was that dreadful smell, rich and fecund, like—

Blood. She was smelling her own blood.

And it was in that moment she remembered: her baby. They had stolen her baby. She'd heard the weak cry through the haze of her stupor and then it had gone. They must have poisoned her again to keep her docile. And now she was in a carriage traveling in the night to . . . where?

But she was not alone, and the voice of her chaperon was all too familiar. Dori opened her eyes the tiniest crack, tears flooding and blurring her vision as she struggled to confirm the identity of the person across the short space from her. The damned priest, Simon, whose presence had turned what should have been the happiest moments of her life—her wedding, the birth of her child—into nightmares, was in the opposite seat, along with a young boy who was carefully hanging the lamp on a hook next to the carriage door. The servant lad showed no interest in her at all as he sat back against the seat, his face turned toward the curtained window.

"How do you fare, my lady?" Simon asked matter-of-factly, as if he was doing nothing more out of the ordinary than greeting her in the morning.

Dori tried to blink away the nonsensical water from her eyes—she wasn't crying, yet the tears continued to flow. "Where is my baby?" she croaked, feeling as if her throat was lined with blades and tasting the film of old vomit in her mouth. She felt a prickling deep behind her ears.

The priest swallowed. "He is safe. He is with your husband."

He—a boy. She'd borne a son.

"Then he is not safe. Take me to him. He needs me. He needs to feed."

"His needs will be attended to."

The rocking carriage caused the bile to rise in her throat and she strangled for a moment, fighting the urge to vomit. "I'm ill," she managed to choke out in warning.

Father Simon rapped on the ceiling of the carriage with his walking stick, the sharp sound sending slivers into Dori's brain. But the conveyance lurched obediently to a halt and the priest was seizing her arms, hauling her through the door the boy held open for them.

Theodora vomited on the side of the road, feeling that her insides were being expelled from her as her skirts were drenched with more blood and Simon gripped her arms from behind.

"The potion will wear off soon," he said from somewhere over her head. "Your bleeding will hopefully slow." The priest pulled her aright and then reached into his cassock as if searching for something. "You will likely recover, but you must try to be as still as you can manage for the next several hours. It will be a challenge, considering—"

Theodora didn't wait to see what he would have retrieved, but reached up with clawlike hands to grab at Father Simon's narrow face. "What have you done with my baby?"

"You must go away now," he insisted calmly, ignoring her question as he pushed her weak fingers away. "Far away. This carriage shall take you to a ship."

"No! Not without my baby!" Dori sobbed now, each breath searing her throat like a torch as she struggled to free herself from the priest's grasp that both restrained and supported her. "He's mine and you know it! They've stolen him! *You* stole him!"

"Listen to me!" Simon gave her a sudden shake and, for the first time since she had known the priest, she heard a thread of fear in his normally emotionless voice. "I have committed a great sin. One that I cannot undo. There is no hope for me beyond God's mercy."

"You are the devil," Theodora accused.

"He told me to kill you," the priest said, shaking her again as if desperate that she should understand him. "That I will not do. And I cannot give you your son. But there is someone who can perhaps help you. You must go there quickly and you must leave tonight. If *he* finds that you are still alive . . ."

Theodora only sobbed, clutching at the priest's robes as he let the thought go unfinished.

"There is a ship at the docks, leaving tonight. In only hours," he said with urgency. "You must see its journey to the end. Up the Danube to the town of Melk, where there is an abbey. Give this to the abbot there—Victor. Tell him who you are and what has been done to you. If there is any help to be had for you . . ." He broke off again, and

Theodora felt him peel away one of her hands and then press a small disk-shaped object into it. "There is a sack of some of your belongings and what coin I could spare inside the carriage."

Dori went very still, feeling the warm, round disk in her hand, like a little ember compared to the cold, wet spring air blasting past her heavy skirts but not moving them, sticking together and to her legs as they were wet with congealing blood. Simon wanted her to go away. He wanted to forget she existed. Of course he did. Likely he hoped she'd die before reaching whatever made-up destination of which he spoke.

The priest continued. "If you do as I say, there may still be hope for you and your child."

"But not for you," Theodora whispered, feeling a strange vibration coming from the road through the soles of her heretofore numb feet, frozen in her thin, sticky slippers. It was like a thread of lightning coursing through her, and she felt strength spreading to her legs, her spine, her arms, her heart.

She realized then that it was not lightning sizzling through her body but a fiery rage, rousing her fully from her torpor at last. And Dori welcomed it.

"You will burn in hell for this," she continued in a low voice, hardly noticing that it had lost most of its rasp.

"Perhaps," the priest acquiesced, and there was a tremble to the word when it passed his lips.

"You may as well go tonight." Theodora raised both hands and shoved Simon with a sudden burst of furious energy, sending the priest backward down the rocky embankment past the edge of the road. His body disappeared into the darkness, taking his echoing shouts of surprise and pain with him.

She stood there swaying drunkenly on her feet, relishing for a cold moment the thought of the priest's bones being broken and snapped, his head crushed on the stones below. But then she remembered she was not alone on the road and turned her head as quickly as her flagging strength would allow to find the servant boy. He stared back at her apathetically.

"You would attack me now, I suppose?" she asked with as much bravado as she could muster, her fire having burned out quickly. He seemed to be perhaps ten years of age, but stocky, likely from the physical exertion placed upon him by the menial labor he performed. Dori knew he could easily overtake her at that moment.

But the boy shook his blond head before looking toward the edge of the cliff where Simon had disappeared. "No, milady. I'll fetch Father back up to the road if I can and take him back to the house." He met her eyes again.

Theodora frowned, but she would not let the boy take advantage of her weakened state. She could afford no sympathy for any child save her own. "What will you tell them when you return?"

He looked back at the embankment, as if so disgusted either by her actions or her appearance that he couldn't long stand the sight of her. "That a woman tried to kill Father Simon. That she left in a carriage for a ship."

"You little spy," Dori accused. "You would betray me even knowing the evil that has been done to me?"

He shrugged, still avoiding her gaze. "I'm not a spy. If I'm turned out, I've nowhere to go." He glanced at the carriage. "You should go yourself, if you would. Before the driver comes inquiring. He expects only one of us to disembark at the docks any matter."

Theodora's hand raised from her side before she knew she was moving it, her fingers pinching the edge of the coin given to her by the priest as if it were an odious thing. "Here," she said curtly. "Perhaps this will change your mind about what you saw tonight. Use it to buy food or something."

The boy opened his palm and accepted the gold, only now daring to glance into Dori's face. "Are you certain, milady? Father said this is the only way you—"

"I trust nothing that viper said. I certainly am not getting into a carriage bound for who knows where so that someone with marginally fewer morals can do the job he was too much of a coward to complete." Besides, the mere thought of getting back into that rocking conveyance made her feel like vomiting again. "You must only tell me: In which direction is Thurston Hold?"

But the boy was now staring at the carriage as if mesmerized.

"Which direction?"

He blinked and then turned to point behind Dori, away from the rear of the carriage and down the dark road that disappeared into the black of the night.

If they had been on the way to the docks, she must be standing on the old Roman road to Chatham. Dori looked all around her, and then up into the clear, cold sky, feeling for any clue as to how far away she was from her home. But she may as well have been stranded in a foreign land rather than standing beneath the sky that had sheltered her since the moment of her birth. The stars seemed to be turning slowly above her, the black bowl of sky rotating as if balanced on a spindle. . . .

The faint moaning of the priest from the abyss near the road startled her back to her predicament. He wasn't dead after all.

Theodora began limping toward Thurston Hold, her steps mincing, dragging, gentle. She paused when she heard the carriage door open and turned in time to see the boy calling up to the driver as he stood on the threshold of the opening.

"We're off," he said. "Don't stop until you reach the ship. The passenger will see himself disembarked." He turned his head to look at Dori as the carriage began rolling away into the darkness. "My thanks for the coin, mistress," he called past his cupped hand. "I hope you get your baby back. A boy needs a mother, even if she's not a good one."

"I am!" she tried to call after him angrily, but her voice had given out again, allowing only a creaky rasp to escape her throat. The carriage disappeared into the black, its jingle and rumble already fading. "I am a good mother," she croaked, and now the wetness that came from her eyes welled from the sorrow she was still trying so desperately to suppress. "I would be. I will be."

"Help me, boy," Father Simon called out from beyond the cusp of the road, his voice breaking as if he struggled physically. "My arm—I think it's broken. Boy? Boy, are you there?"

In an instant, Dori's despair turned into a hard pebble of determination, dropped from the night sky into the storm-tossed sea of her broken heart, endless glittering, concentric ripples of rage radiating from it. She glared toward the chasm, feeling heat pour from her eyes as surely as any rays of light from the sun that would not shine for hours and hours on this cold, dark road.

Perhaps, for Dori, it would never shine again.

She began backing away down the road once more, ignoring the pulling in her abdomen, the freshened wetness on her thighs, the void that consumed not only her body but also her soul.

Theodora Rosemont would get her son back, no matter what she had to do. And she would see those who helped take him from her—who stole her very life—pay dearly.

Especially her husband, Glayer Felsteppe.

Chapter 2

Constantine left the road some distance before the village, choosing instead to navigate the steeply rounded hill on the edge of the wood, slick with new grass and dewy in the setting sun. April had turned the land to green velvet, and the familiar smell of the heavy, cool air teased his nostrils and twisted his heart. He'd sold the black horse upon which he'd ridden away from Melk long ago, but he was glad he wasn't now sitting up high on a mount, forced to look around and ahead at what was one of the largest and wealthiest estates south of London, gazing out across Kent toward the sea.

He was glad, because the breeze carried no sounds of busy planting, no rumble of cart wheels on the road or jingle of harness in a frantic, last-minute rush to get in another quarter hour's work before the sun set. Nay, the squares of fields around Benningsgate lay tousled and wild with many winters' growth. There was no one left to plant for, and so those who planted had gone. Most of them any matter; as Constantine hitched around the mound of the village he heard the occasional bark of a lonely dog, the shout of a woman calling someone to supper. He wondered for a moment if he knew any of the stragglers who had remained in the village, but then he decided it didn't really matter. He wasn't anyone's lord anymore. He wasn't anyone at all. He kept his gaze downward, his rough hood pulled over his head, delaying the first sight of what was left of his home for as long as possible.

His boots seemed to find their way back around to the road on the far side of the village on their own, and soon Constantine walked in the grassy ruts where once hard-packed earth had marked the way to the castle. No carts or riders came beyond the village now. There was no reason to. And so the road was little more than shallow, parallel ditches up the slope. It would curve to the right soon—yes, just here. His feet followed the path, his legs marched in a steady rhythm, his breath hissed and shushed in and out of his nostrils. The sun setting through the blooming trees to his left cast a crackle of black shadows across his route, as if the land had been broken, shattered.

Just like Constantine's heart, his life.

It was four months since he'd left Melk in the night. Four months without the three men who had become like brothers to him at his side. Not an evening passed that he didn't think of Roman Berg and pray for his safe return from the Holy Land. Constantine had heard no rumors on his journey of the king of Jerusalem's murder, and so he hoped the huge stonemason had not sacrificed his own life to save Baldwin.

He thought of Adrian and was glad for the softening of his heart upon marrying Maisie. He wondered if Aid was still content at the abbey, with his duties and his studies.

He thought of Valentine and pondered how long the wily Spaniard would withstand such a mundane life, even with the beautiful Lady Mary and little Valentina to think of. Piracy ran in his blood after all.

God, he missed them all so much. They had become like family when he had still thought to one day return to his own wife and son. And then they had become his only family, because Patrice and Christian were dead.

His feet seemed to stop of their own accord as the ditches flattened and the new grass now poked up through gravel. Constantine stared at it, noticing with fear and dread how the wide apron of the approach to the castle was no longer comprised of only round, gray stone but interspersed with jagged pieces of honey-colored rock, many of the shards charred at their edges. That rock had been carted in from the north more than a hundred years before specifically to construct the tall, square keep Constantine might see if he would only look up. But he couldn't—not yet.

All the bits of rock were pushed down level with the firm mud, trampled by so many feet—feet fleeing Benningsgate that fateful night? Looters going to and fro on the road after the tragedy?

The fantasy of seeing his son running to greet him on this very road upon his homecoming had been the only thing that had kept Constantine sane those years he served King Baldwin at Chastellet, and then after the siege, during his imprisonment and torture in Saladin's dungeon. Had mourners walked this road in funeral procession with the bodies of his wife and son? How long had it been since Christian's little feet had traveled over—

His vision blurred and Constantine crouched down. He swiped at his nose with the back of his hand while he sniffed and then reached out to pry one of the smooth pieces of fine gravel from the mud. He picked the little blades of grass from it, turned it before his eyes and then dropped it into his left palm to roll it around. He swallowed hard as his fingers closed over it, and Constantine at last raised his eyes.

He gasped through his nose even as a strangled whimper escaped his chest. Constantine wobbled on the balls of his feet and then threw his hands behind him as he fell backward on the road, as if the sight before him had reached out with malevolent fingers and shoved him. His satchel slid from his shoulder as he caught himself, its mundane contents clanging loudly in offense.

The keep was no longer a slim, four-cornered tower reaching high into the sky but a thin, jagged triangle of stone. The honey-colored rock was now lashed with black—the remnants of the fire that had consumed Benningsgate—and the once sweet shade glowed scar red in the dying rays of the sun. The wide arch of the entry to the barbican was barely visible behind the piled rock that had fallen from the wall higher up the slope and around the keep, and Constantine could see that the tunnel itself had mostly collapsed. It looked as though the top of the keep had exploded, and he wondered with horror how hot the interior of the dwelling had been to have destroyed walls eleven feet thick at their bases.

A solitary opening remained in the sliver of keep, and he knew by its telltale arch that it was the east window of the great hall, looking out over the wall walk leading around the enclosure on the sloping side of the grounds. The grandest hall south of the king's home, once. Plastered and muraled. If Constantine closed his eyes, he could see the feasts they'd held in that hall; could hear the music wafting up to swirl around the beams in the high ceiling.

Now there was no ceiling, no floor. Nothing to look over from the east window save crumbled walls and sturdy weeds that were quickly becoming trees, nothing to hear save the birdsong surrounding what was left of Benningsgate Castle.

Christian was dead. He had died here. In the one place under heaven that he was supposed to be safe. Each beat of Constantine's heart was a stabbing pain in his chest and the sobs bubbled up from the wellspring of misery that was his soul to shake his physical body.

"My boy," he whispered through gritted teeth, squeezing his eyes shut and raising his face to the sky. His hood fell back and he felt hot tears track into his hairline above his ears. His inhalation was a jagged gasp. "My boy."

Constantine sat up on the overgrown road, raising both knees and laying his forearms atop them. He buried his face in the worn, poor sleeves of the only tunic he now owned and wept.

Dori watched the man sitting on the road below for a very long time, wondering what he was doing at the ruin, who he was, what he was hoping to find. He was a poor man, as evidenced by his rough, drab clothing and his lack of a mount. His tunic was long-sleeved and came to his knees, belted around his waist. His boots appeared to be leather, though, and he wore a hooded cape. She assumed he was a foreigner by the manner in which he wore his hair—in a long, burnished plait that now dangled over his shoulder. He appeared to be resting with his head on his knees, but Dori had heard his sobs.

Perhaps the man had heard of the great estate of Benningsgate and had traveled here hoping for work. Perhaps he had sacrificed every penny he had, left behind loved ones, traveled who knew how far and for how long to come to this place only to find a charred ruin. Even the village was largely abandoned. Surely he had noticed the obvious state of the castle before he came so close.

But Dori understood better than most the manner in which people often sought to fool themselves.

He didn't appear to be an enforcer of the king, or anyone employed by Glayer Felsteppe, although he wore a sword on his belt. Probably home-forged and worth little, she thought. Even a large-framed man such as he could be easily overtaken by a group, and he would be weary and weakened from his travels. He likely posed little danger to her, but she couldn't let him out of her sight until she knew in which direction he would depart. She expected him to return by way of the village to beg shelter and food, now that he saw the ruin was deserted.

Well, deserted save for Theodora Rosemont.

Her foot slid the tiniest bit on the silty walk, sending a tinkling of sand and small pebbles down the side of the wall. Dori froze against the battlement, fearing the man would look up and notice the slightest movement in this place of still death, but he didn't so much as twitch. She exhaled slowly, silently, as she continued to watch his bowed form.

The man raised his head from his forearms at last, but he continued to stare at the level of the barbican gate, as if mesmerized by something there. The evening cold was beginning to affect Theodora now, standing as still as she had been, and her back ached. Yet the strange traveler remained seated on the road. Perhaps he was scarred or obviously deranged. She wouldn't know unless she got closer.

Dori eased herself away from the merlon on silent feet, backing away slowly until she felt the corner of the keep behind her. Then she turned and tiptoed carefully down the set of leaning stone steps that led to the main ward, throwing out her arms for balance, her eyes straining in the growing dusk to make out the gaping chasm where the stairs had pulled away from the keep.

She turned again as she stepped onto the wet grass, the calf-high vegetation tickling her cold, bare skin above her slippers and raising gooseflesh on her legs. She traversed the slope of the ward quickly, descending to the level of the barbican and slipping behind the slide of fallen rock into the narrow space left in the tunnel. Once she reached the barricade of collapsed stone, she hitched her skirts with one hand and reached up with the other, finding her handholds easily in the darkness of the passageway and climbing from memory toward the slivered arch of dusk near the top. From that vantage point, she should be just above the man on the road.

She inched her head slowly above the topmost crumbled stone and looked through the archway.

The road was empty.

Dori's heart froze in her chest and her spine stiffened. For a moment she was unable to move at all, unable even to breathe. There was a stranger about Benningsgate and now she didn't know where he was. Perhaps he'd risen and turned on the road to head back to the village. But perhaps not. And if he found her here alone . . .

Her courage returned to her in a rush and she quickly scrambled back down the pile of the collapsed tunnel ceiling. By the time her slippers touched down on the littered ground, she had freed the little knife from one side of her belt and checked the other for the presence of her larger weapon. The she turned in the darkness, her eyes scanning the shadows of the ward beyond the sloping pile of rubble of the fallen wall. She saw nothing but crept forward in the narrow, treacherous space, rolling heel to toe silently, listening until her ears ached.

She came to the end of the tunnel and raised up on tiptoe to see over the cusp of the rock. Nothing but grass and growing darkness moved beyond, and yet she trod on soundless feet, each step measured and careful. Dori moved around the frozen wave of rock washed out into the ward and again crossed to the set of steps leading to the curtain wall. Not so much as a shadow twitched, nor did even a bird swoop through the space. Dori skipped up the stairs lightly, eager to gain the top of the wall and to see the black form of the man growing smaller as he walked away from the castle toward the village.

She dashed to the nearest embrasure, catching herself on the chest-high stone gap and looked, The road was as empty as it had been moments before.

Dori knew a thrill of cold fright as she pulled herself partway up on the stone and peered over the battlement toward the ground, her eyes darting from shadow to shadow along the base of the curtain wall. Where was he? *Where was he?*

She felt the hard point dimple her skin painfully over her right kidney before she heard the even harder voice behind her.

"Leave the blade on the stone and turn around slowly."

Chapter 3

It didn't matter to Constantine that the slight form turned away from him belonged to a woman—a small, stooped woman whose blade he'd seen as she passed him was nothing more than a broken eating knife of the sort little children were first given. She was a trespasser, an interloper who had intruded upon Constantine's deepest grief and was even now standing upon the sacred ground that had at one time been the center of his world. She trod uninvited on his memories, his pain. Her very presence was an affront.

But the woman had neither moved nor responded at all to his command, and so Constantine pressed forward with his sword until she gave a warbly, frightened cry. "I said, leave the blade on the stone and turn around."

He heard the tinny scrape of the knife against the shelf of the embrasure. The sides of the woman's faded and threadbare cloak lifted even as the deep hood cocked, and Constantine saw that she had raised her hands before her face so that her palms were toward him, shielding her lowered countenance as she turned.

"Please," she whispered. "I beg you, harm me not. I have nothing of value."

"What are you doing here?" Constantine demanded, still leveling his weapon at her as she cowered against the wide merlon. He tried to see past her raised hands in the gloom.

"Only exploring the ruin."

Constantine's eyes narrowed as he took in the details of the woman's costume, illuminated by the misty dusk. The slippers poking from beneath the ragged and filthy hem of her skirts were so thin that Constantine could see the outline of her toes even in the shadows. These were no sturdy peasant shoes; at one time, Constantine imagined they had been quite fine. It appeared that part of her outer skirt had been torn off near the bottom, revealing only one thin under-garment and bare, sticklike calves above white, bony ankles. Her sleeves were also jagged and frayed, and the protuberances at her wrists seemed like bolts, her fingers like thin, trembling twigs glow-ing in the twilight. And yet they served to hide what little of her face Constantine could have seen in the black recess of her hood.

"You live in the village?" he asked.

"Yes. Yes, I live in the village." She paused. "My . . . my husband will be expecting me home. He likely seeks me now."

Constantine felt his brows lower. "Liar."

The hood twitched up as if surprised at his accusation, but she didn't insist upon perpetuating the untruth. "Please don't hurt me," she whispered again.

"Lower your hands so that I might see your face," he commanded. "And step away from the battlements lest that sliver of metal behind you tempt you to foolishness."

She sidled away from the embrasure obediently, her hands falling beneath her pitiful cloak once more, but she angled her face toward the walk so that the soft hood fully concealed her features. Constan-tine glanced over to be certain she had indeed left the blade on the stones and was reassured to see its pathetic length.

He turned his head back toward the woman. "Now, tell me tru—" He hadn't finished the order before he saw a flash of movement from beneath that black cloak, a blur of upward motion, and then felt a stabbing pain explode in the muscles of his right forearm, causing his hand to flex open and his sword to clatter to the stones.

The woman jerked her handled weapon free of his flesh and then turned with a swirl of black to dash into the shadows past the keep, where the stairs to the inner ward leaned.

Constantine recovered quickly, swooping to pick up his sword and giving chase into the growing night. He could hear the woman's slight scraping footfalls over the uneven stone, and whereas Con-stantine still knew and remembered every corner and inch of the Benningsgate in his memories, the reality of the place since it had been abandoned thwarted him with its cants and crumbling stone. The woman ahead of him, however, must have been intimately fa-miliar with the Benningsgate of the present, for she seemed to fly from Constantine's reach with all the fleetness of a forest deer.

But he had been right that she was weak, frail, for when he gave chase in the open field of the ward, her strength flagged and each loping stride brought him closer to the flapping tail of her cloak. She glanced over her shoulder twice, and the second time her hood fell back, revealing a halo of choppy black locks. She must have known that in another moment he would reach out and seize her, for she suddenly stopped and spun around with a fierce cry, swinging her crude weapon in a wide arc toward Constantine's middle.

He arched his body back, but whatever sharp implement she'd impaled on the short handle snagged the wide woven fabric of his tunic and caught the skin of his ribs. He hissed as he felt it slice him but in the same moment brought the butt of his hilt down upon the woman's forearm, causing her to shriek in pain and the weapon to fly off into the night-soaked weeds.

Constantine didn't wait to see if she would produce other hidden armaments from her raggedy costume, stepping forward and taking her feet from beneath her, his left hand already at her throat as he followed her down to the ground. He pinned her legs with his own, held her arms close to her sides as he gripped her narrow neck just below her jaw.

Her breaths whistled in and out of her nostrils even as Constantine's own chest heaved, but she didn't cry out again, didn't beg him for mercy this time.

"Who are you?" he growled.

He flinched as the hot wad of saliva found his eye, and in the next instant the woman's forehead shot toward him, busting his nose. He dropped his sword as she thrashed and bucked beneath him and nearly squirmed free, but Constantine jerked her aright once more, feeling warm blood trickling down his chin. He drew back his right hand and struck her across the face.

The next moment found him effectively blinded as the handful of dirt and rubble she threw at him found its mark in his eyes, and then her knee raised beneath him and drove his vulnerable manhood into his stomach. Constantine gasped and curled into himself as the woman bucked free, but even in his sickening agony, he remembered his sword laying on the ground behind them.

Constantine fell sideways, reaching for the weapon even as the woman dove for it. His hand curled around her arm and jerked her backward; her small, bony fist found his throat. He yanked her again, pushed her behind him as her feet continued to kick out into his ribs, his flank, his left kidney.

Constantine wondered if anything short of death would stop this woman.

He finally felt his fingers curl around the hilt of his sword and he gained one knee as he swung it around to point it at the woman who was now also kneeling on the ground. She stopped her lunge toward him and wobbled for a moment. They each gained their feet as if mirror images, their eyes never leaving one another.

She spat into the weeds and then brought the tail of her cloak up to press it to her mouth. After a moment she held it before her face and glanced down with a grimace.

"Bastard," she muttered and then looked up at Constantine as the moon peeked out from behind a cloud, its pale light glancing off the woman's sharp jawline, the flipped up ends of her strangely cropped hair, the dark slant of her eyebrows.

Constantine stared at the woman, the moonlight revealing such a specter of his long-ago, happy past here in this haunted field of despair.

"Lady Theodora?" he said, the tip of his sword wobbling.

The woman stilled, her eyes widening the slightest bit as her already swollen lips parted. Her fine brows raised above features much too sharp to belong to the only child of Benningsgate Castle's neighboring lord, but too remarkable to be owned by any other.

"At last," she whispered and then looked down at the bloodied hem of her cloak as if to confirm it. Her gaze found Constantine's again. "I've gone mad at last. *You're dead.*"

He shook his head, his thoughts loud and buzzing like a hive of bees. "What are you doing here?" And then, through the deafening hum, the recollection of her name fought its way through the confusion of Constantine's mind.

. . . celebrate the installation of Lord Glayer Felsteppe as Earl of Rosemont, as well as his marriage to our beloved Lady Theodora while on their travels to that Holy City of Jerusalem . . .

Theodora Rosemont began to chuckle, drawing Constantine's attention back to the present. Her laughter deepened and she brought her fingertips to her mouth again. "What am I doing here?" Her hands raised up to cover the ghastly black hollows around her eyes even as her shrill laughter echoed in the ward. "What *am* I doing here?" She dropped her hands to her sides and stared at him, her shoulders still hitching with senseless mirth. "I'm here because I'm dead, too. Benningsgate is the perfect place for those who have lost their lives through unimaginable tragedy, wouldn't you agree? You must, else you wouldn't be here."

Constantine's heart flinched but still held his sword pointed at Lady Theodora; what had they called her all those years ago?

"Dori," he remembered aloud without meaning to.

The name hung between them, and it was as if his speaking it broke whatever spell of desperation and madness gripped the broken woman before him.

Her face went slack, her eyes—black in the night of the ward—empty. "You're too late," she accused, and her voice was so full of bitterness, of resentment, that Constantine felt she was holding him liable for her trials.

What did she mean? That Constantine was too late to save Christian, Patrice? Too late to prevent the destruction of Benningsgate? Too late to stop the marriage of the daughter of a noble ally to his own greatest enemy?

"I know," he answered. She continued to stare at him and so he aired his own grievance against her. "You married Glayer Felsteppe."

Theodora nodded.

"Are you . . . living here? At Benningsgate?"

After a moment she nodded again. "He thinks I'm dead."

"You look as though you nearly are," Constantine blurted out.

She neither agreed with nor disputed the observation as the night chill descended in the ward, as if someone had suddenly thrown a great, cold, wet blanket over the ruin.

"Glayer Felsteppe killed my wife and son."

"I know," she said, repeating his earlier answer.

"I've come to kill him."

Theodora Rosemont shook her head slightly. "You can't do that, Lord Gerard."

And Constantine felt in that moment that he knew what Theodora had experienced when he'd said her pet name aloud. The sound of his title on her lips was a foreign thing, startling and bittersweet; that name belonged to another time, to another person in a different life.

She turned toward Benningsgate's crumbled north wing and began walking away from him, her stooped posture returning. Constantine wondered that this was the woman who had, so recently, seemed more than capable of fighting him to the death.

She called up to the sky. "I hardly think it appropriate that I invite you in to your own home."

Constantine didn't know where she meant to go, approaching what appeared to be nothing more than a pile of rubble where once family apartments and garderobes spanned the curtain wall between the hall and the tall oratory tower. He suddenly found that his own feet would not move.

Theodora Rosemont looked over her shoulder, and when she saw him still standing in the ward, she stopped and turned to face him. She waited.

It took him several long moments before he found the courage, not knowing what devastating memories he would encounter on the other side of the rock. But eventually he lowered his head and commanded his boots to move forward, following Glayer Felsteppe's wife into the corpse of his past.

Chapter 4

Dori's face throbbed and her shoulder ached from her battle with Constantine Gerard as she led the man himself toward the pile of toppled battlements stretched out in the ward like a fallen dragon. She didn't hesitate when she came to the barricade of rock but clambered over the summit and then moved to her bottom, ready to drop over the side. She paused, turning her head slightly to make sure he still followed.

He was right behind her and glanced up as he climbed. "The doorway still stands?" he said, speaking of the small entrance to the middle corridor, partially below ground.

"Yes. But the upper corridor has collapsed," she warned and heard the rasp of disuse in her voice. She hadn't spoken to another living soul in nearly two months. "Mind that you don't disturb it further." She slid in hitches and jerks down the fallen slab that deposited her into the shallow stairwell abutting the doorway, not caring if it sounded as though she was ordering him about; she was. If he caused the tunnel's complete collapse, her refuge would be gone.

Theodora Rosemont hadn't survived the past months only to be thwarted by his high-and-mighty Lord Gerard's return.

Her feet touched down on the crumbled rock spilled out through the doorway from the corridor. She ducked through the arch and into pitch blackness, the gaping holes in the wall walk above too far away to let the moonlight through.

"This way," she called over her shoulder as she began to duck walk over the rubble, one arm stretched out, her fingers skimming the soot-gummed rock for the telltale hole where a wooden beam had once rested.

Behind her, Constantine Gerard coughed, and Dori remembered that the corridor still stank of old fire. She had simply become accustomed to it.

Her fingers found the hole and she cupped her palm around the edge while moving to her bottom and turning her chin over her shoulder once more. "Careful," she warned sharply, feeling the warmth of him come upon her suddenly, sending a little cascade of silt and debris before her. "The way ahead is collapsed. Give me time to go through before you follow."

The only answer he gave was in his labored breaths. Dori didn't think the journey arduous for a man of his strong appearance, so his efforts must have been of the emotional sort. She braced her right hand on the last crumbling edges of the upper corridor floor before lifting herself up and then into the black.

She tottered a bit when she scrambled to gain her feet from the pile and remove herself from the path of Constantine Gerard, who came through almost immediately after her. He tumbled to the lowest level of stone if what she heard was any evidence, little pebbles rattling across the floor around his muffled curse.

Dori sighed to herself. "Are you injured?" She couldn't see him at all now, the lower corridor completely cut off from above.

"No," he answered curtly. "Where are you?"

"Here," she said, turning. "Follow my voice. We'll have light in a moment." She heard the closeness of her words in her own ears. "The floor is mostly clear at this end of the passage." She heard his muffled *oof*. "Mostly."

She found the handle with her outstretched hands and moved the latch. An instant later, what seemed to be golden rays of sunlight poured into the black corridor, although Dori knew it was nothing more than the meager light of a single candle.

"The oratory," Lord Gerard said, although she was certain the words weren't for her benefit.

She passed into the small, square room and closed the door after he entered, bending to drop the slender stake into the groove in the floor. It wouldn't stop someone intent on entering, but it would give her enough warning to prepare to defend herself.

When she looked around at him, she found him staring at the walls, at the altar she was using for a mundane table, the bench that doubled as her cot, made up with the holy cloths from the altar. She knew he was looking at her small pile of hay in the corner and was glad she had burned most of the soiled portion the night before.

He turned his face toward hers in the cold room that never seemed to warm sufficiently. There was a spark in his green eyes from the candle flame, and the light burnished the long plait hanging over his shoulder. "How long have you been here?"

"Forty-seven days," Dori answered without pause.

He stared at her. "Why?"

She responded with her own question. "Have you anything to eat?"

"In my satchel," he said and then glanced toward the door. "I stashed it above when I heard you on the wall walk."

"So you did hear me," she said. "You didn't give sign that you had."

"I know," he said, and then turned to the table and picked up one of the precious long candles she had left to light it on the little stub of flaming wick.

"What are you doing?" she demanded. "Those are my only candles. I must keep one lighted at all times, lest I have nothing with which to start my fires."

"They're my candles, actually," he said and walked to the door, pausing to remove the stave from the floor. "I'd see the true condition of the corridors we traveled, determine whether they're in imminent danger of collapse."

"I can assure you they are," she snipped. How dare he charge in here and assume ownership of everything?

"Then perhaps there is something I can do to shore up the passage." He opened the door and was gone in the next moment.

Dori turned and looked about, but there was nothing with which to occupy herself in the Spartan oratory where the Gerard family had once taken their daily chapel in private. Thankfully, it wasn't as Spartan as a commoners' chapel, else she would have had nothing to survive on. The rich altar cloths, the golden receptacles for the host, the cache of wide candles and their stands had meant the difference between life and death for Dori.

She sat down on the edge of the bench and waited, her fingers twisted together on her lap, her eyes on the thin layer of grime covering the stone floor.

She didn't know how long he was gone—perhaps a half hour. But when he returned he carried on his back the worn satchel she'd spied from the wall walk. He went to an empty stand in the corner of the oratory and affixed the candle to it, doubling the light in the clammy room and seeming to warm it at once.

"Do you not keep a fire?" he asked in an emotionless tone as he dropped an armful of slender sticks before the tiny hearth and then went at once to the table to place his bag upon it.

"Not every night," she said, unable to keep her seat as she saw him withdrawing food from the satchel. "Only when it is very cold, and well after midnight. Even then, I only burn small amounts of twigs and straw."

He glanced up at her as he placed a short, cloth-wrapped cylinder on the table. "You fear someone from the village will see the smoke?"

Dori nodded. "What's that?"

"A bit of sausage." He picked it up and undid the string, pulling the cloth back and holding it toward her.

She snatched it from him, her mouth running with saliva. "A knife," she said curtly. "You made me leave my—" The dull metal glinted in the candlelight as he held the broken blade toward her. She took it and immediately turned back to the cot, walking toward it even as she sliced off a thick disk of the fragrant meat. She delivered it to her mouth with the knife and closed her eyes as she chewed.

Dori sat on the edge of the bench and did not look at him as she quickly worked her way through the short length.

"How long has it been since you've had a meal?" Lord Gerard asked.

She paused and swallowed, her eyes still on the last puckered end of sausage in her hand. "Forty-eight days," she said before placing the bite in her mouth and then raising her face.

He was standing at the table still, a small piece of what appeared to be cheese in his hand. He glanced down at it and then back at her and tossed the wedge.

Dori snatched it out of the air as expertly as a swallow on the wing. The first bite was heavenly. She looked back up at him as she chewed, daring him to feel sorry for her.

"Your husband thinks you're dead," he said instead. "Why?"

"Because he ordered someone to have me killed after I gave birth to my son," she said matter-of-factly, slicing off another piece of cheese. "As far as everyone at Thurston Hold and elsewhere knows,

I bled to death in my childbed." She tried not to dwell on the fact that that fate had actually nearly occurred.

"Why would he want you dead?" Lord Gerard pressed.

"He's gotten what he wanted from me—an heir, a title, an estate. I was far too disobedient to be a suitable wife for him, especially now that I know so much of the animal he is, the dreadful things he's done. I'm certain he's now the heartsick widower, left to bravely raise an infant on his own." She gave a sarcastically sad pout before popping the last bite of cheese into her mouth.

She continued after she swallowed. "Well, not entirely on his own; there's Eseld. She's the one who was responsible for poisoning me for months. And Felsteppe's devil's-spawn priest. Simon."

"Your father—he's dead now, I suppose."

Dori stilled, licked the last taste of salt from her lips. "More than a year." She glanced at his now deflated satchel and then back into his face. "Have you anything else?"

He shook his head. "I'll go fishing in the river on the morrow."

"You'll help me rescue my son, now you're here," she said, not daring to pose the phrase as a question.

Constantine Gerard stared at her for a moment, and his green eyes were glittering, cold, nearly as cold as his tone when he spoke. "You must forgive me for my lack of enthusiasm for rescuing a child belonging to the man who killed my wife and my own son in the very rubble we now occupy. Frankly, Lady Theodora, I couldn't care less what happens to your ill-gotten offspring."

"You'd better," she said, looking him up and down, "if you ever hope to have your lands restored to you."

"What are you talking about?" Lord Gerard demanded.

"Glayer Felsteppe is petitioning Henry to purchase Benningsgate Castle. He's been at it for months now. You're quite behind in your taxes, Lord Gerard." The man's jaw flinched as he stared at her but said nothing, so Dori continued, her heart pounding as if it would leap from her chest. "If you should be successful in your mission to see him dead, you'll have murdered a peer. If Felsteppe has purchased your lands, without proof of his treachery to justify your actions, Benningsgate will never revert to you. It will instead fall to . . ." She let the thought trail away.

"Felsteppe's heir," he finished, seemingly through clenched teeth.

"I don't care, though. My whole purpose in returning to England was to kill Glayer Felsteppe. I don't care what happens to Benningsgate afterward. I don't care what happens to me."

She was nodding, her thoughts turning quickly in her head as she thought of something to say. "I understand. And there is no one else on earth who also wants to see Glayer Felsteppe dead as badly as I. But is that the legacy you wish to leave?" She affected a common accent. "'Oh, aye—that poor boy what burned up in Benningsgate—a mercy, really. You know his father died a murderer and a traitor.'"

"I'm not a traitor," Lord Gerard growled.

Dori rose from the cot and walked toward the table to stand across from him. She trembled in furious panic and it made her words low, breathy. "If you kill Felsteppe before I can reach my son, I'll never get him back. He'll be taken away as a ward and Thurston Hold—and Benningsgate—will be held by the Crown. Glayer Felsteppe will have succeeded in taking everything. From *both of us*."

He continued to stare at her so that Dori felt prickly chills race up her spine; she could see the hatred in his eyes.

"I know things about Felsteppe. Things he did in Jerusalem, people he killed, tried to have killed. My testimony could be the proof you need to ruin him forever. If you help me—"

"I don't want him ruined—I want him dead."

"The proof to justify your actions, then."

His eyes narrowed. "Tell me now."

Dori felt her eyebrows raise, and for the first time in months and months a genuine laugh bubbled at her lips. The sustenance must have made her giddy. "Oh, certainly. I'll tell you everything I know so that you can kill him right off and be on your way."

They stared at each other for a pair of moments before Lord Gerard spoke again. "What's his name?"

Dori's frown faltered. "I beg your pardon?"

"Your son; what is he called?"

Her throat constricted for just a moment. "Felsteppe had him christened Glander, I'm certain—he was set on it from the moment he learned I had conceived."

"What would you have called him?"

"It doesn't matter now, does it?" she said, folding up the cloth and the strings from the food. Who would her son be, if she ever got him back? Who would she be? She raised her face suddenly.

"William." When Constantine looked at her she lifted her chin. "I would have called him William."

He took the folded squares of cloth bundled with the string from her and returned them to his satchel. He cinched the bag and then looked back at her. "At the very least, you must tell me how it is that you came to be married to Glayer Felsteppe; I cannot fathom your father allowing you to wed such a monster."

Dori felt her back stiffen and she turned from him, moving to the cot to straighten her coverlet. "I think I've allowed you enough liberties for the evening. Especially considering you've beaten me. I don't *owe* you anything."

"I believe you've more of my blood on your hands than the other way 'round. I have fed you. And in principle, you're living in my house. Call it a tax."

Dori spun around to fix him with a glare. "Yes? Well, arrest me or shut up."

She thought she saw the corner of his mouth twitch. He grabbed up his bag and slung it over his shoulder before moving toward the door.

"Where are you going?" she demanded.

Lord Gerard paused, bending to pick up the discarded stake and toss it to Dori. "I'll find shelter elsewhere on the grounds. Good night, Lady Theodora."

He pulled the door shut after himself, leaving Dori standing near the cot. The oratory looked just the same as it had before he'd come and yet nothing was the same.

Constantine Gerard had returned.

Chapter 5

Constantine finished lacing the gutted fish onto the slender pike he'd whittled, then stabbed the end of the stake into the dirt before rising from his crouch and collecting his satchel and fishing supplies. The morning sun was at last beginning to warm the ground, and the air grew humid as the bright rays streamed through tree branches thickening with greenery by the moment, it seemed.

He stopped and looked across the peacefully flowing river, its surface sparkling so brightly with silver that he had to squint. His river. His lands. He glanced over at the breakfast he'd procured for himself and Theodora Rosemont.

His fish.

None of it meant a damn thing anymore.

He pulled the pike from the mud of the bank and turned to scale the steep hill below Benningsgate. The smoke from the small fire pit he'd built the night before still curled weakly, showing up in bright relief against the ragged, dark skirts of the woman who stood behind it.

"Could you see the smoke?" he said by way of greeting as he came upon his makeshift camp. He'd prefer not to draw the curiosity of whatever villagers were left below the castle ruins just yet.

Theodora shook her head. "I only smelled it once I was outside the wall. Did you sleep out here all the night?"

Constantine jabbed the staff into the soft dirt again before shrugging out from beneath his satchel and then dropping to his knees to remove the topmost cedar boughs from the fire. Greenery smoldered atop the rocks in the center of the shallow pit.

"I've grown used to sleeping out of doors," he said as he reached behind himself and pulled up the stake of fish. He brought the pole in front of him to lay it across the hot rocks. "It's fair this time of year."

"It's cold," Theodora argued.

"It's warmer here than Bavaria in winter," he rejoined.

"I wouldn't know." Theodora swept her hands beneath her seat before squatting on her heels near the warm smoke, stretching out her pale, knobby fingers as Constantine replaced the cedar boughs.

He looked across the pit at her. "Admittedly, not as warm as Jerusalem."

Her eyes flicked up at him, but she made no comment, and as the sunlight fully revealed the raggedness of her costume, the frailness of her person, Constantine did not press the subject. Her slender neck seemed to be nothing but cord and bone, the hollows at her temples and cheeks deep, the skin covering the undersides of her wrists the palest blue.

Theodora Rosemont was clearly unwell.

"I never wished to wed Glayer Felsteppe," she said suddenly, and although Constantine continued to watch her, she did not raise her eyes to him again. "I hated him from the moment I saw him. I begged my father to retract the betrothal."

"What I cannot fathom," Constantine challenged, "is why your father would have entertained the agreement at the first. Glayer Felsteppe was no match for a woman of your station."

"Not so," Theodora argued mildly, turning her hands in the warming smoke. "He had returned from the Holy Land a hero, with letters to recommend him. He was lauded as the man intent on chasing down the traitors of a besieged Christian fortress. His reputation was that of a champion. A warrior who held great favor with the crown."

Constantine's frown deepened. "Your father could not have known the man's character, and yet he bound his only daughter to him? Was willing to bequeath Felsteppe Thurston Hold and his life's work on the word of speculation and gossip?"

"You've been gone many years, Lord Gerard. My father had been . . . deteriorating in health for some time," Theodora hedged. "I'm sure you know by now how ingratiating Felsteppe can be to those he thinks to profit from. My father was becoming unable to tell the difference between reason and fantasy. Any matter," she looked up at him, then, "I'm certain much the same was said about another lord father when you became betrothed to Lady Patrice. It was through your marriage that you received the earldom of Chase, was it not?"

Now it was his turn to drop his eyes to the fire, realizing the wisdom in Theodora's comparison, if the details of the things were vastly different.

"Patrice's father was not ill. And she and I were agreeable to the arrangement."

"A love match, was it?" Theodora pressed, and he could hear the needling challenge in her voice.

"There are varying degrees of love." Constantine felt his face heating, remembering the tearful confessions, the humiliation of the blatant indiscretions, Patrice's beautiful, bewildered face begging him for forgiveness.

"Hmm." She sighed thoughtfully. And then, "I was at Thurston Hold a week ago. I overheard that Felsteppe planned to journey to London with Eseld and the baby soon." She leaned down even lower to pick at the end of a bough, peek beneath it, releasing a wave of white, fragrant smoke. "Perhaps they are returned by now." She dropped the bough and looked back up at him expectantly.

"How many times have you been back?" he asked.

She hugged her knees, narrow and knobby-looking beneath her dirty, threadbare skirts, and now she met his gaze directly. Her rich, dark hair—Constantine could remember the noble ladies' admiration of the long, thick, shiny locks when Dori was still a child—feathered out around her face like the dark whirls of a new lamb's wool. The black sheep. Yes, that was fitting for Theodora Rosemont.

"Three," she answered. "I wasn't well enough to make the journey for nearly a month after I first came to Benningsgate."

"You don't appear to be well enough for it now," he commented, not caring if it offended her, but by her smooth face and the unchanged line of her wide mouth it did not. "Why did you not procure supplies and food from Thurston?"

She shook her head, and Constantine was momentarily struck by the thought that her cropped hair somehow enhanced the feminine look of her face, rather than given her the appearance of a young boy.

"I can't risk being caught. The servants who are left have no choice but to be loyal to Felsteppe. I risk my life each time I step but a foot onto Thurston Hold lands." She glanced at the smoking vegetation. "How long until we can eat?"

"A bit," Constantine said. "I find it difficult to believe that you've managed not only to survive on your own this long at Benningsgate with no food but you've also made the lengthy journey to Thurston Hold on foot three times."

Theodora rested her chin on her knees, then, and dropped her gaze to the fire. "I managed to take some barley from the stables twice. Last time I found some shriveled roots that were to be given to the pigs. I warmed them in some water in the chalice. I've tried catching fish to no avail. The handful of people living in the village here have so little themselves that it is guarded closely. Now that spring has come, there will be more to forage."

Constantine felt a strange sensation in his middle, thinking of how impossible it was that this young woman had survived until now. A forced childbirth, sheltering in a forsaken ruin, no food, little warmth. Such circumstances would have laid many a mighty soldier down.

He observed that she was starved, cold, her skin holding a bluish tinge. Even her nail beds beneath the jagged dirty crescents of her nails were purpled. While the fish she would soon consume would do much to alleviate her immediate hunger, what she truly needed was rich food, a warm bed, and, likely, a potion.

But then he remembered that she was no longer the celebrated miss of Thurston Hold, the light of her father's eye, the delicate if outspoken angel with the long, twisting locks of dark hair. She was Glayer Felsteppe's wife, and she had borne his child.

Christian was dead because of this woman's husband. And no matter how frail she appeared, no matter what she had endured, although she might not be Constantine's enemy, he certainly didn't trust her enough to consider her his ally. Theodora Rosemont's troubles were her own as far as he was concerned.

She looked up at him suddenly, caught him watching her. His expression must have conveyed his distrust of her, for her own brows twitched downward, her gaze hardened. Theodora didn't consider him a friend either.

"When do we depart?" she asked.

"*We* aren't going anywhere," Constantine said, looping the long strap of his satchel over his head and standing. Theodora gained her feet as well. He met her eyes. "I made a promise years ago; the next time I see Glayer Felsteppe, I will kill him. And nothing or no one will stop me. Not you, not your child, not the king. When I go to Thurston

Hold, it will be to see Felsteppe dead, not to play the gallant." He turned and strode down the slope toward the wood.

"Where are you going?" she called after him. "Lord Gerard?"

Constantine did not answer her.

Dori waited by the fragrant fire pit for what seemed like an hour, watching the fringe of the wood where Lord Gerard had entered. She neither saw nor heard sign of him, and so eventually she stood and made her way to the riverbank for a drink; if she stayed much longer by the slowly cooking fish, she feared she would reach beneath the cedar boughs and seize it, eating all of it herself, piece by piece.

She squatted by the shallows, dipping one hand into the fast, swirling eddies for a drink. She almost couldn't stand the cold on her lips and thought about the last time she had been warm. It had been at Thurston Hold, early in the afternoon before she'd lost consciousness and entered into labor. She'd walked the corridors of her own home, in fine, rich clothes, with servants to attend her, and all the food and drink she could desire. Sunlight had streamed through windows cased with real glass, warming the stones and planks of the floors; there were woven throws of the softest wool for her shoulders, warm stones covered in quilting for her feet. It was like recalling the best dream she'd ever had, but it had been her life.

And then Eseld had come bearing the noxious potion that forced the start of her birth. Dori should have known it was poison, the way it increasingly made her nauseous and caused the pains to start in her abdomen. She should have realized that since Glayer Felsteppe had never given a damn about her, he certainly wouldn't go to any trouble to see that she was given some relief from her agony. No, he had simply become tired of dealing with her, and from her own foolish admissions, he'd known when she had conceived. He'd known when it was safe for the baby to come. And he likely had hoped that by forcing the birth, Dori would indeed die.

Only she hadn't died. And neither had Constantine Gerard.

She stood and dried her frigid hand on her skirts, her flesh feeling thick and gummy with cold. She pulled her thin cloak around herself as she made her way back to the fire and crouched down once more, holding her hands into the warming smoke. The smell of the sizzling fish hidden beneath the boughs was almost too much to bear.

But then Dori heard the crunch of footsteps and looked up to see Lord Gerard emerging from the wood once more, his head down, a fistful of spindly greens in one hand. She watched him stride up the slope, thinking about the differences between them. She was a sickly, frail, desperate woman; he was a strong, hearty, determined man. He sought revenge; she sought respite. She'd been indulged to the point of dereliction as a child; Lord Gerard was wholly self-made.

He was feeding her, but it was clear he didn't want to help her.

Lord Gerard reached the fire and squatted straightaway to move the cedar boughs aside. He pulled at the fish with his thumb and made a little sound in his throat. His hair was magnificent, neatly plaited, long, glinting in the morning light.

She self-consciously ran a hand over her butchered locks.

"Where have you been?" she asked and was surprised at the timidity she heard in her voice.

"In the wood," he answered curtly, rummaging in his satchel and not raising his face.

"No, not just now," she clarified. "All this time. The years you were away from Benningsgate; where were you?"

He withdrew a long, narrow blade and then used it to flip a broken chunk of fish from the stake onto one of the dried, fragrant boughs. He handed it to Dori, who took hold of it with both hands, blinking rapidly at the smoke and the tears of anticipation.

"Syria, in the beginning," he said gruffly, returning his attention to the fish and portioning out his own meal. "Then Damascus. Then . . . the countryside near Vienna."

She lifted the bough to her face and bit into the fish hesitantly with the tips of her front teeth. She drew back quickly, blowing little breaths, and then attempted again. The flesh flaked off into her mouth, seared her tongue. She rolled it around in her mouth, drawing in cool air. Her mouth was scalded, but she couldn't care. She chewed bit by bit, breaking up the piece until it had cooled enough to swallow, and then she started the whole process over again.

She could feel Lord Gerard watching her, and a part of her felt a sting of humiliation at her behavior. She was no better than an animal right now. She swallowed again and let her eyes catch his gaze for a moment.

"It's very good. Thank you."

He took a chunk of fish between his thumb and fingers and held it before his mouth, blowing on it. "Did Felsteppe cut your hair? Or was it the beastly nurse you spoke of?"

Dori chewed and cleared her mouth. "I did it."

He looked at her then, his eyebrows raised, as he popped the fish into his mouth and chewed slowly, seeming to consider her answer. "I remember your hair as a child; all the ladies were wild about it."

Dori nodded, ducked her head as a prickle came into her eyes. "My father was very proud of it as well. My mother died shortly after I was born and he always feared I would lack a certain womanliness. My childhood nurses took great pains with my hair. I remember many a tearful hour beneath their brushes."

"Why did you cut it?"

Dori swallowed again, picked at the tiny bits of fish—all that were left now—that had fallen between the densely packed clusters of greenery. "You don't really care."

"No, I don't," he admitted. "But I am curious as to why."

She held forth her empty server. "Might I have some more?"

Lord Gerard only glanced pointedly at her hair.

Dori felt her cheeks heat. "I had to cut it. It was caked with dirt. And probably blood. I had no utensil to address it. Even when I attempted to wash it, it only matted further once it was dry. I found the eating knife in the rubble one day not long after I'd arrived and used it to cut my hair." She gestured with the bough once more.

Lord Gerard was very still for a heartbeat and then he reached out abruptly, dislodging a large portion of fish and placing it carefully on her bough.

"Thank you," she said stiffly, thinking him embarrassed at pressing her for such intimate details.

"You found the eating knife here, you say?" he inquired mildly.

Dori stilled; even her chewing ceased as she instantly recalled the faint engraving on the battered and scratched hilt of that particular knife: *CAG*.

"It belonged to your son," she realized aloud. "I'm sorry. I didn't—"

"I should have looked at it more closely when it was in my possession," he interrupted and returned his portion of fish back to the pit. "I thought when I first saw you with it that it looked the sort a child would use."

"I shall return it to you at once of course," she said.

"Have you found any other personal items of my family, Lady Theodora?"

Dori shook her head, bewildered at the idea that she could have so soon lost her appetite. She, too, placed her uneaten fish on the smoldering fire and watched as Lord Gerard covered it with the boughs. "No. I've explored as much as I can safely reach. The hall and the apartments are destroyed; the kitchen is buried. I've found nothing else."

"Do you know how the fire progressed?" he asked quietly, sitting back on his hip with his back partly toward her now.

Dori felt an anxious tremble in her stomach at his question as it jostled her warm meal. "No, my lord."

"You're lying."

She frowned and the tremble turned to a lurch. "Why would you say that?"

"Because you called me 'my lord'; are you trying to spare me the details?"

Dori's face heated. "I don't know any details—only the gossip I overheard from the servants."

"Tell me."

She stood swiftly, her head spinning a bit at the sudden motion. "What good would it do to hear gruesome, likely exaggerated rumors? It changes nothing."

"I must know," he insisted in a low voice. "I imagine it constantly— the different circumstances. I know very little, you see? I think I'm owed at least the knowledge of how my family were murdered."

Dori felt her nostrils flaring as she tried to slow her breathing. "But you'll never know if it's the truth. The rumors could be so much worse than your imaginings, and then there will never be any respite from the nightmares in your head."

"It won't be worse I assure you."

Dori hesitated.

"Please," he said curtly, his gaze still directed toward the ever-flowing river.

She tried to clear her throat from the lump that had formed there and then drew a slow, deep, silent breath before beginning. "The soldiers had come because there was rumor that one of the traitors had made his way to Kent to assist an English lady. The king's men turned Benningsgate over, searching for him."

He nodded, not looking at her. "Go on."

"Well, they didn't find him." She pressed her lips together, praying that it would be enough and knowing in that same moment that she had told him nothing he mustn't already know.

"Dori," he said in a low voice.

No one had called her that since her father died, and the pet name coming from his lips in such a fashion made her knees watery. She wished with everything in her that she could just float away rather than divulge the tale she'd heard to the man sitting on the grass below her. Constantine Gerard either knew exactly what he was doing or his instincts were something supernatural. Certainly he had interrogated enough hardened men in his years as a general.

"It was rumored that Felsteppe questioned the Lady Patrice alone for some time."

"Did he harm her?"

Dori paused, closed her eyes. "Perhaps."

"Tell me the—"

"I don't know!" she interrupted, and then forced herself to take a breath. "She might have called for help, but Felsteppe's soldiers prevented any of the servants from entering. When he emerged from the hall, he declared that the countess was lying. He spoke to . . . he spoke to Christian." Dori had to pause here, gird herself. "Then he sent him into the hall after his mother. He ordered the door to be barred and the castle set afire. It is said the men made use of a kind of water that burned. You can see to what extent the blaze completely destroyed Benningsgate."

She took a deep breath. "And that is all I know."

Constantine Gerard didn't so much as move and so, after several moments, Dori gathered up her ragged skirts and moved back toward the enclosed ward, leaving him on the hillside with his grief. She waited until she thought she was out of earshot before giving leave to her own quiet sobs.

Chapter 6

Glayer watched the man hold forth yet another swath of rich velvet, this one in a deep sapphire blue. His lips curved in a slight smile and he held his chalice loosely in his left hand as he reclined in his chair in the lord's chamber. His dressing gown lay heavy and warm against his skin, the material fairly singing with luxury.

"That one is very nice," he said to the anxious tailor. "But have you anything in red?"

He bowed repeatedly. "Certainly, my lord. Certainly."

The man scurried to his pile of goods on a low, wide ottoman, and Glayer observed his enthusiasm to please with great satisfaction. And well he ought—Thurston Hold's lord was keeping the man employed with all the costumes he was commissioning of late. There were feasts and fêtes, tunics cut to impress his calling neighbors, costumes for travel and while petitioning at Henry's court. Why, it was exhausting being of such high rank, considering only the number of times he was forced to change his clothing.

But the idea of it made his smile grow. Glayer Felsteppe had never been so ... *comfortable* in all his life, and not simply in his physical person. True, Thurston Hold was a veritable palace, his furnishings and clothes rivaling Henry's own, but it was his sense of inner peace that brought him the most happiness. His enemies? Banished. Dead, likely, but even if they weren't, there was absolutely nothing that could be done to dislodge Glayer from his much deserved life. Constantine Gerard and everything he'd ever claimed as both a general and as the earl of Chase had vanished as if he'd never existed. And soon Glayer would own the last piece of the man's legacy: the lands of Benningsgate.

He thought he'd leave the castle ruin standing for sentimental reasons.

Yes, Glayer was now titled, rich beyond compare, and working diligently to become a trusted resource to the king in his time of familial and clerical strife. Perhaps there was even a chance Henry would one day elevate Glayer to a dukedom.

The door to his chamber opened beyond the little stooped tailor and Glayer's smile grew. He placed his chalice on the table and held his arms up expectantly.

"Glander!" he called, and the little dark head turned at the sound of his voice. "Come to Papa."

Eseld lowered Glander into his arms and the baby smiled up into Glayer's face. "Good morning, son. Have you had your breakfast, then?"

"It's past luncheon, my lord," Eseld said.

"Is that so?" Glayer said, touching a finger to the little chap's nose. "We don't care one whit, do we? We do not."

The tailor cleared his throat timidly, causing Glayer's smile to falter as he glared at the man for daring to intrude. He continued to scowl until the tailor fidgeted and then at last began gathering up his long lengths of cloth and, giving a hasty bow, scurried toward the door.

"Forgetting something?" Glayer called out after the man and raised his eyebrows as the tailor froze in his tracks and turned back.

"A thousand pardons, my lord," the man said, dropping to his knees before Glayer. His head bent down and then Glayer felt the twin brushes of the man's lips on the tops of his feet. He rose and likewise kissed the tiny, gowned impressions of Glander's feet as well.

"You're dismissed," Glayer said with a wave. "Go on and fashion me a suit each in the blue and the red."

"Certainly, my lord."

"And I'll need both complete costumes by the end of the week."

The tailor hesitated. "Of course, my lord."

Glayer looked at the man pointedly. "Well?"

"Only waiting for further instruction, my lord."

"Get out!" he screamed. Glander whimpered in his arms and so he raised his hand up to cup the baby's ear. "That *was* loud," he allowed.

The door to his chamber shut and Eseld took advantage of the privacy to sit in a chair near his small side table. It was a gross liberty, but Glayer let it go. She was allowed some comfort, he supposed. He stroked Glander's silky hair.

"Preparing for our next visit to the king, my lord?"

"I'd planned for us to travel to court at the end of the week, Nurse, but it will have to be postponed a bit—I've been invited to a fête at Jarlswood to be held in my honor." What an interesting creature this boy was, his son. It didn't even bother him that the child bore such a close resemblance to his mother. Theodora had been a stunning beauty. "Several lords of no little importance will be in attendance, I'm told."

"I thought your priority was securing Benningsgate."

He turned from the baby to glare at Eseld. "Excuse me, but I don't believe your duties extend to the role of adviser. You're barely qualified as a nurse."

The old woman stiffened and turned her eyes away but made no rejoinder.

"There is no race for Benningsgate. No one else can hold such a claim to it as I, although many of our neighbors would love to add the lands to their own. Henry must agree that I am the worthiest of it, considering the obscene amount of money I am willing to pay above its worth."

"Some may put up a fight," Eseld warned timidly.

"And that is why it is so important that I make a good impression on my neighbors, dear Nurse," he said condescendingly. "As young Glander here grows into his birthright, there will be no shortage of allies and those wishing to align with Thurston Hold and the powerful house of Felsteppe." He bounced Glander again. "Isn't that right? We shall claim everything as far as our eyes can see, shan't we? Yes, we shall."

Eseld's already thin lips seemed to disappear in her lined face.

"When you *leave*," Glayer continued pointedly, "locate Simon and send him to me. I've a task for him."

"He's still recovering his arm," the nurse snipped. "You can't think to—"

"You will do as you're told!" Glayer roared, the baby in his arms startling and then beginning to cry. Glayer's face felt afire as he tried to calm himself enough to comfort his son, holding the boy closely on his shoulder and hushing him. He hated for the boy to cry—the sound was piercing and gave Glayer a headache, as well as making the child's countenance a horror.

"You needn't fear that I'll have him rebuilding the sanctuary he's all but deserted. I'm sending him on a journey."

Eseld didn't comment, but Glayer couldn't keep from telling her the details of the thing. It was brilliant really. A complete coup.

"I've found out at last where my enemies have been hiding all these years—under the protection of an abbot at a cloister in Austria. By the time Simon makes the lengthy journey, he should be recovered enough for his task."

"You're sending an old priest to kill your enemies?" Eseld asked with a confused frown.

"Don't be stupi—well, you can't really help that now, can you?" he smirked. "No, Simon's task is not to kill the four men against me—if even they still live. His status as a priest will allow him to beg counsel from his Christian cohort." Glayer patted the baby's warm, smooth, rounded back and spoke softly now; the little fellow had fallen asleep.

"Simon is to gain audience with the man who has sheltered the four responsible for my strife the past five years. Victor, I believe he is called. Shh, shh," he comforted the stirring boy. He looked over the baby's head. "And then he will kill the priest. He's the only one left with enough reputation to possibly vouchsafe for the traitors."

Eseld didn't move, didn't comment, although he could see the fury in her cloudy eyes. Good; he hoped she was vexed, the foolish, delusional fanatic.

"So, go on and fetch him, *Nurse,*" Glayer goaded.

Eseld stood and approached the lord of Thurston Hold and his heir, her spindly arms reaching toward the child.

"No, leave him," Glayer commanded, knowing it would pain her to do so. She hesitantly turned to go and Glayer cleared his throat softly. Eseld froze in her escape.

"Pay your homage," Glayer reminded her in a quiet, happy voice.

The old woman turned and dropped to her knees, kissing Glayer's feet. She reached a trembling hand toward the end of the baby's dressing gown, but Glayer cupped his boy's feet in his hands, denying her.

"That will be all," he said.

Eseld struggled to her feet and quit the chamber, pulling the door closed behind her and leaving Glayer and the baby on the luxurious velvet chaise.

Glayer sighed through his contented smile and stroked the baby's fine gown, covering his shallow, even breaths. "Mothers," he complained on a sigh. "Be glad you don't have one. And you're welcome."

The boy stood for a moment between the pair of massive winged cherubim, soaking up the bright sunshine. He had to squint, even with his hand shielding his eyes. The statues must have been fifteen feet tall, but rather than being intimidating, they seemed to smile down on him.

He dropped his hand and faced forward, looking past tall, wide gates to the courtyard beyond, where it seemed the entire population of the compound was milling about the plots of trees and fountains. He felt a bit of nerves settling in his stomach. He should be relieved, he supposed; now that he'd survived this far, all he had left to do was follow the instructions Father Simon had given the woman on the Chatham road.

If he could find the one Simon had named among so many similarly garbed men inside . . . He swallowed down the shaky feeling in his throat.

But not all the men inside were dressed the same, he now saw, and not all of them were even men. Three couples dressed in the clothing of laity were clustered near the center of the courtyard, an equal number of mounts waiting nearby and obviously equipped for a journey. The men and women were smiling and taking turns embracing one of the robed men in particular, a skinny, balding monk.

Must be him.

He drew a deep breath and started through the gate, glad that no one had thus far noticed his arrival. But that was usually the case with adults and children. Very few grown persons ever paid young ones any heed, unless it was to get up to something dastardly. Up to this point in his journey, it had suited him just fine to be ignored.

He paused and quickly dropped to one knee, wriggling his filthy forefinger beneath the ankle lace of his shoe until he felt the little round coin. He was dismayed that he hadn't taken time to wash up in the river when he'd snuck from the boat. Perhaps the man wouldn't take him seriously if he thought him nothing more than a dirty, penniless orphan.

Well, it was the truth, wasn't it?

He stood once more, feeling a moment of dizziness, and then began his march forward, the gold coin clutched so tightly in his right fist he wondered that it didn't melt.

One of the well-dressed men—he had eyelashes like a woman and a fancy tunic with braiding—caught sight of him over the slight monk's head and gave a quizzical smile.

"Pardon me, Victor," the man said, and his accent was foreign even to this part of the world. "I think there is someone who wishes to speak with you, yes?" The woman at his side, holding a girl child in her arms, leaned 'round and gave a coo and a kind smile of the sort ladies were wont to give as her gaze caught sight of him.

The monk turned around and looked down, his own slight smile on his face. His eyes were red-rimmed and glistening. He opened his mouth and spoke in the language of the towns planted along the winding river below, but of course the words made no sense.

The boy seemed unable to slow his breathing, had to swallow several times. He tried to recall Simon's exact instructions to the woman.

Up the river to Austria, in the town of Melk, where there is an abbey. Give this to the abbot there—Victor. Tell him who you are and what has been done to you. If there is any help to be had for you . . .

"Are you Victor?" the boy asked, surprised at how strong his voice sounded to his own ears, when he was actually more than a little concerned he might vomit before all these finely dressed people staring at him with amusement.

The monk's reddened eyes widened a bit. "I am indeed, my son. Do you require my assistance? I'm a bit occupied now, but if you—"

A huge blond man stepped forward, a falcon sitting easily upon his shoulder, and placed a hand that seemed as large as a cartwheel on the monk's own thin shoulder. "It's all right, Victor. We have a long journey ahead of us. We can surely wait a moment more."

The monk reached up and absently patted the large man's hand before turning his attention back to his visitor. "Well, then. What can I do for you, child?"

The boy wrenched his attention away from the hunting bird and thrust out his arm, his fist opening with what seemed to him to be a creaking of his fingers, the bright sun glancing off the gold in his palm in delirious flashes. Almost finished now . . .

All those gathered around Victor seemed to still. They leaned forward slightly to gaze at the coin offered to the monk and glanced at one another quizzically or with frowns.

Oh, no. Maybe it meant nothing after all. Maybe the woman had been right, and Simon had been sending her on a goose hunt to get her far away.

Victor himself reached out very slowly and retrieved the little metal disk with forefinger and thumb. He looked down at it thoughtfully for a moment before raising his eyes slightly to regard the boy once more. "Where did you get this, child?"

Tell him who you are and what has been done to you . . .

He swallowed down his fear again.

"My name is Christian Gerard. A man called Glayer Felsteppe killed my mother and I think my father might be dead, too. His name is General Constantine Gerard, and he is the earl of Chase. I know that it probably doesn't make very much good sense to you, but I was told if I came here, you could help me."

The abbot made a strange sound in his throat before he was pushed gently aside and a man with long hair stepped into his place and then squatted down before Christian. He reached out his arms, and when his sleeves rose, Christian saw that his skin was painted with spiraling black swirls. His eyes sparkled as he grasped Christian's elbow with one hand and cupped the side of his face with the other.

"Christian?" the man asked, and his voice broke on the word. "Christian Gerard?"

Christian nodded, and the tightly winding spring of fear was somehow uncurling in his stomach. "Did you know my father?"

The man suddenly gave a huff of laughter and he smiled, even as a tear raced down his cheek. In the next moment, Christian found himself pulled into the man's painted arms, held tightly against his chest. No one had embraced him since his mother had died, and even though the man was a stranger to him, Christian could feel the love and compassion coming from him like the warm glow of the sun above. It surrounded him, cushioned him, sank into him. Then the man pressed his lips to Christian's cheek, which he knew had to be grubbier than his hands because he had no way of seeing when it should be cleaned.

Then he felt other hands touching his hair, his back and arms, and the light of the sun was blocked as he was taken into the somehow even brighter fold of these strange and beautiful people, all laughing and whispering his name.

"It's all right," the man holding him said. "It's all right now—you're safe. Thank God, thank God—it's a miracle." His arms tightened around him, rocking him slightly.

Christian curled his dirty fingers into the man's clean tunic, buried his face in his neck, and at last sobbed like the child he was.

Chapter 7

Constantine rapped on the thick oratory door and waited, the charred smell of the collapsed corridor behind and above him causing his guts to twist; how could the woman beyond the door have tolerated it this long?

"Yes?" she called from the stone room beyond, and Constantine pushed open the door.

She was sitting on the narrow bench, but it appeared she'd just risen from a reclining position. He hadn't meant to wake her. She had had color in her face since eating the fish he'd caught for them early that morning, but unfortunately, that color was a faint shade of green.

"Are you unwell, Lady Theodora?"

She pushed a hand through her hair, then shook at her skirts, avoiding his gaze as he came into the room and pushed the door closed behind him to shut out the burned, rotten stench.

"I fear it has been long since I've had appreciable sustenance," she huffed on a laugh.

Constantine frowned, wondering if she had vomited what little she'd eaten that morning. He crossed the room and squatted near the hearth on the stone floor, making a show of straightening the firewood he'd brought.

"How long after you gave birth did you escape to Benningsgate?"

"I awoke from the draught they gave me in a carriage." When Constantine looked up at Theodora, she elaborated. "The priest under Felsteppe's thumb was to kill me. I suppose he experienced an attack of scruples, though, and instead thought to send me far away on a ship. I walked here on the Chatham road."

"Alone?"

"There certainly wasn't anyone I could trust enough to ask for assistance."

Constantine stilled in making the small pile of fuel. The woman had given birth for the first time and walked miles afterward to take shelter at this deserted ruin. It was a wonder she hadn't bled to death. He recalled her telling him her hair had been caked with blood.

But then, he also recalled that he was conversing with the woman who, by marrying the monster she had, had guaranteed Constantine's exile from his own country.

He placed the last stick atop the pile and then turned, sitting back against the wall and looking at her with a sigh. "Does the priest know you still live?"

Theodora shrugged and hesitantly leaned her own back against the wall behind her. Constantine could tell she didn't trust him, and that was fine. He didn't trust her either.

"I'm certain if he survived his fall and managed to gain the road once more to find that I, his servant, and the carriage for our departure to the docks had vanished, he assumed I had taken advantage of the opportunity to leave."

"His fall?"

She met his gaze levelly. "I pushed him over the embankment at the roadside, into a ravine."

Constantine felt his eyebrows raise.

"I'd hoped to kill him," she clarified unnecessarily. "If I'd had any sort of weapon on my person at the time, I would have made certain he was dead."

Constantine remembered the strength with which she'd fought him when he'd cornered her in the ward and had no doubt that what she'd said was true. If only she had used such cunning and will to lay her husband low. "There is no one at all, then, who would have any reason to suspect you are still in the area of Thurston Hold," he pressed.

"There is likely no one who thinks I'm still alive, let alone still in this area."

He nodded. "I'll need money."

She stared at him. "For what?"

"The longer I wait to go after Felsteppe, the greater the risk that either or both of us will be discovered. If I am not to be arrested for Glayer Felsteppe's murder, I must have the means to flee."

"You seem to have done well enough evading the authorities on your own thus far," she pointed out. "Has this become a mercenary task for you, Lord Gerard? Avenging your family?"

"No, but after he is dead, you and your son will once more live in the comfort of Thurston Hold while the king finds a suitable husband for you." He gestured around the small oratory. "I have nothing left. And there are some friends I would help provide for if they are in need of it after all this is over. They, too, have lost their homes, their livelihoods."

"So you are telling me that you will help me rescue my son?"

"No. I am telling you that I will wait to go after Glayer Felsteppe until you have secreted the child safely away from the danger."

He saw her throat convulse as she swallowed and then nodded. A faint sparkle came into her eyes—the first Constantine had seen.

"How much will you require?"

"How much can you lay hand to?"

Theodora was still for a moment, as if considering her words carefully. "I've hidden a shallow trunk in a hollow of the wall behind a stone in the nursery. I hoarded away what coin and valuables I could lay hand to, so that after my son was born and I had recovered, we could flee. There is a considerable amount of silver. Jewels as well."

"That will do," Constantine said.

"Very well. Then we have an agreement," she said.

"You shall have to take more care than you have in the past. It is not above Glayer Felsteppe to torture those he seeks information from, and I'd not have you leading him right to me."

"I'm not stupid, Lord Gerard," she said coolly.

Constantine's mouth thinned. "I suppose, between the two of us, you had a more intimate knowledge of him than I, but I know how he behaves when trapped."

"As do I," she said, and her hard gaze made Constantine wonder for a moment just how deep that knowledge went, and exactly what Theodora Rosemont had done to make Glayer Felsteppe wish dead the beautiful, wealthy woman who was the mother of his child.

It also increased his wariness of her. "Don't think to betray me, Theodora."

"Don't promise what you can't deliver, Lord Gerard," she said, and her words let the unspoken threat hang in the cool, humid oratory, where once, a lifetime ago, Constantine had knelt to receive God's blessing before departing for the fortress at Jacob's Ford.

He stood away from the wall. "It's started to rain. By the looks of the sky, it's likely to continue for some time. I'll collect the fish from the pit and return with more firewood. After that I plan to see who's still about in the village."

"Aren't you afraid someone will recognize you?"

"I am much changed from the time when I was lord here."

"I knew who you were," she challenged.

"I'll be careful," he said and walked to the door. "Old Stacy's cottage might have what we require. If he's gone, perhaps he's left something of use behind."

"Stacy begged for employ at Thurston Hold after the fire," she said. "Most of the villagers did, and my father provided for them. Many have left now, though."

He looked up at her, the question clear in his eyes.

"Felsteppe sent them away. He said they were a burden on the estate." She paused. "Are you searching for food?"

"Herbs. Medicines." He opened the door and paused to look back at her. "You're still quite weak. You'll need to regain your strength before attempting the journey to Thurston. I can't have you being caught or overpowered." *Or dying*, he thought suddenly, unsure why he would remotely care whether the strange young Theodora Rosemont lived or died.

"I do believe this weak woman put up enough of a fight for you, Lord Gerard," she challenged, but the faint shadow of a smile told Constantine that although she had succeeded in maintaining her life thus far, she was beginning to fade and knew it. "I do hope you didn't have too much trouble stitching yourself up," she said, glancing at the ruddy stain on the flank of his tunic.

"But a scratch," he said with a careless wrinkle of his nose. And then he quit the room for the black stink of the corridor, where the gloomy and miserable reality of Benningsgate wrapped around him with its suffocating embrace, obliterating even the hint of levity that had tried to seep between the ruined stones.

Theodora closed her eyes with a shuddering sigh and leaned her head back against the stones after Lord Gerard had departed the oratory. Her throat constricted, but she commanded herself not to cry.

She had already wept enough for a hundred lifetimes and it was a waste of her energy. She took several deep breaths.

He was going to help her.

Probably.

Dori didn't try to fool herself into believing Constantine Gerard's motives were even remotely charitable. By agreeing to wait to kill Glayer Felsteppe, he would secure the entirety of the resources Dori had secreted away while she'd carried her child.

But if it meant she could hold her baby, knowing Glayer Felsteppe was dead, Dori would have gladly given up all of Thurston Hold to the earl of Chase were it in her power to do so. After all, Dori would have her son ever after then, but Constantine Gerard never would have his. The keep meant nothing to her now that her father was dead. Now that . . .

Even the leaning of her mind toward him caused Dori to force herself to her feet to begin pointlessly straightening the few items within the oratory. If she was to share the space with Constantine Gerard, it needed to have the appearance of a common chamber rather than the private quarters Dori had been using it as. She was adding more wood to the small fire when he returned, his arms laden, the hood and shoulders of his cape dark with rain. He brought the sweet smell of spring with him in the breeze of his passing as he walked to the table to deposit the items. He disappeared through the door again without comment, although she'd been certain to leave the little eating knife with its tip broken off and *CAG* engraved on the handle in the center of the table.

Dori rose and walked to the table, curious about the pile of goods he'd brought. A wooden trencher, perhaps, although Dori thought it large enough to be a dough bowl; a spool of twine, nearly spent; several rags, stained but clean, and stiff with the cold spring wind that had dried them on someone's line; a fresh bough wrapped around several fragrant, dried fish.

He was back through the door then, a short, three-legged stool in one hand and a thick, rolled bundle beneath his other arm, which also carried a bucket slightly more than half full of water. He set the stool on its legs near the hearth as well as the bucket and then made room on the table to place the dusty, moth-eaten blanket. He unfurled the ancient thing to reveal a handful of crumbly, dried bundles of herbs, a wooden tankard with a crack along the side; a long handled two-pronged fork; and a rough bag that, although tied tightly with twine, appeared by its deflated shape to be completely empty.

Lord Gerard then swung his satchel from his shoulder and lifted the flap to remove a small covered crock, a forged cup, several metal utensils of various sharpness, and a leather kit that perhaps at one time had contained a gentleman's toilette essentials, being quite finely tooled, but which now Dori suspected held other things.

She looked up at him as he arranged things. "Where did you get all this?"

"The things in my satchel are my own," he said absently, as though she didn't deserve his attention. "The others I scavenged from the village. There wasn't much left in the abandoned houses. I'm certain whoever stayed behind took whatever remained that suited their needs. But I'd wager we'll have enough to get by."

Dori was impressed; the things he'd brought, broken and worn as they were, seemed like treasures to her after living so long in the oratory without little comforts. He shrugged out of his wet cloak and hung it on a peg likely meant for the priest's stole and added even more wood to the crackling fire before returning to the table.

She watched him as he began to break off pieces of the dried herbs and sprinkle them in the metal cup, where they slid to the rounded bottom with little shivers of sound. Then he unwrapped one of the fish and, taking hold of one of the slender bladed knives, deftly severed the head and peeled the spine from the flesh before folding it into the cup atop the herbs. He loosened the cover from the crock to reveal jagged rocks of cloudy salt, of which he chose a piece and added it to the cup.

Then he picked up the wooden tankard and walked to the hearth, where he dipped it into the water bucket to below the crack. He returned to the table and poured the water over the ingredients in the metal cup and mixed the contents with the blade of his knife. The utensil made a sharp ringing sound when Lord Gerard tapped it on the cup and Dori startled a bit, realizing that the growing heat of the room and the graceful surety with which the man moved had enchanted her for a time.

He picked up a square, handleless blade and placed it atop the cup before returning to the hearth with it. He dragged the stool before the warming blaze and sat down, reaching out to snuggle the cup into the graying coals on the edge of the fire. Then he rested his elbows on his knees, held his palms toward the fire, and seemed to forget she was in the room.

Dori stood at the table staring at his darkened outline for several moments, feeling the heat of the fire seeping into her bones and making her flesh feel heavy. Even her toes were beginning to warm. Constantine Gerard obviously had no use for her at this time, now that he'd made his soup and was waiting for it to cook. She glanced behind her at the bench, the embroidered cloth beckoning to her.

A moment later, she had curled up on her side as soundlessly as she could, pulling the cloth around her and using her bent arm for a pillow. The comfort of the coverlet in the warm chamber nearly made her moan with pleasure. She stared at Lord Gerard's back as her eyelids grew heavy, realizing that, for the first time since coming to Benningsgate, she needn't fear anyone finding her, intruding upon her secret shelter. He wasn't her friend; he wasn't her savior; he wasn't even her ally really. But she somehow knew she was safer now than she had been for several months. He might not go out of his way to protect her from an intruder, but he would certainly defend what little was left of his home from any further trespass.

She finally let her eyes close and sank into the pitch black of sleep, so much brighter than the despair and fear that had been her constant companions.

Constantine watched the flames leaping and waving in the shallow square of the hearth, letting the warmth seep into his clothes and dry them, relax his tightened muscles. Steam began to curl from beneath the small metal plate he'd set upon the cup to keep ashes from the brew, and rose and stepped to the table to retrieve one of the rags to protect his hand. He saw the little broken eating knife laying perfectly perpendicular to the edge of the tabletop, as if it had been placed there with great care, and then glanced at once to the bench where Theodora Rosemont was fast asleep. He didn't know how long she had been that way, but her face seemed more serene than at any time since he'd come upon her on the wall walk. He glanced back at the gilded eating utensil, its shiny coating mostly worn away, the creases in the braid of the handle packed with black.

Soot? Dirt?

Constantine picked it up carefully, reverently, with the rag and let it lay across the palm of his other hand. He turned back to the stool soundlessly and sat down. The firelight flashed on the little blade, the shadows of the shallow engraving of initials seeming to deepen in the light, and Constantine ran his thumb across them.

Christian Ambrose Gerard.

How many times had Christian's little fingers grasped this handle, awkwardly gaining the skill to feed himself? Hadn't Constantine himself placed it in his very hand many times, helping adjust the boy's grip, guide it to his mouth? He turned the blade toward himself and brought it closer to his eyes, examining the broken edge. The metal there was not sharp and raw but rounded and dull; this damage had occurred long ago. A result of play, perhaps? Likely Patrice had fitted him for a larger one as he grew any matter, and Christian had reserved this for his own boyish uses. Perhaps when he pretended at being a Templar knight, as Patrice's last letter had relayed.

He is very proud of you, Constantine—his papa is a hero in his eyes. He looks for your return each day, as do I . . .

Constantine closed his fingers over the eating knife and looked back to the flames. The chill of his memories had banished the warmth of the crackling fire before him, and he hunched into himself on the little stool.

God help him, he was going mad. He had thought that perhaps being at Benningsgate would renew him, stoke the fire of revenge in his belly until it burned so furiously that it obliterated any thoughts beyond his eagerness to watch the life seep out of Glayer Felsteppe. But it seemed as though the opposite was happening; the despair he now felt was greater than any he'd experienced the night he first learned of the fire at Benningsgate. Holding this possession of Christian's—the only one he now had—caused his heart to ache so that he wished he could reach into his chest and extract the thing, perhaps even toss it on the flames to be devoured.

Anything, anything to take away this pain. This guilt.

Please don't go, Constantine; please! I swear to you, it will never happen again. I swear it! Please don't leave us—we need you here.

A spluttering and hissing interrupted his reverie and he blinked away the watery, stinging memories to see the liquid in the metal cup bubbling and spitting through the narrow opening left by the cover. Constantine wound the forgotten rag around his hand and used the broken tip of Christian's knife to lift the lid a bit and then turn and

slide the cup itself farther from the heart of the fire. The boiling settled and the smell reached his nostrils.

It would be better if it had cooked for longer, but he didn't think
Theodora Rosemont's condition warranted waiting.

He went again to the table, retrieving the cracked tankard and the
meager amount of twine. Constantine cut a length of the hairy thread and
wrapped it around the top of the tankard, looping it back on itself so that
by pulling one end, the twine tightened and closed the crevice near
the rim. He knotted it securely and examined it; it would have to do.

He took his supplies back to the fire and squatted by the hearth
next to the tankard. First he slid the cup out of the coals and then
lifted the lid away carefully and set it aside. Then he wrapped the rag
around the cup and placed the blade along the rim, holding back the
solid contents as he poured the steaming liquid into the tankard. Constantine set the tankard aside to cool while he added to the metal
cup's contents and then returned the new batch to the coals.

He rose, setting the blade and rag on the table before walking to
the bench to stand over Theodora Rosemont's sleeping form, the
tankard in his right hand. He watched her for several moments, wondering if she was dreaming, what she was seeing. She was curled into
herself tightly, as if she needed to defend herself even in her sleep.

Constantine knew that feeling well, and for a moment he thought
how bad her life might have been since her father died. She was still
so young. . . .

He shook himself. Theodora Rosemont's plight was no matter to
him in the least. She was a means to an end, and her sorrow, her future, that of Glayer Felsteppe's *child*—here he grimaced and cocked
his head—would cause no rise of sympathy in him. He couldn't
allow it. He *wouldn't* allow it.

"Theodora," he said, and his voice was gravelly, cracked. She did
not stir. He cleared his throat. "Dori."

Her eyelids fluttered open and she blinked, squinted up at him.

"Yes?" she whispered. "Is something the matter?"

Constantine looked down at the tankard in his hand. *Damn it.*

"Get up. Your broth is ready."

Chapter 8

Tonight was the night he would kill himself.

Yes, he thought so. He had fasted nearly to the point of starvation during Lent, partaking of only bread and water once a day for more than forty days, so that his already long, gaunt face seemed that of a specter, the graying widow's peak of his hairline retreating farther on his skull, his voluminous robes unable to conceal his thinness. He had prayed in every private moment—hours on the hard cold stones—to be delivered from the torment of his life, to have this demon excised from his soul. He had partaken of self-flagellation, holding in his mind's eye the faces of the people he had harmed, betrayed, thrown to the abyss in order to do his dark tormentor's unholy bidding as he cut his own flesh with the whips. He had prayed unceasingly for escape, for mercy.

But he had celebrated the risen Lord at Thurston Hold himself. There would be no escape for him, save that which he enacted himself. So be it.

Simon heard the chapel door creak open behind him and closed his eyes with a silent sigh, blocking out the sight of the crucifix he'd been concentrating on and closing the worn-thin prayer book between his palms.

It didn't matter—God hadn't been speaking to Simon any more than he'd been praying.

"Father?" the timid, watery voice called out. "Am I disturbing you?" *Eseld.*

He turned his face only enough so that his voice would carry to the back of the room.

"No," he lied, the word thick with mucus and the despair of the ocean of tears he'd not wept. He cleared his throat quietly. "What is your need?"

The door creaked again as the stooped nurse entered the chapel. She bobbed and made the sign of the cross in the direction of the altar, although she didn't venture any further inside.

"It's not my needs I've come for," she said. "The lord is requesting you."

Simon's heart—if indeed he could still claim even a part of that gentle organ—shriveled in his chest. Glayer Felsteppe asking for him could only mean that there was yet another crushing, splintery burden to lay across Simon's shoulders. He wondered what horrific, grotesque defilement the man wished performed. Simon could hardly think of anything much worse than what he'd already done for Glayer Felsteppe, but that meant little; if there was one thing Felsteppe had always been wealthy in, it was the endless array of appalling acts he wished to have visited upon those he despised.

He didn't realize he was shaking his head, already futilely refusing the unknown duty, until Eseld stepped closer and spoke again.

"Would that you not let it sit so heavily upon your heart, Father," she said softly. He looked up at the old woman as she glanced over her shoulder and pushed the chapel door halfway closed. She turned back to him and gave him what she likely hoped was an encouraging smile, her teeth—what few she still claimed—yellowed and black, her thin lips drawing out the pursed wrinkles around her mouth.

"I know it's a great burden you've borne, aiding his lordship. But surely you see that you will be paid back for your loyalty a hundred-fold when your life on this dismal earth is over."

Simon felt the prickle of tears in his eyes. The poor daft woman. "You truly believe that, don't you?"

Eseld rushed forward and dropped to her knees on the floor, grabbing at the edge of the bench upon which Simon sat to steady her descent, and he winced as he heard the crackling of her joints. He wanted to jerk her to her feet, shake her. But it was she who pinched his cassock with her bony fingers.

"With all my heart. It seemed only a fortnight ago that he left my cottage, naught more to commend him save the farm we only partly claimed. He left for his great crusade, to be a champion for God, and he saved the king of Jerusalem! Despite his enemies' best efforts to see him ruined."

Simon stared down into her face, so lined and weary and gray, her hair so thin beneath the black linen cap that he could see her scalp shining in the dim candlelight of the chapel.

"And he sent for me," she continued, her smile gentling. "His old mother. He needed me in his grand new house, to help raise his precious baby—my grandson! What a gift he has given me, given both you and me, by allowing us such small parts to play. Do you see?"

The bile rose in Simon's throat so quickly that he couldn't speak lest he be sick all over the old woman.

"And his work is not yet over; nay, nay!" She inched closer to him on her knees. "He is yet wresting his reward from those enemies who sought him dead. He is winning England for the just! And for me," she said, her voice softening. "He is atoning for my sins, my failures. Because he loves me."

"No," Simon at last managed to strangle out and reached across with his right hand to grasp the woman's forearm. "He cannot atone for your sins. No one can do that save yourself and Christ."

"Oh, but he is," she vowed solemnly. "He's told me he is, and I believe him. And just as you were asked to do that which pained you—delivering him from his wretched enemies, like that hateful Rosemont woman who would have denied my son his own precious, perfect child—I, too, must persevere in the knowledge that we are doing God's work as he has put it to Glayer. *To his lordship*," she corrected in a whisper with wide, rheumy eyes.

"Eseld, listen to me," Simon said, his voice trembling with fury and dread as he tightened his fingers around her bony arm. "Your son did not call you to Thurston Hold to save your soul, just as I am not in his employ because I am a loyal servant of God." He swallowed and could feel the perspiration at his hairline.

Shut up! Shut up!

But he could not. Perhaps he *was* possessed by a devil inside him, not just the one residing in the lord's chamber across the bailey. It didn't matter really—he would be dead soon.

"Glayer Felsteppe is compelling me to do his most offensive tasks because what he knows of my past would see certain people I love very much destroyed. He is using my status as a priest to cover up the crimes he is committing—is forcing me to commit—and I vow to you now that the only one reaping glory and bloodstained reward from both our labors is him."

"That's not true, Father," she said with a pained look and a sympathetic shake of her head. "His lordship loves y—"

"He doesn't love me, and he doesn't love you either," Simon said through clenched teeth, rising from the bench and dragging the nearly weightless Eseld up with him. Her eyes widened in surprise now, but Simon couldn't stop. "He brought you here to rub in your face all that he now commands; to treat you like a slave and humiliate you—why do you think you are not permitted to call him by his given name or reveal to any other than me that you are his *mother*?"

"I'm certain the king's mother doesn't call him Henry in his own court now, does she?"

"Glayer Felsteppe is not the king!" Simon insisted.

Eseld's eyes narrowed at last and she jerked her arms free from Simon's hold. "But he is the lord," she emphasized. "And that's as close to a king as the likes of you and I are ever to serve." She leaned toward him, reaching her bony nose toward Simon's own. "I know what you did," she whispered. "His lordship told me how he saved you from ruin when the affair would have been revealed. How he secreted you away. He protected you—he continues to protect you— and you would repay him by turning his graciousness into a s-s-sin," she hissed, the word moistening Simon's lips so that he winced.

Damn Glayer Felsteppe; he had revealed just enough of the truth to the woman to convince her that everything he said was a certainty. Isn't that what he always did, though? Build his lies and treachery around the existing good he wanted? It was like hiding a man's silver in horse dung and then thanking him to load the manure for you. Robbing everyone he came across of their wealth, their homes, their sanity and reputation—their lives, in too many cases.

"He was not protecting me," Simon said levelly. "It was he who threatened to reveal me. I had no choice but to cooperate with him."

"And you'll cooperate with him now," Eseld said, shrinking back to her stooped posture and fixing him with a stern glare. "It's for your own good. And Glander's. So you go on to him now, as you were told to do. And you do whatever it is he asks of you." She turned to walk back to the chapel door but stopped before exiting, her fingers wrapped around the handle. She turned back to look at him.

"And if I should ever again hear such slander against my son from your lips, Father"—she paused, and her gaze bore into his with an intensity that accurately portrayed the relation of mother and son—"I'll tell him." She bobbed toward the altar, repeated the sign of the cross, and then shut the door with nary a sound.

Eseld Felsteppe had always been a reverent woman.

Simon turned back toward the crucifix affixed to the stones above the altar, his knees trembling, his stomach roiling. The candles to either side of the ornate dais still flapped with the breeze created by Eseld's soundless departure. He glanced down and saw his prayer book tented on its stiff pages on the stones in front of his feet.

He bent down and picked it up, smoothing its worn leather cover, pale and supple with age. It had been a gift upon taking his final vows as a priest. A gift from Bledsoe.

Simon flung the small book at the crucifix with a roar of fury. The scream went on until his lungs wheezed in agony, and Simon staggered on his feet as he at last drew a breath. He stood in the tomb of the chapel with his chest heaving, glaring at the symbol of his lifelong delusion. The icon for which he had devoted his life; the representation of all that had been taken from him, taken from those he loved.

He believed none of it any longer. It was naught but a story he'd desperately wanted to see proven true. Like a bedtime tale meant to comfort and assure a child anxious in the dark. Simon had berated the desperate Eseld for believing such fantasies about her son, but at least her idol was a living, flesh-and-blood man. Whatever Christ had been—if he had been at all—now he was nothing more than the likeness of a dead man hanging in macabre decoration in chapels all over the world.

There was no difference between the nurse's delusions about Glayer Felsteppe and Simon's pathetic whims about God. Except perhaps that Eseld was infrequently rewarded for her unwavering devotion.

Simon left the chapel with the door standing open and made his way toward the keep to answer Glayer Felsteppe's summons.

Chapter 9

Dori watched Constantine Gerard stack the wet firewood near the hearth and felt another pang of guilt as she kept her seat on the bench, the ever-present tankard of broth in her fist. She'd tried several times for the first few days of her recovery to offer her assistance to the man who was so dependably—if brusquely—tending her. Each of her inquiries as to how she could help him had been met by increasingly stinging rebuffs, causing her to feel foolish and humiliated, and so she'd stopped offering. They rarely spoke now, unless it was a hesitant inquiry or a curt response regarding the weather beyond the walls.

They'd been sharing the little oratory for more than a week and it had rained constantly all those many days. A blessing that had allowed them to enjoy a warming fire, even though the great torrents outside had flooded the river and made fishing almost impossible, and the ground and the very air were so saturated with water that the walls inside the oratory had begun to trickle, lending the shelter the feel of a subterranean cave.

Dori felt much improved; her mind was clearing, as was her vision; her skin was not so blatantly transparent as it had been for weeks. The constant cry of her baby—trapped in her ears since the blurry moment of his birth—quieted somewhat, allowing Dori to recall it at will rather than be at its mercy while it haunted her unceasingly, causing her heart to gallop and her thoughts to thrash against the inside of her skull. She no longer felt that she was barely clinging to sanity, liable to leap from the edge and run toward Thurston Hold and to whatever bloody end Glayer Felsteppe would serve upon her. As she grew stronger, her thoughts became more methodical, more calculating. She was coming back to herself; she could feel it. And each day in the oratory bolstered her confidence in the idea that when she went to collect her son, she would not fail.

She was nearly ready.

"The rain must surely stop soon," she said to Lord Gerard's back, ever toward her.

The shadow of his head bobbed in response.

She grimaced and gave a silent sigh. "I'd go to Thurston Hold at its first break; perhaps before. The rain will do much to hide my journey. I'll discover whether Felsteppe is in residence and see what else I can learn of the goings on."

He didn't bother to face her. "You're still too weak."

"I'm not," Dori argued. "I'm nearly well."

The shadow shook to the negative and then was still for some time. Just when Dori thought he was set on ignoring her completely, Lord Gerard turned sideways on the stool.

"You'd come down with fever and die."

"No," she said calmly. "I wouldn't."

"Or you'd be caught."

"*No.*" She could feel her temper rising, heat coming into her cheeks, and so she took a moment to breathe. "I can't simply sit here forever while Felsteppe is allowed to go on about his life with my son however he pleases."

Lord Gerard shook his head and turned his face back to the fire, although his large body remained perpendicular to her on the stool. "Too weak."

"Well, I'll never recover completely living on nothing but fish and broth in this dank prison," she snapped.

Lord Gerard rolled his head back to regard her with somewhat of a wry expression. "You're welcome."

Now Dori's cheeks did heat. "I didn't mean to sound ungrateful. I know you likely saved my life."

He looked away again. "I did save your life."

Her frown deepened. This was not going at all the way she'd planned. And yet she couldn't keep herself from rising to the bait he seemed intent on dangling before her. "After you tried to kill me."

"You tried to kill me, too," he replied mildly.

Dori gave a low growl in her throat. "If only I had."

"Yes, if only."

Another deep breath. "I'm not asking your permission. I'm telling you that I am ready to make the journey to Thurston Hold."

He was silent for several moments, and when he did begin to speak, he kept his gaze on the fire to his right.

"If you were to depart now, while the rain fell, or after it stopped, you *would* be caught. The deluge of water has kept many indoors, and at first respite the farmers will be anxious for their fields and stables. You, in the same clothes in which you last left Thurston Hold, and shoes that are so thin as to be breathed through, would be as obvious on the road as a scarlet unicorn. Especially after you fainted on your face and someone discovered you."

"I wouldn't fai—"

"If you are determined to leave now, I will set out in the same moment. I will reach Thurston Hold before you, in order that I might do what I returned to do before your discovery and capture could possibly alert Felsteppe that something other than your purported death has gone awry and he becomes even more careful than he already has."

"You'd never have the proof you needed to condemn him," Dori reminded him, but her stomach had fluttered at his matter-of-fact description. "To restore your reputation."

He shrugged his wide shoulders and turned toward her once more. "Given the choice between Glayer Felsteppe dead or incriminated and on the run, I'll choose dead. And my reputation took quite the flogging before I left for Syria any matter."

Her eyes widened at this mention of his past, of the rumors Dori had only vaguely heard, being of such a vulgar nature as to have made her servants and keepers attempt to shield her from the gossip.

"So I'm little more than your prisoner," she said, trying to cover her discomfort. "Perhaps you have more in common with your enemy than you'd like to admit. He, too, commanded my comings and goings."

She regretted her words before the accusation was completely spoken. He had cared for her, nursed her, and she had thanked him by comparing him to Glayer Felsteppe—the man who had murdered Lord Gerard's family. Constantine Gerard's face closed down even further, while Dori's own throat clenched, unable to let words out even if she had thought of some poor apology. But that was Theodora's nature, unfortunately. Hasty. Given to fits of temper.

And so she only lifted her chin and met his gaze.

His voice was so quiet it was little more than a whisper above the crackle of the fire. "You are free to go whenever you wish."

Dori swallowed. "You don't mean that." *Please, don't mean it.*

"I do. You may rise from that bench, walk through yonder door unimpeded. Go in whatever direction your heart desires. Only know that once you go, I will do exactly as I have told you. My aim is the same, and I shall achieve it with or without your childish cooperation."

The barb stung, so often had its kind been flung at her and found its mark. Spoiled, immature, selfish, demanding Theodora.

She got what she deserved, Dori could hear the gossips just as surely as if they were whispering the rumors into her own ear.

"I'm sorry I compared you to Glayer Felsteppe," she said suddenly and in a rush. "I didn't mean it. You're nothing like him."

"A rather poor and tardy attempt to cover yourself, Lady Theodora," he said as he stood. He picked up his satchel from the table as he walked toward the door.

Dori scrambled from the bench, dropping the tankard and rushing to him. "Wait! Lord Gerard," she cried, and grasped his arm with both her hands as she reached him. He looked down at her with ill-concealed contempt. "I didn't mean it. You have to understand—speaking that way, it's a habit I developed to protect myself. To stand up for myself."

He jerked from her grasp and opened the door.

"Please," she cried after him.

Lord Gerard stopped and turned his head slightly, not actually looking at her. "I'm only going fishing, Theodora."

"You swear it?" she pressed, sounding so like the child he accused her of being that she cringed inside.

"Only fishing," he repeated and then left the room, leaving the door standing open.

Dori grasped the edge of the wood with one hand and laid her other palm along the stones of the doorway, watching as Constantine Gerard disappeared into the murk of the corridor. She heard the scrabbling of his footsteps on the stones, but then even his footfalls faded away. Dori continued to stare into the darkness, her heart in her throat, her knees quaking beneath her.

What a stupid, idiotic fool she was! Constantine Gerard could easily set out for Thurston Hold immediately—he had his satchel in his possession. Indeed, he'd left none of his personal possessions behind in the oratory each time he had gone fishing or foraging. Perhaps he had learned to be ready to depart for other destinations at a moment's notice or been prepared to go another way should he determine he was being followed. She'd thought nothing of the habit before this day. But now . . .

By the time Dori accepted that Constantine Gerard was not returning to the oratory, he could have reached Glayer Felsteppe and accomplished what he set out to do, leaving her baby in the hands of whomever was left alive at Thurston Hold. Her son would become a ward of the king and Dori would have no way of knowing where he was or with whom. She might never see him again.

Lord Gerard had said he was going fishing. But who was the last man she could think of who was completely trustworthy? Dori had also dealt him a grave and humiliating insult only a moment before; what would her reaction have been if he'd compared her morals and loyalty to Patrice Gerard's?

Dori left the doorway to fetch her raggedy cloak from the bench and then she, too, set off into the blackness of the corridor.

It was still drizzling as Constantine made his way across the swampy, reedy ward toward the low wall overlooking the river. The sky was gray with low clouds, but they seemed thinner, of less substance than they had on previous days. The air was warmer, too, and Constantine thought the rain would stop very soon. He stepped onto the threshold leading through the wall and hopped down into the long tangle of grass bent low with water.

He tried not to see Theodora Rosemont's face, hear her voice in his head as he made his way down the slippery hill toward the churning, roaring river. Her hair was dark, not blond; her lament was not an argument about Constantine's loyalty to his rank. And yet he couldn't help but hear Patrice's tone in Lady Theodora's accusations.

You're away for months at a time and I am left alone!

I am lonely, Constantine. Will you not at last make a life with me at Benningsgate?

You have a son now; we need you. The estate needs you.

I'm finished being nothing more than a battle trophy for you! Of waiting for you to return!

You forced my hand, Constantine. And this time I am not sorry.

He knew the vile things that had been said about Patrice. But that was only through her growing lack of discretion and poor choices of companions. Few men could resist boasting of having possessed a woman of such beauty. But even though the rumors spread through her own fault, what had driven her to such scandalous behavior was Constantine's own lack of attention.

He came to the edge of the weeds and stepped one foot onto a large outcropping of rock on the bank and looked over the churning water. He should have listened to her. Patrice's actions had grown more outrageous the longer and more frequently Constantine had been away, and he could see so clearly now, so obviously, that her imprudence had been nothing more than a desperate bid for his attention. He should have stayed home and been thankful day and night for the blessings of such a grand estate, such a beautiful, noble wife. Such a strong, handsome son, who did, indeed, favor Constantine, despite the vilest of the rumors.

But accepting the commission at Chastellet had in part been Constantine's way of punishing Patrice. He would give up the sword, yes, but not until this last tour. On his terms. And now his wife was dead. His son was dead. His home was destroyed. His life was over.

Neither he nor Patrice had gotten what they'd wanted.

He heard Theodora coming down the slope as if she was a herd of goats, her breathing choppy and loud as she scrambled over the wall. Stan waited a moment, composing himself before he turned.

She slipped and skidded to a halt on the wet grass above him, the air so thick and humid that her breath steamed. Theodora's hood had fallen back, her short hair flipped up like a dark cherub's. Her eyes were still shadowed, her cheeks still thin, but now a flush of life bloomed on her pale face. Her thin, dark brows were wrinkled together and he wondered what she would rail about now.

"I said I was sorry," she all but shouted.

"And I heard you the first time," he said. "What do you want, Theodora?"

She paused, as if considering the question. "I came to make certain you weren't going ahead to Thurston Hold."

"I told you I was going fishing."

She held up her palms toward him and looked him up and down pointedly.

Constantine felt the corner of his mouth twitch. "I was getting around to it."

Theodora dropped her hands back to her sides. "My father didn't know who I was when he died." The abrupt admission caused Stan's eyebrows to rise. The lady continued. "For nigh a year he had grown increasingly confused. Combative. I had to follow him about on his business and sit in on his meetings so he didn't say something ridiculous, and so I could remind him of things he had agreed to, or conversations that had already taken place. I often had to interrupt negotiations of one sort or another with hysterics to save him from some ignoble trick to part him from his wealth or land. People began to speak of me as being unreasonable, spoiled, demanding. They blamed me for his odd behavior. It wasn't obvious when he didn't recognize a servant or a villager, but when he began to ask people who I was when I walked into the room, they attributed his words to some form of humiliation for the embarrassment I was causing him. Sometimes he thought I was my mother."

She paused here to swallow, and Constantine made no comment. "Felsteppe knew, though. He had heard the rumors and knew my father was ill. And my father agreed to the betrothal in order to get rid of the daughter everyone seemed to suddenly find so difficult and disrespectful. I begged him to recant, but he had me removed from his chamber, calling me a trespassing adolescent village brat. I would usually return to him later when he had such a fit of delusion, but that night he had hurt me, humiliated me so deeply, I didn't. I stayed in my chamber and fumed. That was the night he left the keep, walked into the river—this river—with nary a stitch of clothing on." Her chin lifted the slightest bit. "And he drowned."

The rain had slowed so gradually while Theodora spoke that Constantine hadn't noticed its cessation until she looked at him with her lips pressed together and her chin lifted, her dark lashes wet with the very air. The roar of the river behind him seemed to have come alive now, knowing what he did about the lord of Thurston Hold's death. Was it difficult for her, he wondered, standing on its sodden bank, listening to its hungry rumble? Did she think of her father's last moments, perhaps struggling for his breath in its wet embrace?

"You had no recourse for the marriage agreement after his death," Constantine realized aloud.

Theodora shook her head.

Constantine turned back toward the river, bringing both his boots to the outcropping of rock and crossing his arms over his chest as he gazed at the overgrown, misty fields on the far side of the rushing current. He felt more than saw Theodora Rosemont join him on the perch he'd claimed, and he had to force himself not to glance down, extend a hand in case she should happen to lose her footing on the wet, mossy rock.

"I'd hoped you would tell me Glayer Felsteppe killed your father," he said. "Perhaps then we could have enjoined to Henry in a common plea."

"As much as I hate to disappoint you in that my father wasn't murdered," she said wryly, "there were many witnesses to the goings-on at Thurston Hold the night he died. And Felsteppe had been in the Holy Land for weeks by then."

He had perhaps been feeling the beginnings of sympathy for her before she'd reminded him. "You went to him there."

"Yes."

"Did he send for you? After receiving word of your father's death?"

Theodora was quiet for several moments, and Constantine thought perhaps there was something—anything—about her actions that could redeem her in his eyes.

"I went of my own accord."

"And you married him in Jerusalem."

"I did," she said, and those two words seemed to place the final details together in a neat, snug bundle with the rest of the tragedies that had led to this day.

Even though the facts as he'd known them had now been nothing worse than confirmed, Constantine's mind was a whirl of bitter regrets, and his black, angry thoughts buzzed around his head like hornets. For although the decision to wed Felsteppe hadn't been her own, Constantine could not allow himself further kindness to Glayer Felsteppe's wife.

"Please don't go to Thurston Hold without me," she said at his side, and Constantine could hear the plea in her voice, although he refused to turn to look down at her waiflike face. "I know you hate me, and I understand why. But I swear to you that once my son is safely away from Glayer Felsteppe, I will do everything in my power to help you. Anything you ask of me, from this point forward, until you release me of my debt. I swear it."

"I don't need your help, Theodora."

"Perhaps not," she allowed. "But we need yours."

We. Theodora and her infant son—Glayer Felsteppe's infant son.

"And perhaps, just perhaps," she interrupted his dark thoughts, "we will prove useful to you yet."

At her strange tone, he did look down at her. "What do you mean?"

"I don't know," she admitted, and although Constantine wouldn't have acknowledged it aloud, her gaze as she stared up at him was clear and without any hint of subterfuge. Guileless, like the young girl she likely had been before being forced to parent her ill father; before Glayer Felsteppe had corrupted her mind with his games and her body with his child.

Constantine felt his principles struggling against some faint whisper of intuition.

"Perhaps I could start by preparing the meal tonight? It's true that I have no experience as a cook, but I doubt even I could ruin boiled fish." Her wide mouth curved up the tiniest bit.

His own lips wanted to return her ghost of a smile at the absurdity of her suggestion, but the moment was interrupted by the abrupt barking of a dog, and Constantine looked over Theodora's head in the same moment that she turned to behold the long-legged gray animal bounding down the riverbank toward them, sounding its deep, staccato alarm.

And coming right along behind the animal was a rotund village man, his arm already raised in greeting.

Constantine looked around for a brief moment, considering their options for flight—the river, the woods, or back to the ruin. With the river they'd be swept away; to the wood, the dog would only give swift chase. Should they retreat to the ruin, the man would gather whatever reinforcements there were to be had in the village before searching the rubble.

Theodora turned back to look up at him, the panic clear in her pale face. "Should we run?"

Constantine looked back to the man walking ever closer to them, what appeared to be some small traps across his back, his long stick helping his waddling progress. The dog was nearly upon them now, his wiry coat flinging water with every leaping stride.

"Constantine," Theodora insisted. He glanced at her again and saw that she had picked up her pathetic, ragged skirts in one fist and now her hand lay on his chest. "Do we run?"

He shook his head. "I'm finished running." He took her elbow and pulled her from the rock behind him as he made his own way down. Constantine turned just as the dog gave a final whining bark and leaped at him.

Chapter 10

The prow of the skiff nodded wildly through the thick mist above the choppy water in the bay. It was dawn, but only barely, and the fog made it seem as though night still surrounded the small boat bounding through the waves with each pull of the oars.

"Careful, there," Adrian said, half-rising to place a steadying hand on Christian's shoulder when the boy would have been tossed into the air. "Hold to the underside of the seat, lad."

Constantine's son looked back at him with a grateful if uneasy smile. "Yes, sir."

Adrian sat fully next to Maisie once more and turned to her as she slid her fingers into his hand and leaned her mouth closer to his ear. "He's nae going anywhere, Adrian. You fuss like a mother hen."

"He's my responsibility until we hand him over to his father," Adrian argued, not the least bit perturbed by his wife's teasing.

"I think we all share in that responsibility," Maisie said. "At least Valentine and Roman feel they do. You are being too selfish with the boy."

Adrian now turned to look past the oarsman and their belongings behind him and found the smoky outline of the second boat, carrying the other two couples. Satisfied that they weren't lost in the mist, he faced forward once more, smiling to himself as he caught sight of Christian leaning this way and that, trying to see ahead through the fog.

"I don't intend to disparage their sense of obligation," he said. "But I will behave as I see fit. As far as I'm concerned, I am Christian's guardian. Stan would want it that way." Although he hadn't intended the statement to have such connotations, a chill made its way up his spine, as if a finger of the damp fog had found a way beneath his heavy cloak and tunic.

Maisie only squeezed his hand, and so he knew she'd heard the worry in his words. What if they were too late? What if they returned to England only to find that Constantine had achieved what he had set out to do, not knowing that his son lived, and had met his own death in seeking his revenge of Glayer Felsteppe?

But Constantine could not be dead, not now. Not when Adrian was bringing to him the person he'd loved most in this world and thought lost forever. No, Adrian would not allow that possibility to enter his mind. Or Christian's.

"Adrian," Christian said, pointing his arm through the mist. "Look!"

The black hull slowly emerged as the skiff strained through the waves, the larger vessel itself bowing and rising deeply in the water.

"Is that our ship?" Christian asked, and Adrian could hear the uncertainty in the boy's voice.

"I do doubt any others are anchored so far from the docks, even in this chop," Maisie muttered wryly.

The boy glanced around with a worried frown. "The merchant ship I sailed on was much larger. This seems too small a vessel to take on passengers." He looked back at the swarthy oarsman suspiciously before turning sideways on the seat and leaning over precariously to whisper, "We could be led into a dangerous situation, Adrian. Brigands of some sort. Perhaps even pirates. It's a scheme of theirs to lure unsuspecting passengers out to open water under the excuse of securing passage. They rob them before tossing them all into the sea."

Adrian smiled. "It's all right, Christian. We aren't unsuspecting in the least."

"Aye, lad," Maisie said. "Unfortunate though it may be, we know exactly the sort that lie in wait of us."

An ear-piercing whistle sounded from the oarsman, causing Christian to startle and frown doubtfully once more at the dark-complexioned man before raising his fair eyebrows at Adrian and his wife.

"Certain about that, are you?"

Adrian only laughed.

Christian shook his head and turned forward on his seat in the skiff just as the *Azure Skull* began to emerge fully from the fog. Adrian saw Christian's head tip back as he caught sight of the man standing on the rail of the ship, one hand grasping the rigging as he leaned out over the roiling waters. He swept his plumed hat from his head in a merry greeting.

"Welcome! Welcome, my friends!" Francisco Alesander called out with a broad smile. "Let us hurry you aboard and raise anchor before the fog is gone, yes? I have managed to fit in a bit of work before your arrival and I would hate to delay your voyage with a battle at sea."

"Or by getting you out of the jail," Valentine called out from the skiff behind them, causing Christian's head to whip around, his eyes like an owl's.

Roman's laugh echoed over the water. "Val, I think we all know that although your talents are many, orchestrating prison escapes is not one of them."

Francisco brought his elaborate hat to his chest to cover his heart. "They have no yet constructed a cage capable of containing *La Ave Mortal*, cousin."

Back and forth Christian looked between the two men before his wide gaze went to Adrian. "Are we . . . are we going home on a *pirate ship*?"

"Would that please you, young Christian?"

He nodded. "Yes, sir."

"Then I would suggest that you turn 'round and take hold of the rope dangling there before you," Adrian said, motioning past the boy with his finger.

Christian spun around and was scrambling from his seat in the next instant, swiping at the swaying knot and causing Adrian to stagger to his own feet to prevent the boy from being pitched into the breach between the two vessels. He grasped the rope and held it steady while Christian took hold and then wrapped his arm around the boy's middle, hoisting him up to stand on the knot while, above them, two of Francisco's mates began to pull, lifting Constantine Gerard's son through the air.

Adrian stood with one hand braced on the edge of the pitching skiff, watching closely while the boy was helped over the railing. Christian spun around and leaned against the wooden rail, looking down at Adrian with his face split in a wide grin.

He gave a high-pitched whoop with a little jump and then drummed his palms on the rail. "Come on, Adrian!"

A second rope had been dropped to the left of their dinghy and Adrian glanced over to see Lady Mary and Valentina being carefully lifted into the air. Adrian thought the look on Valentine's wife's face closely matched that of young Christian's.

"I'll join you in a moment, lad," Adrian shouted up to the boy as he took hold of the rope once more and motioned for Maisie to come to him.

"I should have at least tried to summon a crawler," she muttered as he lifted her high enough to gain a foothold.

"Hold on." He grinned at her and then let her go as she rose above the water.

Adrian himself was aboard *The Azure Skull* in time to help the crew haul up the massive form of Roman Berg as well as the belongings of the friends. The two oarsmen didn't bother waiting to be pulled on the ropes, ascending with the expertise of swarthy spiders, leaving the oars in the bottoms of the skiffs that were already drifting away from the pirate ship. Adrian looked questioningly up to Valentine, whose boots had now taken the place of his Spanish cousin's upon the railing.

"Those weren't even Francisco's boats, were they?"

Valentine shrugged a shoulder and gave Adrian a grin. "Something makes me think they were no."

Adrian shook his head and turned toward the center of the small ship, which was alive with festive movement even as the vessel itself began to turn in the fog. The crew scattered across the deck and rigging at their tasks, save for an old man seated upon a squat barrel, whose sole responsibility, it appeared, was to play the slender pipe in his hands. A merry, birdlike song flavored the sea air with the bright promise of an English spring only days away.

Roman had replaced the falcon on his shoulder with Christian, and they stood on the upper deck next to Isra and Lou, and behind Lady Mary, who appeared to have taken control of the wheel of *The Azure Skull* while a particularly brutish-looking fellow bounced Valentina on his arm. Maisie was presently at the opposite rail from Adrian, holding a long cylinder to her eye under the close guidance of Francisco, who seemed to be directing her gaze over the choppy gray waves.

If he hadn't known the man was completely devoted to Valentine's lovely sister, Teresa, Adrian might have been jealous.

But as it were, he turned back to the railing alone. Although the fog was still thick over the water, he could see the far-off hills of the countryside.

"Good-bye," he whispered, although precisely to whom or what he was bidding farewell, he couldn't have said. Perhaps to dear Victor and Melk and all the brethren they had come to know so well. Perhaps to the wretchedness and sorrow, the death and injury he had known. Perhaps to the man he had been upon his arrival there so many years before.

But he suspected that, more than anything else he could be leaving behind, it was to Constantine Gerard himself. For even if they found Constantine alive in England, Adrian doubted he would be the same man he had come to know and to love as a brother. No longer the general; no longer the earl of his estate. No longer the man nearly broken by his imprisonment in Damascus or devastated by loneliness and despair once he'd learned of the tragedy at Benningsgate. He feared Constantine could only be the man he'd been the night he'd left Melk without so much as a note for the friends he'd left behind.

Adrian had been that man once, not so very long ago. And so he knew the depths of apathy and how deceivingly benign it could appear to the casual observer. He knew how it could consume a heart whole, tinging even the act of inhaling and exhaling with bitterness.

As Adrian watched the continent fade away, he remembered Constantine praying aloud while chained to the wall of a Damascene dungeon by his neck. He remembered lying on the floor of the prison, his body—filled with fever and maggots—slowly dying but still feeling such scornful pity for his friend, who had resorted to superstitious nonsense in his desperation.

Christian's laugh echoing over the decks brought Adrian back from that wretched past. And then Adrian closed his eyes and prayed.

"There you are, there you are," Glayer said as he handed the baby to Eseld, who had already taken her seat in the carriage. He was not in the habit of allowing the old woman to be seated before him—especially not in the grand conveyance that would carry them all to London—but it was important to Glayer that he arrive at Henry's castle as a family. A wealthy widower lord and his infant son. A valuable ally now for the king and a ready source of financial and political support. Once Henry scratched his back by allowing Glayer to purchase Benningsgate at an outrageously inflated price, Glayer would be more than happy to acquiesce to a politically beneficial marriage.

He'd need a wife to tend his home and child, after all. And Glayer was especially good at persuading those who would have their women relatives cared for to do as he suggested.

Little Glander whimpered at the separation. "Papa shall be along directly," Glayer assured the infant and then gestured to the door with a flick of his eyes so that the footman closed it. He then turned to the reason for his delay in alighting as Simon came to a stop before him.

The old priest had been looking quite raggedy of late; Glayer supposed the winter had been harsh on the fool. And he'd seemed to take disposing of Theodora Rosemont rather personally. She must have fought with amazing strength for a woman nearly bled to death on her childbed and poisoned to her very eyeballs with pennyroyal and nightshade. Old Simon had staggered back to Thurston Hold full of mud and with a broken arm.

But the spring air following the torrential rains seemed to have enlivened the man—or perhaps it was the task Glayer had recently set the priest to. Was it possible that the once-holy Simon was now fully loyal in his duties to the lord of Thurston Hold?

"What is it?" Glayer demanded of the man. "Can't you see I'm leaving?"

"Why, I've only come to bid you farewell, my lord," Simon said. "And to bless your journey."

Glayer raised an eyebrow at the man. "Really?"

"No," the priest said in an emotionless voice. "Everything had been arranged."

"Very well," Glayer said. "When do you depart?"

"Perhaps a week."

"A week?" Glayer repeated with a frown. "Why the delay?"

"I've need to secure provisions for the orphans left at the rectory, my lord. They will need looking after until my return."

"Oh," he said, not caring to keep the distaste from his tone. "Well, I suppose that is necessary, for I certainly don't wish the charge of them. Very well. But you must be on that ship when it sails."

Father Simon gave a shallow bow.

Glayer would have rebuked him for such a paltry display of homage, but he let the slight go. He would consider it the priest's going-away present.

Glayer glanced at the door again and the footman opened it at once. He ducked into the plush interior and was closed into its hushed opulence with the old woman, who had at least managed to secure more appropriate garments befitting the nurse of his son. The carriage began to rumble and sway as it circled in the yard and Glayer pulled off his gloves in order to take the baby onto his own lap.

What a devoted father he was.

"Will we be long away from Thurston Hold, milord?" Eseld asked, and although he did not like it when she questioned him on any matter, her tone was one of curious deference and so he thought to oblige her. Also, it made him happy to relay his brilliant plans. Plans that he could execute or not at his very whim, with all the fortune of the estate growing only marginally smaller as the fine carriage whisked them down the road.

"As long as it takes for Henry to sign the documents granting me Benningsgate Castle," he replied mildly, nestling the boy in the crook of his arm and pulling the heavy curtain aside with the back of his hand so that Glander could watch the misty countryside of his father's realm roll by. "He hardly remembers my petition lest I am beneath his very nose, and his court is a proper circus on any given day. This time I shan't leave until the deed is in my hand. I daresay my stalwart presence shall be a breath of sanity to our harried monarch."

"We'll surely return to the keep before Father Simon, though, will we not?"

Glayer looked to the old woman with a sigh. It irritated him so when she acted as though she had a brain inside her wizened raisin head. "I've no idea, and I really couldn't care less. Glander and I shall not be rushed. We will have a leisurely journey to the city, and while we are there, we will avail ourselves of Henry's every courtesy. Even if Simon survives the journey, it shall likely be no fewer than two months before his feet touch English soil again. Why on earth would it possibly matter?"

"My confidence in the man has been shaken," she said with a dreary frown. Everything about the woman was dreary, as if she'd steeped so long in sheep dung that it had flavored her very person.

Glayer fancied he could still smell the filth on her, the same smell that had been soaked into the dirt floor of the single thatched room that had been his childhood home, turning his thoughts decidedly dark even as Eseld seemed to be expressing concern for the worn-out Simon.

"Perhaps he no longer has your best interests at heart, my lord. When I fetched him for you, he seemed as though he could turn . . . defiant. Perhaps once he is away from Thurston Hold he will go elsewhere rather than toward that to which he was directed."

"It's none of your concern," Glayer said, frowning down at the boy, who seemed to have lost all interest in the acres of land they passed through, pointing to Glayer's power and wealth. The little spit had fallen asleep. He handed the awkward bundle back to Eseld with little ceremony. "Simon is firmly under my control, of that I am supremely confident. He will perform the task I have given him precisely as I have set it forth. And if for some reason he dies en route or chooses to betray me—again, highly unlikely—it matters not."

Eseld's already wrinkled gray brow crinkled even further above where her eyebrows should have been as she rocked the infant on her lap.

What a disgusting creature.

Glayer sighed. He couldn't resist telling her, though. She would be so impressed with his cunning and brilliance.

"I've a sealed message on my person, swearing in my own hand to the naughty misdeeds of Father Simon as regards his beloved Bledsoe. The priest will be ruined before he reaches Austria and he won't even know it. If he survives the journey, he'll likely kill himself upon his return. Either end is perfectly acceptable."

Eseld's eyes widened, and Glayer felt a swelling of pride. He'd known she'd be impressed.

"Why would you want that, milord?" she asked faintly. "I thought Father Simon dear to you."

"He was necessary at one time, true. Now he has become superfluous. He knows too much of what I've had to do to gain my current position, and unless he is ruined, his testimony might carry some weight. After he and the simple abbot are neutralized, there shall be no one of any reputation who can speak against me. Simon was a loose end, Mother dear, that's all. But he's all tied up now."

Eseld's face was slack until his last words, and then a bright smile crept across her face and she pulled his son in an even-closer embrace. "I do so love it when you call me mother."

"Ugh," Glayer grimaced and turned back to the window to avoid her repulsive countenance. "Shut up."

Chapter 11

Dori couldn't help her scream as the huge dog took Constantine Gerard to the ground. Some sort of wolfhound that seemed nothing but long limbs and exaggerated head, covered in wet, gray fur as its mouth lunged toward the lord of Benningsgate's face. Constantine seemed to be trying to wrap his arms around the beast for some sort of leverage, and she expected to see blood flying at his guttural shout.

The owner of the dog appeared in no hurry to rescue them from his beast; in fact, Dori feared he must be of the diabolical sort, for she could hear his laughter at their predicament even as he sauntered on toward them. If there was any hope for Constantine to survive this attack—indeed, for Dori to survive after the animal was done mauling the man on the ground and before the dog's evil master was upon them both—Dori would have to provide it.

She looked around the steep, sodden bank and her eyes caught sight of the thick, black tree branch, half rotted where it had been washed onto the grass by the flooded river. She had no other weapon and so she dashed to it, wrenching its heavy mass from the tangle of weeds and using all her strength to raise it above her head. She gave a cry of determination as she staggered toward where Constantine Gerard still lay beneath the animal, and she saw a brief flash of his face, his teeth bared in a terrible grimace.

"No! No!" he shouted, but the dog paid him no heed.

"Get away from him!" Dori screamed and swung the branch.

"Dori, no!"

The branch was jerked from her grasp by the man who must have found a burst of speed to have gained her side so swiftly. Dori spun in the slippery grass to face him, hardly noticing his plump, bewildered expression before her fist shot out and she punched the man in his bulbous nose.

Her attacker dropped the branch and his walking stick to bring both hands to his face with a wounded cry, his cages and traps sliding to the ground behind him as he staggered backward and nearly tripped on the things. Dori took the opportunity to reach down for the long, flexible-looking cane and, taking it in both hands, spun toward where she'd left Constantine Gerard at the mercy of the beast, ready to fight off the monster as best she could.

But Benningsgate's lord was sitting up in the grass, the great hairy animal sprawled across his lap and Constantine's arms wrapped around its neck. Perhaps he was trying to choke the animal to death, but he didn't appear to be making much headway as the animal seemed quite content, its long, flopping tongue hanging out of the side of its mouth in a vulgar fashion as it leaned into the man's chest.

And, actually, Constantine Gerard was looking at her with a rather confused expression.

"What are you doing?" he demanded.

"I-I—" she stammered and slightly lowered the weapon in her hands. "The dog was attacking you. I—"

"Glory, missus," the man standing to her right mumbled through his hand. She turned her head in time to see him give a swiping pinch of his even more swollen nose before he raised his eyes to her. "I can understand you not fancyin' dogs, but Erasmus wouldn't harm you or your man. See? He only—"

Here the stranger held his bloodstained fingers forward and glanced at Constantine, wherefore his speech abruptly stopped.

Dori looked to Constantine and saw the dog craning its neck back, rubbing its matted-looking face against Constantine's in what appeared to be a desperate attempt to lick the man from chin to hairline.

Constantine chuckled, and Dori realized that perhaps the grimace she'd witnessed when he'd been mauled by the dog had been a smile.

"Good day, Jeremy," Constantine said to the man. "You're looking well."

The man—Jeremy, apparently—gave a choking gasp and staggered forward to fall to his knees in the wet grass at Constantine's side.

"My lord?" he asked in a quiet voice. "Is it really you?" He tried to shove the wide head of the dog away before grasping two fistfuls of Constantine's tunic. Then he actually shook the lord of Benningsgate as he shouted, "Is it really you?"

Constantine grinned. "I worried for a moment that Erasmus wouldn't recognize me, He was little more than a pup when last I saw him."

Jeremy gave a shout of joy and drew Constantine to him in an embrace. Dori was surprised to see the plump man's shoulders shaking with—well, laughter or sobs, she supposed. But she had been a poor judge of emotion only a moment before, and so she wasn't entirely certain. Although she was relatively sure Constantine was no longer in danger.

She bent her knees and laid the man's cane on the grass as inconspicuously as possible, straightening and then using her foot to push it farther away from her person.

Jeremy drew back, grasping Constantine by the shoulders and looking into his face. His expression was still.

"My lord, Lady Patrice; our young master . . ."

Constantine's throat convulsed. "I know, Jeremy."

Dori's chest tightened, but she was startled from her compassion by a warm, hairy dampness on her hand. She jerked her arm away and looked down to find that the monstrous dog had sidled up to her left elbow and was now looking up at her with black, mournful eyes.

No, she mouthed down at the beast.

It scooted slightly closer to her on its haunches and gave a soft whine.

"Come now, Erasmus; let the lady be," Jeremy said as he grasped Constantine by his arm and pulled him to his feet. "You've already thoroughly wet his lordship through." The man turned to her and gave a bow, his eyes only barely flicking over her conspicuously short hair. "My apologies, my . . . er, milady. Jeremy's the name— loyal swineherd to the house of Chase since I was a lad."

Dori felt a twinge of shame at her appearance, a foreign sensation after being so desperately alone for so long with her thoughts consumed by little more than survival. She could only imagine what she looked like to this man.

"How do you do?" Dori said stiffly and glanced at Constantine. "I apologize for striking you. I misunderstood your intent."

Constantine stepped forward and reached out to scratch the dog's head. The animal went willingly back to his side, much to Dori's relief. "It's a habit of hers I've found, Jeremy, upon making the acquaintance of men."

Dori's cheeks tingled. At least he hadn't told the swineherd her name.

"This is the lady Theodora Rosemont of Thurston Hold."

The man's hooded eyes widened. "Lady Theodora? But I thought—"

"Yes, well, I'm quite alive." Dori bristled, her stomach clenching as she glared at Constantine Gerard. Was he out to ruin everything? "Apparently."

The corners of Jeremy's mouth turned down and he gave a knowing nod. "That does explain a lot," he said, but his eyes were no longer kind on her. "Your actions, I mean."

Dori frowned, and a hot rush of humiliation washed over her. Even the simplest villager not of her own home thought her a horror. He hadn't even said he was glad she wasn't dead.

Would there be anyone who was glad of it?

The man gave her anther brisk bow and then turned back to Constantine. "When did you return, milord? There have been many inquiries as to your whereabouts the past several years; have you been to see the king yet? Does he know you've returned?"

Constantine let a long silence fill the air as he scratched the enraptured dog's head. "No one save yourself knows that I or Lady Theodora are alive, let alone at Benningsgate. I arrived more than a fortnight ago and have been making my plans."

"I see," Jeremy said, in a tone that conveyed he might not. He glanced at Dori. "What's she doing here, if you'll forgive my asking, milord? You still have my loyalty, and the loyalty of what few of us remain below in the village, but I'd wager not many would be willing to help her after what she drove her poor father to. You might not know that she left a new babe behind at Thurston, although the right bastard she married let it be thought she'd died." He said it as a challenge, as if daring her to deny it.

Dori stiffened and waited for Constantine's response with her eyes fixed on the hillside. It was clear by the contempt in Jeremy's tone that he thought her of the same ilk as Glayer Felsteppe. She would not acknowledge the swineherd's comments, but she was curious as to what Lord Gerard's reaction would be, when she had only just explained to him the events that had led up to her father's death.

"Lady Theodora is . . ." Constantine began and then paused. She could feel his gaze on her, as if using the spare moments of his silence to come to a weighty decision. Dori's chin lifted.

"She is helping me recover Benningsgate," Constantine finished, and Dori didn't know she'd been holding her breath until it began to leak out in a cool rush through her nose.

"Is that so?" Jeremy had the audacity to question in a more than slightly suspicious tone. Or perhaps he was only intrigued by this turn of events. It had been so long since anyone had said anything kind to her that Dori couldn't be sure.

"If such a recovery is at all possible," Constantine said. "And so we must strive to keep our presence secret until such time when revelation can no longer be avoided. I will make my return known to all once I have settled on a course of action against my enemy."

"Well, we who've stayed have done so because we couldn't imagine living out our days anywhere else save Benningsgate. Loyal to the family to the end, we are. Certainly I am at your every command, milord," Jeremy said with a bow. "Where do you sleep?"

Constantine took up his fallen satchel, which had been knocked from his person by the enthusiastic beast that was even now dancing at his heels. He glanced toward the wall behind him. "Here."

Dori's anger simmered again.

"About the ruin, milord?" Jeremy said. "But it's not at all safe; all the interior corridors have collapsed. When we tried to get to the hall afterward—" He broke off, and his florid complexion mottled further. "I imagine the walls have crumbled further with the passing seasons."

Constantine looked at the man for perhaps a heartbeat longer than was warranted. "Parts of it are yet sound and should suffice for the time being. But Lady Theodora has been quite ill. I would press you at once for a potion and perhaps some meat. I've no bow."

The man glanced at Dori. "I fear Stacy is the man you'd want for the purpose of medicines, milord, and he took to Thurston Hold some time ago. We've seen little of him." The statement somehow seemed an accusation at Theodora, and she could no longer tolerate the strain of the man's less than silent judgment as her eyes swelled with watery anger and unreasonable hurt.

Why did she care what this Benningsgate villager—a swineherd of all things, who had stayed behind to live in the shadow of a ruin the rest of his friends and neighbors had wisely abandoned—thought of her?

She stepped around the men without a word and began walking up the hill toward the wall, taking great pains to step carefully lest she slip on the wet grass and further humiliate herself by falling on her face.

There was a lull in the conversation, and Dori imagined both men watching her walk away. Perhaps the dog had thought to follow her, for Jeremy gave a sharp whistle.

"Erasmus, to me—the lady don't want you." And the meaning behind his words was clear: *And we don't want her, either.*

"I'd be honored to provide for you, milord," Jeremy said to Constantine after calling the dog back in Dori's wake. The man looked over his shoulder at the numerous traps strewn about the hill where he'd dropped them. "Not much hunting goes on at Benningsgate these days. The forest is plentiful with game."

"I will meet you in the ward before dusk, then," Constantine said, trying to push from his mind the sight of Theodora's face as her reputation was aired before her. "Have you married, Jeremy?"

The man's expression grew jolly once more. "I never have, milord. Few women would tolerate old Erasmus here supping at their table and soiling their rugs." He clapped the dog about the shoulders and then looked back up at Constantine. "It's fine to see you again, milord. I never thought to."

Constantine could not tell the man that he, too, was happy to have returned to this place, so he only nodded. "Perhaps you could lay hand to some clean garments for Lady Theodora? A pair of slippers? Her wardrobe has taken some wear since leaving Thurston Hold."

"The items will be hard to come by with everyone having so little. And I have no admiration for the woman, I confess," Jeremy replied.

"You only know her as well as the rumors about her perhaps," Constantine chided.

"You know her better?" Jeremy rejoined with a raising of his eyebrows. "Milord?" he added deferentially.

"I'll appreciate whatever you can lay hand to" was all Constantine would say. "As will Lady Theodora. Be sure you aren't followed when you return later."

"You can warrant it," Jeremy said, gathering up his traps and his long pole while Erasmus ran in loping circles around the man. "No one dares come to the ruin after midday—any hour really." He dropped his eyes as if he'd misspoken. "Good day, my lord. Come along, Erasmus."

Constantine watched the man navigate the slope into the fringe of the wood, his dog bounding to the fore and aft like a hairy pendulum. Once Jeremy had disappeared into the fresh, dripping greenery, he turned on his heel and followed in Theodora's trail in the weeds toward the wall.

He didn't expect her to be waiting for him as he stepped over the threshold. She sat on a large rectangular stone that had tumbled a far distance into the ward from where it first had fallen. Even after being returned for weeks to the reality that was Benningsgate, he still could not fathom the catastrophe that had taken place here. Besides the obvious signs of the fire that had structurally destroyed the tall keep, it was as if a great fist had seized the enclosure, bending and cracking its walls, shaking its pillars and arches to the ground.

When we tried to get to the hall afterward—

Perhaps crushing the burned bodies of his wife and son in its grip, leaving their remains trapped somewhere deep inside the rubble.

No one dares come to the ruin after midday—any hour really.

Did they think Benningsgate haunted by Patrice and Christian? Was it?

Constantine stopped and waited to see what Theodora Rosemont had to say, for obviously something was weighing on her mind. But she only stared at Constantine, and the longer her dark, sad gaze bored into his, her wide mouth still and silent, the higher Constantine felt unreasonable ire rising in him.

"I'm surprised you didn't strike poor Jeremy again for speaking so poorly of you," he said, hearing the bait in his own words.

"Because he wanted further proof of my bad behavior?" she rejoined, but her words were without bile. Indeed, she sounded subdued, resigned. "'Spoiled, rude Theodora. Never made to mind her manners. Treated as a princess, with her every whim granted. The ruination of her father, God rest his poor, weary soul.' I wouldn't want to disillusion him into considering I actually am one of his betters."

Constantine heard her words against the backdrop of his destroyed life as she spoke them from her weak and battered body, her costume worse than rags.

"Everyone envied me for some reason or another," she went on, and still her voice was flat, lifeless. "Usually something ridiculous, like my hair or my father's station. How many horses I had to ride at my pleasure. As if I had any control at all over those things. As if I had control over anything."

"Patrice mentioned several times that everyone thought you'd marry royalty," Constantine spoke the memory aloud before he could think better of it.

Theodora huffed a mirthless laugh. "And look at me now. I'm supposedly dead. Everything has been taken from me: my health, my beauty, my fortune, my family, my home. My son. Even the basest slave has more to boast of than I. Theodora Rosemont, who had every freedom, is now little more than a ghost. A hated ghost."

Her tone caused Constantine's defenses to rise. "Was I supposed to defend you to my loyal man, who served my family and knew me well?"

Her eyebrows raised. "I don't know. Were you?" she challenged him.

"You're twisting this into some lack of chivalry or honor on my part," he accused her. "Before coming back to Benningsgate, I hadn't seen you since you were a girl in short skirts. You came to my wedding with your father. You'd never even met my son."

"I've said nothing of chivalry or honor," she replied coolly and then rose. "And to my knowledge, after your wedding to Lady Patrice, you were not in residence at Benningsgate for a length of time such as would allow a visit from my father or anyone else. So perhaps it is your own conscience you hear berating you rather than me. Are you ready?"

He was frowning in earnest now. He had come back to the ruin from the river intent on doing that which he hadn't known was still necessary, and he didn't need Theodora Rosemont trailing after him like the sickly, pathetic waif she was, her big eyes holding him responsible for all the wrongs that had perhaps been done to her, even as he wanted to denounce her for his own trials.

"Ready for what?" he snapped.

"For me to show you through to the hall," she said, looking into his eyes. "That's where you want to go, isn't it?"

Constantine's stomach became an icy pit. "You know a way?"

"I could see your reaction to the loyal Jeremy's slip that no one had been able to reach Lady Patrice or your son after the stones had cooled enough to attempt a retrieval. You thought they had received a great ceremony befitting the noble house of Chase, did you not?"

Constantine could only stare at her and nod his head once, sharply.

Theodora Rosemont shook her own head to the negative, and he thought he saw a spark of anger in her dark eyes. "Patrice was marked as a traitor in league with you—as hiding one of your co-conspirators within Benningsgate and refusing to divulge your whereabouts. The king ordered the ruin abandoned, the village emptied, until such evidence as to your guilt or innocence could be provided."

Constantine continued to stare at her until his vision blurred and he was forced to look away. His rage was so great that he felt as though his mind and body had been enveloped in a white-hot haze, buffering him from the earth, burning him inside this fiery cocoon.

"Show me," he rasped.

She turned without further word and began walking toward the tilted stair that led to the wall walk and Constantine followed her, his heart screaming in his chest, his footfalls so heavy he thought it a wonder they didn't leave chasms in the twisted overgrowth of the ward.

They gained the walk and Theodora went to the most intact wall of the keep. Hugging it close, she stepped on to the stones that had fallen against its south side, forming a sort of bridge. Constantine thought they looked more than a little loose, but none of them so much as shifted under Theodora's slight weight. If they did, she would tumble down into the ward atop the pile that had already met that same fate long ago, becoming buried herself.

As if she heard the unspoken warning, she turned her face back toward him. "Step lightly." And then she was gone around the far side of the charred remains.

Constantine followed, the stones beneath his boots sighing and groaning, whispering to one another as he made his careful way after the woman. Perspiration sprang out along his forehead, both from the exertion of keeping his footing and the nightmare into which he was heading. Part of his heart was screaming at him to stop, go back. He didn't want to see.

But he reached the hidden corner of the keep that appeared from below to be collapsed. It largely was, the wall cracked in a long seam along the stones of a doorway lintel and shoved back as a whole, revealing a partially collapsed gap inside, filled with stone and what appeared to be a long, oiled piece of finely turned wood.

"I'm not going in," she said, drawing his agitated attention.

"I didn't invite you," he snapped.

Her pale face regarded him for a long moment. "If it collapses around you . . ."

"Lucky for you," Constantine said.

"I didn't do this, Lord Gerard," Theodora said, and the sadness was back in her eyes once more. "I'm sorry you think me your enemy. I'm not." She paused. "Be careful."

Then Theodora Rosemont braced her hands on the collapsed walls and moved around him, back along the treacherous path of the fallen stones to leave him to his miserable discoveries or his painful end, whichever he might be more determined to find.

Constantine lowered himself carefully into the chasm, reaching one booted foot upon the conspicuous piece of hewn wood. It wobbled and flipped under his weight, obviously no good foothold, and he spilled to his knees, sliding sideways into the wall with a shout of alarm. But his fall was arrested and he turned over onto his stomach to take hold of the piece of wood that had caused his slip.

It was the crucifix from the oratory, the crumbly remains of a wreath of long-dead flowers still affixed with faded ribbon around the scarred head of Christ. Flowers Benningsgate's priest would have laid. Or perhaps even the lady of the keep, Patrice.

But how did the crucifix come to be . . .

Constantine glanced at the triangle of daylight beyond the pile of rubble, thinking of the woman who had come upon this place so ill and weak; the only person who had been determined enough to attempt to enter the place his wife and son had lost their lives through the cruel evilness of the man she had married. And even as fragile and unwell as she had been, Theodora Rosemont had wrested the crucifix from the wall of the oratory and somehow managed to bring it over the treacherous path through the ruin to lay it at the threshold of the place where his family had been left without ceremony. To try as best she could to make a proper tomb for his little boy. Spoiled, horrid Theodora Rosemont, Glayer Felsteppe's wife.

She'd been the only one who cared.

Constantine swallowed down the thorny lump in his throat and crawled on through the black chasm.

Chapter 12

Constantine would have vowed familiarity with every twist and turn within Benningsgate's keep. But being trapped in the narrow gap of the collapsed stairwell was like trying to navigate a foreign shore at night. He flipped over onto his back to slide through a particularly shallow opening between slabs of charred red stone, and as the solidness of the masses pressed against both his chest and his back, for a moment he had the panicked sense that he didn't know up from down. If the rocks shifted the tiniest bit from his movements, he would be killed.

Or perhaps not killed, only pinned under tons of rock, the breath squeezed out of him little by little for hours or maybe days. Imprisoned, just as in the dark cell in Damascus.

The thought caused him to freeze in his movements, as if already trapped, and he could feel the perspiration causing his tunic to stick to his skin as surely as if he'd walked into yonder river. That idea in turn called to mind Theodora's dead father, the drowned Lord Rosemont.

But he shook himself. Christian was inside the ruin somewhere. He and Patrice lying alone in such a sad, desolate place for years without him. Still waiting for him. He could not fail them again. And so he shoved down the panic when his next deep breath was arrested halfway, and used the anxiety to fuel his motion through the gap.

He turned his head to look up and ahead of his path and saw a line of daylight. Pushing once more with only his toes in the narrow place, Constantine's head inched from the crevice to emerge in open air, the sky suddenly blue above him through the gauzy curtain of high, sheer cloud. Black darts swooped and circled through the column of charred stone, diving diagonally to and from their secret nests tucked practically inside the injuries of the keep.

Constantine craned his neck to look beneath himself and saw the square of rubble that had settled into the foundation of the tower keep, perhaps fifteen feet below his head. Wriggling to the side, he withdrew first one arm, then the other, from the crevice and reached above to find handholds, mindful of the fact that any downward pressure he exerted on the detritus in the doorway could cause it to collapse fully on his lower half. He pulled tentatively at first, trying to allow most of his weight to remain on his back while he slithered from the gap. Once he could slide his right knee out and gain a foothold with his boot, he drew a deep breath, gripped the stones with his fingers, and stood in one sliding movement.

The stones held, even though he did hear the crumbling, skittering sounds of pebbles running mazelike around him. He looked down the steep wall to the rubble below—too far yet to jump. He'd break his leg at the very least if he landed upon something solid. Worse, if the debris shifted. Constantine turned his head to look down his right side and saw the jagged, black remains of a wooden beam perhaps two feet below and one foot farther to the right than his boot. It was just what he needed to move in a zigzag fashion to the bottom of the doorway. He slid both feet as far to the right as his perch would allow, and then, hanging on with only his left hand, he stepped out and down with a quick intake of breath.

He lay flat against the stones like a spider, balancing awkwardly on the jagged end of wood that was already crumbling, collapsing like a sponge beneath his sole. He looked back to the left at the narrow ledge of masonry threshold just deep enough for his fingers. Constantine closed his eyes for a moment, the side of his face against the cool, damp stones. Then he looked once more to the ledge as his left arm slid down the shallow depressions in hitches. He was only perhaps a foot from reaching it now. He took a deep breath and let his body fall.

His left hand slipped off the threshold and his arm swung away. He couldn't help his shout of alarm as his right hand arrested his fall, and he quickly brought his left hand up to cease his wild swinging over the floor. He dared to look down again and guessed that the soles of his boots were perhaps ten feet above the rubble now, and so he inched to the left, the toes of his boots scrabbling against the wall for purchase until he was suspended over a wide-looking, slanted piece of rock. Then he let go.

The drop was farther than it had appeared, and his right knee twisted before his legs buckled to the unevenly resting stone slab. His shout of pain echoed up in the jagged column of the ruin, startling the birds from their hidden nests and sending their panicked tweets bouncing inside the keep. Constantine rolled to his back with a groan, bending his right leg and raising his head as his hands went to his knee. He hissed as he extended his foot along the stone and then drew it back again; he didn't think it was broken, just turned. And so he scooted back to a sitting position, his hands braced to either side of him and looked around.

He'd never thought to be in this hall again. Especially after he'd heard of the fire that had destroyed Benningsgate. But here he was, the only person to have entered this place since the night Glayer Felsteppe murdered Patrice and Christian. He was finally where he should have been these many, many years.

The rubble was deep—Constantine knew from the height of the lone window above him that the debris had filled at the very least the first floor chamber abutting the gatehouse below the slope of the ground outside the wall. The doorway he'd slid through into the ruin had belonged to the antechamber leading to the great hall itself and the corridor of apartments belonging to the family. He'd dropped somewhere midway into a receiving room, which led to the lower corridor in the bottom half of the wall. Had the way been clear—and the west wall still intact—Constantine could have trod the entire length of the passage beneath the wall walk to the oratory.

Had Theodora Rosemont returned there after leaving him to his macabre duty?

Constantine looked up again to the narrow opening in the wall some thirty feet above his head—the window that had decorated his great hall. It held no colored glass now, only the remnants of last summer's vines. Then his gaze fell back down to the rolling field of jagged stone before him.

How much of the keep walls lay atop the layer of the hall floor?

Constantine stood up, favoring his right knee, and limped across the rubble to the center of the space and turned in a slow circle, his eyes taking in the remaining walls, up to the pinnacle of the stone as it stretched toward the bright sky around the island of wreckage on which he was now marooned. Nothing slid, nothing shifted. The stones were packed in solid with their weight, baked in place by fire and the suns of summers past, solidified by rain and snow and wind. Not a speck of material that had not been chiseled from the earth could be seen. No wooden beams or floor boards, no charred furniture, no bleached scraps of tapestry.

No white bones.

"Where are you?" he whispered to the shadows crouching beneath the stones.

Was he just to leave his boy here, his wife? Could he allow them to lay where Glayer Felsteppe commanded they fall?

Constantine dropped to his left knee, stretching his right leg out before him. He picked up a stone the size of a round of bread in both his hands and hefted it there for a moment, feeling its weight as he looked around himself at the thousands more like it. He tossed the stone to the left with a huff, and it tumbled and bounced across the field of debris until it came to rest near the wall.

Then he picked up another.

Dori sat in the yard for hours, leaving her post only a handful of times to fetch a drink of water or to seek the tall weeds later to rid herself of it. She'd gained the wall walk twice, placing her hand upon the remaining wall of the keep and pausing to hold her breath and listen. She thought she'd heard a rhythmic scrape and tumble of rocks, little more than whispers of sound on the wind. But there had been no shout of alarm, no plea for help, and so she'd gone back down to her hard seat in the ward.

Likely Constantine Gerard wouldn't have called out even had he found himself in dire straits, whether because his injuries prevented it or because he didn't wish to be rescued. She thought he would choose instead to remain in the open-air crypt that was Benningsgate Castle. Dori didn't know how long she would have to wait in the ward for his return.

As long as it took, she supposed.

The sun was welcome heat on her skin. It had been months since she'd been out of doors in the bright light, and her body seemed to drink it in through the pitiful thinness of her clothes. Her lips became raw and tingled under the rays and the brisk wind, but she didn't care. Her only concern at Constantine Gerard being in the keep for hours now was that soon the sun would dip behind the ruin, washing the ward in purpling shadows and despair once more, and she would be alone, with no way of knowing if he was ever coming back.

She was surprised to see the great gray beast of a dog bounding across the threshold of the wall. And as if he had come to the ruin with the express intention of seeking Theodora, he ran straight at her, his unhinged tongue flapping from the side of his mouth, his matted hair now dry and wiry-looking over his sinuous back, apparently unbothered by the lack of attention she'd shown him earlier. Or her sincere plan to have brained the dog with his master's own cane. She sat still while he bounded across the ward, the rotund Jeremy following at some distance, not at all fearful of being attacked by the beast now.

But she became slightly warier of Erasmus's enthusiasm when the animal failed to slow as he galloped ever closer. Dori frowned and at last held her hand down to below her knee, snapping her fingers as she'd seen her father do with his hunting hounds when she was a little girl.

"Here now," she called out sternly. "Mind yourself and lie down if you must."

But her eyes widened as the dog seemed to take her speaking as encouragement and increased his speed.

"No," she called out and held her hands before her to ward off the collision that seemed imminent. She'd waited too long to rise.

Erasmus leaped at Dori in much the same manner as he had Lord Gerard, but her slight form held no leverage against the dog, who weighed more than she did, and both woman and beast went over backward on the stone with a shriek and an ecstatic whine.

The breath was knocked from her body, and even as she tried to gasp for air, her nose and mouth were covered with heavy, wet attention from the wide head before hers. She shoved at the animal, but her fists slid ineffectually off his solid muscles and sinewy limbs.

"Get . . . off!" she wheezed and then, a moment later, a blessedly cool rush of air whooshed over her as the daylight once more reached her face and Jeremy was pulling her to her feet.

Dori jerked her hands away and then bent over, bracing herself on her knees as she gasped. Once she had command of her respirations, she stood and glared at the village man and his dog, who appeared to be cowering behind his master's back.

Jeremy held up his palms and gave her a sideways look.

"What?" Dori demanded.

"Are you going to strike me again?"

"I should!" she shouted, and then looked down at the ducking animal to give him a glare all his own while she shook out her skirts. She was fairly certain she'd heard a rip as she'd gone over backward, and there was a decided looseness about the waist of her poor underskirt. It was likely tearing free from the ties at last.

Erasmus whimpered quietly.

"He's only happy to see you," Jeremy informed her in a chastising tone. "Although why I can hardly say, as you've been naught but cross with him."

"Excuse me," Dori said, "but you seem to have forgotten that you're addressing a lady."

"You're not *my* lady," he said snidely. "And this ain't your house, so . . . ?" He gave her a pointed look. "Where is my lord?"

"I might not be your lady but neither am I your servant to be ordered about or inquired of in such a rude manner," she said. "So you can find him yourself."

"Ah," he said with an air of interest. "So that's how it's to be, is it?"

"I suppose it is," she said with a lift of her nose and turned away from him.

They stayed like that in the ward, not looking at each other or speaking for the better part of a half hour. Dori eventually found her way back down onto the stone, but she turned her head sharply as she sensed the gray beast sidling through the grass to attempt to lay at her feet.

At her narrowed gaze, his advance stopped, but neither did he retreat.

Behind her, Jeremy cleared his throat. "Lord Gerard didn't attempt to gain the interior of the ruin, did he?"

Dori didn't so much as twitch.

"*My lady*," he added, it sounded, to Dori, through gritted teeth.

She turned her head only enough to glance at him. "He did."

"But there's no way in," Jeremy argued, and she could hear the concern in his voice. "How could you allow him to go, you daft woman? He could be trapped!"

Dori gained her feet and spun around, stepping first onto then over the rock to bring herself nose to nose with Jeremy.

"If you speak to me in an untoward manner *once . . . more,*" she warned, her finger under the nose that still bore the evidence of their first meeting, "you will soon find out whether I am as bloodthirsty and vicious as the rumors you seem so eager to perpetrate purport, do you understand me?" she demanded. "I've not survived thus far because I'm some spoiled, weak ninny who's been waited on hand and foot, and you will show me the respect I'm due if only owing to the fact that, one, I'm *not* dead, and, two, I haven't exercised my *completely justifiable* urge to take a switch to you *and* your ill-mannered, smelly beast!" She paused, and when there was no response, she leaned even closer to his face, looking at him sideways and bringing her finger up level with her own nose. "Do you understand or not?"

Jeremy's own eyes narrowed. "Aye. I understand, *milady.*"

Dori stood aright from the man. "There is a way into the keep. I found it." She paused. "And Lord Gerard *has* been away for several hours. I do feel it would be best if we could perhaps determine his safety, but the only way into the keep is treacherous." She glanced up at the birds swooping expertly through a window facing the ward. "Unless you can fly, that is."

Jeremy looked thoughtfully at the remnant of the tower for a moment. "I can't fly," he said at last and then looked at her with his arms crossed over his chest. "But I know where there is a ladder in the village."

"High enough to reach the window?"

He nodded. "From the outside, aye. But . . ."

Dori's eyes narrowed again. "What?"

"My form is too . . . muscular to attempt to gain such a height." He turned to face her. "*You'll* have to climb it." He said it as if it were a challenge.

She shrugged. "Bring a length of rope as well. A long length." She paused. "Two of them."

Jeremy hesitated. "I'm not your servant, lady."

"No, but you are Lord Gerard's, by your own passionate vow," she reminded him and then gave a sigh. *"Please."*

He turned on his heel and headed across the ward to the threshold in the wall. "Back in a thrice," he said.

"Don't let anyone see you!" she called out.

He raised an arm over his head but did not reply.

Dori stood on her tiptoes and cried, "You forgot your dog!"

Jeremy stepped over the threshold and was gone.

She looked down at the dog who, at her first glance, gained his feet and wagged his tail enthusiastically.

"What?" she demanded of him.

The tail slowed to a stop.

Dori sighed and looked back to the keep, wondering what she would find when she dared climb to the window and look inside. Constantine Gerard's body broken or crushed in the rubble? Or perhaps clutching the charred bones of his family?

Dori shuddered, wondering if his predicament could very easily become hers did she not return to Thurston Hold soon and save her own son. But first she had to help Constantine Gerard, whether he thought he needed her or not.

Chapter 13

Thirst seemed to eat at Constantine's throat from the inside out even while perspiration poured from his skin, but he did not slow in his labors. If anything, his irritation grew with every stone he moved, as it seemed the rubble refused him any downward progress.

He chose to focus on his memories of Patrice and the last time he'd seen her—here, in this very keep. Her beautiful face had been tear-streaked, although she had kept her composure while they'd said their farewells over their son's head. Her bloodshot, shadowed eyes had spoken louder than any words she might have repeated, continuing to beg him, as she'd done late into the night, to stay. Stay. Please, stay.

Christian had just recently turned four years old. And so he hadn't understood the idea of Papa going away for so long a time. Constantine could now see what a fool he had been—it was so clear to him here atop the destruction he had wrought. Regardless of Patrice's betrayals outside of their marriage, Constantine had punished everyone he loved by going away. The brave general, so full of pride. So sure of himself. He'd acted little more than a child himself.

Yes, Glayer Felsteppe had given the command for his family to be killed, but that wouldn't have been possible if Constantine had been where he belonged the entire time—at his home, protecting those he loved. For he *had* loved Patrice, even though her infidelity had changed that love. He had remained faithful to her, after her betrayals and even in faraway Syria. It was a duty he had sworn to after all.

But God had determined that Constantine deserved neither his wife nor his son and had taken them both away.

He paused in his labors and let his palms—dirtied and bloodied—

rest on his filth-caked chausses as he stared into the shallow depression before him.

"My lord," a woman's voice called, and a chill raced up his spine as his body stiffened. "Lord Gerard."

It sounded as if the voice was coming from the sky.

"Would you *shut up*? *Please*? Yes, I do see him. *Constantine!*"

He turned his head slowly and looked up to find Theodora Rosemont's gamine face looking at him through the tall window.

"All right down there?" she asked, as if they were perfectly ordinary activities the two were engaged in.

He nodded dumbly. "Yes," he called up, realizing she might not see the movement from such a height. And then he appreciated that she was thirty feet above him. He wasn't actually surprised at her appearance—he was beginning to suspect Theodora Rosemont usually got what she set out for. But he was curious. He cleared his throat. "How are you up there?"

"Jeremy stole a ladder from the village," she said and then turned her head to look behind her. "It doesn't belong to you, does it? Fine." She looked back down at Constantine. "He *borrowed* a ladder. It shall be growing dark soon, my lord—do you think you might want to come out now?" He could tell she had tried to make the statement matter-of-fact, but Constantine could hear the gentleness of her tone, a quality he'd not noticed in her voice before.

He thought of the crucifix atop the rubble.

Constantine gained his feet with a groan and rested his hands on his hips as he glanced up toward the collapsed doorway through which he'd entered. He was surprised at the indigo shadows that indeed now painted the inside of the keep. He looked back to where Theodora Rosemont watched him from the window.

"I don't think I can return the way I came," he said. "And there are no handholds to reach the window."

"All right," she said with a shrug. "Never mind, then. Good night." Then she actually grinned at him before she threw down a long coil of rope that unfurled and swung and slapped against the stones.

He wasn't certain which he needed most in that moment—her levity or the rope—but he suspected both.

"Shall I stay to cheer you on?" she teased.

Constantine looked back to the pathetic progress he'd made. *I'll be back on the morrow*, he vowed silently, realizing with a glad heart that Theodora Rosemont had supplied the means of ingress and egress for him to return.

Then he dusted his hands together and limped over the broken rubble toward the rope. He stood at the bottom and looked up at the window, where Theodora rested her forearms and leaned over to look down at him.

"It's a long climb," he admitted, his hands on his hips once more, thinking of the weariness in his arms, the pain in his knee.

"Sooner begun . . ."

He gave a sharp nod. "Right." Constantine approached the rope, reached up with both hands, and gave it a jerk. "What's it tied off to?"

"The most substantial thing in the ward—Jeremy."

Constantine thought he heard a muffled bit of words on the wind, but Theodora only glanced over her shoulder with a grin before looking back down at Constantine.

"Pardon me—*muscular*." Her expression became pointed. "Lord Gerard, my slippers are thin and the rungs are hard."

Constantine grasped the rope firmly and stepped the bottoms of his boots onto the wall.

Dori knew something was wrong before Constantine was even halfway up the wall. Each time he placed his right leg higher to move his left, his grimace grew deeper, his strides shorter.

He must be injured.

Now his right foot slipped altogether and the tawny-haired man gave a growl of pain as he placed his boot back against the stones forcefully. He paused to look up at her, and she saw that sweat ran down his face.

"My knee," he explained.

Dori knew a shiver of unease. She licked her lips and leaned farther into the opening of the window, making a show of looking beyond him to the shadows that were now roiling like a dark ocean along the rubble of the keep.

"It's half of it, either way you go," she said matter-of-factly. "But if you don't move soon, you'll likely have the decision made for you when you fall."

He gave a guttural shout and adjusted his feet on the wall. She could see the seams of his tunic over his biceps straining and she thought about how tired he must be physically after his exertions;

how tired mentally the chore had made him. He was a strong man, true, but even the strongest men had breaking points, and most of the time they were not failures of their bodies.

"You're wasting time, Constantine," she said sharply. "*Move!*"

He tried to raise his right leg again, but this time, it fell from beneath him, causing his left boot, too, to lose its grip. Constantine's body went vertical to the wall, swinging out, spinning and then returning to collide with the stones.

Dori only just contained her gasp, expecting the rope to slide through his hands until the friction of it caused him to release it and collapse onto the jagged debris below. Her heart pounded in her chest.

"What happened?" Jeremy demanded, likely having felt the jerk on the rope in his hands even though it was also looped around a stone pillar.

She waved a hand behind her, putting him off, not wanting to take her eyes from the man dangling below her even for a moment. Constantine looked up at her, his face red, his mouth pulled in a wide grimace as he tried to work the rope in a spiral around his left leg. His eyes met hers.

"Come on," she encouraged.

He began to climb. Hand over hand, so slowly that Dori feared she would go mad. After what seemed like an hour, he was so close to the window that Dori could have reached out and touched his topmost hand. But she daren't, knowing that she hadn't any strength to lend him.

"Almost there," she said quietly instead and backed down one rung on the ladder, her legs shaking, the ladder trembling.

He was breathing forcefully through his nostrils when he threw his right forearm over the thick window ledge. His left followed and he heaved his chest onto the stone casing with a growling shout, lying there for a moment. Dori knew what desperate strength he had mustered would leave his muscles wobbly soon, throwing him off balance.

"Don't stop now, Constantine," she said and backed down another rung. She had a moment's mad fear that the ghosts buried inside the keep would suddenly decide to claim ownership of the man struggling to escape, and she would see Constantine's arms slide back into the blackness before hearing his body hit the stones.

"Come along!" she insisted. "It's getting dark and . . . and I'm hungry. And my feet pain me." Her voice was shrill, demanding. She sounded the same as she had so many times with her father, making a fool of herself in her desperation to extricate him from whatever trap was laid in his path.

She saw Constantine's head appear as he raised himself up onto the ledge with his hands. Dori backed down another step as he drew his right knee into the opening and then dropped his foot along the outside of the wall, straddling the sill and leaning his back and head against the stone casement with his eyes closed and his chest heaving.

Dori let her breath out of her mouth in a long, low whoosh, and when he rolled his head against the stones to open his eyes and look down at her she couldn't help her relieved smile.

Constantine Gerard looked at her thoughtfully, the corner of his mouth twitching upward in a bemused, weary grin, and it flustered Dori unreasonably.

She felt her eyebrows draw together. "I told you it wasn't a good idea to go in there."

"That you did." He looked beyond her and lifted his hand, Dori assumed to Jeremy, but she didn't trust her own balance at this point to turn to make certain.

She looked down at her own skirts falling through the rungs and carefully began stepping down the ladder, one slow rung at a time, grateful that her downward-directed gaze would hide the tears prickling in her eyes.

Jeremy acted as though nothing untoward had gone on the past hour as he wound the rope around his arm and walked alongside Constantine, and for that he was doubly grateful to the man. Erasmus expressed his usual enthusiasm, nearly taking Constantine's legs from beneath him a second time that day.

"I've brought the things you asked for, milord," he said, motioning behind him and then glancing twice at the empty ward. He turned back to Constantine with an irritated expression. "I suppose you know where she's gone?"

Constantine hadn't noticed Theodora leaving either, but she was so small and dark in the rapidly approaching dusk that he really wasn't surprised.

"I do," he admitted. "Although I'm surprised Erasmus didn't think to follow at her heels. You have my thanks."

"The lady probably kicked at him or some other such cruelty," the man said. "Any matter, it was my pleasure, milord. I should be able to lay hand to more when you have need. Perhaps even going to the village at Thurston Hold for what I can't procure here." The man waggled his eyebrows as he met Constantine's gaze.

Constantine nodded, grateful for Jeremy's willingness to be of assistance; the man's cooperation had already helped save Constantine from almost certain injury.

Although he knew there was one even more deserving of his gratitude than the girthful villager before him.

"I'd best be getting back before I'm missed," Jeremy said, tossing the large coils of rope behind a fallen stone before moving the ladder to the weeds nearby. "With so few of us in the village, anyone's absence is noticed. I'm in the wood most fair days, if you have need of me before I return."

Constantine grasped Jeremy's hand and then gave Erasmus a rub behind his ears before watching the pair disappear through the wall into the dusk. Then he turned toward the low tumble of stones and limped across the long grass toward the hidden door.

It took him a little longer than usual to reach the lower level of the corridor where the oratory was located, but he felt a queer sense of peace and welcome at the open door and the light shining from within—someone waiting for him. It was an odd feeling he hadn't experienced in years. Even odder that the feeling would have been prompted by the presence of Theodora Rosemont.

He stepped to the doorway and waited, watching her as she unpacked the bundle Jeremy had brought with eagerness clear on her face. The glance she gave him upon noticing his arrival didn't cause her enthusiasm to fade as had typically been the case since their meeting, and that made Constantine glad. She'd said she was hungry after all.

"A pot!" she said with a half smile. "And a portion of oats! Oh, my mouth does water at even the feel of them in my hand. There's a roast of venison as well. And what's this?" She pulled up a long length of muddy-colored cloth and shook it out over the floor in front of her. "An apron?" She turned to lay it on the bench before swinging her faded cloak from her shoulders. Then she slipped the apron over her head.

The thing was a tent on her slight frame, and when she looped the strings crossed over each other and around her middle twice, Constantine couldn't help his breath of laughter.

Theodora turned toward him with her arms out, looking down with satisfaction at her new, humble garment. "It's quite sturdy, isn't it?" she said. "And there's even a bit of embroidery here at the bottom." She looked up at him. "I doubt anyone would take me for a missing lady in it. But then again, I'm not supposed to be missing, am I? I might not look quite as dead in it any matter."

It sounded as though she was becoming more flustered by the moment, although Constantine could not tell if it was from the ordeal they'd just come through or her discomfort with the items Jeremy had brought. He doubted Theodora Rosemont had worn anything even resembling an apron in the whole of her life.

But whatever the case, Constantine had a duty to fulfill, and he found that, this time, he didn't have to remind himself to persevere. He limped toward the table until he stood before Theodora. She stopped her fidgeting and looked up at him, but her eyes were still darting, nervous; her wide mouth pressed tight into itself.

He reached out and took her hand, stiff and cold and small, into his own dirtied, cut fingers. He held it firmly when she twitched as though she would snatch it back, looking down at its ridiculous frailness inside his own grasp, so pale and slight, and he thought of the honor she had paid his family when she herself had lost so much, had yet been so ill and alone. When the urge struck him to lift that small, white hand to his mouth, he followed it.

Constantine closed his eyes as he pressed his lips to the backs of her fingers for a moment, breathing a long sigh into her cold skin. When he opened them and looked up at her over her hand, he saw that Theodora Rosemont was watching him with wide eyes, her lips parted.

"What . . . what are you doing?" she stammered in a quiet voice.

"Thank you," he said and at last dropped their joined hands, although he did not release her yet. "For what you did for Christian and Patrice."

She did not play coy, forcing him to detail the reason for his gratitude, and Constantine's respect for the woman grew.

"It certainly wasn't doing me any good," she said of the crucifix, and although her tone was wry, her face was still solemn and she continued to hold his gaze.

"And thank you for what you did for me," he added. "You were right—it was foolish of me to enter the keep when I had no idea what I would face once inside and no good plans to extricate myself."

"You needed to go," she said. "It is not very different from the times I dared return to Thurston Hold. It was too dangerous by far, and I never really achieved what I set out to do either time."

"We've both learned our lessons, though, haven't we?" Constantine said softly. "With the tools Jeremy brought today, I'll be better able to enter and exit the keep."

"And now I have you," she said, and although he knew she'd meant it as a rejoinder to his intention of returning to the keep, once the words were loose in the air between them, they seemed to take on an entirely different connotation.

Constantine felt a stirring in his chest as he looked down at Theodora Rosemont, at least ten and five years his junior. Her pale face looking up at him in earnest, her fingers still in his grasp. Her hair flipped out around her head in such a way that seemed to make her eyes twice as big in the candlelight of the oratory. She appeared so frail that a hard fall might break her slight body, and yet she had already endured so much—and Constantine only knew a fraction of her hardships.

"What are you going to do when you have your son returned to you?" he asked suddenly, finding that he was curious about her future.

Theodora blinked, and it seemed to break whatever spell of intimacy that had bloomed between them. She pulled her hand from his, but very slowly, and turned back to the table to continue to look through the supplies.

"I don't really know," she said, loosening the drawstring of a muslin bag and then bringing it to her nose to smell it. She reached inside with her forefinger and thumb to retrieve a pinch of the contents and rub the crumbly herb between her fingertips. "I suppose it depends on whether you kill Glayer Felsteppe or not."

Constantine frowned. "I will kill him. On that you can depend."

"Hmm," she said, flicking the bits of dried matter back into the sack and pulling the string tight once more. She picked up a jug and twisted at the cork with no little effort. "Well, I suppose if the king allows it, I will remain at Thurston Hold. It's a wealthy property, and he will want a suitable guardian to manage the estate until my son is old enough to inherit."

A cold fist seemed to grip Constantine's neck and he felt angry at his foolishness. How quickly he had forgotten that the woman before him had lain with his greatest enemy—the man he'd come back to kill. She had borne him a son, he who had taken Christian from Constantine, and even as she stood before him, Theodora Rosemont was still that man's wife.

He'd looked into her eyes and felt . . . what? Attraction? Sympathy? Camaraderie? Gratitude? He did owe her thanks for her assistance today, and for the respect she had shown the crude resting place of his family, but that did not mean he could treat her softly, as a woman deserving of his gentleness.

Even if it was through no fault of her own, she was still married to Glayer Felsteppe. And even if the boy was now in the hands of that depraved monster, at least Theodora Rosemont knew her son was *alive*.

"Constantine," Dori said inquiringly, but he could barely afford her a glance now, his stomach was twisted so with anger and bitterness.

"What is it, Lady Theodora?" he snapped as he limped to the bench and sat down, stretching out his leg with a groan. His body felt as though he'd just been taken down from the rack. She didn't answer and so he looked up with a sigh to find her standing before him in her ridiculous peasant's apron that pooled around her feet, clutching the still-corked jug to her bosom like a little girl playing at pretend.

She thrust the jug toward him.

He looked at her for a moment and then took hold of the container, twisting the cork loose with a hollow pop. She took the jug and cork and turned back to the table at once, busying herself with the chalice, her hands fluttering over the items spread before her.

"You may call me Dori if you like," she said in a quiet monotone. Then she glanced at him from the corner of her eyes, and he saw the flush come over her pale cheeks.

Constantine wondered, then, if he was not in greater danger now than he had been in the ruined keep. He was at such odds with himself when it came to her. Did he hate her? Did he respect her?

She walked toward him once more, the chalice in her hands. She held it toward him.

"It's wine. I think perhaps your leg would prefer it to fish broth."

Constantine waited a heartbeat of time before taking hold of the cup. "Thank you," he said, but he didn't look at her before she turned back to the table. He brought the cup to his lips. "Dori."

Jeremy made his way back through the wood at the rear of Benningsgate to come out below the village on the road, Erasmus bounding along with his usual enthusiasm. The poor beast had been cooped up for so long in just the cottage and barn with the rain; today had been quite the treat to have received so much exercise. Indeed, Jeremy's limbs were feeling the exertion of it all.

But, oh! The honor of being the first and only soul to know of the lord's return! He felt his already considerable chest swell with pride. What a time he would have when all had been returned to Constantine Gerard and Jeremy could at last confess that he had known of the earl's plans to reclaim Benningsgate from the bastard currently in residence at Thurston Hold.

He paused on the path to catch his breath and indulge in a bit of fancy. Perhaps Lord Gerard would even recognize Jeremy's service before the household. Wouldn't that be grand?

That Rosemont woman, however; she was a trial.

He slowly began moving up the road once again, his legs and back aching from the strain of the rope and the many steps he'd walked that day, but the discomfort of his body did nothing to diminish the satisfied smile on his face.

"I'm coming, I'm coming," he said to Erasmus, who ran back to him repeatedly, seeming to urge him forward. The large animal was probably more than ready to eat, as was his master.

He entered between the first two cottages and a golden specter stepped out from the right, her thick arms crossed over her chest.

"And just where have you been?" Nell demanded. She glanced down at the loping dog. "Yes, I see you as well; good evening, Erasmus."

Jeremy staggered to a halt, his hand to his chest. "Glory, woman! What are you thinking, jumping out at me like that?"

"You've been gone all the day," she accused, her eyes narrowing in her broad face. "Save when you was skulking through the village with Harmon's ladder. And now my best apron is missing from the line."

Jeremy swallowed and his heart beat faster, although he waved the woman away and continued on through the village. "What use have I for your apron?"

"What use have you for Harmon's ladder's a better query, I should think," she countered, trailing along behind him. "It's not as though you can climb it."

"What mean you I can't climb it?" Jeremy demanded and stopped in the street to turn to face her, feeling his cheeks heat. He knew he must look a dreadful fright, being about the lord's business all the day—and Nell's hair was in its typical, round-the-head plait beneath her slight kerchief, the golden strands blending in such a comely manner with the gray. "O' course I can climb it, lest I'd never have taken it!"

"So you *did* take it," she said, looking at him sideways. "For what?"

"I don't see how that's any of your concern," he said and turned back around to continue on to the safe haven of his cottage.

Nell didn't follow him, but she did call out after him. "I've made a stew. I might need a bit o' convincing on what to tell Harmon when next he comes 'round askin' after his ladder."

Jeremy stopped in the street again and half-turned to look back at Nell. "Why should you have to tell him anything? I took his ladder to place a trap."

"Why didn't you bring it back, then?" she demanded.

"Because I'll need to get it down, won't I?" he said with his arms spread, feeling rather proud of himself at his quick thinking.

"I don't believe you," she said simply, this time putting her hands on her hips. "I think you're up to something." She looked him up and down. "Something at the ruin."

"Why on earth would you think that?" he said, wondering how she could have so accurately guessed his whereabouts.

"You've soot all 'round your tunic," Nell said, and he couldn't stop himself from glancing down at his middle. "I thought it was only mud from afar, but I see that it's not. It's clearly soot."

Jeremy looked up at her, his tongue seemingly stuck to the roof of his mouth.

Nell quirked an eyebrow, and Jeremy had to admit her comeliness was no match for his brain. "I'll expect you when you've had the chance to wash up."

Jeremy nodded sheepishly and then turned toward his cottage.

It was only Nell after all. And she could keep a secret.

Chapter 14

Mary lifted her skirts and mounted the steps to the little guard-house, Valentine reaching in front of her and courteously wrenching the door open with a familiar screech. He swept his other hand before his stomach and bowed.

"After you, *mi amor*," he said.

Her heart still thrilled at him, especially when he was outfitted so splendidly as he was now.

Mary swept into the guardhouse, startling the young man from his stool. He gained his feet.

"Good day, milady," he said, turning as Mary barely paid him any heed beyond a smile. His voice called after her and she could hear the indecision in his tone. "I beg your pardon, but you just can't—milady?"

He caught up with her and lightly took her elbow, causing Mary to spin around with wide eyes. But she needn't have worried, for before she could come full circle, her husband had pressed the lad against the wall of the guardhouse, a knife point under his chin.

"Perhaps you have no been taught that you do no touch a lady—especially no the lady of Beckham Hall, and especially no *my wife*," Valentine said in a chastising tone, looking through his lashes at the guard.

The young man gulped, his eyes going from Valentine to Mary and then to the commotion of footfalls trampling up the steps to the door.

"L-lady M-Mary?" he stuttered. "B-but, the lord said—the king said—I—"

"Oh, it's quite all right, dear," Mary said, gesturing to her husband to let the guard go. "I'm certain Beckham has been through a trial in my absence." She reached out and patted the young man's forearm, if only to distract him from the variety of individuals now filing past him in somewhat dubious raiment. They'd done their best, but there was only so much that could be accomplished with one's costume when one was wearing an eyepatch.

She continued, "I've all the necessary documentation, so I need only inform Lord . . . oh, I'm afraid his name has slipped my mind again."

Valentine smirked at her. "You are so silly."

"I am," she agreed and wrinkled her nose at him before looking back to the young guard. "Lord . . . ?"

"Quimby, milady," the lad finally managed to stutter. He stood away from the wall and moved as though he would overtake Mary into the hall. "I'll go and—"

"No, no," she trilled on a laugh and gave the young soldier a sweet smile as Valentine shoved him back into the guardhouse and then gave him a gentle pat and made a show of brushing off and tidying the guard's tunic. "No need for that! I remember the way to my own quarters well enough, I daresay."

The hall beyond was filling with raucous commotion as the crew from *The Azure Skull* infiltrated the place, jolting the few soldiers quartered at Beckham Hall from their complacency with wide-eyed expressions. Some of Francisco's men had managed to secure a motley collection of clothing meant to mimic military garb, but if one only looked, the striped sashes, ornate and foreign swords, and odd jewelry were quite obvious.

And of course there was the fellow with the unfortunate eyepatch.

Maisie Lindsey stepped onto one of the benches and then sat her bottom directly on the tabletop in the far corner of the hall, Valentina on her knees. Mary watched the woman's keen eyes and knew that Valentine's and her backs would be safe from unlikely attack. Maisie raised one of Valentina's hands and waggled it in their direction.

Mary blew the pair a kiss as, behind her, the more authentically clothed members of the crew filed from the guardhouse and through the doorway leading to the garrison and storeroom below, their arms laden with crates and trunks and baskets. Roman Berg's intimidating presence as foreman discouraged any argument from the surprised and confused contingent of Beckham soldiers coming up from the lower quarters.

Adrian Hailsworth breezed through the opening and cut between the line of men and cargo, a sheaf of parchment in one hand and a hammer and tacks in the other. He peeled off one of the sheaves and handed it to Roman without a second glance. Mary doubted the ink was even dry as the man began to hammer one of the other authentic-looking proclamations to the door of the guardhouse.

Isra Tak'Ahn urged Christian up the steps to the hall before her, the boy doing his best to walk carefully while carrying a hooded Lou on his right forearm in the too big gauntlet. The lad was propping up his elbow with his other hand, and Mary thought Roman and Isra's idea to keep Christian focused on something other than the forcible seizure of Beckham Hall quite ingenious.

Francisco was the last to sweep inside, nodding to Roman as he took charge of his crew, and Roman turned on his heel and walked toward Mary and her husband. Roman handed Valentine the parchment, meeting his gaze and giving him a nod of his own.

"Let's do this."

Valentine looked down at Mary as he tucked the parchment inside his fine velvet tunic. "Shall we, *mi amor*?"

Mary smiled at him, and together the three walked to the door at the foot of the stairs, which Mary noticed had been replaced with one twice as fortified as that which Glayer Felsteppe's men had broken down when she and Valentine had fled Beckham for their very lives. The door was suitable for a fortress indeed, and looked to be virtually impenetrable.

Had the present Lord Quimby bothered to engage it, that is.

"I don't think they saw us coming, my darling," Mary murmured through her smile as she mounted the first step.

"All the time, they are underestimating us," he said ruefully. "Have you your blade, *mi amor*?"

"I'm seldom without it. Oh, Valentine, what wonderful fun this is!"

"It pleases me that you are so happy, Maria. I still think you should have worn the hat," he murmured, and she felt his hand slide over her hip as he followed her up the stairs.

"Later," she promised, and then called up into the brightness above their heads in a cheery tone. "Hello? Hello-o? Good day, Lord Quimby. Are you about?"

Mary heard a wheezing gasp and then a short fit of coughing before she came to the top of the stairs. Apparently they had interrupted someone's nap. She prepared herself for the sight of her old, bare hall, where she had spent the whole of her life with only her nurse, Agnes, and the kind Father Braund for company. She feared the memories that would flood her upon gaining the upper floor might throw her off her game.

But she breathed a sigh of relief that quickly turned to a gasp of pleasure as she came into the tall, columned room while a man of perhaps three score struggled to push himself up from the upholstered chair before the hearth. Gone were the stark floors and walls, replaced with thick, dark rugs that seemed to ripple in the bright sunlight streaming through the tall windows like lush, magical lakes. Colorful tapestries and gilded urns decorated the spaces between the windows and braided cords wreathed around the columns. It smelled of warm beeswax and pipe smoke and it took a bit of self-control for Mary to refrain from a happy jog on the spot.

"I beg your pardon, my lady," the old man said with a rusty clearing of his throat. "Someone should have announced you."

Mary rushed toward him with her hands outstretched, leaving Valentine and Roman standing near the top of the stairs. She shined her brightest smile at him as she reached him.

"Lord Quimby, at last," she said and clasped the old man's hands.

His smile was pleased if a bit bemused. "Again, I must beg your pardon, my lady—it is clear that you are familiar with me and yet I cannot for the life of me place the how of it. Surely even in my old age I would not forget a face as comely or a voice as gracious as yours."

Mary cast her eyes to the carpet in a show of humility—goodness, it was rich; she could just imagine her bare toes sinking into it.

"You are even kinder than your reputation would paint you," she said, dragging her gaze back up to the old man's jowly face. "But it is I who must apologize for my lack of attention. Surely you must think I had no care at all for you and your plight here at Beckham Hall."

Now his hoary brows drew together, and although he kept hold of Mary's hands for far longer than was appropriate, she allowed it. "My plight? If you mean the weevils, I must say that it really wasn't that bad, and it was only that one instance at Eastertide. By spring all the flour has a bit of them. It was Lady Elmsbeth, was it not? That old gossip! I knew I shouldn't have let her invite herself. Cook has assured me that—"

Mary gave a laugh that was genuine. It seemed the dowager lady had been keeping a close eye on Beckham in Mary's absence, and she did hope to meet the woman again soon.

"No, Lord Quimby, I was not speaking of the weevils, although I am aware of the havoc the loathsome creatures can wreak on one's holy day feasts!" She shook and pressed his fingers with another little laugh and then deftly slipped her hands from the old man's papery grip. "I meant your plight in holding Beckham in my stead until I returned to England. While extremely noble in service to the king, I'm sure it was hardly convenient for you to take on such a task without knowing the terms. You have my deepest gratitude and I will be certain to relay it also to the king."

Now the old man frowned in earnest. "Holding Beckham until you returned . . . ? There must be some mistake. I—"

She heard the footsteps behind her, and by Lord Quimby's wide gaze darting over her shoulder, Mary knew her support was nearby. She turned slightly and took the parchment that was already at her elbow only to hand it directly to the old man.

He snatched it from her, almost all traces of his earlier courtesy gone. "You can't be . . ." he muttered to himself as he held the parchment close to his nose. "*Lady Mary Beckham?*" He jerked the parchment down with a rattle and glared at her.

Mary forced her expression into one of gentle surprise. "Lord Quimby, I can't help but think that you are dismayed—nay, shocked and dismayed!—at my return. I can't fathom why that would be."

"You," he said, the parchment trembling in his hand, "were rumored to have abandoned your home with a known traitor and then thought dead! Save for a handful of letters that could not verify your whereabouts, there has been no sign of you for nearly two years! Henry couldn't *pay* someone to take Beckham now—the harbor's overrun with pirates! No soldiers of any worthy spirit agree to be stationed here, and the sheer lunacy of the types of pilgrims we see through the village now marks the place as little better than a barbarian purlieu!"

She gave him a sideways, chastising look. "Oh, don't be so modest.

The hall is simply lovely." She leaned up straightaway and tapped the scribbled calligraphy on the parchment with her fingernail. "As you can see, it plainly states that I have returned to Beckham with *my husband*," here, she rolled her eyes up to indicate the men behind her, "and that the estate is to be returned to me immediately." She drew her hand back to fold her fingers together primly before her waist. "Which would be right now."

"This is outrageous!"

"Why, Lord Quimby, you behave as though you didn't receive your own copy of this decree from the king a fortnight ago."

The old man sputtered. "I most certainly did not!"

Valentine leaned around Mary and used his forefinger and thumb to pluck the page from the old man's hands before he could tighten his grip. "Excuse me. I am sorry, but this one belongs to me." He straightened behind Mary once more.

"What an embarrassing mistake. I'm afraid you'll have to speak to the king about it," she said with an air of grave seriousness. "I wouldn't dare go against a royal decree myself."

"Speak to him I certainly shall!" Lord Quimby said in a trembling voice and drawing himself up to his full height. "I'll depart at first light for the king's court and—"

"I couldn't agree with you more. This is a simply shocking turn of events and I think your plan most appropriate." Mary stepped closer to the old man and took hold of his elbow. She began walking toward the stairs, her arm linked with his. "I shall have your personal belongings sent to the inn right away, and any private servants you have employed."

"What?" The old man jerked to a stop. "The inn? I'm not going to the *inn*; I'm staying here, in my home!"

Mary clasped her hands again and gave him a sweet smile and a wrinkle of her nose before she shook her head. "I'm sorry, but . . . no."

She heard a door open and the pale, thin Father Braund emerged from the chapel at the end of the hall.

"Lady Mary?" he said, his kind voice full of amazement. "Is it really you?"

Her smile deepened as she rushed toward the priest, breaking into a run the last few steps and embracing him.

He drew away and his gaze beamed down at her. "I daresay you look much improved over the last time we met. Have you come home?"

"I have. And not only I, Father, but also several others I've brought with me whom I can't wait for you to meet."

"*She. Has. Not!*" Lord Quimby shouted with a stamp of his slippered foot.

"Lord Quimby is rather put out with me, I fear," Mary said in a pseudo-whisper.

"Shall I try to appease him?" Father Braund muttered, only barely moving his lips. "He's rather inhospitable on his good days."

"I understand. But I'd hate for something untoward to happen to him if—"

The old man stalked toward Mary and the priest, already shaking his finger at her, his face alarmingly red.

"You will get out of my house this instant, young woman!" he shouted. "Or I'll have you forcibly removed! I don't know what sort of trick you think to put over on me, but—"

Mary saw Valentine and Roman exchange glances before coming up behind the irate Lord Quimby. Before the man knew it, they had flanked him, seizing his flabby arms and lifting him from his feet.

"What? Wha—? Put me down this instant!" he screeched, circling his feet over the rug—it was so lovely and deep. Almost an indigo color. Why, you could nap comfortably on a rug of such thickness. Even make love on it.

Oh, that most certainly would happen, very soon.

Valentine and Roman turned and carried the man toward the stairs, while Father Braund took Mary's arm and escorted her in their wake. She looked over her shoulder at the design along the edge of the rug—fern leaves, if she wasn't mistaken. How elegant.

"*Put me down!*" Lord Quimby's shouts echoed in the stairs.

"How did you find the continent?" the priest asked her with interest.

"Rather boring in general, I must confess, although it did have its moments," she said with a rueful smile. "Father Victor sends his regards."

"Kind of him. I've always wanted to visit Melk in the autumn."

"Oh, you must!" she insisted. "The river is simply lovely."

They ceased their conversation as they made their careful way down the steps—the old man's shouts rendering all attempts at speech pointless—and came into the hall.

"Help me, you idiots," Quimby demanded of the ranks of Beckham's soldiers, who were lined up in the hall before one of the tables. But they only looked at him briefly before their gazes turned back to the head of the table, where Adrian Hailsworth sat, a small open trunk of coin near his elbow, fresh parchment and quill and ink beneath his hand. A pirate stood to each side behind him as Adrian took individual soldiers' marks and then doled out the stipend for their continued service to Beckham Hall's rightful mistress.

"Maria," Valentine called, gaining her attention to where he and Roman still held the struggling old man aloft. "To the inn, yes?"

She nodded and blew him a kiss.

Roman was holding the old man with only one hand near his armpit. "I think we should tie him up, Val. He's kicking me on purpose now."

"We do no wish to convey the idea that we have *detained* Lord Quimby in any way. However, I should advise you, my friend," Valentine said as they made their way toward the guardhouse, "if you think to kick me—" Mary heard his intake of breath. "Yes, that is what I mean. Roman?"

The two men stopped at the top of the stairs and released the man with a little toss. Roman turned away and came back into the hall at once, but Valentine stood on the top step, his arms held wide.

"I tried to warn you, my friend. And now you will have to walk to the inn and carry your things yourself. They will be waiting here for you by the time you have secured other accommodations. Ah-ah!" he said in a warning tone. "If you should come back inside, I will have the soldiers arrest you." He paused. "Or worse."

"*They're my soldiers!*" Mary heard Lord Quimby wail.

"Good day to you, sir," Valentine said with a bow and then stepped inside and slammed the door. He dusted his palms together and then placed his hands on his hips to regard Mary with his warm gaze.

"You," he said with a grin, "were magnificent, *mi amor*." He put his hands together in applause as he crossed the floor toward her, and soon the whole of the hall was clapping—even the soldiers, who weren't entirely sure why but were fairly thrilled with the unexpected wages that now weighed in their hands.

Mary felt her cheeks tingle and she gave a short curtsy to the hall before Valentine snaked his arms around her waist.

"Excuse me, Father," Valentine said to the priest, who looked on with an indulgent smile. "I must kiss the lady of Beckham Hall now."

"Valentine," Mary said quietly, drawing his attention to the blond boy who stood just beyond his elbow.

"Yes, Christian?" Valentine said.

"Is it time now?" the boy said, looking from Mary and Valentine to the faces of the people around the hall he knew, the only people he could now trust. "Can we go find my father?" He dropped his gaze back to the falcon he still held but glanced at Adrian a final time.

Everyone's eyes went to the man still seated at the table, his sleeves rolled up to reveal his tattooed arms.

"Soon, Christian," Adrian promised with a nod. "Soon."

Chapter 15

Dori awoke the next morning with a decidedly strange feeling of warmth about her person; her toes weren't numb, her chest didn't hurt, there was no ache in the pit of her stomach nor ringing in her ears. The absence of them all was so startling that for a moment she simply lay on the bench staring at the wall, wondering that she had become so used to the discomforts that the deficiency of them was akin to being reborn into a different body.

The oratory was warm, but she had nearly gotten used to that since Constantine Gerard's arrival and so she attributed her returning health to the fortifying food they'd eaten the night before, and the strong, piney tea she'd drunk. The heavy, ornate altar cloth slid from her shoulder soundlessly as she pushed herself upright and turned to face the room.

Lord Gerard was sitting before the hearth, the small fire crackling cheerily. His right leg was stretched out before him on the stool and he was stirring the contents of the pot the two of them had nearly consumed in its entirety the night before. She hadn't yet made a sound and so she thought she should greet him to let him know that she was awake rather than suddenly intrude on his grim pensiveness. But in the perpetual evening of the windowless oratory, his outline was black against the glow of the fire, the silhouette of his face strong and peaceful, and she couldn't help but take the opportunity to study him. His lashes were darker than his brows or his beard or his long, tawny braid; his eyes reflected the dancing sparks before him. His upper lip was deeply bowed in the center.

Dori felt a stirring in her middle, looking at him at her leisure while he was unaware. He was a very handsome man, older than her, true, but no one could accuse her of childish fancies any longer. She was a woman now, and as she looked at him through a woman's eyes her mind turned to Patrice Gerard and the horrid rumors that had been the favorite fodder for the gossips before the woman died.

What wife in possession of her right mind would even consider straying in her fidelity to a husband such as Constantine Gerard? And then, in the very next instant, indignation rose up in her chest and Dori wanted to defend the woman; Lady Patrice could have been prompted by any manner of secrets in their marriage, Dori supposed. Perhaps Lord Gerard had beaten her or had had lovers himself.

Perhaps he didn't even prefer women.

Heaven knew Theodora Rosemont had kept secrets no one would ever guess. Didn't people likely think her worse than Patrice Gerard? If Dori had felt the choices she'd made were unavoidable, what corner had the countess of Chase been pressed to inhabit?

Dori indulged herself a moment longer by imagining that it had been this man she'd married, his child she'd borne, and her heart beat faster in her chest. What would her life be like now? What boundless opportunities would await her son with a man like Constantine Gerard to bring him up to manhood?

But he'd rarely been in residence at Benningsgate, had he? The sudden thought cooled her enthusiasm for the fantasy she'd been constructing in her mind.

"Good morn, Dori," he said without turning, and his low, gravelly voice surprised her so that she blinked the last of her musings from her imagination and sat up straight.

He'd somehow known she'd been awake and watching him the entire time.

And he'd used the name she'd bade him call her.

"Good morn," she said briskly and swung her feet to the floor. "How fares your leg this day?"

He answered with a sigh and glanced at her as she gained her feet and began to fold the cloth into a neat square. "I'd hoped to return to the keep, but it's doubtful I could climb the ladder for either entry or exit. I'd be in little danger if forced to shelter in the place overnight, but—"

"It would be foolish to attempt it and then have no choice but to stay there because of an injury," she interjected sharply—more sharply than she'd intended, but the idea of him sleeping alone in that damned place, at the mercy of the spirits of those he loved free to torment his dreams all the night, caused Dori's stomach to flutter. What memories would they share?

She placed the cover neatly on the bench and then walked to the table to pour herself a cup of water. "You'd likely only make it worse," she said stiffly, but at least her tone wasn't so panicked.

"This is still warm," he said, and when she turned her head to look at him, he was holding the metal cup toward her. "You slept so well last night, I assumed the brew suited you."

Dori set down the wooden tankard and was struck dumb for a moment. She stepped toward him and took the cup.

"Thank you," she said hesitantly.

He nodded and looked back to the fire.

"I assume you did not sleep well?" she said, and then blew on the surface of the fragrant tea before raising it to her lips and sipping, watching him closely over the rim.

He stirred the fire with a long poker. "I've much on my mind after yesterday," he said. "And my knee pained me so as to make finding a comfortable position a trial."

Dori was certain that sleeping on the floor hadn't helped, even if he'd made his pallet before the small hearth. The stones were still damp and sucked the warmth from anything that touched them. And yet he hadn't complained about the location of his bed.

"Lord Gerard—" she began.

"You called me Constantine yesterday," he interrupted, and the idea that he'd noticed her use of his given name shocked her so greatly that she fell back into silence.

Could he perhaps begin to see her as someone who was not at odds with his goal? Not Glayer Felsteppe's wife, not detestable Theodora Rosemont, but as she saw herself—Dori, someone he could trust?

He glanced at her. "It's doubtful I'll recover Benningsgate or my title any matter. Once I've accomplished what I came here to do, it's possible the king's men might apprehend me. I'd likely be hanged."

"But," Dori stammered, "I promised you that I would vouch for you. And I will. I will go to the king myself and testify to Felsteppe's misdeeds. You'll surely be exonerated."

Constantine turned his head with a sniff of incredulous laughter. "Henry's not going to believe *you*."

He might as well have struck her. She felt the breath go out of her lungs and her fingers tightened around the warm cup still in her hands. The tea he'd made her. She looked down into its dark, murky depths to avoid his amused gaze and then stepped to the table to set the cup down carefully. Her eyes burned with humiliation as she stepped to the peg on the wall to remove her cloak, now little more than a long, hooded rag.

"Have I upset you?" he said behind her.

Her fingers paused for only an instant as they struggled to fasten her cloak at her throat. "How could you have possibly upset me?" The blasted loop was so worn and stretched that the knot wouldn't stay hooked. "You only suggested that my testimony would be completely worthless and unreliable. Am I known as a liar now, too? I fear I've been out of the circle of gossip, so I can't be sure what's been said of me since my fortuitous *death*."

He sighed. "That's not what I meant."

The cloak wouldn't fasten, so she jerked it from her shoulders and threw it to the stones before turning around to face him.

"You didn't mean the king couldn't possibly believe *me* because of my reputation before my father died? Because I journeyed all the way to the Holy Land to become married to the very demon I would accuse? Because I allowed everyone to believe I was dead while I cowered in this hellish, ruined *hovel* and my infant son is at the mercy of that beast and his servant dog?"

"No," Constantine said levelly. "That's not what I meant. That's what *you* think."

She gasped. "What?"

Constantine rose from his stool with a hitch as he pulled his leg beneath him and then walked toward Dori with a slight limp. She held her ground, her wounds so raw and painful that they were easily covered by anger. She would not shrink from him.

He stopped before her and bent down, picking up her cloak and shaking it out. He swirled it behind her and then looked down his nose while he worked the closure at her collarbone.

"That's what you think," he clarified. "I meant that Henry isn't likely to release my estate back to me at your word when it's your son who will inherit both Benningsgate and Thurston Hold after his father is dead. It would be in the king's best interest to retain a modicum of control over both houses, which he will be able to do upon realizing that you have been resurrected as a widow."

His hands fell away from her throat and his gaze met hers. "If Henry were going to do justice for me, he already has received letters testifying to my innocence and to Felsteppe's treachery. He stands to benefit from Felsteppe's purchase of Benningsgate, and once I see that one dead, it will again fall to his guardianship. He shall profit twice."

"But you've been gone for years," Dori argued quietly, not certain which emotion was the right one to feel out of the tangle of them that mired her thoughts. "Perhaps it is only your presence he needs to attest to your fidelity."

He looked at her thoughtfully. "Perhaps. But even if that were so, I have lost everything. Henry will know soon enough that I've nothing with which to rebuild this place," he ended on a whisper. "Not even the will."

"Then why did you agree to help me?" she insisted. "If I am so worthless to you, why not just chase down Felsteppe now that you are so close to him and do that which your vengeance demands?"

He pressed his lips together, and Dori's eyes lingered on his upper lip, where the sensuous curvature she'd noticed only moments before was nowhere to be seen.

"I don't know," he said, his voice low, and now, as his eyes looked into hers, Dori didn't know if it was regret she saw there or only a reflection of her own fears. "Perhaps it's because if I had a chance to save my own son I would. If I had a chance to see that he was cared for and"—he paused here and swallowed, and the obvious pain of it caused Dori to wince—"safe, I would wish him in the hands of one who could protect him. Even if those hands weren't my own."

Dori felt her eyes welling with tears. "I'm sorry, Constantine," she said. "I wish I could have been that person for you. For Christian."

He raised his hand and smoothed back a lock of her hair behind her ear, which had been bent against her cheek while she'd slept. How stupid of her to have cut it. She had been impetuous even so near death. What must he think of her appearance, this general, this earl, who had been married to one of the greatest beauties in all the land, who had surely seen the most enchanting and exotic of women in his many travels?

And yet here he was before her now, still staring down into her eyes, and Dori could not look away from him. Even if he thought her ridiculous in her appearance, a foolish child, she didn't care. The strength and depth of his gaze was more potent than any food, any warming potion she could consume, and it rendered her unable to move at all.

"I believe you," he whispered, his thumb grazing the underside of her jaw as he withdrew his hand.

The phrase was like some magical incantation, for when she blinked, he was no longer simply Lord Gerard, Earl of Chase, the brusque, handsome general who had come back to avenge his family. No, it was as if his words had kindled a fire behind his eyes, a glow within him that Dori was suddenly drawn to like a dumb, helpless moth; as if he was a portrait of manhood exquisitely rendered but then gasped to life and crawled out of the still frame to stand before her so close, breathing the same air that she did.

He was a man who owed her nothing, had no reason to placate her. She was entirely without influence in any area of her life, at the mercy of God and fate and—truly—of Constantine Gerard himself. And he'd said he believed her.

This is when he shall kiss me, she marveled to herself, and even felt her lips part in anticipation. *What a strange turn of events.*

Constantine's gaze went to her mouth and then she saw his own lips quirk, a rueful smile coming over his face. He reached up suddenly and raised the hood of her cloak over her head.

"It's raining again," he said and then stepped away from her to limp back to the stool, where he sat with a weary sigh.

Dori stood in the center of the floor for a moment, as if she'd just been dropped through the ceiling. He hadn't kissed her after all, and she wasn't quite sure what had just passed between them, but she was certain the air in the oratory was somehow different—that their lives were now different because of each other, and that perhaps their futures would be, too.

Different because he believed her.

It was too much for her to ponder in his presence, so she turned to the door, opened it, and was gone into the black, stinking corridor.

Constantine dropped his forehead into his palm after Theodora had closed the oratory door and then smoothed his hand over his head with a sigh, looking up into the flames before him.

She'd expected him to kiss her. And hadn't he thought about it? This fairylike woman-child with her pixie's hair and elfin face, her wide mouth that should have been sensuous but was made innocent by its honest expression of expectation. How could she have had such stars in her big eyes when they were in a cell below the ground?

Theodora's beloved father had deserted her with his mind long before his body had died, and now that Constantine was here, perhaps she thought to cling to him in Lord Rosemont's stead. She was little more than a girl who'd been made vulnerable by her circumstances.

And yet she was the girl who had married Glayer Felsteppe. By her own admission, she had run to the Holy Land after him once her father was dead. Why? Because, as now, she had no one else to look after her? Was she so unsure that she needed someone, anyone—even Glayer Felsteppe—to claim her rather than be left to her own devices?

But she'd come to Benningsgate alone. She'd stayed here when it probably should have meant her death rather than seek help and risk any chance of her ever going after her son without Felsteppe knowing she was coming. That didn't seem like the actions of an insecure girl but rather the gamble of a determined woman, willing to wager her own life against Glayer Felsteppe winning the prize of her child.

It didn't matter. She had still married the fiend and nothing could ever erase that fact. Even after Felsteppe was dead and Constantine had his revenge, Theodora Rosemont would still be Glayer Felsteppe's widow. Her boy would forever be Felsteppe's son. Each time Constantine looked at his red hair, he would think of the blond little boy who should have his place.

The thought caused a wave of nausea to rise up against his sternum. How could he have entertained the thought of kissing Dori when his wife and son lay dead and buried under the rubble of their ruined home only hundreds of feet away?

Constantine decided he was only sad and lonely, touched by the obligation of love he would perform in the ruined keep, as well as the absence of his friends, so far away. They might not forgive him for his desertion, if he was so fortunate as to ever see any of them again. He didn't blame them.

The oratory door burst open and Dori rushed back inside, closing the door quickly but quietly, reaching down for her ridiculous stake and then shoving it into the groove in the floor. She rose up at once and pressed her back to the door, her wide eyes staring at him in horror.

"What?" he said, gaining his feet. "What is it?"

Her mouth came open, as if she would answer, but no sound issued forth. She pushed away from the door and began gesturing sharply with her hands, as if gesticulating a conversation she was incapable of having.

"I was . . . there is . . ." She took a deep, gasping breath and swept her hands toward the door, then back toward Constantine. "In." She closed her eyes for a moment and took another deep breath while making tight fists of her hands. She at last looked at him once more and loosened both forefingers from her fists. "The ward."

He winced at her. "What?"

An escalating, humming noise came from her throat, clearly a sound of distress, but Constantine could not decipher the cause for Dori's panic. She clasped her hands together, lacing her fingers as if she would fall before the commandeered altar and pray the jumble of words that sounded as though they were trapped behind her teeth.

Constantine thought perhaps seeking divine intervention wasn't a terrible idea, the way she was behaving.

"Do you need to sit down?" he asked.

"*N-n-no!*" The word finally forced its way between her lips in the same moment her hands forced themselves apart. She rushed to him and grasped his tunic, and he found himself catching her with his hands on her waist. "Constantine, there are . . . *people!* In . . . the *ward!*"

"People?" he repeated while looking down into her face.

She nodded tightly, her eyes wide with fright, and then emphasized on a whisper, "In the ward!"

"What sort of people?"

"What sort of—?" She broke off and winced at him. "The sort with arms and legs. What do you mean, what sort of people?"

He gave her a frown. "Are they men, women, soldiers?"

"I don't *know,*" she insisted and jerked on his tunic. "I didn't think it wise to put forth an inquiry."

He saw her point. "How many?"

"Ten? A score? Does it matter?" she said. "There are supposed to be *none!*"

"Did they see you?"

"I don't think so."

Constantine took Dori by the arms and backed her to the bench and into a seated position so that if she was going to faint he wouldn't have to tend catching her while he took a moment to think.

People in the ward. Could be anyone—envoys of the king, of Glayer Felsteppe. There could only be two groups of individuals with any reason whatsoever to congregate in the deserted ward within the broken walls: they had won Benningsgate or they were hunting Constantine.

He reached down automatically to feel for the hilt of his sword. Theodora had said ten or perhaps twenty people; Constantine could never hope to prevail against so many if they were indeed here to take him.

If they were here to claim Benningsgate, did Constantine care if he survived or not?

And what if Glayer Felsteppe was in the group?

He turned his head to look at Dori, still seated on the bench as Constantine had left her, but her eyes had followed him as he paced the oratory.

He stopped before her. "I'm going up."

"What? Are you mad? They'll see you!"

"There's no helping it. They've either come to claim the estate, in which case we'll be discovered eventually, or they've come seeking me. I'll not be cut down in this oratory with my back to a wall, unable to escape."

"What about me?"

"You may stay here if you wish," he said, tightening his belt and removing his cloak—it would only hamper his movements. "I won't divulge your presence."

"Oh, so *I* can be cut down with *my* back to a wall when I'm discovered?"

Constantine stopped to look at her. "I must face this. Its's my duty."

She stood, swirling her own cloak from her shoulders. "Then I'm coming with you."

"You don't even have a weapon," he argued.

"And whose fault is that?" she snapped with her hands on her hips, all of her earlier panic seeming to have vanished. "I looked over the ward yesterday and it was lost to the weeds, where you threw it. Have you any idea how difficult that was to fashion?"

"Well, I couldn't allow you to keep it after you nearly spilled my guts with it, could I?"

"I should think it would come in rather handy now," she said with a lift of her nose as she crossed her arms over her chest. "I suppose you'll have to give me one of your knives."

"You're sincere in this, aren't you?"

She only looked at him, her mouth set.

Constantine sighed and then limped to his satchel, in a corner by the stool. He bent at the waist to retrieve it and then held it by one hand as he reached inside and sorted carefully through the contents. He located the one he sought at last, the blade long, parchment thin, and tapered, meant for taking meat from bones, and Constantine thought the woman could do a lethal amount of damage with it before she was stopped, thinking once more of their first meeting in the ward with her handcrafted defense.

He dropped the satchel back to the floor and looked at her. "Stay behind me, out of sight in the corridor. Should I be overpowered, you might yet have an opportunity to escape."

Her only answer was to hold out her hand, and Constantine placed the handle of the long, deadly-looking weapon there.

"Thank you," she said in a haughty voice, dropping her arm to her side and concealing the blade within the folds of the voluminous apron. She looked back up at him. "Whenever you're ready."

He gave her a nod and walked to the door, bending to remove the stake from the floor.

"Constantine?" Her voice was just behind him.

He turned and looked down at her and she rose up on her toes suddenly, grasping his chin with the hand not holding his knife and pressed her mouth tightly to his. Her breath whistled in her nostrils as she leaned up and into him, and then she withdrew with the sort of breath one takes when coming out of water.

Dori cleared her throat delicately. "In case one or both of us are killed." Then she reached past him for the door. She pulled it open, but it hit his boot, where he had failed to move.

He felt an odd heat on his ears. "That was inappropriate, Theodora," he said gruffly.

She smiled up at him. "Have you any idea the number of times I've heard that exact phrase issued at me?"

Constantine turned and took hold of the edge of the door and opened it, leaving her to follow him from the oratory and into whatever battle awaited him in the ward.

Chapter 16

Dori followed Constantine as he made his stealthy way up through the collapsed maze of the corridor beyond the oratory. He behaved as though she wasn't behind him, but she'd expected that. He'd already warned her that he could not be responsible for protecting her if she insisted on following in his wake.

She pulled herself over the rubble as quickly as she could, hurrying over the wreckage just in time to see his black outline pause against the grayness of the doorway. He seemed to listen for a moment, and then he drew his sword without a sound, ducked through the doorway, and was gone.

Dori took his place in the doorway, her ears straining, her fingers rotating the handle of the knife against her palm nervously. If he was overtaken, she could not consider going to his aid. Absolutely not. Doing so might mean her death or, at the very least, her discovery.

Dori closed her eyes at the memory of his touch on her face.

I believe you . . .

A roar sounded suddenly from the ward beyond the corridor, and her eyes flashed open as she jumped. It sounded like the battle cry of scores of soldiers, and Dori immediately thought of Constantine's green eyes gazing down into hers, the warm, smooth feel of his lips when she'd kissed him.

No matter who they had been before, the lives and family and status they had enjoyed, they only had each other now.

She slipped around the door frame and darted to the fall of stone, scrambling up it in a crouch before withdrawing her blade and standing fully upright, ready to fly down upon whatever fiend had Constantine subdued.

She saw below her not an army of men intent on destroying the earl of Chase but a motley group of folk with bowed heads, dropped to one knee before the man who stood before them.

Peasants. Villagers.

They rose as one and then seemed to mob Constantine, although their intention was obviously benign as the lord returned his sword to his sheath and clasped hands with several men and was embraced by one large woman. The rotund Jeremy hung to the rear of the advancing group, his expression anxious as he neared Constantine.

"Forgive me, milord," the man was saying, his stringed hood twisted in his hands, revealing the mass of curly brown hair atop his head. "It was Nell who dragged it out of me—sorceress of a woman, she is! She must have used some foul charm, milord." He dropped his head before Constantine.

"Foul charm," the large woman sniffed as she drew away from the lord and turned to look at Jeremy with her hands on her wide hips. "You were thick enough to come traipsing through the village at midday with Harmon's ladder, looking as though you'd just discovered St. George's lance."

Jeremy sent the woman a sideways glare. "You said you wouldn't tell," he hissed.

"You stole my best"—the woman stuttered to silence as she caught sight of Dori standing atop the pile of stone, Constantine's blade still gripped in her hand—"apron."

All eyes shifted up to her and Constantine turned.

Dori felt a lump of ice forming in her chest as the Benningsgate villagers stared at her, their eyes wide and wary, their distrust of her obvious as they took in the ill-fitting article of clothing wrapped several times around Dori's middle. The apron seemed to suddenly weigh a hundred pounds.

"Milady," Nell said stiffly and followed the greeting with an equally rigid bob.

Constantine looked to Jeremy with one tawny eyebrow elevated. "I assume they know about Lady Theodora as well."

"A sorceress, milord," Jeremy insisted in a desperate whisper.

Constantine only shook his head and then looked back to Dori. "Benningsgate folk, the lady Theodora Rosemont of Thurston Hold."

No one made a sound, although they continued to stare at her openly. Dori couldn't help but see hostility in their gaping, and she wondered how the rumors had been twisted by the time they had made their way around to Benningsgate.

She lifted her chin and her eyes scanned the individuals in the crowd just as brazenly as they regarded her. Besides Jeremy and Nell and Erasmus—bounding around the ward as usual—there were five other men and one old woman, wife to the most elderly of the males in the group if her leaning on his arm was any indication. It was the tall, thin man with a dark, bushy beard who chose to step forward from the group and give a short bow.

"I'm called Harmon, milady," he said solemnly. He turned sideways and motioned toward the rear of the gathering, where a pimply-faced adolescent boy stood next to a short, squat man with eyes that didn't quite point in the same direction but rolled in opposing circuits, seeming to scan the heavens and the horizon at once. "Dunny and his uncle, Garulf." The boy bowed, but the older man only stood, his gaze seeming to wander about the ward aimlessly until Dunny yanked on the sleeve of his rough shirt.

Harmon then gestured to the other grown man, blond and middle-aged, his left sleeve tucked oddly across his chest and into his belt, beneath which Dori could only just see the ends of shriveled fingers. "Leland."

"Milady."

To the elderly couple, "Edgar and Edie." They bobbed in Dori's direction, but they did give her the brightest smiles of the group.

Finally, to the wide woman who still stared at Dori as if boldly taking her measure. "This is Nell. And you've met Jeremy," Harmon finished.

"Unfortunate for her, I'd wager," the man called Leland muttered just loud enough to be heard.

Dori's cheeks tingled as the fat Jeremy turned to give Leland a glare. She felt the panic building in her stomach. She would never be safe here at Benningsgate now and these villagers obviously knew it. Dori was very aware that she and Jeremy had been at odds almost since the moment of their first meeting, but she'd thought that after cooperating with each other to safely extract Constantine from the keep they had entered at least into a truce. But it seemed Jeremy couldn't keep the lord's presence to himself for even a full day before the few folk remaining in the village had known about it. Not only known about it but had descended upon the keep en masse to see for themselves.

It wouldn't be long before the news spread to Thurston Hold.

An awkward silence filled the ward as Dori looked over the motley assortment of people staring up at her expectantly. She looked to Constantine suddenly and saw that he was watching her. Her breaths were coming more quickly now and she didn't trust herself to speak. So she turned atop the pile of rubble and skittered down the back side with as much dignity as she could before walking around the end of the wash of stone and striding across the weedy ward to the opening in the wall.

She heard Erasmus bounding after her, and a moment later she saw his great, gray mass loping near her side. She didn't warn the dog away, fearful of the sound that might escape her throat were she to allow herself to speak.

She stepped over the stone threshold and made her way toward the wood.

"She won't hurt Erasmus, will she, milord?" Jeremy asked suddenly, drawing Constantine's attention away from the opening through which Theodora had disappeared.

"No, Jeremy," Constantine said.

"Did you see the blade she carried?" the man protested. "It was bigger than she was."

"I gave it to her," Constantine said. "It was Lady Theodora who was first aware there were visitors in the ward. She came to warn me. You must understand that it places her in great danger that anyone knows she is in hiding here."

"Yah, Jeremy," Leland said. "You great idiot."

"It weren't *me* what told all you that the lord was even here," Jeremy burst out and spun around. He thrust a stubby finger at Nell. "I only told her. And I certainly didn't invite you all up to the ward so as to put 'em both in a panic!"

The bearded Harmon stepped forward, holding his palm up to Jeremy before looking to Constantine. "We would never betray you, milord," he said solemnly. "Nor the lady either, if it's your wish that we do not."

Constantine looked around and saw that all were watching him expectantly. He chose his words with great care.

"Lady Theodora's husband is the man responsible for this." Constantine swept his arm around the ward to indicate the old destruction. "It was he who ordered Benningsgate be set afire and now he who is lord of Thurston Hold."

Young Dunny piped up from the back in his squeaky voice—Constantine couldn't recall the lad at all; when last he'd left Benningsgate the boy would have been barely older than Christian.

"Is she a spy, milord?" Dunny asked. "Sent here by her husband in case you returned?"

Constantine paused. The thought had never crossed his mind. Although perhaps it would have if Dori hadn't been so ill.

"Why else would she leave her child?" Nell added in a low, pressing voice. "The lord of Thurston Hold announced that she died in childbirth."

"The man currently in residence at Thurston thinks Lady Theodora *is* dead," Constantine said. "She only seeks help in regaining custody of her infant son before it is revealed that she lives. She was very ill when I discovered her here. I didn't think she would survive."

Nell brought a hand to her expansive bosom. "But her father, the old lord . . ."

Again Harmon interjected. "We will honor your wishes, Lord Gerard." When Constantine looked at the man, he saw nothing but sincerity on his face. "All at Benningsgate—even those who moved on to Thurston Hold—have prayed for your return. Now that you have, you won't want for loyalty."

Constantine's chest tightened and he nodded, once more clasping arms with the man who had once made the carts for Benningsgate. He wondered for a moment why Harmon hadn't followed his wife and daughters to Thurston Hold to work in the keep there; Patrice had valued the women highly.

"Come to the village, my lord," the elderly Edgar piped up. "The lady as well. There is no shortage of dwellings to be had—several still in good order. We all shall be better able to look after you there, and you will more quickly know if strangers approach Benningsgate. Our good, strong men—Jeremy and Dunny and Leland and Garulf—could have you outfitted this afternoon, I'd wager."

Constantine looked around and saw the other males in the group—

obese and blind and crippled and adolescent—puff with pride. This was the whole of their village now; they'd only had one another to depend upon for years.

And now they wanted to help Constantine, the lord who had abandoned them.

But Edgar had failed to mention Harmon in that group, and so now Constantine looked to that man.

As if sensing the question on Constantine's mind, Harmon glanced to the jagged outline of the keep. "I've brought more rope and other supplies with me. I figured you and I had a task to finish. It's best that we get right to it, is it not, milord?" He met Constantine's eyes.

He hadn't thought to gain the keep again until his knee healed, but with another man to help him, Constantine felt the burden lift slightly from his shoulders.

He nodded at Harmon. "It is. Much of the rubble may be too large for even both of us to move. Would that we had an ass or a horse to which we could affix a rope should we require it."

Nell piped up brightly, "Why, Jeremy's got an ass!"

"Aye, milord," Dunny added with enthusiasm, "Jeremy has a big, sturdy ass!"

Leland snorted. "Verily, his ass is huge. Forgive me, milord, but I'm surprised you haven't noticed it before now."

"That's it," Jeremy growled, pushing through the small gathering of folk toward the blond Leland. "I'll rip that shriveled branch from your body and beat you to death with it, you yammering bastard."

But Leland whooped through his broad grin and leaped nimbly around the perimeter of the group to evade the lumbering man giving chase. Edgar and Edie turned as one and crept along in Leland's wake, continuing to clutch at each other and display their unfathomable happiness through their largely toothless smiles.

Nell smiled up at Constantine. "With your permission, milord, I'd prepare your rooms. Would you be choosing the cottage yourself?"

Constantine shook his head. "My thanks, Nell, but the lot of you would know better than I."

Jeremy paused, bent over, his hands on his knees, and gasped for a moment, holding up one fat forefinger. "I'll . . . fetch Pearl. Send her . . . up . . . with Dunny."

"Back home again, Garulf," the boy said, taking hold of his uncle's hand and guiding it to his shoulder.

"Oh, aye. They're coming," Garulf said as he shuffled obediently behind Dunny. His voice was shockingly steady and deep for one of his decrepit appearance. "Like mine, like mine. Happy teeth. Happy claw."

"Don't mind him, milord," Dunny said, glancing at Constantine with a look of humility. "He talks out of his head. Says the same things over and over."

Constantine raised his hand in farewell and watched the boy depart. When he looked back to Harmon, he saw the bearded man was also closely watching the boy and his uncle as they slowly traversed the ward, but his brow was furrowed.

"What is it?" Constantine asked.

Harmon looked to him quickly, the frown falling from his face. "Beg pardon, milord. Lost in my thoughts, is all. Shall we begin?"

Constantine clapped Harmon's shoulder and slowly started toward the keep, seeking to preserve as much of his leg as he could for what would likely be a long day ahead. But he couldn't help but hold in his mind's eye the look of concern on the bearded man's face at, according to Dunny, what was typical behavior for the affected Garulf.

And he chose to concentrate on that rather than the memory of Theodora Rosemont charging into what she likely thought was certain danger, his blade in her hand, ready to come to his aid.

Dori jerked her ragged skirts free from the wet, thorny canes shooting forth from the verdant forest floor like tethered arrows. She couldn't take five steps before she was snagged again, and trying to hold them gathered together before her only resulted in her shins becoming colder and wetter and crisscrossed with stinging red welts. The thin, razor-sharp blade was of no use against such limber ropy vines, and so she tucked the knife into the double loop of the apron she wore and trudged on, seeking to gain as much distance as she could from Benningsgate without actually becoming lost.

At last she spied an old, wide stump, its weathered top indicating the tree had been harvested some time ago. Dori half-fell onto it on her hip, yanking her skirts after her a final time before letting them fall in a sodden heap against her legs. Erasmus ran around her in two full circuits before coming to an uneasy halt, his blockish head erect, his tongue lolling from the side of his mouth.

"Go back and leave me be," she grumbled at the dog.

The sounds of his heavy pants seemed to ricochet off the humid air of the forest.

Dori flapped her hand at him. "Go on. Go back."

Erasmus flinched to the side, as if he was eager to take off bounding once more through the trees, but when Dori failed to gain her feet and follow he hesitated. The dog yawned widely and shook his head, licked his muzzle noisily, and then turned in a half circle to flop down in the long weeds with a sigh. But he wasn't still for long as his ears twitched and he turned his head, his eyes bright and his posture stiff. Dori couldn't hear anything, and yet a moment later the dog leaped to his feet and galloped away, leaving her alone with only the dripping leaves and the faint roar of the river for company.

She was perhaps in greater trouble now than she had been on the night she'd come to Benningsgate. No fewer than eight people knew of her existence now, and those people hadn't been too keen on finding her with their lord and master, Constantine Gerard. She didn't know how much longer she could delay her return to Thurston Hold. If Glayer Felsteppe discovered she was still alive and had been hiding all this time little more than a stone's throw away, he would certainly realize that Dori was only biding her time until she could retrieve her son. He was depraved and evil, certainly, but he was also cunning, and at the merest hint of Dori's survival he would take flight with her child.

And then, Dori knew, Glayer Felsteppe would make sure Dori was hunted like one of Jeremy's half-wild forest swine until she was cornered and cut down.

"Lady Theodora?" The unmelodic female voice cut through the wet air, interspersed with the crashing strides of Erasmus.

Dori sighed and pressed her lips together. Was it not enough that she had been humiliated before everyone there, being seen in the peasant woman's apron? Nell would press the point by chasing Dori down and taking the garment from her?

Dori stood from the stump and picked at the knot, her ire rising as she remembered the goggling gazes of the villagers. They were all likely pleased to see that she had fallen to such a state.

By the time Erasmus led Nell to her, Dori was unwinding the wide apron and pulling it over her head.

"There you are, milady," Nell panted as she came to a stop.

Dori wadded up the apron and threw it at the woman, who barely caught it before her face. Then Dori picked up her skirts and tromped past Nell, heading toward Benningsgate once more.

"Lady Theodora?" Nell called after her.

But Dori did not slow, jerking her skirts free from the clinging vines. Erasmus bounded nimbly in and out of her path as she struggled forward.

"Lady Theodora, please wait!"

She was jolted to a stop by her traitorous skirts yet again, and this time her yanking did not free her. Dori pulled and leaned back against the resistance until she heard the fateful rending of the cloth, but then it was too late, for the angle of her body was so severe that she could not correct it in time. She gave a strangled cry as she toppled back into the weeds.

"Hold on, milady!" Nell called out. "I'm coming!"

But Dori was attended to immediately by the great gray beast that was Erasmus, the dog stepping across her midsection and thrusting his wide, damp head into Dori's face, sniffing and snorting with great interest.

Dori threw up her hands, pushing at the long muzzle with gasping shrieks, but it was like trying to shoo away a sinking ship, and Erasmus seemed encouraged by the sounds coming from Dori's mouth.

"Get off, you!" Nell shouted. "I said get . . . off!"

Dori gasped as the air before her face opened up at last. She looked up and saw the wide, rosy-cheeked Nell bent over her, a meaty fistful of Erasmus's scruff in her left hand, and yet the animal didn't seem chastised in the least, his ever-present pink tongue flopping from the side of his mouth in time to his pants.

"Are ye injured, milady?" the woman asked with a concerned frown.

"No." Dori swiped at her mouth with the sleeve of her right forearm, but it did little in the way of cleansing, as it seemed the entire back half of her person had pressed down into the thick, soft forest tilth. She held her arms away from her body and looked at them with dismay.

"Come on, then."

Dori raised her gaze back to the village woman, who circled her fingers at Dori and then reached out with the same hand and grasped her left arm just above her elbow. Dori couldn't help but draw comparisons with the way the woman seized the dog, and although her pride made her want to jerk from the woman's hold, it felt as if all the energy had burst out of her and flowed away along the ground when she'd fallen.

And so Dori reached across with her right hand and grasped the woman's stout forearm, which was much like taking hold of a tree branch, and held tight while Nell pulled her to her feet.

"Mercy," Nell said as she hesitantly let Dori go. "I've picked leeks thicker than you."

Dori didn't respond to the slight as she was too busy staring down at the asymmetric puddle of her skirts. The rip she'd heard the day before had been only the start and now Dori could feel the relative coarseness of her overskirt against the skin over her hips.

"Damn!" Dori said with a stomp of her foot. She raised her head to glare at the woman. "I hope you're at last pleased."

"Wha?" Nell looked up from regarding the same catastrophe with an expression of concern.

"You couldn't wait to put me in my place by demanding your stupid apron back immediately, could you?" Dori accused, trying to muster all the anger she could to cover her humiliation and fear. "You had to . . . you had to pursue me even into the wood!"

Nell's eyes went wide for a moment and then narrowed. "I followed you because I wanted to help, even as poorly behaved as you were. And I'll have her highness know, the embroidery on that apron took me a year of saving scraps of thread and another year to sew! It's my best piece, and better than anything you're wearing at present."

"I never said it wasn't! And I happen to have admired the needlework very much to Lord Gerard!" Dori shouted.

"Well, I thank you!" Nell barked.

"You're welcome!" Dori yelled.

Erasmus's head had swiveled back and forth as if it was on a pivot throughout the exchange, and now that there was at last an uneasy silence, the dog gave a high, breathy whisper of a whine.

Dori looked back down at her skirts with a sigh. She bent over and tried to pull the remainder of the cloth that was still hanging somewhere near midthigh from beneath her overskirt, but it was stubbornly attached and only caused her to wobble on her feet. She stood on the thing with one foot and lifted the hem of her overskirt to gain a better hold but nearly fell over again, so she let the whole lot drop back to the ground as she stood aright and brought her hands to cover her face.

The first gasping sob took her so by surprise that she simply gave herself over to it. Dori bent her knees and sank to her bottom on the forest floor and wept loudly. It didn't matter now that Nell saw her. Dori couldn't be anymore humiliated if she tried.

She felt a warm, heavy weight collapse into her and push her sideways, and when she peeled her hands from her face to look, she saw that Erasmus had come to sit behind her and prop his great mass against her flank. His panting breaths jarred her so that she couldn't even cry properly. She gave the dog her elbow unenthusiastically, but it only prompted him to turn his muzzle back against her face so forcefully that she saw stars, and then he licked her.

Which only caused Dori to wail all the more.

"Now, milady," Nell said awkwardly. "There, now. It's not so bad as all that."

Dori dropped her hands and looked up at the woman.

"Well, it may be," Nell allowed with a grim set to her mouth. "But sitting here in the mud shan't improve anything." She held out her hand again with the same circling motion. "Come along now. We've much to do before this eventide."

Dori placed her hand in Nell's and let the woman pull her out of the mud for the second time since their meeting only an hour before.

"What do you mean?" Dori asked.

"It's a wonder you didn't run yourself through with this horrid thing," Nell muttered as she reached out and pulled Constantine's blade from the tie at Dori's waist and then bent to the ground. Lifting the hem of Dori's overskirt, she cut the sagging, threadbare material beneath away and then wadded it into a ball as Dori stepped out of it. She handed the rags and Constantine's knife back to her.

"Lord Gerard is coming to the village. I suppose he means the same for you, if only to keep an eye on you."

Dori's eyes narrowed at the woman.

"Any matter," Nell continued, "I'll not be waiting on the likes of you as if I were a lady's maid, so you'd best be prepared to lend your hands to the task."

Dori looked her up and down. "I doubt anyone with knowledge of such matters would mistake you for a lady's maid."

"Not if you were the lady, I reckon," Nell retorted and then started back through the wood.

Dori watched the woman's wide back retreating for a moment, feeling an odd twitch at the corner of her mouth. She realized Erasmus stood pressed against her leg and looked down into the dog's mournful gaze.

"Good boy," she whispered.

Chapter 17

Glayer openly watched the young woman getting dressed at the side of his bed as he reclined on the luxurious bolsters. The girl was pale and wide-eyed in the bright candle glow of the guest apartment, her hands visibly trembling over their own shadows as she struggled with her fine, heavy kirtle. When the hem at last dropped to the floor, she looked to him.

"You'll speak with my father soon," she pressed, her fingers twisting around themselves. "And then you'll come for me."

"Straightaway," Glayer promised, although he couldn't quite keep the smirk from his mouth. He didn't even know who the girl's father was. Actually, he couldn't bother recalling her name now either, after finding out she was birthed of such a small estate. "Right to Glenmarrick."

She frowned, and Glayer saw her throat work as she swallowed. "Glen*covent*."

He always seemed to forget that virgins—while physically delightful—were much too exacting for his tastes.

"Of course. Glencovent," he corrected himself, giving his smile free rein now. A rap sounded on the chamber door and he gestured toward it before stretching to the side to retrieve his cup. "Admit my caller on your way out." He lay back once more but paused in bringing the chalice to his lips as he saw that the girl stood staring at him as if rooted to the spot.

"You're not going to speak to my father at all, are you?" she demanded in a shocked voice, her expression the epitome of innocence destroyed.

It put a warm, happy feeling in Glayer's stomach.

He cocked his head. "Do you really wish me to? It might put a quick end to any potential pimply-faced suitors awaiting you in the wilds of Glencarmack. If I keep my silence, you'll have all the way until your wedding night to think of an explanation for your scandalous indiscretion."

"It's Glencovent," she insisted through her teeth. "And I doubt there's need for any explanation."

Glayer rolled his eyes and waved his cup at her. "Be gone, child." He drank.

Her complexion, previously a beguiling shade of porcelain, took on a ruddy hue. "You'll pay for this. You . . . you monster."

Glayer nearly choked on his wine, he was so amused by the threat. He held his wrist to his mouth while he snorted and swallowed. "Lofty aspirations, I assure you, poppet—men far bigger and braver than you have sought retaliation against me and fallen dismally short of their marks."

The rapping came at his door again, this time more insistently.

He smacked his lips together and then sighed. The novelty of her was wearing off. "Shoo, shoo! I'm an important man with important business to attend to."

The girl whirled on her heel, tears already coursing down her face as she wrenched the door open and stormed past Eseld and little Glander, jostling them most rudely.

Eseld turned and watched the young woman's flight before closing the door carefully and turning her questioning gaze to Glayer.

"A hanger-on," he said with a dismissive wave of his cup. "I'm positively harangued of late by women hoping to attach themselves to me."

Eseld's wrinkly face relaxed and her smile was prideful. "What maid with any sense wouldn't wish to get herself in your good graces, my lord? You must choose carefully your next bride."

"Indeed," Glayer said, lighting from the bed and slipping his arms into his silken gown. He tightened the belt and then walked to Eseld to take Glander from her. "She will not only need the finest pedigree but be of meek and gentle nature to be worthy enough of the title stepmother. I'll not consider anyone seriously until Henry signs over the deed to Benningsgate; the addition of the estate shall open up a higher tier of nobility to choose from. Good day, Glander."

"She won't take my place though, will she?" Eseld pressed worriedly. "You'll still retain me as nurse."

"Yes, yes. Of course," Glayer said in an irritated fashion, walking away from the annoying old woman. "We should have our answer any day, I expect. Henry is covered over with contemporaries of the Younger and their demands this week. I believe the tournamenting has addled them all with political ambition but no sense of strategic alliances."

"Not all men can carry the blood of such strong sires," Eseld said, once more with pride in her voice, but this time Glayer ignored her. "Certainly Glander will be of such stock as his father and grandfather," she continued in a happy, musing tone. "Great-grandfather."

Glayer pressed his lips together, his neck stiffening, and walked toward the window to look down upon the unclean street below.

"I thought we agreed you would no longer mention that," he said through his teeth.

"I don't see what harm it could bring you," Eseld said, walking about the room and picking up discarded articles of clothing. "It's much the same with any royal family."

"You weren't a royal family," he pointed out. "Your father was a lecher who lay with his daughter because he was too lazy to leave the farm and find a proper wife after his had died."

Eseld turned to face him, her chin held high. "He wanted to keep the line pure."

Glayer winced. "The line of what?"

"Our family was powerful in the north before the sickness destroyed the tribe. Your father provided well enough for you to go on Crusade, did he not? And look what you've made of yourself. If that doesn't show breeding, I don't think anything would."

Glayer felt the rage boiling up inside him, but he fought to keep control of his temper while he held the child. He was a different man now. He was titled, respected, with an heir and a wealthy estate. *He was a guest of the king of England.*

But he would not allow this woman, little more than a peasant, to think she could ever talk down to him again. To think herself free to discourse on the sordid facts of their earliest years with some sort of *pride* when it had been the thing that had nearly meant the ruination of Glayer's mind.

It was a miracle he was still sane.

He walked past her calmly toward the bed, where he reached out with one hand and made a careful nest for Glander. He tucked the baby into the sumptuous coverings with a smile and a tweak of his nose and then turned to walk back to Eseld.

Glayer drew his left arm across his body. The old woman had no idea what he meant to do as he swung with all his might, the back of his hand striking the side of her face and spinning her on her feet before she fell to the floor. He straddled her body and put his left hand around the loose folds on her skinny neck, and even though she struggled with both her hands on his wrist, it did not cost Glayer much effort to cause her face to purple.

Behind him on the bed, Glander whimpered.

"Your lascivious sire," Glayer said calmly, looking down into her face with as little expression as he could train his face, "did not provide me with shite. When I asked him for my earnings to depart that desolate spit of land and seek my greater fortune, he laughed at me. *Laughed at me.*" Here he shook her neck so that her skull banged against the floor. "Said he wouldn't let loose free labor and that anything I ever earned would belong to him." Glayer leaned close to her face, now clammy and pebbled with sweat, Eseld's eyes bulging. "That was the day he fell. Only he didn't fall—*I killed him.*"

He released her throat and stood, stepping back and watching her as she writhed onto her side with a wheeze.

"The only reason I didn't kill you, too, is because I was in too much of a hurry to leave. But I have all the time in the world now, Mother. You'll do well to remember that." He turned and walked to the bed to pick up and hopefully quiet the child, who had begun to cry in earnest.

"That's quite enough, Glander," he soothed. "It's over now."

Eseld had gained her hands and knees but moved no further, crouched there on the rug, rocking herself.

"You're dismissed until I send for you," he said to her. "Show yourself out."

"No," she rasped and looked up at him, her expression stricken atop her swelling face. "Please—don't send me away. I'm sorry. You needed to teach me, I see. Please don't take him from me—my grandson. Glander. Please, don't take him."

She was crawling toward him now, and the sight so disgusted him that he felt his stomach lurch. And so he met her halfway across the floor, moving the still-crying Glander to his left shoulder while he grasped the back of Eseld's faded black kirtle. He dragged the old woman to the door while she cried out in a wheeze and dropped her in a heap before he opened the door.

"Quiet!" he barked at Glander, who startled into silence, his fist in his mouth.

Glayer regained his hold on Eseld long enough to toss her into the corridor. "You'd also do well to consider the limitations of your station. There are all too many nurses eager to take your place," he warned in a cold voice and looked up to see a noble couple pausing on their way down the corridor. He met their gazes directly, almost hoping one of them would challenge his actions.

But, to his surprise, the lady tilted her head and gave Glayer a sympathetic smile, and her lord husband nodded approvingly as he led his wife around the blubbering pile of rags that was Glayer's mother.

Glayer pulled himself together and gave the couple a short bow. "My apologies."

"Not at all, my good man," the lord said heartily. "Refreshing to see her sort put in her place."

"They grow more insolent each year if you don't arrest it right away," the woman said. "Well done, I say."

Glayer bowed again as the couple continued on their way and then kicked out at the talons that clutched his bare ankle. He backed into his apartments and shut the door.

Eseld inched her hand up the solid thickness of the door that had been closed to her, her son and her grandson on the other side. She knocked lightly.

"Glayer?" she whispered in a small voice, and even that breathy word caused daggers of pain. "My lord? Please . . ."

She looked for his shadow approaching beneath the door, but it did not come. He meant to leave her there alone in her humiliation.

She lay the sharp edge of her temple against the wood to roll her forehead along the door with a low moan and then paused with her eyes closed.

"You're just like him," she accused in a soundless whisper.

There were only three of them on the road, Adrian recognized, and it was no thoroughfare of stone and packed sand. The sun that shone down did so almost lovingly, the verdant air around him soft as a caress. And yet his mind was thrown back to another road, years earlier, a road that had seen him on the verge of death, walking to a place that should have been his tomb. The sun had been white, blinding fire, the earth an open oven powered by the fires of hell presumably just below the surface of the never-ending sand. Whips and scourges, maggots and chains . . .

The black markings on his skin seemed to tingle.

"He'll be there," Maisie said lightly, drawing his attention back to the lush greenness of the day surrounding the road to Clifty Wood.

Adrian looked over the neck of Christian's small mount to his wife, who rode on the far side of Constantine's boy. He could never hide anything from her.

Adrian nodded. It was rare that Maisie was mistaken in matters she chose to speak of deliberately, but he also knew she wished for this as much or more than Adrian himself.

"Adrian, look," Christian said and nodded up the road.

He could just see the dark gray outline of the roof of Clifty Wood manor, the house set beyond the little valley where he knew a lake lay hidden. A stacked timber fence bordered the rise, interrupted by a wide pass through on the road and although Adrian could never remember there being one before, he could clearly see the light, freshly hewn timbers of a gate that—at least in the present moment—stood open.

Open to allow another trio of riders though, being seen off by the two rough-dressed men on foot standing between the mounts.

Guards and a gate across the road to Clifty Woods?

Adrian wasn't spurring his horse on any longer. In fact, the reins had gone limp in his hands as they rested on the fore of the saddle, and he watched the rider in the middle, the rider with the long gray beard. . . .

The old man looked up, then, and all his company turned to regard the approaching visitors. But the bearded man didn't raise an arm in welcome, didn't ride out to meet them. He seemed to freeze, his gaze likely not able to make out the distinct features of Adrian's face, shadowed by his hood, and yet he dismounted slowly, pushing his reins into the hands of the man standing nearest his horse, and began walking with halting strides.

Adrian's own mount stopped and, somewhere far away it seemed, Maisie called her and Christian's horses to stand. Adrian swung down from the saddle and heard his boots crunching the gravel of the road he hadn't walked in ten years. Faster and faster, his hood fell back . . .

"Adrian!" Herne Hailsworth choked as he opened his arms wide.

"Da."

His father seemed so much smaller than Adrian remembered as he embraced him; gone were the barrel chest and stout appendages, leaving a man who while not quite frail was physically diminished and showed that the years had rolled across the meadows of Clifty Wood just the same as they had floated past Melk on the Danube, or blasted across the burning sands of Syria.

Herne drew away but kept a tight grip on Adrian's biceps, his beard split by his smile while his eyes glistened.

"I knew you'd come back," he said emphatically and then turned his head to look over his shoulder at the man approaching them.

Adrian raised his own gaze and saw Alastair. And it seemed that for every hand by which Herne Hailsworth had been diminished, Adrian's older brother had increased. Alastair Hailsworth was even larger, more solid, the ends of his now long dark hair plaited and pulled back at his nape.

"Little brother." Alastair smiled, glancing at Adrian's rich cape, his eyes taking in the tattoos creeping down his forearms where his sleeves had crept up. "Given up your dry studies at last, I see."

"Never," Adrian said, returning the smile, and then stepped into his brother's embrace.

"But Adrian," Herne called, drawing the brothers' attention, and Adrian saw his father's gaze alternating between the red-haired woman and the blond boy still mounted. "Who have you brought home with you to Clifty Wood? Dare I hope . . . ?"

"Da, Alastair, this is my wife, Maighread Lindsey," Adrian said. He turned to Christian. "And while I would be proud to claim him as my own, this fine young man is Christian Gerard, the son of my good friend, the earl of Chase."

Alastair froze in the act of giving Maisie a courteous bow to look at Christian, as Herne reached up to grip the boy's shoulder.

"Christian Gerard?" Adrian's father said, amazement loud in his voice. He turned to look at Adrian as if to be certain he understood the gravity of what had been revealed.

Adrian nodded but didn't have the chance to expound, for Christian chose to speak for himself.

"We're going to find my father," he said clearly. "To help him."

The elder Hailsworth men exchanged glances before Alastair broke the tightening silence following Christian's proclamation by raising his arm and hailing the last mounted rider still waiting at the gate, who urged his horse forward at once.

As the rider drew near, Adrian saw that it was a boy of about Christian's age, with the same dark hair and wide, solid features as Alastair.

"Come down, boy," Alastair said and then stood him facing Adrian, grasping him by the shoulders. "Walter, your Uncle Adrian has at last returned to us."

Walter's eyes widened as Adrian squatted down and held out his hand. "Good day, Walter."

The boy stared at Adrian's hand for a long moment and then launched himself past it, wrapping his arms around Adrian's neck.

"Welcome home, Uncle," Walter said. "Da and Grandda's been so worried about you. And just wait until Mam hears—she'll have the chapel bells rung. Now I'll have someone to show my renderings to." The boy pulled away and looked up at Maisie. "Is she my auntie? Are you my cousin?" he boldly addressed Christian.

Adrian chuckled and looked up at Alastair. "Renderings?"

"It seems studious pursuits must be in our blood, although I obviously lack that peculiar inheritance, thanks be to God."

Herne laughed. "Aye, young Walter has designed several pieces for the farm, Adrian, including yonder gate."

"You can pass through it with your horse at a gallop from the inside," the boy offered enthusiastically. "But it swings to of its own accord and latches shut behind you."

Adrian felt his eyebrows raise. "Indeed, I will be very happy to look at your designs, Nephew."

The boy beamed up at his father, who smiled down and said, "All right then, Walter. Why don't you take young Christian here to the kitchens? The two of you may ask Cook for a bite and then you can show him the barns, eh?"

"But we were going to see the king again," Walter protested with a frown. "Now that Uncle Adrian's returned, shouldn't he go with us and speak for himself?"

Adrian looked up at his own father as he gained his feet.

"Perhaps," Alastair said vaguely. "Right now, do as I ask of you, Walt."

"All right, Da. Come on, Christian," Walter said, letting his father boost him up to his horse. He took the reins and turned the small mare back toward the gate. "Cook makes the best pasties. If we're polite, she might give us some milk to drink with them."

Christian looked at Adrian as if for permission, and Adrian could see the question in his eyes as clearly as if he'd spoken it aloud.

Am I safe here?

"Go on," Adrian said softly. "We'll be along for you later."

Christian urged his horse from the group to walk alongside Walter's and the adults watched the boys retreat in silence. When they were through the gate and heading past the manor house, Adrian turned back to his father and brother.

"Going to see the king again?" he prompted. "And what need have you of a gate and guards on the road to Clifty Wood?"

"Much has changed in your absence, Adrian," Herne Hailsworth said. "Your brother and I, we have never stopped fighting to restore your good name. It has garnered us some enemies for certain, and made it necessary to choose carefully who is admitted onto the estate."

"We've had to defend against raids," Alastair offered. "Twice the parties included soldiers of the king."

"They meant to set fire to the house," Herne said, glancing down the road to where the boys had disappeared. "Just as they did to Benningsgate Castle. Although the king's men weren't party to that particular event."

Alastair added, "But we have tried to stay in Henry's good graces by pleading our case regularly. It's kept him from sending soldiers here again thus far."

"Thus far," Herne added darkly. "We've had no visitors for nigh on six months, and we think it's due to the rumors that the man responsible for the accusations against you will gain Benningsgate lands any day."

Adrian felt his jaw tense. "Constantine Gerard has come back to kill the one of which the rumors speak; his name is Glayer Felsteppe.

He is prepared to do whatever it takes to see the man dead. But he doesn't know his son, Christian, lives. Our friends—"

Herne nodded as he walked to Adrian, pressing his arm and smiling up at him and then Maisie. "Let's go home, shall we? You can tell us about your plan once we see you settled. You do have a plan, do you not?"

Adrian smiled, and some of the anxiety he felt building inside him at learning what his family had suffered in his absence—and on his account—faded. He placed his hand atop his father's.

"We do have a plan, Da. It's already been set in motion."

"I thought as much." Herne squeezed Adrian's arm again and then began walking down the road to retrieve his mount.

Alastair gained his saddle and looked to Maisie, who had been quietly observing the men the entire time. "My lady wife will be much pleased with your arrival, Lady Maighread. Although I must admit that if my brother chose you for his bride, you likely don't wile away your hours laboring at the needle."

Maisie smiled at him. "I'm certain I've nae idea what you're talking about, Lord Alastair," she said as she urged her mount forward and passed him, choosing to ride alongside Herne Hailsworth.

Adrian swung into his saddle, then kicked at his horse. He tried not to notice the jarring sound of the gate when it closed behind the riders, a reminder of the danger that had reached across oceans and years to stalk them all still.

He only hoped the brotherhood found Constantine first.

Chapter 18

"**M**y lord."

Constantine straightened, breathing hard, a large piece of rock suspended in his hands. He propped the jagged edge on his thigh and twisted slightly at the waist to look behind him at Harmon. The man knelt on one knee, his bent back to Constantine, the single window of the hall high above him.

Constantine thought briefly of when he'd dangled from that very window only the day before, through which Theodora Rosemont had delivered him to safety.

He tossed the rock to the side, then swiped his arm across his wet brow. He rested his hands on his hips while he attempted to regulate his breaths before answering.

"Yea, Harmon?"

The carpenter looked over his shoulder but didn't say anything, and Constantine felt his skin freeze over, his heart stop in his chest. Above him, the birds swooped and sang their sweet songs, slicing the air with gay abandon. The sun was gentle, warm, suddenly sending long beams of golden light into the ruin and filling it with a tender glow.

Constantine began slowly walking over the uneven rubble toward Harmon, his chest growing tighter with each scuffling, sliding footfall. He wanted to run toward the man and whatever he had found; he wanted to flee to the farthest corner of the world to avoid seeing the discovery with his own eyes.

At last he was just behind the man, unable to bring himself any closer at the moment. Harmon stood at once and turned away, averting his face from Constantine's as he passed and leaving him alone above the slight depression in the rubble. Constantine kept his head cocked, his eyes on the charred red stone of the wall proper while he listened to Harmon's footfalls echoing across the debris floor.

His gaze came around in jerks and starts, as if a great hand had taken hold of his skull and was forcing him to look. Amid the gray and black rubble he saw the charred, curved anomaly among the shapes, the bone-white patch streaked with black, and his breath fled his lungs as his knees buckled and he collapsed near the depression, his hands catching him on either side of the discovery.

Constantine reached out with his right hand and touched the curve with shaking fingertips. It did not rock—Harmon had obviously ceased his excavations at first sight of it—and so Constantine shifted the stones around it aside. He pulled the bone from the rubble, turned it toward himself. It was the top half of a slender skull, the front teeth long and white.

She had smiled up at him so on their wedding day . . .

Her gentle looks of love for the new babe she cradled in her arms . . .

The flash of her grimace as they'd shouted at each other . . .

"Patrice," Constantine whispered.

The birds above his head started from their secret nests and all together, causing him to startle and look upward. He pulled the skull to his chest, cradling it, the vision of the birds' graceful flight above bulging and blurred with the tears in his eyes.

"I'm so sorry," he gasped on an inhalation. "Please forgive me."

He didn't know for how long he sat like that, but it was some time later that Constantine sensed movement on his left and he glanced down at the rubble to see Harmon's sturdy, well-cared-for boots. The man set a long, floppy-sided basket near Constantine's hip. A blink sent some of the haze from Constantine's vision, and he saw the fine embroidered linen cloth on the bottom of the basket, pressed to a formal crispness that drew attention to the birds and swirls flying in a static circuit around the perimeter.

"It was a gift from Lady Patrice to Isley the Christmastide before . . . before," Harmon said. "I thought it fitting it should be returned to her. She should be wrapped in something belonging to her. Something fine."

Constantine's chest tightened again, and it was a moment more before he could bring himself to speak.

"Are you certain Isley won't want it as a memento of her time with Lady Patrice?" He looked up at the bulky, bearded man.

"Isley'n the girls perished in the fire as well, milord," Harmon said gruffly.

And then Constantine understood why the man had remained behind in the deserted village at Benningsgate, with the rest of the cripples and outcasts. Harmon's beautiful, golden-haired daughters . . .

"Your loss pains me as much as my own, friend," Constantine said, his voice thick with emotion. "How did you know where to look?"

"When we found the others—the servants who'd been locked inside the keep when the fire was laid—they had died pressed against the doors that were barricaded against them. In the upper corridor." Harmon paused, and Constantine let the man be, marveling at his willingness to aid him after already providing this same act of love for his own family and friends. "If Lady Patrice had any consciousness in her, she would have tried to escape the hall by any means she could." Harmon glanced up at the window above them, prompting Constantine to do the same. "You were already searching closer to the door, milord."

"Thank you," Constantine said. He ran his palm along the smooth surface of the skull, then laid it gently in the basket atop the beautiful linen. He let his thumbs caress the high cheekbones as he released her, wishing that he had used the motion to wipe the tears from her face when last he'd seen her. Wishing he had set aside his pride— damn his pride!—and stayed, stayed, *stayed*.

Harmon gave a sigh and then knelt across the depression from Constantine. When Stan looked up the man's gaze was steady, without pity, without embarrassment, and Constantine understood at once that he and Harmon had been through the same war together, although their battles had taken place in different locations, years apart.

"Let's find Master Christian now, shall we, milord?" Harmon suggested.

Constantine nodded and once more began removing the rubble, with each stone laid aside, each small fragment of charred and broken bone placed reverently atop the linen, his guilt was exposed to the air and breathed life in macabre contradiction to the woman whose remains would not fill a small woven basket.

* * *

"I'm sorry for the way I spoke to you earlier," Dori said as she stood in the doorway of the cottage's only other chamber, causing the round Nell to turn from her work at the bench in the center of the room and regard her with wide eyes. "I know I've done nothing to belie my repute. Thank you for what you've done for me, and what you're doing for Lord Gerard."

The woman blinked, a knife in one hand, a bunch of radish greens in the other. The small hearth in the cottage crackled, and although it was no royal chamber, Dori knew the remaining villagers at Benningsgate had given up the best of their own possessions to see that Constantine was well-furnished.

"You're welcome, milady. Wasn't no one going to wear those things again any matter. Certainly not me," she said gruffly, and then she turned her eyes back to the bench, where she tossed the greens into a small pot.

Dori glanced down at the slim gray kirtle and short brown apron she wore. The sleeves and length of the skirts were too short for her by at least three inches, but otherwise they fit her thin frame well. After bathing in a bowl of warmed water in the back room of the cottage and donning the clothes, Dori felt as though she were dressed in the finest garments ever to be tailored, even with the moth holes and unraveling hems.

"They belonged to my daughter," Nell continued, trimming another handful of the white roots. "Fever took her and my man more than ten years ago. That there was her everyday dress. I couldn't bear to part with 'em. Kept 'em folded with my own things. Think of her every day as I dress." She paused, and her cheeks flushed, as if embarrassed by the unmistakable emotion behind her curt words. "I hope the shoes aren't too small."

Dori held forth one foot to show Nell the short leather boot, still serviceable although stiff and brittle with age and disuse. "You've cared for them well. There is enough give in the leather to accommodate my feet. I'll see they are returned to you."

"I'll thank you for it."

Jeremy appeared in the open cottage doorway just then, rousing Erasmus from his slumber before the hearth. The rotund swineherd was panting, his cheeks flushed.

"His lordship and Harmon's coming down from the ruin. Carryin' a basket."

"Mercy," Nell whispered and made the sign of the cross. She turned to Dori. "You must see to finishing the meal, milady. I'm the only woman to help prepare for the burial—Edie is too old."

Dori glanced at the food strewn about the bench, the pot not yet even hung on the swinging arm. The panic must have been evident on her face, for Nell gave a grimace.

"Never you mind; I'll throw this on as is and tend to it as well as I can when I return. I've said for the longest time I wished some task to set my hands to. God has answered my prayers most generously."

"I will assist Lord Gerard," Dori volunteered before she had thought better about it. Jeremy and Nell and even shaggy, gray Erasmus turned their heads to look at her, and she felt her face heat. Partly in humiliation for her intimidation at preparing a simple stew, but also by their suspicious expressions. They likely didn't think her capable of doing anything. It made her eyebrows draw together and her chin lift.

"How many nobles have *you* buried?" she snipped with a raised eyebrow.

Nell and Jeremy exchanged guilty, if doubtful, glances.

"Very well," Dori said curtly and then started toward the door. "Excuse me." She stood, looking pointedly at Jeremy, who was still filling the doorway.

"Milady, I—"

Her eyes narrowed. "*Move.*"

Jeremy stepped outside of the cottage and Dori swept past him, walking straight up the village path several yards to stop in the middle and wait to meet the two men descending from the ruin.

Constantine walked ahead of Harmon, and Dori's stomach clenched at the basket he held against his chest. He looked straight ahead, his expression determined, but his gaze seemed to cut through Dori as if she were invisible. Indeed, Lord Gerard walked past her and on through the village without a word, although Harmon came to a stop at her side.

Dori turned and watched Constantine continue down the path, noting how the remaining villagers—Edgar and Edie, Nell, Jeremy, Dunny and Garulf—had come to the edge of the path, watching in respectful vigil as their lord made his grim procession past the cottages. Even Erasmus stood watch, and Dori heard his low whine, soon matched farther down the path by the strange Garulf. Only Leland was missing, and Dori wondered for a moment if the crippled man was ever expected to attend much in the village.

"It's our lady, alone," Harmon said, prompting Dori to turn and look up at the man. It took her a moment to comprehend what Harmon was saying. "We haven't yet found Master Christian."

Dori straightened her spine in order to give the illusion of confidence. "I see. I'll be preparing Lady Patrice for burial."

Harmon nodded, accepting her declaration without question. "His lordship is going on to my cottage—I've some linen ready on the bench, although there's no oil or balm."

Dori recalled the small basket hidden beneath the altar table in the oratory. "I can lay hand to something," she said. "I'll join Lord Gerard shortly."

"Very well, milady," Harmon said deferentially. "I'll go on to the burial ground and prepare the plot. His lordship likely wants some privacy with his wife before she is laid to rest any matter."

Harmon's thoughtful comment gave Dori pause. The basket Constantine carried held what was left of his wife—the woman he had married, had made a child with.

His wife.

"I realize that," Dori said, her tone sharper than she'd intended.

Harmon only gave a short bow. "I knew you would, milady." He headed deeper into the village while Dori turned and walked toward the ruin.

Once she'd gained the ward, it took her only moments to descend to the oratory; her feet and hands found the holds and steps as surely as any path she'd once trod at Thurston Hold. When she pushed open the door, the hearth was cold and dark, the candle on the table little more than a rim of transparent wax, the flame seeming to float atop the puddle of clear liquid from the tall taper left there hours before. And so Dori lit the last remaining candle stub, intending to make sure she took everything she needed from the dank, dungeon room—she hoped never to set foot in it again.

She retrieved Constantine's satchel, setting it atop the table and opening the flap to return the miscellany to it—pausing a moment to look down at the vessel from which he'd given her sustenance. He'd saved her life. She tucked the cup inside and then quickly added his other things. Then she crouched down and felt along the shelf at the back of the table, her fingers seeking the little woven basket latched with a wooden peg and a leather thong.

Dori laid hand to it and rose, setting it on the table and opening the container to reassure herself of the contents before setting it atop the other things in Constantine's sack. She stuffed the few stiff linen cloths she'd used while living in the oratory at the top of the bag and secured it tightly. Then she put her hands on her hips and looked around the room for anything she'd missed.

There was only the ornately decorated altar cloth—heavy and slick and stiff—folded neatly on the bench where she'd left it. Dori picked it up and then the satchel, ducking her head through the strap before extinguishing the light and leaving the pitch-black room.

When she'd gained the ward, she crossed the tall weeds, which were at last beginning to dry out and straighten respectably, to exit over the stone threshold on the side of the castle ruin above the river. She paused for a moment, taking in the small stone ring, already beginning to be overrun with fresh greenery, where Constantine Gerard had smoked fish the morning after he'd come. She walked past it down to the river's edge, where she took one of the worn and dingy linen cloths from the satchel and dunked it in the frigid water.

Then Dori turned and trudged up the slope to the patch of flowers on the edge of the cliff just outside the wood, where she spread the dripping cloth on the grass and then removed his satchel, setting it aside. She slid the knife he'd given her earlier from the sheath on her apron tie.

She piled the cloth with wild early violets, stems of tiny-leaved mint and slender fern. The few delicate snowdrops she found persevering beneath the north side of a moss-covered boulder she saved for last, placing the bright blooms atop the bouquet before carefully knotting the corners of the cloth in the middle. She returned the blade, ducked back into Constantine's satchel, and picked up the damp bundle.

It wasn't difficult to locate Harmon's cottage after Dori had returned to the village. Many of the smaller dwellings had fallen into disrepair, and the ones that were still habitable clustered together along the road, save for the larger swineherd's cottage and attached barn, which was located on the outer edge of the town. This time, there were no observers as she made her way down the path, not even curious and enthusiastic Erasmus. She leaned in the window—one shutter half open—and saw the back of Constantine Gerard's head as he sat on a stool, his back to her.

Dori left the window to hesitate a moment before the closed door, then knocked firmly.

A long beat of silence, and then, "Come."

She pushed the door open and stepped inside, closing it silently behind her. Dori placed the bundle of flowers on the table and paused, hesitant to intrude upon him even after he had granted her entry.

"I had never failed at anything in my entire life before I married Patrice."

She glanced up at him, but Constantine wasn't looking at her as he spoke, instead fixing his eyes on the shallow basket in the center of Harmon's table.

"It seems as though I failed at everything ever after."

Dori directed her gaze downward once more as she lifted the strap of Constantine's satchel over her head and set it on the other side of the basket. She slid the folded altar cloth from its bulk and smoothed its edges as she laid it on the table.

"I failed as a husband; as a father. As a lord."

Dori pressed her lips together firmly as she began attending to the ties on the satchel.

Constantine huffed a mirthless laugh. "I'm still failing Christian. He's somewhere buried in that ruin and I can't so much as find his *body*."

Dori paused again after retrieving the basket of oils, unsure of what to say or do. Should she suggest that, because of the boy's young age and small stature, his body could have been burned to nothing? Or crushed to oblivion in the rubble? It didn't sound comforting to her own mind, thinking how she would feel if the same consideration were made to her about her own son. But Theodora Rosemont had never been in the situation of comforter before and so she continued to lay out her supplies carefully and silently on the tabletop.

After what seemed a long while, he asked, "Why are you doing this?"

Dori at last looked up at him, startled to see the dark hollows beneath his eyes, the creases that seemed to have pressed into his forehead since that morning.

"Because I don't know how to make a stew," she blurted out and then felt her face heat. She dropped her gaze to the tabletop as she took the bottles out of the basket. "I have experience burying my father at least."

There was nothing else for her to prepare or procrastinate over and so she looked up at him again and found him watching her.

"You're very kind, aren't you?" he asked suddenly, as if making an unexpected discovery.

She shook her head slightly. "No."

It was only an hour later that Patrice Gerard, Countess of Chase, was laid in her grave. The linen kerchief she'd so lovingly gifted her favored maid was the shroud for her bones, a flower wreath to cover her bare skull woven by a young lady in peasant's garb who was presently rumored to be dead. The basket was wrapped with the embroidered altar cloth from the oratory before being placed gently in the dirt.

Constantine presided over the ceremony, lacking any priest, and his words were low and gruff as he recited long prayers obviously from memory. Besides the two in attendance still dubiously of the nobility, the burial was attended by eight villagers and a dog.

When Harmon began returning the earth to the depression he'd recently excavated, Dori saw Constantine's reddened eyes, his flaring nostrils. She looked away courteously but raised her right hand, slipping it into Constantine's. He squeezed her fingers.

Dori held on.

Chapter 19

Theodora pulled her hand free from Constantine's as the villagers approached them, and he felt the absence of the warmth of her slight hand like a physical hole in his flesh. She turned away and headed down the slope toward the village.

Alone, except for the rangy gray beast who loped after and caught up to her in moments. Constantine watched as she took a halfhearted swipe at Erasmus's rump, which only sent him into ecstatic circuits around her.

Constantine began following her, flanked by Nell and Harmon, and it was the latter who spoke. "I've left a jug of mead at the cottage for you, milord."

"And supper is on the fire," Nell added. "I don't think even *she* could endanger it this far along."

Constantine looked down at Nell. "Lady Theodora has done me—done all of us—a great service today in seeing that Lady Patrice was laid to rest with as much dignity as any of us are capable of."

The woman's eyes grew round. "Beggin' your pardon, milord. I didn't—"

Harmon interrupted the woman's awkward apology. "I'll be ready at your call in the morn, Lord Gerard."

"My thanks, Harmon," Constantine said, pausing to grip the man's shoulder as they stood at the edge of the village, and then the carpenter turned away to his own abode.

Constantine continued on to the borrowed cottage alone and pushed through the partially open door. Dori was already at the bench, hacking a round of bread through the middle, and Erasmus was already lying before the hearth, his wooly eyes squeezed shut as if in deep slumber.

Constantine could have sworn the animal peeked at him with one eye.

He walked over to the dog all the same. "Go on, now—back to your master," he said, shooing the dog through the door and ignoring his doleful look. He shut the door and then turned back to the room, where Theodora seemed to be doing an excellent job of ignoring him.

But that idea only proved to Stan how far off his perception was, for in the next moment, Dori spoke.

"When did you last see your family?" she asked calmly, at last succeeding in parting the bread into halves.

He was surprised by the question, and even more surprised that he was not averse to answering her. "Six years ago." He sat down in a wooden chair with a low back. "Christian had only just turned four." She didn't pose any further questions, and so he grew curious himself. "Why do you ask?"

Dori shrugged and then picked up one of the halves she had scooped out and turned to the hearth so that her back was to him when she answered. "I couldn't remember when you left Benningsgate, is all. My father had mentioned you were gone on Crusade, but I rather didn't care."

She turned back and set the bread trencher before him without comment and then retrieved the other half.

Constantine stared down at the food. It smelled delicious, but his head pounded, and he kept hearing the gravelly tumble of rocked echoing off the ruin walls in his mind, as if taunting him to return.

A chair scraped and he looked up to find Theodora taking her seat. She glanced up at him, and he noticed that her expression was tense, angry. He hadn't realized until now that it was how she'd looked when Constantine had first discovered her at Benningsgate, and he hadn't realized that the look had gradually faded until today.

She picked up a chunk of the bread and dipped it into the stew. "How long will you work in the ruin?" She took a bite.

Constantine thought it best that he follow her example and eat, even if he didn't feel like it. He needed to preserve his strength for the hard work that yet lay ahead of him. He picked up his own hunk of bread.

"As long as it takes."

After a long pause, Dori asked, "Have you given up on your cause against Glayer Felsteppe, then?"

Constantine felt his gut clench. "No," he said levelly. "But I will lay my son to rest properly first. I'll not be turned from it. And you'll not question it if you wish my aid."

He could feel the tension rolling across the table as if it were a prickly tide. He glanced up and saw that Theodora was no longer eating but only staring down at her trencher.

"What is it now, Theodora?" he asked, feeling the spiral of anger begin at the base of his pounding skull.

"Nothing." She stood from her chair and picked up the half-eaten round, then walked past him. He heard the door open. "I thought you'd be waiting," she said to someone outside the cottage. "Here you are, then." The door closed.

"You're angry with me," Constantine ventured, "because I'm delaying going to Thurston Hold. You would harangue me on this of all days?"

"I'm not haranguing you in the least. I've not said another word about it, have I?"

"No, but you're still angry," he repeated. "Is that the only reason why you did what you did today? So that I would feel guilty if I didn't—"

He hadn't anticipated the slap she dealt him, although he should have been more familiar with her demeanor by now.

"*Your guilt*," she said in a trembling voice through clenched teeth, "is of your own making. Whatever *failures* you've accumulated have nothing to do with me."

"You really are a brat, aren't you?" he accused, feeling his rage at her rising, although he couldn't have explained why.

"A brat now, am I?" Dori accused with wide eyes. "Because I'm not cowing to your every whimful edict? When I was wrapping Patrice's body, I was *kind*!"

Constantine stood from the chair. "That was a ruse."

"My patience is too far past its end for engaging in games, Constantine. Since you've come here, I've never really known whether you would help me or not. Now you seem content to play at lord again, over your handful of subjects in this"—she looked around the small room—"*house*."

"I nursed you from the brink of death."

"Did that make you feel noble?" She smirked. "I assure you, I was closer to the brink of death before you arrived, and I would have survived had you not."

"If you don't need me, why the pout?"

Her gaze was full of daggers. "I supposed it would be much more convenient should you kill Glayer Felsteppe for me."

"As it was convenient for you to marry him after your father died?"

"Rather more as it was convenient for you to run away to the Holy Land rather than be humiliated by Patrice's infidelity."

Constantine raised his hand and Dori stepped toward him. "It's painful, isn't it? The truth? Especially when you're not using it to deprecate yourself like some . . . some *martyr*."

"Shut up, Theodora," he warned.

"*You left* your family, your home; *you left* the friends who helped save your life. All to serve your own agenda. When all I ever wanted was to *keep what I had*."

"Shut up," he repeated.

"And now I'm to wait on you as well, until it's absolutely convenient for you to *keep your word*!"

He reached out and grabbed her by her arms, his fingers meeting around her slight biceps encased in the rough gown. She struggled, but when she saw that she could not pull away, she stilled and snarled up at him.

"You wish to strike me?" she dared, turning her face up to him. "Go on, then, if you must. But I've been someone's pawn all my life and I'm finished waiting for you."

Constantine thought he only kissed her to ensure her silence, but in that moment after he dropped his mouth on hers, the only thing he could think of was tasting those lips that had condemned him so thoroughly, of touching a bit of that righteous indignation and, yes, perhaps to humiliate her as she had done to him.

She breathed in through her nose with a loud wheeze and then pressed her body to his, her hands going to his waist. He released his grip on her upper arms, wrapping her in his embrace, lifting her to him, deepening their kiss. He tasted salt and pulled away to see the tears on her face. He brought his hands up to cup her face, kissing her cheeks.

But she sniffed and shook her head, pulling him closer and bringing her mouth back to his. His hands raked back through her silky, springy hair, holding her face before his, and then he bent and picked her up in his arms and carried her through the doorway at the back of the cottage.

There was a single rough bedstead in the tiny, windowless room, made up with thick blankets. He lay Theodora Rosemont atop them and then lay down beside her, kissing her once more. He worried he would hurt her, she was so slight. He ran his hand up the front of her kirtle, sliding his palm over her small breast. She gave a happy sigh as the tips of her fingers dug into his ribs.

Constantine brought his leg across hers, pulling her into his groin, cautioning himself to go slowly; it had not been many months since—

He stilled so suddenly, it was as if he had frozen into solid ice. Even his heart seemed to frost over in his chest.

Since she'd given birth to Glayer Felsteppe's son.

The last man she'd made love with—likely the only man she'd ever made love with—was Glayer Felsteppe. The one who'd put Patrice in her grave more surely than the devoted villagers at his side this day.

He rolled away from Dori and sat up on the side of the bed, his elbows on his knees, his head in his hands.

"What?" she said in a breathless voice, and he felt her sitting up behind him. "Constantine, what is it?"

"I can't," he groaned, squeezing his eyes shut and hating the sound of his weakness. When he felt her tentative touch on his back, he shot to his feet with a growl. He turned to look at her and her face was pale, solemn, her eyes too big for her face, her innocent-looking mouth turned down.

"Can't because of Patrice or can't because of me?" she asked quietly.

"I can't reconcile any of this!" he shouted, pacing the floor. "You weren't supposed to be here; you weren't supposed to be kind to me. I've hated you since the moment I heard you had wed that monster." He paused and looked at her. "Dori, he took the most precious things in my life."

"Yes, he did," Theodora agreed. "He took mine from me, as well. *He* did, Constantine. *I didn't.* You didn't. Why should we be further punished for his evil?"

Constantine shook his head. "It matters not. I touch you and my head goes mad with thoughts of him touching you."

"If you cared for me," she said carefully, "if you wanted me, truly, you would not let Glayer Felsteppe stop you from claiming me. From claiming anything you wanted." She scooted to the edge of the cot and stood facing Constantine, the several feet still separating them feeling as wide and deep as a black, bottomless chasm. "Do you care for me, Constantine? Could you care for me, as I am, once the situation in which we now find ourselves no longer exists? In a future where there is no Glayer Felsteppe?"

Constantine felt an ache in his chest as he looked at her, Theodora Rosemont, as demanding as the rumors painted her, but this time what she was demanding was nothing more than the truth.

He tried to imagine returning to Benningsgate and meeting her again, had she been unmarried, and he felt hope leap in him. A rush of excitement at the idea of pursuing her, with her delicate fairy face and secret kindness, her will and physical stamina that could rival the mightiest soldiers he'd ever known. The way she wanted to protect. Perhaps in time he could forget . . .

But then he recalled her child. Felsteppe's child. Constantine could not raise the boy in good conscience after having killed his father. Even if he had been the man who had murdered Constantine's son.

Once Constantine had made good on his vow to exact his revenge, it was unlikely he would live very long any matter. It was better for Dori, more merciful, should he end any thoughts of a future with her now.

He looked at Theodora, waiting patiently before him, and she must have seen the answer in his eyes before he spoke, for her expression hardened once more.

"I can't," he said.

Her chest rose and fell shallowly with her breath. "You *coward*. Glayer Felsteppe has already bested you."

She walked past him from the chamber.

Constantine turned in time to see the door close behind her as she left. He returned to the front room and sat down at the table, reaching for the corked jug Harmon had so courteously left for him. He opened it with an echoey thunk and turned it up to his mouth. He swallowed and sighed, looking at the empty chair across from him.

Let her work out her anger at Nell's, then. Eventually she would see that his decision was best for both of them.

Constantine repeatedly turned the jug to his mouth until the mead was gone from the vessel. And still Theodora Rosemont's beautiful, wide eyes accused him as he lay down once more on the narrow bedstead, this time alone.

Dori ducked back behind the edge of a cottage as she came around the corner and saw Jeremy and Erasmus disappearing into Nell's cottage. She was only barely keeping her composure after her confrontation with Constantine, and now the only place she could think of to escape was closed to her. She needed supplies, and although she wasn't sure how she had planned to wheedle the necessary items from Nell, it no longer mattered.

Then the thought occurred to her that if Jeremy and Erasmus were dining with Nell, the swineherd's dwelling was untended. Dori emerged from behind the cottage and crossed the path diagonally, intending to cut behind the farthest row of little houses to come upon the rear of Jeremy's plot.

"Looking for something, milady?"

Dori jumped and spun around with her hands raised to find Leland, his withered arm tucked beneath his belt. He leaned against the rear wall of a cottage, holding a pipe to his mouth with his good hand.

Dori stared at the crippled man as she lowered her arms and tried to calm her breath. "Just out for a walk," she said. "Clearing my head after the day. Not that it's any of your concern."

"Mmm," Leland said with a sage nod. He pointed his pipe stem in the direction in which Dori had intended to go. "Might be dangerous, should you walk too far past Jeremy's."

"Certainly," Dori said, and then cleared her throat. "It would."

"Have you your blade yet?"

Dori nodded.

Leland drew on his pipe again and looked away from her, as if she no longer interested him, although he added, "Enjoy your walk, milady." He pushed away from the wall and ducked around the front of the cottage toward the center of the village.

Dori let out her breath in a whoosh and then carried on toward the swineherd's cottage in the glow of the setting sun. For a village boasting only eight inhabitants and a dog, escaping unseen was proving rather impossible. Her heart pounded with the fright she'd suffered, and yet she sensed that the embittered Leland would not tell anyone in the village that he'd seen her. She likely had at least until the morning before Constantine might bother to discover she was missing.

It was just enough time to reach her destination.

The sky was still magenta at the horizon when the small, dark shape that was Lady Theodora Rosemont skittered through the shadows along the road leading away from the blubbery swineherd's cottage and Benningsgate village. Leland watched her from across the square of freshly turned earth atop the rise of the burial ground until she was lost to the deepening night, his pipe smoke curling lazily in the cool air.

He clenched the stem in his teeth before bending to pick up the satchel at his feet and ducked beneath the strap. Taking his pipe bowl in hand once more, he started down the hill toward the road, a jaunty spring in his step.

Isra pushed her way through the crowd in a wandering fashion, her head held high, her expression haughty as she felt the numerous stares and lingering looks sliding over her from the courtiers she parted. In her fine English ensemble, her hair piled atop her head with a tall frame beneath her embroidered wimple, the fat, sparkling jewels about her neck and wrists, dangling from her ears, she resembled the royalty she portrayed.

"... princess. From..."

"... Turkish. Her father—"

"—husband—"

"—brother—"

"Good day, my lady." The young man stepped directly into her path with a rakish smile and a bow as deep as the crowd of people and beasts would allow. He was dressed in the finest velvet with hammered gold adornments at his shoulders and waist, as well as over the insteps of his low, cuffed boots, so that with each movement, he jingled conspicuously.

"Forgive my boldness," he continued. "But I must confess that my companions and I have been watching you. It has come to our attention that you are without attendant."

He *was* bold, even for a young, wealthy man, and Isra lifted her chin and narrowed her eyes at him. "And you think perhaps to take advantage of the situation for your amusement?" she challenged, allowing her accent to thicken. "I assure you," she said, her hand going to her waist to rest atop what appeared to be a rope of thick braid but was actually the hilt of a deadly-thin dagger, "I am skilled enough that you would heartily regret it."

"Oh, nay," the man insisted in delighted and amazed laughter and pressed his hand to his chest. "I only wished to invite you to sit with us. My friends and I command quite the best position in the room—only look, that's our dais right over there—and it would honor us greatly if you would join us. Would be quite an accomplishment—you've set the room agog with your presence."

Isra projected an air of indifference. "In my court, if a man should dare speak to a member of the royal family without introduction, it is grounds for execution."

"Thank heavens for me we are in England, then," the man said with a rakish lift of his eyebrows, and Isra couldn't help the indulgent smile that curved her lips. He was young and brash and carefree and rich beyond compare.

Perfect.

"I am Ethan Carmichael; my father is Lord Bledsoe. You've likely heard of him." The man bowed again. "At your service."

"Ethan Carmichael, I have *not* heard of your father," Isra insisted. "Likely he is only one of the pagan Irish."

He threw back his head and laughed at Isra's taunt, even as he turned and placed her hand in the crook of his elbow confidently, leading her through the crowd and preening under the attention they garnered.

"Quite the opposite of pagan," young Carmichael insisted as he led Isra up the dais step to a wide, sumptuous cushion amid several young couples. He helped her to sit and then dropped to one knee at her side. "He owns several churches and a monastery in fact. He's right . . . over . . ." The young man scanned the shifting crowd of nobility and musicians and dogs and horses who suddenly parted, and those around the perimeter of the chamber, including the youths in Ethan Carmichael's group gained their feet. He assisted Isra in standing once more.

The king entered, flanked by his retinue and his army of snuffling, scrabbling hounds, waving away bids for his attention with a disgruntled air.

"Ah, there!" Carmichael said, kneeling once more at Isra's side when she was seated. "On the king's left. Now right. Now left again."

"Your father owns churches and a monastery?" Isra queried, genuinely surprised.

"Oh, yes," Carmichael assured her. "Quite profitable. Although it's my mother who runs them really. Devout woman. *Devout.* As any of her seven children will attest."

Isra allowed him a sincere smile. "You English are very strange with your selling of God."

"Hmm, yes, I suppose. Rich, though," Carmichael said with another lift of his brow. A familiar, twanging melody rang through the chamber. "They're about to begin; marvelous. Simply marvelous. Only wait until you see. Completely famous. You'll sit with us again on the morrow, won't you?"

The double doors on the far end opened once more, prompting those occupying the middle of the floor to clear and a man swept into the space, his green velvet tunic fitting him like a second skin, his ebon hair rising into a crest high above his forehead, his breathtaking smile wide as he held his hands aloft and spun to address the crowd.

"Prepare yourselves, my lords and ladies, for the most *thrilling* displays of amusement from *all* corners of the earth. Allow me to present to you van Groen's Magical Mankind Menagerie!"

Isra clapped politely, feigning disinterest, although, at her side, Ethan Carmichael and his friends were frenzied in their enthusiasm.

Asa had made quite a name for the troupe, it seemed.

Many of the acts circulated through the crowd at once, so that the applause and exclamations of delight rolled through the room like waves. Helena and her dogs were a huge success, her little darlings' songs prompting accompaniment by the king's own numerous canines and setting the whole court to peals of laughter.

"The king appears somewhat aggrieved," Isra murmured, leaning slightly toward Carmichael. "Perhaps your father is to blame?"

"Oh, nay, my lady—my father is beyond reproach, to that I can attest. The king always appears aggrieved. Today it is certainly only due to a silly matter of a vacated estate that was purchased. The lord was accused of some treason while on Crusade and stripped of his title. Terrific scandal, I tell you. The castle was burned to ruin and has sat empty for ages. Worthless rubble now—even the peasants have all gone. The disgraced lord is presumed dead, although there is now some question as to the degree of his guilt. The king was to have unburdened himself of the property this morn at a healthy profit."

"Why the grimace, then?" Isra asked, trying to keep her expression detached while, inside her chest, her heart raced.

"He had a sudden attack of scruples, of all things, my father said last night at supper," Carmichael scoffed. "Father encouraged him to look at the matter from a vantage of practicality."

"The lord who purchased the property," Isra said, "is he called Glayer Felsteppe?"

Carmichael's bright eyes widened. "Even you've heard of him! The man's as slimy a pretender as has crawled up from the dregs, I say. But he's come into a vast estate at Thurston Hold. Almost as rich as me." Carmichael sent her a beguiling grin. "Even Lady Eirene has been seen chasing after his heels, and the little infant he parades around like a nappied banner, and *she* is the heiress of Glencovent."

"*She* might be an idiot," Isra muttered.

Carmichael's face brightened in camaraderie and he nodded. "Ah! So you've met."

Isra's thudding heartbeat seemed to shake her very frame, and she wondered that none of the young, wealthy nobles seated around her noticed her trembling. She kept her eyes on the master of ceremonies on the floor below her, waiting for the moment when she could catch his eye. She had the information she needed; now she only had to make her escape.

"It seems the king *is* rather more disgruntled than usual," Carmichael murmured at her side.

"Hmm?" Isra watched as Dracus expertly shot a faux partridge off the head of one particularly unamused servant to the howls of utter delight of the nobles in the crowd.

"He's just received a message. Which he's now handing to my father." Carmichael's voice seemed intrigued and Isra reluctantly turned her face to regard the monarch even though she'd just given Asa the signal.

The man at the king's side, currently holding what must be the message Carmichael mentioned, looked up suddenly and seemingly right at Isra. Her breathing stopped, lodged in her throat. But then Lord Bledsoe's stricken gaze slid from Isra to his son, still kneeling at her leg.

"Whatever it is," Carmichael said with amused gravity, "must be dreadful."

"And now I require the assistance of a beautiful lady," Asa called from the floor, startling Isra's attention back to the entertainment. His dark gaze seemed to scan the crowd with consideration, while behind him, Gunar and Nickle carried the long, saffron-colored curtains now attached to a circular framework.

"One who is fearless, brave!" Asa expounded, prompting several handkerchiefs to wave in the air.

"Go on," Carmichael encouraged Isra. "You'll be famous. I've heard the man keeps tigers. Man-eaters."

"That is preposterous," Isra scoffed.

"Only the very bravest!" Asa insisted.

Carmichael shot to his feet. "Here, sir; here is your brave lady!"

Asa smiled at her and held out his hand. "Would you indulge me, my lady?"

"Very well." Isra sighed and stood, drawing applause from the crowd. Carmichael courteously helped her alight from the raised platform and delivered her into Asa's hand with a bow.

"Make sure she is returned to me," the young man cautioned Asa with a grin.

Asa returned Carmichael's smile with a wink as he squeezed Isra's fingers. "I can make no promises, my lord." Then he looked to Isra as he led her to the golden draped cage. "Would you happen to be Egyptian? The rumor is Turkish."

Asa drew open the curtains on both sides of the frame so that the entire crowd could see that it was empty before he helped Isra step inside and then turned immediately from her, his hands held high above his head.

"Ladies and lords, I do hope you shan't be overly distressed at what you are about to witness! In a spirit of precaution, I beg you to be seated if at all possible. Brace yourselves, at the very least."

Gunar winked at her before he whisked the curtain closed. Isra felt a whoosh of air behind her as well. She turned quickly and looked for the seam.

A quarter of an hour—and much aggrandizing from Asa van Groen—later, the cage was turned on its side and collapsed down to its frame, seemingly still empty of the lady who had disappeared, despite the menagerie leader's best attempts to retrieve her. The man's assistants picked up the enchanted container under their arms and carried it from the shocked chamber and the Turkish princess was never seen at Henry's court again.

The assistants slid the frame into the back of a wood-sided wagon and then pounded on the bed, signaling to the large blond man in the driver's seat, who was accompanied by a falcon on a perch.

Roman flicked the reins and the wagon rolled away.

Chapter 20

The child's laughter was bubbly, like the water in a woodland spring, trickling giggles erupting suddenly into a fountain of mirth, and it stirred Constantine from his slumber with all the abruptness of being dropped from a great height.

"Pa-pa," the voice called in a singsong.

"Christian?" Constantine looked around the small bedchamber of the cottage, but he was alone.

"Pa-pa!" More giggles.

The call sounded as though it was coming from outside, and he ran to the shuttered window in the front room, pushed the wooden closures wide.

And in the center of the dirt road of Benningsgate village stood Glayer Felsteppe, with his leather hauberk and heeled boots, his wooly orange-red hair and hooked nose, turning in circles with a small blond boy at the end of his outstretched arms.

"Faster, Papa!" Christian laughed.

"No," Constantine shouted from the window. "Christian, I'm your father! I'm right here!"

Christian only giggled as Felsteppe swung him faster and faster, his little shoeless feet rising higher and higher above the dirt.

Constantine left the window and leaped to the cottage door, flinging it wide and charging forward, but he ran into long, wrought bars of the very sort that had held him prisoner in Saladin's dungeon. He grasped them with his fists and shook them with a roar.

"Christian!"

He ran back to the window, only to find that iron cylinders had grown there, too, imprisoning him in the cottage, and he was help-

less to do anything other than watch the horror unfolding on the path before his eyes.

Felsteppe suddenly let go of Christian's hands and Constantine's son was flung out of sight in the direction of the ruin, his high-pitched scream ripping at Constantine's heart. Felsteppe laughed and began strolling in that direction.

"No, Papa!" Christian pleaded faintly, and although Constantine pressed the side of his face to the bars, he could see neither his boy nor Felsteppe.

But he heard the muffled wails, the sound of blows upon flesh, like the whip that had scourged Constantine's own back. He saw the red glow of flames reflected on the cottage walls across the narrow road, could feel the heat of the fire.

"Get away from my son!" Constantine screamed and shook the bars, feeling the muscles in his neck at the verge of tearing. "Get away from my son!"

Constantine sat straight up in bed, gasping as though he hadn't drawn breath for an hour. He was covered in perspiration—even the thin, prickly ticking beneath him was soaked with it. He pushed himself to his feet, staggered into the front room of the cottage, and made his way to the door by the faint glow of the fire dying in the hearth. He tore the door open and charged through, then stood swaying in the street and turning 'round as the spring night air slipped into the hot crevices of his body like icy blades.

He gasped a final time and then leaned over with his hands on his knees, fighting the sob in his chest as he accepted the nightmare. His inhalation was a shuddering sniff.

God, he was going mad.

He stood aright and looked up the black path to the outline of Nell's cottage, where Theodora had likely gone, and then his gaze rose farther to the skeletal stone finger of Benningsgate Castle.

If Felsteppe had possession of Christian, what would Constantine not do to get him back? He would rally armies, defy kings, fight his way through ranks of armed men in order to pull his precious, innocent boy away from that monster.

He looked back at Nell's cottage.

The same monster who now held Dori's infant son in his very real clutches. Dori, who hadn't the power to challenge king or steel, but had persevered within a life linked with Glayer Felsteppe's, seeing him in her home; in her beloved father's place, with his title. She had withstood God only knew what sort of hellish existence before defying death itself in hopes of one day returning for that little helpless child.

That precious, innocent boy. Only a baby.

Constantine looked back toward Benningsgate with a pain in his chest so deep it nearly brought him to his knees in the street. Christian was gone. Gone to heaven with his mother years ago. He was safe and loved and happy, and although Constantine accepted that the guilt of his own failings would haunt him for the rest of his life, he knew Christian didn't need him anymore.

But Theodora Rosemont's son did.

He began walking toward Nell's cottage.

Dori walked for hours without lagging, fueled by her anger and hurt. She couldn't remember much of the other journeys she'd undertaken from Benningsgate, save for that she was now very thankful for the balmy weather and her sturdy, borrowed peasant's shoes.

The moon was barely a sliver overhead, coyly skittering from cloud to wispy cloud in the starry sky, and didn't seem to give forth much light until Dori walked through the patches of woods, whose branches before had been early spring bare and like walking beneath a web of thin shadows. Now in full leaf, entering the wooded sections of road was like traversing caves through a forbidding mountain range, where every woodland sound was magnified off the walls of thick greenery, and the nocturnal animals were long out of their hibernation and more than willing to investigate the presence of a trespasser in their domain.

She heard the crack of a stick and glanced with wide eyes over her shoulder at the black nothing behind her before facing forward once more and half-running the remainder of the forest path. Her breath only began to slow when she emerged from the wood between open fields. She fumbled with the blade in her hand and had to stop in order to properly return it beneath the ties of her apron lest she stumble and fall upon it, doing Glayer Felsteppe a great service by dying a second time.

She looked up and began walking again, but slowly now as she saw the blocky outline of Thurston Hold on the rise, the tall, black rectangles of the keep and inner buildings like a keep-shaped hole in the sparkling night sky.

If Glayer Felsteppe was keeping as close of a watch as he had before he'd thought to have her killed, the portcullis would be closed at the barbican, and she'd have to wait for the morning until the town was about its day. That would be many times more dangerous, for she would almost certainly be recognized, even with her chopped hair and peasant's garb. Should she manage to gain the keep without detection, she would certainly be stopped as soon as she attempted to breach the family wing.

"Good evening, milady."

Dori couldn't help her strangled shriek as she spun around, pulling her blade from her apron once more and wielding it at the black shadow now standing before her on the road.

"Stay away from me!" she ordered, backing down the road.

The shadow seemed to grow an arm. "Don't be frightened—"

"Drop your weapon," she demanded.

"I don't have one!"

"Show me your other hand!" Dori insisted.

"It's fixed in me belt!"

Dori paused and lowered the blade, but only slightly. "Leland?"

"Great gods, I thought you'd know it was me," the man said in exasperation. "Glad I am I thought better of calling out to you in the wood!"

"You'd have at least one hole in you by now had you," Dori said with a sigh, standing aright and returning the blade. "Why are you following me?"

Leland stepped closer and the fingernail of moon showed itself between the clouds so that Dori could make out the man's features.

He shrugged. "Didn't have aught else to occupy my time." His face turned toward her. "Figured it'd be best if you didn't go alone. No one'll miss me in the village."

Dori frowned at him, unsure as to whether she felt annoyed or thankful by his presence.

He waited a moment, perhaps to see if she would turn him away, before asking, "You're going back to Thurston Hold, are you not?"

Dori hesitated. "Yes."

"Hmm," he said, as if she'd just told him something of high curiosity, although the man had surely guessed her destination when he'd decided to follow her from Benningsgate. He began walking. "All right, then."

Dori felt as though she had little choice but to catch up and then walk along Leland's left side, deciding she was rather glad she wouldn't have to traverse the final stretch of wood, perhaps only a quarter mile ahead of them, alone. They walked in awkward silence for several minutes, but when he did not press her or chat idly, as if they were true companions, Dori's shoulders began to creep down from her ears once more, and it caused curiosity about the man to rise up in her.

"What happened to your arm?" she asked. "If you don't mind my inquiry."

Leland glanced over at her, but Dori couldn't make out his expression in the dark. "I don't suppose I do, milady. Nothing at all happened to it. I've had it since birth."

"I see," Dori said. "I'm sorry."

"Nothing to be sorry for, I reckon," he said in an easy voice. "It's saved me a lifetime of labor. Me mother left me and my father when I was a lad. It was just the two of us for a few years. Then he caught the fever that took Nell's man and girl. No one ever expected much from me after that. I worked the portcullis most often. The pulleys made it an easy job. Sometimes I delivered messages. I was more trouble for the effort of giving me a task as not," he finished, as if he was talking about nothing more important than the weather, but Dori could hear the underlying resentment in his words.

No wonder the man had developed such a caustic personality; he'd basically lived off Benningsgate folks' charity his entire life, with no family, no purpose to fulfill him. Dori had the realization that it was how many noble children grew up, without responsibility or care for a task or other person, and she suspected it caused part of their souls to turn black and die. She realized it likely would have been her lot, too, had her father not become ill, and had Glayer Felsteppe not swooped in like a carrion bird to feed on them both.

"Do you hunger, milady?" Leland asked suddenly, reaching down with his right hand to lift the flap of his satchel. "I've brought a bit of ham and some other things."

Dori felt her stomach rumble at the mention of food and remembered she had not finished her supper with Constantine Gerard. Thoughtful of the man to have brought enough for them both.

"Thank you," she said. "In my haste to depart the swineherd's cottage without being seen, I fear I didn't think to take much in the way of sustenance."

"Likely not much to be had in that glutton's abode," Leland muttered while rummaging in his bag. "Blast it." He looked up at her and glanced at the knife on her apron. "Beggin' your pardon, milady, but could I bother you for your blade?"

"Certainly." Dori reached down and pulled it from the sheath and handed it to him as they entered the edge of the black wood. As his only good fingers wrapped around the handle, the last slice of moonlight flashed across the blade before being extinguished by the trees overhead, and Dori felt a frown move likewise across her forehead.

Her legs were abruptly and painfully kicked out from beneath her and Dori landed on her back, her skull bouncing against the dirt road and the breath knocked from her lungs. The point of her own blade—of Constantine Gerard's blade—rested in the notch of her collarbone, pointed downward by Leland's warm fingers, wrapped around the handle and laying alongside her cheek.

"Shh, now," he whispered near her temple in a trembling voice, but she could detect no fear in his tone, only evil excitement. He squirmed against her, already thrusting his groin into her midsection. "It will be over soon, if you're still and good."

His heart was black and dead after all.

He'd played her well, asking if she was armed and then following her from the village. No one would know Dori was missing until well after sunrise, and Leland would be back in his own house before then.

And once her body was found, the crippled villager would likely be the last person ever suspected of her rape and murder; everyone knew Theodora Rosemont had died in her childbed months ago after all. There was no one to vouch for her existence save a handful of motley villagers and their lord, who was himself wanted as a criminal.

Her breath came back to her in painful wheezes, the jerking motion of her chest causing the knifepoint to prick her repeatedly, tiny stabs that, along with her coughs and fear and anger, caused tears to leak from the sides of her eyes and track into her hairline.

"Now, I wish to feel you moving beneath me, so I'll ask you kindly to raise up your skirts—I'm at a disadvantage in doing it myself, you see," he confided. "However, if you're defiant, I'll just open up a little hole in your throat. You'll eventually run out. I might have a struggle at first, but I'll get what I want."

"You'll kill me either way," she rasped.

He licked her neck. "Raise your skirts."

"No," she said and tried to pull away from him even as the pressure on the blade increased. "I've never been taken without my consent and I'm not about to give it to the likes of a filthy, one-armed, lying parasite."

Leland stilled against her. "That's just fine, milady. Just fine. We can do it the other way certainly. For if you think such weak taunts move me after a lifetime of ridicule and pity, you're wrong. And once everything is over, I'll be the one who walks away." He placed a noisy kiss on her cheek.

"Do you think so?" she asked.

"I do."

"Then before you continue on to what you are certain is your great triumph, allow me to divulge to you a little-known fact," Theodora said.

"What's that, lovely?" Leland said in a mockery of patience.

"Jeremy wasn't the first to discover Lord Gerard at the ruin," she said. "I was. And he, too, thought to subdue me, although with motivations much less criminal than yours."

"And so you willingly gave it to him so that he wouldn't kill you," Leland finished with a darker tone. "Everyone in the village already knows it. Is that supposed to make me jealous of his lordship? I'm getting what he got, and I won't have to put up with your mouth afterward."

"You want what I gave him?" she asked.

"I do."

Dori slammed her forehead into Leland's face and shoved him off her as he screamed, but even though his right forearm went instinctively to his broken nose, it didn't stay there for long, and he slashed out with the blade before Dori could completely drag her lower half from beneath him. She felt the cold slice on her left hip and thigh and kicked out wildly with her right leg, which found its mark by the man's muffled shout.

She gained her feet and began to run, heading farther along the road into the darkest part of the wood, no longer feeling the knife wound on her leg, no longer caring about the darkness or its inhabitants, only seeking to escape the malevolent creature who had attacked her after feigning friendliness.

"You stop right now! Right now, you bitch!" Leland shouted, and Dori could tell by the jarring of his voice that he was running after her.

And just like that night in the Benningsgate ward when Constantine Gerard had chased her, Dori could feel her legs slowing.

"I'm going to kill you!" Leland promised in a furious voice that seemed right on her very heels now.

But then Dori heard the man give a strangled yelp, and there was a scuffling sound behind her. Dori thought he must have fallen, and the idea of it seemed to spur her flagging strength the tiniest bit, although the next sounds that reached her ears caused her to slow and turn, still staggering backward on the road toward Thurston Hold.

"No, no!" Leland was shouting. "Please, no—I'm only a poor cripple!"

"I know exactly what you are now," a familiar deep voice said in the darkness.

Dori stopped, swaying on her feet. "Constantine?"

"Did he harm you, Theodora?"

She could feel the wetness on her leg, trickling down her calf, although it still did not pain her.

"He has your knife!" she warned

There were more scuffling sounds, then a series of anguished cries from the crippled man.

A shadow emerged from shadow, moving toward her, but this time Dori did not run.

"Did he harm you?" Constantine repeated, and Dori could barely make out the shape of him as he came to a halt still some six feet away.

"I've a cut on my leg," she said.

Leland's voice cried out in the darkness. "Don't leave me here, milord! I beg of you!"

"I should go back and kill him," Constantine said. "How bad is it?"

"I don't know," she admitted. "I can tell that it's bleeding, but it doesn't pain me."

He was quiet for a heartbeat of time and then said, "I'll need to look at it."

"All right," she acceded.

Constantine took two steps toward her, until Dori could have reached out a hand and laid it on his chest, which she knew would be solid and warm. But it was he who reached out to her, scooping her up into his arms once more and carrying her from the black wood.

He walked with her in this manner until they were far enough from the forest that Leland's pathetic cries had faded away. Then he tilted her to her feet near a rock at the edge of the road and helped her to sit.

The clouds had fled the sky, leaving the sliver of moon and glittering stars strewn across the field of black above them. He shrugged out of his satchel and knelt before her, his hands going to the skirts over her left leg. Dori looked down and saw the darker patch of wet in the already dark material and then met his gaze.

"I need to see it," he reminded her.

Dori nodded and inched up the long skirts, bunching them in her hand until the length of her white, thin leg glowed in the meager moonlight. She saw the tracks of her blood, which looked black in the night, and the long, thin, arcing cut in her skin. It began to throb as soon as her eyes took in its full measure.

Constantine took her lower leg in his hands, his fingertips skimming alongside the wound, his warm, smooth palms cradling her flesh. She raised her eyes to over his head, looking at the dark barbican of Thurston Hold, her heart dropping into her stomach as she observed the lit torches on either side of the gate, the stones between them conspicuously bright and unadorned.

"It's not deep," Constantine said at last, lowering her foot to the ground and pulling her skirts down. He looked up at her. "I think it will be fine."

"He's not there," she said and then turned her gaze once more toward the castle. "The banner is furled. Glayer Felsteppe isn't at Thurston Hold." She couldn't bring herself to mention the little boy he kept always with him, her son, to the man before her. Constantine had already shown how little consideration he felt for her child.

"Well, I should say that makes things a bit easier for us," he said to her surprise.

"Easier?"

"We certainly have a very good idea where he is, if he's not at Thurston Hold, do we not?"

"With the king, I assume."

"It must be," he said, and then paused for several heartbeats. "Think you he would have left . . . your son behind?"

Dori shook her head.

"I'll find out for certain," Constantine said. "We must have mounts."

Dori stared at him for several heartbeats. She could no longer contain the question. "Why did you come, Constantine?"

He met her gaze. "Because you were right in what you said at the cottage."

She continued to look into his eyes, wishing him to say more, but her pride would not allow her to press him. Instead, she asked, "How did you know I had gone?"

"Christian told me."

Dori blinked at him, and she knew her frown was obvious.

But Constantine only rose and placed the strap of his satchel over his head and then looked to the eastern horizon. "We have perhaps an hour before the sky begins to lighten." He looked back at her. "Stay here. If you hear anyone approaching, hide as best you can."

"Wait," Dori called out. When Constantine paused and half-turned back toward her, her thoughts stammered with the sheer number of questions she wanted to ask.

Do you love me?

Will you love my son?

Where will we go?

She cleared her throat. "What did you do with Leland? I don't want him sneaking up behind me after you've gone."

"I doubt that will happen. I tethered his leg to a tree, then made a noose and hung it around his neck attached to his arm. If he attempts to get loose, he'll likely choke to death."

"Won't someone come along and free him? Take pity on him for being a cripple?"

Constantine shrugged. "Leland's future is not my concern."

"How will you get past the portcullis?"

Constantine gave her a smile of the sort she had never seen cross his face before—sly and charming and confident, transforming his already handsome face so that Dori's heart stuttered in her chest.

"I've learned a thing or two from my friends," he said. And then he abruptly stepped toward her once more and leaned down, cupping her jaw and kissing her lightly on the mouth. "It's time I utilized that knowledge. What sort of general would I be otherwise?"

Dori's lips were still parted as he turned and walked boldly down the center of the road toward Thurston Hold.

Chapter 21

Constantine rode through Thurston Hold's open portcullis, the second mount tied behind him, in less than an hour. He wasted no time in urging the horse into a run after clearing the bridge, hoping to be past the keep once more by the time the sun had truly risen. In moments, he reined to a stop by the boulder, behind which Dori rose from where she'd been crouched.

Her expression was one of disbelief as she took in the pair of mounts and the equal number of bags across the saddles. "How did you manage this without being seen?" she asked as Constantine swung down from his horse and moved toward her.

"I didn't." He took her hand and guided her to the side of the horse and helped her into the saddle, mindful of her injured leg. He loosened the reins and placed them in her hands. "I was counting on Felsteppe's arrogance and lack of leadership. The men left behind at Thurston Hold had no clear orders about their duties. I told them I'd been sent to fetch extra mounts for the lord's return journey from London and the entire stable was mine for the taking."

"And so now we know for certain where he is," Dori realized as he swung onto his own saddle.

Constantine gave her a grin as he turned his horse. "Now we know for certain. No one should stop us, but if they do, don't say a word. We'll ride hard until dawn and then rest a bit. I plan to reach London by nightfall. It will be best if we can meet with the king after most have gone on to their evening pursuits."

He paused and met her eyes, looking for signs of doubt or fear; any indication that she was not completely committed to the path they would take, both literally and figuratively.

"Well? What are we waiting for?" she demanded.

Constantine kicked at his horse's sides. "Hah!"

He led them swiftly as the sun rose in the sky, their speed making conversation impossible, even if either of them had been wont to speak. Constantine knew that seeking the king before killing Felsteppe might be suicide for him.

But he also knew it was the best option he had of securing Dori and her child's safety. Once the king saw that she lived and heard her tale, there could be no doubt in Henry's mind of Felsteppe's inherent evil.

What the king would choose to do about it—if anything—Constantine could not say.

They stopped to rest the horses and themselves once the sun was bright and fully in the sky, eating what food they had beneath the shade of a beech tree. Their backs were against the wide trunk, their shoulders nearly touching.

"You're worried, aren't you?" Dori asked, glancing at him as she pulled a piece of bread from the hunk in her hands. The breeze caused the upturned ends of her hair to dance and shadows of the leaves overhead to flutter over her gamine face in such a way that Constantine felt he was in the presence of fae royalty despite her peasant attire.

He wouldn't lie to her. "There's no telling Henry's mind after so many years. He's been against me for many of them, believing in the tower of lies Felsteppe has constructed. I can't say how he will react to our arrival."

She huffed a breath of laughter. "I should think two dead people appearing suddenly at his court and begging an audience will at least gain his attention."

Constantine's mouth curved while he chewed and swallowed. "I was once party to a woman pretending to be a corpse in order to escape detection. A pattern, perhaps?"

Dori's face turned toward him, her fine, arched brows raised. "Did it work?"

He shrugged and looked away to take a drink from the skin. "I don't know. I left before they could return." The silence settled around them for several moments.

"I'm worried."

He turned to look at her, but her gaze was for the bright yellow fields glowing in the sun beyond the perimeter of their shady, breezy retreat.

"He won't know who I am."

Constantine frowned. "The king?"

"My son." She looked at him. "I've never held him; never fed him. I don't know anything about caring for an infant."

"It's largely instinct, isn't it?" Constantine offered, returning things to his satchel.

"Hmm. I suppose."

When he was finished, he looked back at Dori, who hadn't moved from her contemplative pose, and he was surprised to see tracks of tears on her cheeks.

"What if we're already too late?" she asked, her easy tone belying the glistening trails of sorrow on her face.

"Then that will forever be a burden across my own shoulders, not yours," Constantine said, turning her face toward him. "Theodora, you've done everything you could on your own."

"Do you mourn Chastellet?" she asked suddenly.

Constantine swallowed. "Yes. I will always mourn Chastellet. Many good men died there."

"You didn't, though," she said, staring so intently into his eyes that Constantine felt she was trying to look into the core of his soul.

"Perhaps I am not a good man," he offered. "My actions have cost me my family, my home, my livelihood. My reputation. That has to stand for something."

"I find that the more you blame yourself for the actions of Glayer Felsteppe, the more convinced I am that you are a good man," she said.

"I'm not blameless, Theodora," he cautioned.

"I never said you were."

"The reason I refused you at the cottage, why I said such things to you, is that my mind tells me that I must soon set you free," he said, letting his gaze play over her face as he smoothed a lock of hair from her forehead. "For both our sakes."

"What does your heart say?" Dori whispered.

He leaned close and kissed her softly.

"My heart says the same thing," she whispered against his lips.

Constantine pulled her against his chest where she rested her cheek, his arm around her shoulder protectively.

"Close your eyes if you can and rest," he suggested. "We'll ride again in a while."

She didn't reply, but Constantine felt her body slowly relax, felt the warmth of her breath on the back of his hand where he clasped her forearm.

His duty commanded that he see Glayer Felsteppe's end.

His heart insisted he must keep Dori and her innocent son safe, protect them, love them, no matter their connection to the man who had destroyed Constantine's life.

And under that tree, in the bright light of day and while holding the wife of his greatest enemy, General Constantine Gerard at last realized that he wished to honor both requirements.

Father Simon came down the curving staircase, doing his best to keep his chin up and his feet moving forward despite his urge to collapse against the thick banister in his despair and fatigue. If he stopped to look around him, this house he knew so well, stopped to think about who he had left in the bedchamber above, he would not be able to walk through the door for the final time. Even breathing had seemed to require much more effort than usual since his arrival in the city, as if a heavy, melancholic fog had settled over his chest.

But he could not indulge his sudden weakness of body; there was an important guest of the bishop due to arrive by ship today—the same ship Simon himself would board and depart England on the morrow, never to return. The vessel had been delayed by the torrential rains along the coast, causing the bishop's guest's arrival—and Simon's own departure—to be delayed.

Not that the priest minded. Indeed, he would hold the memory of this day in his heart for the rest of his life. He must; it would be all he had left.

He heard the shouting and clattering commotion swelling outside the house before he'd reached the bottom of the stairs. In the next moment, the double doors on the far side of the entry below burst inward, admitting two footmen carrying the limp body of Lloyd Carmichael, Lord Bledsoe, whose wife Simon had just left.

Ethan Carmichael was on their heels. "Take him upstairs!" he commanded, leaving the doors swinging wide behind him. "The surgeon's on his way."

Simon pressed against the railing as Bledsoe was hurried past him. He looked at the man's gray, slack face, the jowls thin and collapsed against his wrinkled neck where once, years ago, plump, robust flesh had circled. His eyelids were only partially closed, and yet Simon could see nothing but bloodshot whites.

"*You.*"

The word was shot at him with all the deadly force of an arrow, and Simon looked around to see his beloved Ethan at the bottom of the stair, one fine, decorative boot on the first riser, his fist gripping the banister.

"What happened, Ethan?" Simon asked.

Louisa's distressed cry echoed faintly above, but neither man looked away from the other.

"He collapsed in the carriage en route from court," Ethan said. "After he'd received a troubling message while with the king."

The surgeon came through the open door just then, his heeled boots clicking across the marble beneath his swishing robes as his assistants scurried behind him.

"Lord Bledsoe?" he queried, approaching the stairs without slowing.

"Yes, above," Ethan said, standing aside so that the man might pass.

Simon waited for the man to ascend to the upper floor before turning back to Ethan. "Is there anything I can do?" He came away from the banister and stepped down one level toward the young man who was ascending the stairs slowly.

Ethan reached inside his tunic and withdrew a wad of parchment. When he was on the same riser as Simon, he shoved the crumpled page into the priest's chest so hard that Simon slammed back into the railing.

"*This* is the message that was delivered to him," Ethan hissed.

Simon looked down and smoothed the paper with trembling fingers, fingers that soon lost all their sensation as he read the words scrawled boldly there.

The declaration was signed by none other than Glayer Felsteppe.

He swallowed as his chest constricted painfully against his next breath and then looked up at the young man whose eyes stared into Simon's at exactly the same height.

"You blasphemous son of a bitch," Ethan snarled, and then grasped Simon's cassock in his left fist, drawing back his right. "You mocked the friendship—"

"Ethan, what on earth are you doing?" Louisa shouted from the top of the stairs, and both men turned to look up at the woman standing there, still in her thick, embroidered chamber robes. "Come up immediately! He's awake and asking for you."

Ethan sent the woman a glare but released Simon's cassock and ripped the parchment from his hands before leaning close to Simon's face.

"I'm not finished with you, *Priest*," he growled and then took the stairs two at a time, sweeping past his mother without a further glance.

Simon looked up at her stricken face, her pale hand at the neck of her gown, the elegant gray at her temples, the starburst of creases at the outer corner of her eyes—folds from her years of gentle smiles. Now her pale lips pressed together in a grimace of fear for the man who might be dying in her chamber. A searing pain seemed to be weaving itself through Simon's chest, growing stronger on the loom of his ribs.

"Simon," she said in a strangled voice, and he knew it was taking all her considerable will to remain calm. "The bishop's guests . . ."

Simon nodded. "I'll meet them."

"They were to stay with us, but—"she broke off and glanced behind her.

"I'll take them to the palace," he suggested. "Give them over to the cardinal."

"Thank you," she whispered, then seemed to hesitate.

"Go, Louisa," Simon ordered, fighting to make his words even and gentle. "Bledsoe needs you."

She brought her fingertips to her lips and sent him a kiss.

Simon tried to smile, but the attempt crumbled when she turned away and was gone down the corridor. He clutched at the banister as he made his way to the marble entry, turning and grasping the handles to pull the double doors closed behind him as he left the house.

Simon walked to Bledsoe's carriage, still waiting before the doors.

"Good day, Father Simon," the driver called out with a surprised smile. "Haven't seen you in an age. 'Tis a miracle you're here—the lord's in a bad way."

Simon only nodded as he grasped the handle and opened the carriage door. "I'm to fetch the bishop's guests from the docks. We'll be taking them to the palace."

"Aye, Father."

Simon pulled the carriage door shut and then collapsed against the seat as the conveyance began to rumble and sway. It smelled of fear inside. And anger. Simon should know; it had been his own personal scent for two years now.

. . . to inform you of the base indiscretions of your priest, Simon, who had carried on blatant infidelities with Louisa Carmichael, Lady Bledsoe, which I have both personally witnessed and heard the confession thereof by the adulterer's own voice.

Now the worst had happened. Actually, worse than the worst—the secret had been exposed, and Bledsoe was perhaps on his deathbed because of this revelation. Simon withdrew the elegantly shaped cask of wine from the side wall of the carriage and uncorked it, helping himself to some of Bledsoe's famous grapes. From the smallest estate Bledsoe had set aside for Ethan to run.

Poor Ethan. The lad would take it hard should Bledsoe die, being the youngest. The rest of the children would as well of course; and Louisa. And well they should—Bledsoe was a good man.

Simon stared out the window as the carriage bore him slowly through the narrow, twisting, smelly streets toward the docks, forced to yield to people and goods, small flocks being herded down the crowded avenues. Deep down, Simon must have known Glayer Felsteppe wouldn't so easily turn loose anyone who knew so many of his filthy secrets. It had likely been the fiend's plan all along to reveal his and Louisa's complicated relationship, ruin and discredit him after he'd used him for every vile service he could wring out of him.

After all he'd done to try to protect them . . .

He squeezed his eyes shut for a moment against the hot, angry flood of tears that threatened, and his chest constricted even further, seemed to stick there.

Simon certainly couldn't stay in England now. Once the bishop learned the truth—if he hadn't already—he would see him excommunicated, ruined. Possibly imprisoned.

And yet, how could Simon abandon those he loved to bear the worst fury of the aftermath of the scandal, which had the potential to destroy not just the life of Louisa—the woman for whom he'd forsaken his vows for forty years—but also the lives of her and Simon's seven children?

He hadn't come to any good conclusion by the time the carriage rocked to a halt, and Simon blinked with a bit of surprise as he realized he'd arrived at the docks. He pushed the door open and climbed out slowly, feeling as though he'd aged a score of years in the brief ride.

"They'll have trunks," Simon called up to the driver halfheartedly, rubbing at his chest with the heel of his hand as he turned to walk down the sloping quay toward the milling crowd gathered before the tall-masted ships docked in the water.

"I'll keep me eyes sharp for your signal, Father," the driver called out after him.

Simon raised a hand in acknowledgment and threaded his way into the fringe of the stinking tapestry of merchants and sailors, prostitutes and travelers.

He caught glimpses of a flowing cassock coming down a gangplank through the crush of individuals hurrying to and fro on the ship. Simon pushed his way to the end in time to see a priest and the two monks who followed him come ashore. The skinny, balding superior seemed to scan the crowd, perhaps seeking Lady Bledsoe, as the pair of brethren behind him—looking almost identical—jostled a trunk between them.

"You must let me carry the trunk, Brother."

"No, I insist that you conserve your strength."

The priest's profile turned toward Simon at last, causing his already lurching heart to leap painfully into his throat.

"Victor?" he whispered. And then, louder, "Victor! *Victor!*" Simon ignored the drawing pain in his arm and shoulder to wave above the crowd.

Victor turned at the sound of his name and his eyes widened, his face brightening, as he saw who had hailed him. He pushed his way forward.

"Simon?" he said in happy disbelief, his kind face—so much older now—split into the smile Simon remembered from his youthful studies.

The two priests met with a clasp of arms and then a full embrace, laughing.

"Simon!" Victor repeated in his soft accent, noticeably lessened now, as he leaned back and beamed into his old friend's face. "You've no idea how glad I am to see you. This is Brother Ladislav and Brother

Vladislav—they've come to assist me on some special abbey business."

Simon nodded to the monks and tried to swallow down the painful lump that had manifested at the base of his throat. "Good day, Brothers."

"Good day to you, Father," the robed men spoke over each other.

Victor drew his attention once more. "But what are you doing in London? The last news I had of you, you had retreated to the countryside. I'd thought to have need to beat bushes to find you."

"It's only temporary," Simon said, rising up on tiptoe to look over the crowd and signal the driver, who began maneuvering the conveyance farther down the quay to meet them. "I've come on Lady Bledsoe's behalf; the lord suddenly took ill. I've just left them at the manse."

"Is it serious?" Victor asked as they moved slowly through the crowd.

Simon cleared his throat with some effort. The lump was growing thorns and spreading further behind his shoulder blades. "I'm afraid it looks that way."

"My sympathies to you, Simon," Victor said earnestly. "I know how devoted the three of you have been to one another these many years."

Simon couldn't bring himself to comment further and so only nodded in acknowledgment as he led the way to the carriage. But as the twin monks argued over who would lift the trunk to the top of the coach, Simon took the opportunity to grasp Victor's sleeve and lean in, speaking while he could; the pain in his chest seemed to be stealing his breath, and sweat poured down his temples.

"Did you receive a woman at Melk in early spring?" he asked, hearing the breathiness of his own voice. "A dark-haired woman, perhaps a boy with her?"

Victor frowned. "A woman? But—"

"Yes, a woman," Simon insisted. "She was in trouble. I—I sent her to you."

The abbot grabbed for Simon as his knees threatened to buckle. "A boy as well, you say?"

"Yes, a blond English boy. Orphaned by a fire at one of the estates. I was looking out for him. I'm worried something happened to him. To both of them." He gritted his teeth against the cry of pain as his left side seemed to spasm.

Victor called out to the bickering monks in his own language, but Simon couldn't concentrate on the words enough to translate what the priest was saying. In a moment, the burly twins had helped him into the carriage and followed him in. Victor called up to the driver before joining them, shutting the door firmly and turning toward Simon as the two brethren fought over who should pour the wine.

"We're taking you with us to the bishop's palace," Victor said, and Simon didn't have the strength to argue against it for his own well-being. He was too busy fighting off the waves of pain Victor's confused look had brought.

Simon had caused Theodora Rosemont's death as surely as if he'd followed Glayer Felsteppe's orders precisely. And the bright, young, quiet boy's, too. The child may as well have died in the fire that took his family, the less cruelty he likely would have suffered.

"Simon, can you hear me?" Victor demanded, drawing his attention from the chasm of despair Simon wanted to throw himself into. "I want you to tell me about the woman. *Look at me.*"

Simon raised his eyes to the priest.

Victor's gaze was intense. "Tell me everything."

And so Simon did.

Chapter 22

Constantine felt as though he had entered into another foreign country rather than the London he had once known so well. The sights and sounds that were familiar to him as General Gerard, and then as the earl of Chase, seemed hostile to him now as he led Theodora Rosemont through the streets on their tired mounts. They drew suspicious stares from the night walkers prowling the growing shadows—two people of poor dress but traveling astride—and Constantine kept his senses attuned and his sword beneath his hand as they drew ever closer to their destination.

It was evening, but the king's household was still engaged in raucous activity, if the stream of people going to and fro the wide building were any indication. Constantine thought to ease past the guards into the courtyard unnoticed, but one sharp-eyed sentry seized the bridle of Constantine's horse at the last moment.

"Where d'you think you're going, mate? The fair's moved on—naught for you to see nor buy any longer, if you had a penny to your name."

Constantine had to steel himself from jerking his horse free. He spoke calmly. "I've come bearing important news for the king. The lady I travel with requires an immediate audience."

The guard leaned sideways and eyed Dori with a smirk before straightening and looking askance at Constantine. "Lady, you say."

"Yes, lady. We've been traveling the whole of the day. Our horses require shelter and feed, and we must see the king at once."

"Your horses are of the better sort, and your speech is fine, but many connivers' are." By now the milling crowd about the torchlit courtyard had turned toward them in blatant curiosity and were watching the exchange with hungry gazes. "But if I interrupted the king with every beggar who wished to bend his ear, I'd be tossed from my post into the gutter."

"Your post won't be endangered in the slightest. Only announce our petition to the king," Constantine suggested as calmly as he could. "He will want to see us, I assure you."

The guard gave a bored sigh and then signaled to one of the pages along the wall behind him.

"Deliver a message to court," he told the lad, and then paused and looked up at Constantine. "Who shall I say is calling upon His Majesty?"

"The earl of Chase and the Lady Theodora Rosemont."

The guard's eyebrows drew together as he stared up at Constantine and then Dori in turn, his arm waggling as the horse he still held shook its head in impatience.

Constantine did not elaborate, nor did he break his gaze with the sentry.

"You heard the man," the guard said to the page, this time with much less scorn in his voice. "Announce the earl of Chase and Lady Theodora Rosemont. Return as quickly as your feet can carry you."

The boy was off through the crowd in a flash, although Constantine saw the lad pause twice at different clusters of people gathered in the courtyard, his mouth moving rapidly before holding out his hand for payment and dashing away.

A rumbling hush swept through the space beyond the gate as the guard drew Constantine's attention.

"If you'll dismount, my lord, I'll have your horses seen to." Constantine swung down, recognizing the guard's cunning. If Constantine turned out to be who he said he was, the man would ingratiate himself to a noble; if Constantine was lying, he would be unable to escape and would likely be thrown directly into prison.

He moved to Theodora's horse and reached up to take hold of her waist as she slid down into his arms.

"What's happening?" she whispered into his ear as a large retinue of riders exited the gate near them, a noble of obvious importance somewhere in the center of the group outfitted with great pomp, not to mention accompanied by a goodly number of the king's own men.

"We're being announced." He set her on her feet and placed her hand in the crook of his arm when she fidgeted with her skirts. "Only a few moments."

"I think I might be sick. What if he won't see us?" Her fingers tightened on his arm and she leaned in to speak near his shoulder. "They're all looking at me, whispering."

Constantine turned his face to look down at Theodora, her heart-shaped face a mask of dread. "It's because you're beautiful, Dori," he said with a smile. "It's why they've always whispered."

"Lord Gerard?"

Constantine turned at the sound of his name being called and was met with the sight of a pair of the king's personal servants. They bowed, first to him and then to Theodora.

The spokesman looked to them each in turn. "This way, if you please."

Constantine guided Dori through the courtyard of finely dressed revelers, who parted for them most graciously as they continued to whisper in salacious delight that court seemed to become more interesting with each passing hour.

Glayer Felsteppe rode out into the London street surrounded by the king's men, feeling as though he might simply float away into the fragrant night air with giddy pride.

It was done: Benningsgate was his.

He was a new man this night, a powerful man, and everyone knew him. Even as he had passed through the courtyard with the king's borrowed men to secure the stragglers at the ruin's ramshackle village, the guests milling in the king's gardens had recognized his passing, filling the air with whispers of "the earl of Chase."

They'd even thought enough of him to mention his exquisite—if mouthy and, thankfully, dead—bride, Theodora Rosemont.

It was good to be adored.

To celebrate, he would pause for an hour before departing the city proper in order to secure a bit of adult companionship. The court maidens were clean and proper, certainly, and made for interesting sport, but just at that moment, Glayer wished for entertainment of a more . . . toothsome nature.

Only an hour, though; he did have the time of the king's soldiers at his beck and call to consider.

Two hours, at the very most.

* * *

Dori's skin was a blanket of gooseflesh as the servants showed her and Constantine through the ornate double doors. The wide corridor outside the chamber was crammed with an inconceivable number of nobles, and their hot whispers seemed to swirl about her head, making her dizzy and her legs weak. In contrast, the room they entered was cavernous and cool and quiet—although it did rather smell like a barn—and Dori thought it empty until the lone voice called out from the dais.

"I didn't think it was true." The words had a slight echo, and Dori found herself clutching Constantine's arm as they both looked to the right and saw the imposing figure of the king lounging in his chair, surrounded by what appeared to be a pile of furs about his feet.

Henry was wearing riding attire, his red hair lying over his shoulders, his light eyes seeming to pierce them from across the room.

Constantine gently withdrew from Dori's grasp and walked toward the king, stopping several feet before Henry and dropping to one knee. The pile of furs rose up in points, and Dori realized they were hounds.

"My liege."

"Well, stand up, Constantine. I must have a good look at you if I am to be convinced of your resurrection. You know the courtiers are already swooning. I had to eject them all lest they fall upon the both of you and begin cutting at your clothes and hair for relics."

"No resurrection, my liege," Constantine said, gaining his feet.

"No?" Henry turned his head, and Dori felt the full weight of his stare. "Surely that cannot be the case for this one. The ghost of Thurston Hold, if I'm not mistaken. Or shall I better address you as Lazarus?"

Theodora remembered herself and stepped forward, sinking into a low curtsy. "Forgive me, my liege," she said.

"Forgive you for not being dead? Or for barging into my court?" Henry turned back to Constantine. "It takes quite a bit of courage to show yourself here, after all this time."

"I would think you would always wish those loyal to you to come to you without fear."

"Ah, yes—those who are loyal to me. Do you know of any such individuals, Lord Gerard? From where I am sitting, they number too few, even in my own family, both here and abroad."

"I have always been loyal to you, my liege."

"Is that so?" Henry goaded, abruptly sitting forward in his chair and causing the dogs at his feet to stir once more. "When you practically demanded I send you back to Syria to serve the leper, although I had yet to bring the anarchy in the farthest reaches of this land to heel? They're not calling me castle breaker because I've challenged the lords to tourneys of chess. And when I indulge you, you manage to bring the whole of the Holy Land down upon your own head! Killing hundreds of Englishmen! Causing the king of Jerusalem to condemn one of my favored lords as a traitor." He sat back against his seat once more. "Your actions reflected poorly on me, Constantine."

"I am not guilty of the horrors accused of me," Constantine said, his voice low and steady, and Dori knew he was trying to keep hold of his temper. "Baldwin—"

"You should have come to me!" Henry shouted

"I couldn't!" Constantine replied, throwing out his arms. "You had employed an army of mercenaries to hunt me and my friends down and kill us for the bounties on our heads!"

Henry looked away in a bored manner, shaking his red head with a sigh.

Constantine continued. "You condoned the murder of my family! Patrice and Christian!"

"I did not," Henry corrected, looking back at him. "Lady Patrice failed to cooperate."

"Of course she wouldn't cooperate with a maggot like Glayer Felsteppe; he wasn't worthy to lick her shoes!" Constantine paused to take a breath. "I ask you now, my king: Has the man who killed my wife and son petitioned for my title and home or not?"

Henry stilled, looking at Constantine with an intensity that ignited a spark of hope in his soul.

"I signed the decree this afternoon. I'll ensure you receive a copy."

"No," Constantine whispered. Then he rushed forward a pair of steps. "*No.*"

The dogs raised their heads again, and one gave a warning growl. But Henry looked to Theodora now.

"Which means your son could one day be entitled to both Thurston Hold and Benningsgate. Although I'm not at all certain how pleased your husband shall be to learn the mother of his child obviously feigned her own death. He seems rather fond of little . . . Glander, isn't it? Odd name."

Dori was already shaking her head, and although her posture was proud, Constantine could see the nervousness on her face. When she glanced at him, he thought he saw a hint of pure dread. She looked back at the king.

"It's not Glander; it's William. And Glayer Felsteppe is not his father."

The dark-haired, almond-eyed woman ducked out of the door and scurried past Dori and Reg, attempting to cover herself as best she could with the sheer scarves of her costume. Reginald tried to shield Dori from the sight, but she couldn't have been scandalized by any-thing connected to Glayer Felsteppe by that time; the more she had learned about him, the more convinced she was that she had made the correct decisions. Had her father still been alive—and in posses-sion of sound mind—he would have been proud of her.

Glayer Felsteppe was an evil man. And, after that day, she would never have to see him again.

It made the long, long journey from her cool, verdant England to this hellish land more than worthwhile. The heat in the stifling car-riage had made her nausea so much worse.

The door creaked open again, and the priest stepped aside to admit them, his slender face devoid of expression.

"Come in."

Simon, Dori thought he was called.

Felsteppe was still fastening his belt around his leather hauberk, his wooly hair a bit disheveled, but his face still bearing a surprised smile.

"Theodora!" he exclaimed, crossing the floor. "I didn't think it was possible when Simon said you had come."

Reginald—dear, honorable Reg—stepped in front of Dori before Felsteppe could reach her with his outstretched hands.

"Forgive our intrusion, Lord Felsteppe," Reg said. "But we felt the news we bore was of such import that we could only deliver it personally."

"Good heavens," Felsteppe said with widened eyes, the corners

of his mouth turned down. "This does sound serious. Although you obviously know who I am, I don't believe we've met."

Reg gave a short bow. "Lord Reginald Calumet, Baron Amberly. I am a cousin of Lady Dori's."

"Ah, yes... Lady Dori," Felsteppe said with a slight roll of his eyes. "A pleasure, Lord Calumet. Please..." He gestured to a grouping of woven reed chairs at the far end of the chamber, before a wide, white-curtained doorway leading to a long veranda.

Reg led Dori to a chair and then claimed the one beside her while Felsteppe sat across from them, one heeled boot resting on his opposite knee. A servant appeared to pour a fruity-scented liquid into metal cups and left them on the low table between them.

As soon as the boy departed, Reginald opened his mouth to speak, but Dori placed a hand gently on his arm. She had to do this herself. She'd come this far.

"My father is dead," Dori said without preamble.

Felsteppe's surprise seemed to deepen, but he did not offer any contrived condolences. "I've the feeling this is not the grave news you wished to deliver in a personal fashion."

"It is not," Dori acknowledged. "Reg came up from Amberly for his funeral and"—she had to pause, draw a deep breath—"I cannot marry you, Lord Felsteppe."

Glayer Felsteppe's eyes narrowed and one red brow arched. "Really."

"I am sorry," Reg began with a sincere expression. "We are very much in love. Have been for some time. Well," he looked at Dori with tenderness, "at least I have been for years."

Dori felt a tenderness in her heart for the young man as she tried to return his smile. But then she looked back at Felsteppe and saw the priest, Simon, standing in the shadows of the room.

It was just as well that there was a witness to the final blow she was ready to deal.

"I'm carrying Reginald's child. We shall be married as soon as we return to England."

Now the surprised look returned to Felsteppe's face and he huffed a shocked laugh. "I see." He uncrossed his legs and recrossed them in the opposite direction, adjusted his seat in the creaky, woven chair. He laughed again as he looked at both of them in turn. "You don't say."

"Truly. Very sorry," Reg insisted, and Dori had the urge to shout at him for his polite apologies.

"The king knows of this, then," Felsteppe inquired.

"No," Reginald admitted. *"We wished to inform you first. Save you the embarrassment of a scandal."*

A smile crept across Felsteppe's face as he cocked his head at Dori's cousin. *"Remarkably courteous of you. I can scarce believe you would think to spare me so."* He looked to Dori briefly and then stood. *"Well, far be it for me to stand in the way of true love,"* he said to Reg and held forth his hand. *"I wish you both all the happiness you deserve."*

Reginald stood with an audible sigh. *"Very relieved at your taking this so well, Lord Felsteppe."* He gripped the man's hand enthusiastically. *"God bless y—"*

Felsteppe thrust the knife into Reginald's ribs so quickly that the movement was little more than a blur to Dori. She screamed and shot to her feet as Reg gave a weak cry and a grunt, collapsing forward onto the table.

Felsteppe jerked the blade free, letting loose a thick red stream of blood that splashed onto the floor.

Dori flew to his side, slipping in the growing crimson pool as she went to her knees, gripping his young, handsome face in her hands. *"Reg! Reginald! Answer me! Reg! Reg!"* she shrieked.

But his eyes were already rolling away, glassy, empty.

"No!" she screamed. And then her cry was wordless and she felt herself being lifted to her feet by her hair.

"You thought you'd be so clever," Felsteppe gritted through his teeth as he dragged her from the alcove toward the main part of the chamber. *"Steal what was rightfully mine and give it to some ninny of a pup. You think it concerns me that he thrust into you first? Naaaay, milady."* He flung her onto the bed, and Simon moved toward her.

"Simon," Felsteppe warned, and the priest froze in his tracks. He looked back to Dori and seemed to consider her, shaking his head. *"No. It's not you I wanted in the first place—it's Thurston Hold. And I will have it. You've done me a great service by coming here in your attempt to ruin me. Ha!"*

He reached toward her, and although Dori screamed and held up *her hands to shield herself, Felsteppe still managed to grab a fistful of her hair through her veil.*

"Get up. Get. Up!" He dragged her to her feet and shook her.

Dori kicked at him, swung her claws, raking his face and arm.

He hissed in pain and then punched her in the face, causing her cheek to explode in agony, white starbursts flashing behind her eyes.

Dori heard the sobs being wrung from her body. Reg was dead. Dead! And she was alone in a foreign land with this . . . this monster.

"Simon," she heard Felsteppe say. "Marry us."

"What?"

"I said marry us. Are you deaf?"

Dori struggled to free herself once more. "I'll never marry you. Never! Never!"

Another blow to her face made her ears ring, and Dori could do naught but hang by his grip for a moment, trying to clear her vision.

"You'll do exactly as I say, from this moment forward," Felsteppe hissed, straining to pull her face up to his. "For if you don't, I will take yonder knife which I used to dispose of your erstwhile suitor and cut out the little fish that wriggles inside you. Do you understand? I will gut you and then feed your innards to the hyenas that roam outside the walls."

Dori could only whimper.

"Do you understand?" he screamed in her face. "Do you?"

"Yes, yes!" she shrieked. "I understand!"

"Good," Felsteppe said, taking a deep breath and calming himself considerably. He looked to the priest. "Carry on, Simon."

The priest began stammering, but Dori couldn't understand what he was saying. Her ears rang, her mouth filled with blood.

And Reg was dead.

"Let's honeymoon in Dubrovnik," Felsteppe whispered in her ear.

The chamber was tomb silent as Dori finished her tale, keeping her gaze on the king rather than risk looking at Constantine.

"He kept me prisoner until my state was obvious," she said. "We returned overland to the Channel and then by ship to England. He had sent for his mother—the hag who acted as my son's nurse. It was she who slowly poisoned me under the guise of offering me a strengthening potion."

"What of your death?" Henry asked. "Lord Felsteppe genuinely believes you to have been dead these many months."

"He believes me to be dead because he charged the priest to take me from my home and kill me. Simon."

"Simon," the king muttered. "Of course. It could only be Simon." Then louder, "Apparently, he did not."

"No. He urged me to flee the country rather than have another death on his already black conscience," Dori said. "I instead went into hiding at Benningsgate."

"Rather close to the danger you narrowly escaped, wasn't it, Lady Theodora?"

"It was my intention all along to return for my son," she said defiantly. "Baron Amberly's son. Felsteppe and I were never married in truth. The union was never consummated."

"Were I you, Lady Theodora, I would refrain from sharing that bit of information with anyone else just yet." Henry turned to Constantine, and Dori dared a sideways glance at him. He was not looking at her.

"You found her there at Benningsgate, I suppose, and the pair of you thought it more effective to besiege me with your tales of woe together."

"I had no intention of coming to you at all, my liege. I only returned to England to kill Glayer Felsteppe. Send for him now and I shall prove it to you."

To her surprise, Henry threw back his head and laughed. "Constantine, Constantine. Honest to your own detriment, as always." The king sighed and then raised his palms into the air for a moment before letting them fall back to his thighs. "There's naught I can do. Lord Felsteppe departed with a band of my own soldiers not an hour ago."

"What?" Dori blurted out.

The king rolled his gaze toward her, almost reluctantly, it seemed. "Baron Amberly has been dead for more than a year now—another sad victim of the Holy Land's vicious ways, as it was reported. Besides yourself, Lady Theodora, and a disgraced priest, there are no witnesses to his supposed murder. Obviously you're alive and well. There is no proof that Lord Felsteppe has wronged you in any way. If anything, he's done you a great service by claiming your child—the boy's been christened and officially marked as his heir. If you return to your husband and promise to be the meek woman he desires—no matter how difficult a task that would prove—perhaps you will be allowed access to your son. I am not completely without sympathy for you, and so I am willing to have my secretary pen a letter of apology on your behalf."

"To apologize for not being dead?" Dori demanded in shock.

Henry shrugged. "During the course of my reign there have been several men I would be greatly put out to have turn up alive."

"Myself for instance," Constantine accused.

The king sighed and turned his head, leveling a look at Constantine. "No, Lord Gerard. Not you. But I cannot simply give you leave to hunt down and assassinate Glayer Felsteppe. You'd be arrested and tried for murder, as you have no proof Felsteppe intentionally caused the deaths of Patrice and Christian. Even if the charges against you from the Holy Land have been dismissed, the rumors have followed you, and they will carry weight should you be accused of killing a peer in cold blood. I'll not volunteer to take another whipping for condoning a man's death—even one who might deserve it."

"You're going to stand by and let him get away with murder?"

"You have no proof."

"My word should be proof enough for you!" Constantine pointed at the king. "You were my friend!"

The king looked at Constantine without anger at the accusation, and Dori thought she saw a spark of compassion in his gray eyes.

"I am still your friend, Constantine. But, more importantly at the present, I am your king. As far as I and my realm are concerned, you are as yet innocent of any treachery here or at Chastellet. You are free to go; none shall detain you in my name. But I warn you, Constantine, the only way you can see Glayer Felsteppe dead by your hand is by the letter of the law, which does not condone what you wish to do. I'll rouse my secretary in order to provide you a copy of the decree before you depart."

"I don't want it," Constantine said.

"Yes, you do." The king looked at Dori. "Do you desire my letter of recommendation to your husband, Lady Theodora?"

Dori's stomach churned and she couldn't hide the sneer she was certain twisted her mouth. "No. Thank you. My liege."

"Then I've no desire to see either of you again until you have something of actual worth to present; my hall is too crowded as it is." He stood and waved toward the guard at the door. "Admit them or not. I'm going to bed any matter."

The chamber was awash with a flood of draped, chattering, perfumed nobility in moments, swirling around Dori and separating her from Constantine. She was jostled, plucked at, faces staring at her from only inches away, taking keen interest in her poor attire, her strangely short hair.

She felt a hand grip her arm, but it wasn't Constantine's wide palm. She jerked away instinctively and looked around to see a young blond woman with hard, glittering eyes.

"Come with me, my lady," she said, leaning near Dori's face. "Now. We must hurry."

"Why?" Dori demanded, even as the nobles around her pressed more boldly, their taunts and observations full of ridicule.

"Come," the woman insisted, reaching down and taking Dori's hand and pulling her through the crowd.

Dori looked back over her shoulder, but she could not see Constantine above the wall of grotesque faces towering over her. She reached up with trembling fingers to jerk her hood over her head and then lowered her face and allowed herself to be pulled through the pressing crush by a stranger, reaching up several times to hold her covering in place when it was snatched at.

They came into the entry hall, cool, fresh air at last filling Dori's lungs, but instead of being led toward the doors of the courtyard, the young woman was skipping across the smooth floor, deeper into the maze of corridors. They mounted a narrow stair.

"Who are you?" Dori demanded. "Where are you taking me?"

They dashed down a wide upper corridor and then the girl came to a sudden halt before a door. She dropped Dori's hand and turned to face her.

"I heard the rumors about you," she said boldly. "What your husband said happened to you." Her young, plain face was hard. "Lord Felsteppe. He's a liar."

"Who are you?" Dori asked again, completely confused at what was happening.

"Eirene of Glencovent," she said. "Helping you hurts him, does it not?"

Dori nodded, wondering at what the girl was about.

"This is the only thing I can do," Eirene said. "I hope it's enough." She banged on the door suddenly with her fist, the noise startling Dori and causing her already raw nerves to scream.

But then the door opened and an old woman's face appeared.

"Yes?" Eseld said, her eyes going from the blond Eirene to the shadow inside Dori's hood. "His lordship's already gone. What is it you want?"

Somewhere in the room behind the old woman, a baby cried.

Chapter 23

Constantine waited along the wall of the corridor outside the secretary's alcove of a chamber, connected to the hall from which he'd just been summarily dismissed. His arms were crossed over his chest, his gaze fixed upon the joinings of stone and mortar across from him. He didn't know where Theodora Rosemont was.

And he didn't care.

It's not Glander; it's William. And Glayer Felsteppe is not his father.

Felsteppe and I were never married . . . the union was never consummated.

The king's young secretary emerged from the doorway at Constantine's shoulder, still appearing disgruntled at having been roused to another piece of work. In one hand he held forth a piece of parchment, still curled at the ends; the other grasped a candleholder. The man shook the page pointedly and Constantine took it. The secretary immediately turned and pulled the door closed, securing it with a key from his ring before turning smartly in the corridor and stalking off without a word, leaving Constantine alone in the passage, the shadows flickering from the torch at the far end.

He didn't want to read the decree; didn't want it in his possession. Whatever it said would make no difference once Glayer Felsteppe was dead. Constantine would also be in his grave, in prison, or once more—and forever—wanted as a criminal.

All he needed do now was follow Glayer Felsteppe back to Thurston Hold and run him through. He would pay for the evil he had orchestrated by the only means acceptable to Constantine—with his pathetic life. What happened to Constantine in the moments or days or years following didn't matter.

The image of Theodora Rosemont bloomed in his mind, unexpectedly and undesired.

What would she do now? And what about the boy?

Constantine told himself it didn't matter as he started down the corridor. He didn't care.

You cared only hours ago, when you still thought the child was Felsteppe's. Now you know the monster did not sire the boy and has no real claim on Dori, the woman you love.

He stopped as so many more images flitted through his memory—the way she'd fought him in the ward, the crucifix she'd borne all the way to the ruined hall in memory of the woman and boy lost there; how she'd rushed out with his blade to defend him when she'd thought he was in danger from the villagers. The way she'd lovingly prepared Patrice for her final rest.

She'd left Benningsgate alone, after Constantine had gone back on his word to her, to save her son.

Constantine at last admitted it: he did love Dori. That was why he'd come after her, brought her before the king, accepting her son to be Felsteppe's, accepting Dori was his wife. Accepting all of her, just as she was.

She lied to me.

No. She never lied, he realized.

Dori would never do as the king suggested and crawl back to Felsteppe on hands and knees, begging to be part of her son's life when it was Felsteppe who had ordered her death. Although Henry had been uncharacteristically obtuse compared to the ruler Constantine had previously known, surely the king must realize Felsteppe would only make certain Theodora truly was dead the next time.

Henry must know that, just as surely as he knew Constantine would never rest until Glayer Felsteppe paid for all he'd done.

Constantine looked down at the parchment in his hand. He slowly walked toward the single torch in the corridor, holding the hastily scribbled words closer to the light. After a moment, Constantine lowered the page and raised his eyes to stare into nothing.

The king knew.

The shuffling sound of someone approaching drew his attention, and Constantine looked up to see an old woman walking slowly down the stairs. She appeared in a trance, her eyes—set in discolored purple wells in her face—were locked on some far away sight that perhaps only she could see and her lips moved in a soundless soliloquy below her distinctive hooked nose. She reached the bottom of the stair and turned to walk toward him and Constantine saw that she was without shoes, although her dress was that of a better servant.

"Beggin' your pardon, sir," the old woman said in a breathy, dreamy voice. She looked up at him, but her gaze seemed to take in the air around his head rather than meet his eyes directly. "Have you seen my son?"

"No, mistress," Constantine said with a wary frown. The woman was clearly unwell. "Is he a young boy?"

"Oh . . . no," she said, turning on her feet in a slow circle, looking around at the walls and ceiling and floor of the corridor, as if she expected her missing progeny to manifest from the stones. "He's a great lord, now. Grown. He must have forgotten his old mother again. I'm not to call him son."

She looked up in the general vicinity of Constantine's face once more. "In which direction lies Thurston Hold, sir?"

He recognized the profile, then, softened by feminine features and years but still the same hooked nose, the same pointed chin, the same narrow eyes.

Eseld. Felsteppe had left his mother, the nurse caring for Dori's son, behind. Which meant—

Constantine looked up the stairs.

"Sir?" Eseld queried again. "Won't you help me? I must know how far Thurston Hold is from here."

He looked back down at her, wondering at the bruises on her face, the evil she'd endured.

And enabled.

"South," Constantine said. "Thurston Hold is south of here. Three hours by horse."

"I thank you, sir," she said and then turned away in her dreamy manner and slowly walked down the corridor on her bare feet.

And then Constantine dismissed any thought of Glayer Felsteppe's mother from his mind as he ran to the foot of the stairs and ascended them two at a time.

Theodora threw herself against the door in the same instant that Eseld recognized her and sought to slam it in her face.

"Help me, Eirene!" Dori cried.

The girl added her weight with Dori's and the door flew open, sending Eseld stumbling back into the room.

"Close the door and bolt it," Dori said to the young woman behind her, all the while never taking her eyes from Eseld.

The old woman turned as if to move toward the bed, where the crying had come from.

"Don't you dare," Dori warned in a low voice. "Don't you dare think to touch him ever again. I'll kill you with my bare hands, I swear it."

"You don't command me," Eseld said. "Glander is my grandson. He is in my care. His lordship will see your end himself this time, rather than leave it to that pathetic, faithless priest."

"Your son is gone from London," Dori said. "And *my baby* is not of his issue. His name is William Calumet. He is not your grandson."

"You lie." Eseld glared at her. "Glayer impregnated you in the Holy Land, when you ran after him and begged him to marry you. You threw yourself atop him. He told me."

"Glayer Felsteppe killed the father of my son and claimed him for his own. He thought to have me killed so that no one would ever know."

"He can't impregnate anyone," the accusation came from behind Dori, and Eirene stepped forward. "I should know. He can't make love in a normal way. He's sick. His manhood is . . . broken."

"*You* lie because my son turned you away," Eseld said and faced the bed again. She took a hesitant step and then glanced back at Dori, her brows drawn together. "He *is* my grandson."

"I'm telling the truth and you know it, if you'll only admit it to yourself," Dori said. "You cared for Felsteppe as a baby as you cared for my son. There can be no resemblance; it's impossible. I was three months gone when that farce of a marriage took place."

"This child is perfect. And he has my blood in his veins," Eseld whispered frantically. "He must."

"He doesn't," Dori said. "And I'm taking him with me, where he belongs."

"No!" Eseld cried and rushed forward, her hands out.

Dori threw up her own arms, ready to defend herself, but the old woman dropped to her knees on the floor.

"You can't take him," she gasped. "You can't. He's all I have left. If he's gone, I'll have no purpose. Glayer will send me away. He'll send me back. I'll *die!*"

Dori looked down at the disturbed woman, then walked in a backward circuit away from her, putting herself between Eseld and the bed. "You poisoned me while my child was yet in my body. You stole him from me the moment after I bore him. You allowed your monster of a son to commit such atrocities that even hell's darkest fiend would condemn. Evil he likely learned from you."

"No! No, no, no!" Eseld tried to follow on her knees but fell forward onto her hands. She crawled after Dori. "Not from me. I showed him naught but love. I loved him! I still love him. And I love Glander."

"That's not his name," Dori said, staring in horror at the rapid deterioration of the woman at her feet.

"Take me with you, then," Eseld pleaded suddenly. "Wherever you go. I can serve you. I can care for the babe. I'll love him so much. You can beat me if you wish."

Dori pulled her skirts from the woman's claws. "No!" she shrieked. "Get away from me! Get out! You're mad!"

Eseld dissolved into a pile of weeping on the floor. "I know, I know," she moaned into her shaking hands. "He doesn't love me. None of them did. None ever."

"Eseld," Dori said, her voice trembling. "Eseld, you must leave. You must go now."

The old woman rose to her feet as if her body had become boneless and was tethered to an invisible rope that pulled her aright. Her sobs were soundless, issuing from her gaping mouth. She turned in a slow circuit and slid toward the door, collapsing against it for a moment while struggling with the bolt. She pulled it open at last and walked through the doorway.

Dori looked up into the wide eyes of Eirene of Glencovent, a stranger to her. A stranger who had given her a gift of inestimable value.

"Thank you," Dori whispered.

The blonde glanced beyond Dori's shoulder toward the bed and then met her eyes once more. "How long has it been since you've seen him?"

"Since the night he was born." She turned and saw the very top of a rounded head covered in dark hair among a nest of creamy bed-clothes. "I've never held him." She felt the young woman come to stand close behind her.

The pile of blankets suddenly gave a sharp yelp and Dori jumped.

"I'm a bit nervous," she admitted.

She heard stomping footfalls through the open doorway and her heart leaped into her throat. "Close the door," Dori said, lunging for the bundle on the mattress. She scooped up the surprisingly heavy baby and brought him close to her chest just as the male voice called out in surprise.

"Who are you? Where is the child the old woman was caring for?"

Dori recognized Constantine's voice, but she could not look away from the big, slate-blue eyes staring up at her from the folds of the coverlet. William frowned at her, his little face solemn even with his rounded, flushed cheeks, frosted with pale down.

"Get out or I'll scream," Eirene threatened in a shrill voice.

"It's all right, Eirene," Dori said, still transfixed by the little face before her. His mouth was like a knot of red ribbon, his ears like flower petals. "He's a . . . friend. I think." She looked up then, but Constantine's form was blurry. She blinked, felt the wetness on her cheeks, and could see him at last.

"I found him, Constantine," she whispered. "And Eseld's gone. I sent her away."

Constantine nodded and Dori noticed he carried a parchment. But she didn't care that he did, or what it said, as she turned around to ease into a seat at the side of the bed, looking back down into her son's face.

"I saw her. She's unwell, Dori. And I think she means to return to Thurston Hold."

"It doesn't matter," Dori said, bringing up a trembling hand to tentatively touch the silky strands of hair across William's forehead. His shallow breaths were fast and sweet in his perfect nostrils as he looked around himself, as if seeking the source of the deep voice he'd heard. "I'm not going back there."

"Dori."

"Yes?" She trailed her finger down the side of his impossibly soft cheek.

"I have the decree Henry signed, granting Glayer Felsteppe Ben-ningsgate."

"I'm sorry, Constantine," she said distractedly.

"I'm not," he said, and his answer, along with the tone in which he spoke caused her to look up reluctantly. "It's an assignment of inheritance, Dori. It bequeaths Benningsgate to Glayer Felsteppe in the event of my death without an heir."

Dori blinked. "But . . . you didn't die. The king knows that—we just had an audience with him."

Constantine nodded. "Benningsgate still legally belongs to me, with all rights and privileges."

"Which means that the moment Glayer Felsteppe trespasses upon it with the intention of claiming it for himself or harming anyone who belongs there . . ."

"I can defend my home."

Dori felt the breath go out of her and she pulled William even closer. He gave a little squawk so that she started and looked down. "Oh, sorry, sorry." Her gaze found Constantine's again. "You must go."

"Come with me?"

Dori looked at him for a long moment and then her eyes went to the rapt Eirene, who seemed to be enjoying watching Constantine. Dori couldn't blame her; he was breathtaking.

"Could I trouble you for yet another favor?" she asked the young woman.

Eirene gave her sly smile. "If I have liberty to later speak of it. My companions will be beside themselves at my daring."

"I'm in need of a proper costume," she said and glanced down at the baby in her arms, still watching her with his great, blue owl eyes. "I can't have William's mother looking like a beggar. I shall compensate you for it after I return to my home."

"And send up one of the king's servants to me, if you would, my lady," Constantine added. "I have a message for Henry, and a small request I think he will be all too eager to grant."

Once Eirene of Glencovent had all but skipped from the chamber, Dori looked back at Constantine.

"You want me to return with you now because I never was Felsteppe's wife and William is not his son."

"No," he said. "I want you to return in spite of those things." His expression went hard. "Why didn't you tell me, Dori?"

"Because I didn't think you'd care if you knew he wasn't Felsteppe's child, if he had no legal claim to Benningsgate. It would have been easy for you to just . . . leave me there to die. Leave William in Felsteppe's hands, and then in whoever's hands the king placed him."

"You think that's the man I am?"

"I did when first we met," she admitted.

Constantine's face was stricken. "Because I left Patrice and Christian."

Dori shook her head. "No! Because I know avenging their deaths meant more to you than saving the life of spoiled, foolish Theodora Rosemont." She looked down at the child now somehow asleep in her arms. "It meant more to you than the possibility of someone loving you in the future." She looked up. "The possibility of us loving you."

Constantine walked across the floor to stand before her. "Might you love me in the future?"

She shook her head. "No. Constantine, I love you now."

He reached one hand toward her but was interrupted by a rap at the door. He turned away.

"Come."

A servant entered and gave a stiff bow. "How might I serve you, my lord?"

"I have a message for the king and, with his permission, several items my lady and I are in need of."

"His Majesty has already given his permission for whatever it is you ask, my lord."

Constantine looked over his shoulder at Dori, and for the first time since they'd arrived in London, she saw his mouth curve in a smile.

The joy Glayer Felsteppe had experienced upon his departure from the king's court and after easing himself with a particularly interesting couple found in one of the darker houses near the palace had gradually worn away, until he was fussy and impatient when Thurston Hold came into view. He wanted to go inside the luxurious house, crawl into bed, and sleep for a pair of days. The idea of watching the last few houses still standing in Benningsgate village burn in the night was appealing, but he had underestimated his fatigue after such athletic pursuits. And, any matter, the sun would rise in a few hours. By the time they fueled the huts, killed any resisters, and got everything going properly, it would be daylight, and not nearly as dramatic.

Hot, too.

But then the shadow came lurching from the wood toward his mounted party on the road, causing his heart to leap into a gallop even as the armed guards to either side of Glayer drew their swords, ready to protect the new earl of Chase.

"Lord Felsteppe! Lord Felsteppe! Aaaghh! Don't strike me!"

The man cowered on the road, his right arm raised up over his head, the dark splotches on his filthy tunic and mottling his light hair appeared to be blood. His leathery twig of a left arm, normally hooked inside his thin belt, swung freely, causing Glayer to wrinkle his nose.

"It's all right," Glayer said to the guards at his side. "He poses no danger to me." He looked down at the man, who seemed to have either fallen down two successive cliffs or been beaten to within an inch of his grubby little life. "Good God, you mean to tell me the villagers haven't killed you by now? Flealess, isn't it?"

"Leland, milord," the peasant corrected.

"Leland, yes," Glayer said with a wave of his hand. "What are you doing so close to Thurston Hold? You think because you did me one infinitesimally small favor years ago by admitting me to Benningsgate Castle, you now have leave to beleaguer me when I'm in the vicinity? I paid you that night, didn't I?"

"Nay, milord. And aye, milord. I've only come to warn you, as I promised." The man stepped closer, and although the soldier to Glayer's right said nothing, he held his sword before the man's chest, preventing his advance. Leland glanced down at it before looking back up at Glayer. "He's back."

Glayer sighed. His back actually *was* aching, now that the cripple had mentioned it. "What are you talking about?"

"Lord Gerard," the peasant insisted. "You told me to warn you if anyone came 'round asking after the earl. No one's done that, but the lord hisself has come."

Glayer went very still atop his horse as his mind suddenly shook off its fatigue. "Did you see him? Perhaps from afar and you merely thought it was Lord Gerard? You are at a physical disadvantage."

"It's me arm that's crippled, not me eyes!" the man shouted. "I not only seen him, I spoke to him. I watched him bury the bones of Lady Patrice what he dug out of the keep with his own hands." Leland paused. "And with the help of one Lady Theodora Rosemont. The bastard wanted to beat me to death for the sake of that mouthy bitch."

Glayer's eyes narrowed. "Now I know you're mad. My beloved bride"—he looked dramatically heavenward—"God receive her soul, has been dead these three months. Unless she is a reawakened corpse, you have clearly been imbibing of tainted drink. Even if she were otherwise—which she isn't—Lord Gerard would certainly have nothing to do with her."

The man shook his head until his hair arced out around him. "No. She's been hiding in the ruin at Benningsgate all this time. 'Twas Lord Gerard discovered her." He stepped forward again, pushing against the flat of the sword still held to his chest. "They've gone to London. Together. To find you."

Glayer didn't believe him. "Well, obviously I'm not in London. I think perhaps it would be better if you forget this little fantasy before I lose my temper. Good night, Flealess." He was about to move on when the man reached inside his tunic, prompting two more guards to draw on the peasant.

But Leland only produced what appeared to be a piece of cloth and held it up. "Leland, milord."

Glayer wrinkled his nose and withdrew his own sword, hooking the peasant's offering with its tip and then flipping the object up in the air to catch it with his other hand.

It was a thin embroidered piece of footwear, perhaps once quite fine, but now worn thin and stained with great black splotches that appeared to be blood.

Theodora's slipper.

"I stole it from the pile of ruined clothing she discarded before she left the village," Leland said. "The earl said he's coming for you, milord. And that naught will stop him. Not even the king."

That did rather sound like something Gerard would boast of.

"*I* am the earl," Glayer muttered, ignoring the sudden galloping of his heart in his chest. "Fine." He turned to one of his soldiers. "Ride on to Thurston Hold and rouse the rest of the men so that they might prepare. I want Constantine Gerard—if he actually still lives— cut into teeny, tiny pieces and sprinkled over what's left of that pathetic town. And then I will choke the breath out of Theodora Rosemont myself. That bitch. She'll ruin my status as an eligible widower."

He wheeled his horse around. "What are you waiting for? Go!"

"Milord?" Leland pressed.

Glayer gave a groan and looked down. "What now?"

"What shall I do?" Leland looked up at him expectedly.

"Hmm." Glayer, sidling his horse away from the man, looked at him as if considering. "Probably not return to Benningsgate. Perhaps drop yourself down a hole?" Glayer kicked at his horse, and it leaped toward the black outline of Thurston Hold.

"Lord Felsteppe!" the cripple cried after him. "Wait! I've nowhere else to go! My lord! Please!"

Glayer looked over his shoulder to see the man trotting down the road, holding his useless arm against his side, likely to keep it from flopping about.

"My God, is he following me?" Glayer muttered. He sighed and turned 'round. "Go back and take care of that," he said to the hired sword on his right. "Once I get out of this saddle, I simply must sit down properly, and yet I can't have him alerting the entire country-side."

The mercenary wheeled his horse from the party, drawing his sword as he turned.

"What are you doing?" the man called from the road, his voice growing fainter beneath the sound of the pounding hooves and the distance Glayer was putting between them.

"What are you doing? No! No! Plea—"

Glayer didn't bother looking back.

Chapter 24

Constantine watched Theodora place the now sleeping baby in the low cradle as the maid left the chamber, closing the door quietly after herself. The baby had been fed and changed, Dori insisting upon wiping the whole of the child down with warm, sweet water, as if she would cleanse little William of the memory of those who had held him before his mother. She had done her awkward best with the infant, and to her credit, William had not once cried out in fear.

Now that they were alone in the smaller, less-ornate chamber the servant had shown them to and the baby had been tended, Dori moved to the small table where Constantine sat with his cup resting on his knee. She reached out to pick up the other cup, then plucked a piece of cheese from the small repast provided them.

"Shall I leave while you attend your toilette?" he asked, his eyes flicking to the plum-colored velvet Eirene of Glencovent had provided, which was presently laid across the end of the bed.

Dori held his gaze while she chewed, even over the rim of her cup. She lowered it and licked her lips. "Do you want to leave?"

He shook his head. "No." He held his cup forth as she picked up the decanter and she filled it without comment. "But if I am to stay, we must discuss the future."

She set the vessel back on the table. "All right."

"I've nothing to offer you," he said. "No home save the pile of rocks that is now Benningsgate. No wealth. Perhaps not even the dignity of my name, as badly battered as it has become."

She watched him, her gamine face cocked, as if considering what he'd said. "I don't suppose you can claim any of those things yet," she admitted. "But I believe you will have all of them restored to you in time."

"Perhaps," he agreed. "It is certainly my desire now to rebuild Benningsgate. I'll find a way."

"Then we might talk about what I will bring to you," Dori suggested, and the fact that she had not moved close enough for Constantine to be within his reach irritated him, like an itch he was prevented from scratching. "Rather than the lack you perceive on your part, I bring a surplus of things you may have no interest in. A home of my own. Another man's child. The taint of my—quite deservedly earned—reputation."

Constantine grinned. "I happen to admire your reputation very much."

"Do you want me, Constantine?" she asked boldly, and set down her cup before stepping into the space between his knees. "Not just my body—I'm not so naïve as to be oblivious to our attraction to each other. But I come with my past, mistakes and ugliness. Obligations and burdens. Uncertainty."

Constantine stood, causing Dori to turn her face up to his in order to look at him.

"I could argue that the mistakes of my own past are uglier than yours. And they, too, might rear their heads in our future, providing even more obstacles for us to overcome."

"I suppose we've already proved that we can overcome anything the world throws at us," she reasoned, bringing her palms to his chest. "Even death."

Constantine wrapped his arms around her shoulders and looked into her eyes. "I love you, Theodora."

She raised up on her toes as he lowered his head, and their joined mouths were warm and wet, gentle and welcoming. The sounds of their long kiss were loud in the room, accompanied by the crackle of the fire in the hearth.

Dori touched his face as they parted. "I love you, too."

Constantine looked into her eyes. "I will do my best to raise William as a father. To love him as he deserves to be loved. As I know his own father would have loved him."

Her big eyes reflected the candlelight behind him. "And I will always respect the place in your heart where Patrice and Christian still live. I don't expect my son to take his place, Constantine. But I know William will be a better man because you first had Christian."

Constantine's breath caught in his chest and he forced himself to swallow. "The man I have been since Chastellet, before Chastellet, is also dead. And I need to bury him."

Dori nodded. "I'll help you."

He took one of her hands and brought the backs of her fingers to his lips. Then he released her and pulled the rough brown tunic over his head. Dori slipped out of her peasant's shoes and untied the coarse apron and tossed it aside, and then Constantine turned her away from him, dropping his mouth to the curve of her neck as he pushed the kirtle from her shoulders. Dori loosened the ties of her underskirt and it fell in a puddle around her feet.

He led her to the stand where the wash bowl sat and dunked, then lathered a soft linen cloth. He ran a trail of suds over her chest, the thin bubbles racing down over her small breasts while she untied the laces of his chausses. Then around her neck so that he could pull her naked torso to his and kiss her once more. Then he spun her in his arms, supporting her with his forearm while he washed the narrow length of her back, over the rounded cheeks of her buttocks. Constantine brought the cloth over her hip and slid it between her legs while Theodora reached up for him, turning her face to the side and seeking his mouth.

Constantine dunked the rag again and then squeezed it atop her head while she turned in his arms, closing her eyes and raking her fingers back through her cropped hair. Then he tossed the rag back into the bowl and pulled a length of linen toweling from its folded stack, wrapping it around her shoulders and then kissing her as he backed her to the bed.

Dori lay across the coverlet, the ends of her hair already curling up as they sent silvery droplets of water across her chest. Constantine hesitated, ready, then, to crawl atop her and love her, but he was not yet worthy of her. Instead, he turned to his satchel on the floor. Crouching near it, he withdrew one of his knives, then returned to the stand. He removed the rest of his clothing and boots, conscious the entire time of Theodora watching him from the bed.

He washed himself quickly, leaving only his hair unclean. And then he picked up his knife and began carefully cutting away his beard and then scraping the stubble from his skin. Constantine reached behind himself and pulled his long plait over his left shoulder. Holding it close at the base, he sawed through the rope with his blade, letting a curtain of tawny hair swing back around his cheeks.

Then he poured fresh water over his head from the pitcher, scraping his lessened locks back over his scalp before he turned to face the woman on the bed.

"You're beautiful," Dori said to him with a smile.

Constantine crawled onto the bed, feeling his damp skin prickling with cool air and desire and nervousness; anxious to touch her and yet feeling undeserving to do so.

She held out her arms and he came into them.

His freshly shaved skin was hot and erotically smooth against her breasts where he kissed her, and Dori was breathing heavily through her nose while his mouth slowly traveled up to her own lips and his hand moved over her stomach to her most intimate parts. She had been conscious at first at the change in her body since giving birth to William; she hadn't seen the whole of it at once in months and the curves and planes were foreign to her. There were marks and scars, still red from the deadly battles she had fought in her war to survive Glayer Felsteppe and to bring her baby into the world, bring him back to her.

Constantine seemed to worship each one as he took his time stirring her to passion. She drank in the smell of his skin, gulping her breaths with her mouth pressed to his damp chest, pulling his muscled body as close as she could.

He kissed her as he at last joined with her, and their coupling was firm and simple as their fingertips dug into each other. There were no words. Just their hot breaths and the sound of Constantine giving himself to her body again and again.

It was over in a sweaty, sweet rush and they lay tangled together, hearts pounding, muscles twitching; their foreheads touching as they faced each other on the bed. He turned his head and kissed her upper and lower lips in turn, pulling them into his mouth, licking the seam, once more seeking entrance. She felt him coming alive inside her again and she pulled him closer with her leg as he was already rocking against her.

"More," he said in a low growl.

"Yes," she whispered. "All right."

And then, in the still of the chamber, William cried out once sharply.

Constantine rolled atop her and pushed himself deep and then stilled. "Shh," he whispered in her ear.

The baby called again, this time in a staccato cry.

She didn't want to refuse the man inside her; indeed she wanted him again, but...

Constantine rolled away with a sigh, his forearm over his head on the pillow. He smiled at her in the candlelight. "We should leave soon any matter."

And she loved him even more as she left their bed to tend to her son. Perhaps their son.

Simon walked slowly along the darkened London street alone, his footsteps shuffling, his head down. He never before would have dared to do such a dangerous thing, but it didn't matter now. Any of the criminals who would have at other times accosted him perhaps sensed that he was ill and penniless, for surely his heartbreak rolled off him like the miasma seeping along the stones from the quay.

Victor would find that he was gone at morning prayer, but it was acceptable. Simon thought his friend had suspected when he'd heard his confession and then delivered him absolution. He was forgiven.

His sworn testimony had been taken as well, damning Glayer Fel-steppe and everyone connected with him. Perhaps it would do no good, he thought as his feet echoed on the wooden planks of the bridge, but perhaps when delivered by Victor's hand and the abbot's own tales...

Bledsoe was recovering, thanks be to God. Louisa and the children would make certain he rested until he was completely well and could once more take over the duties of his title. Simon had wanted to leave his friend a personal note, but he knew it wasn't necessary. Bledsoe would understand, and although he and Louisa would mourn, perhaps they would also both feel relief for the sons and daughters they loved so much and called their own.

Only Ethan would know the truth. And likely that young man—the youngest, and Simon's favorite—would convince himself to forget all he'd learned, as if it were nothing more than a bad dream. He'd go to his own grave—many, many years from then, Simon hoped—as Ethan Carmichael.

Simon stopped in the center of the bridge and looked down into the black, inky water, still swollen with the weeks of rain they'd endured. His chest seized in pain again and Simon gasped, digging his fingertips into his cassock and squeezing his eyes shut. He'd better get on with it, before he collapsed in a faint. It would be his luck that the lone Samaritan in all the city would be out before dawn to deliver him right back to Victor's capable hands.

Once he could breathe shallowly again, Simon stepped onto the bottom of the railing and threw his leg over with some difficulty. He turned 'round and grasped the railing with his arms spread, feeling the swaying structure urging him away from the side of the bridge.

He closed his eyes and let the cool breeze blow across his sweaty brow as he brought to his mind images of Louisa and Bledsoe, Ethan and his brothers and sisters; Simon's own parents, long dead now. He thought of Victor; Theodora Rosemont; the little blond orphan boy. He sent them all the love he could muster in his lurching, damaged heart.

"Thank you, Lord," he whispered into the wind, raising his face. "Thank you for my good life."

Then Simon let go of the railing and disappeared beneath the peaceful black water.

Chapter 25

They came through the final stretch of woods below the village still in the dark of night and began the final ascent up the road toward the ruin, invisible to them yet from where their horses walked, although Constantine could feel it ahead of them in the black sky—that solitary finger of stone.

William was quiet, once more sleeping after Dori had fed him a skin of goat's milk. Her actions with the baby were awkward and unsure, but she had not once asked for help, and Constantine was certain her determination and the love she felt for the boy would quickly make up for her lack of experience. And although it caused a bittersweet pain in his chest, Constantine could remember holding Christian at that age. They would manage.

The ruined keep came into view at last as they neared the far end of the village, and the odd glimmer on its ragged edge caused Constantine to frown and pull his mount to a stop in the center of the path. Dori came alongside him, and he didn't have to explain why they'd stopped, for she, too, was looking up at the castle.

"Torches," she said, her gaze locked on the faintly flickering stones.

Constantine looked about the houses to either side of him now—Nell's cottage and, farther back, Harmon's. The doors stood open, and yet no hearth light could be seen within the darkened doorways.

It was as if they'd meant to leave a clear sign: there is no one here.

He looked back toward the ruin. Perhaps they had gathered there, and it was his own people's torch glow he saw. But why would they leave the comfort of their homes before dawn unless urged to do so? Constantine had not brought Theodora back to Benningsgate by way of Thurston Hold, so he had no way of knowing if Glayer Felsteppe had only gone as far as Dori's home, or if he had chosen to come straight to Benningsgate, thinking it his, to claim it at once.

His gaze dropped to the road beneath him, but he could not see any evidence in the night shadows of a large party of riders passing through the town, if even it was there.

Although he could not fathom whether it was for good or ill, Constantine knew that Benningsgate was different than when he'd left. And he also knew he must prepare Theodora as best he could before he proceeded.

"If I should fail . . ." he began.

"You won't fail," she interrupted, and he knew she had already worked out on her own the possible scenarios that lay ahead of them in the ruin.

"Listen to me, Theodora," he ordered sharply, looking at her in the gloom of predawn. "*If I should fail*, you must return to London as quickly as you can. Beg Henry's protection in seeing you and William away from England as soon as possible."

"Constantine . . ." she pleaded.

But he would hear none of it before she gave her word. "Promise me."

"All right," she said. "I promise. Of course."

Constantine swung down from his horse and then walked to Dori's side. She held the baby close to her bosom while he helped her slide to the ground.

"I'm going up on foot," he said. "Felsteppe left London with a retinue of the king's men. I'll need to get as close as I can without being seen."

"You can't seek him out when he has armed men at his command! You know he will set the soldiers on you rather than face you. He's a coward!"

He looked down into her eyes and smoothed a lock of her hair from her forehead. "Go into the back room of Nell's cottage but leave the door open as we found it. I'll tie the horses inside Leland's, across the way; his door is still shut and won't incur suspicion. If I don't come for you, wait until you hear them depart and then go. You don't want them behind you."

"I'm not going to cower in a cottage while you're possibly killed. If Felsteppe and the king's men are there, I'd as soon know it and leave for London immediately."

Constantine shook his head. "You're not coming past the village."

"Yes, I am," she insisted. "Only part of the way. I must."

"No."

"You can't stop me, Constantine," she said shrilly. "I'll just wait until you leave and follow you."

He pulled her into his chest and stroked her hair as she began to cry. But William soon objected to the close quarters and roused with a squawk, prompting Dori to pull away from him.

"I'm not going to endanger myself or William," she said, bouncing the baby to quiet him as she swiped at her nose. "But I can't allow you to think that you are alone any more. I won't. Because you're not. And if you know that the two of us are behind you, perhaps you will try just a bit harder to come back for us." She glared at him, as if he had committed some terrible slight against her.

But Constantine knew she was only very afraid.

"All right," he conceded.

Her nostrils flared and she continued to glower at him. "I love you."

He leaned down and kissed her lips lightly, unable to help his smile. Then he bent and pressed his mouth to the blanket covering William's head. "And I love you."

He closed the horses inside the crippled villager's sty of a home and then met Theodora in the street once more. They left the village side by side, and Dori, true to her word, fell behind him gradually as they ascended the rise leading to Benningsgate Castle. He was grateful for that, for believing she would hide herself away when she ought. Constantine knew Theodora loved him, but he also knew she would not risk the son she had come so close to dying trying to save.

He could see the outline of the ruined keep and walls now, yellow light rippling up from the ward beyond. Many torches would be needed to create such a bright glow, and the thought of Felsteppe trying to use Benningsgate as a fortress against him caused a new, fresh fury to rise up in Constantine.

A smaller flare of yellow was now bobbing along inside the partially collapsed tunnel of the barbican, reflecting on the wall behind the fall of stones washed out on the road. Constantine's mind went briefly to that day, weeks and weeks ago now, when he had first returned to Benningsgate and wept on this road with the gravel in his hands.

A black shadow grew within the yellow glow—a sentry perhaps.

"Who goes there?" a man's voice called out with authority, and Constantine stopped in the center of the road. "Announce yourself or prepare to be cut down."

A lump formed in Constantine's throat as a sneer twisted his mouth. Despite the years that had passed, the regrets he held, the mistakes he had made and could never atone for in this life, in that moment, Constantine had returned to protect his family.

Patrice and Christian.

Dori and William.

He drew his sword and began walking forward once more.

"It is the master of this hold who approaches," Constantine said in a low and deadly voice, his weapon at the ready, his steps sure. "And I have come to reclaim what is mine."

"The true master of this hold is rumored dead," the voice taunted.

"The rumors are false. I am General Constantine Gerard and—"

He broke off as a piece of the yellow glow from within the barbican separated itself from the larger radiance and crept around the edge of the rubble. A single torch emerged and Constantine's heart hardened further when he saw that it was a young boy who carried it. It was clearly not this lad who had warned him away.

Constantine stopped. "Fetch your lord, boy," he growled. "He is using you. You'll only be hurt. Run, I say."

The boy shook his head, the torchlight glinting off his unruly blond hair and stared at Constantine.

Constantine looked sideways quickly as Dori appeared near his arm, holding William.

"What are you doing?" Constantine growled. "Go back to the village before you're seen, Theodora, for the love of God!"

But Dori also ignored his command. "It's you," she said, looking at the boy as if seeing a ghost. "I thought you got on the ship that night. The ship to—"

"Fallen Angels Abbey," the man's voice from earlier finished, and a tall shadow appeared from behind the rubble and stepped to the boy's side, placing a hand on his shoulder.

Constantine feared in that moment that he would faint, for the man's arm was tattooed with swirls and points of black.

"Adrian?" he choked.

Into the torchlight at Adrian's side stepped Maisie Lindsey. Then, on his other side, Valentine and Mary and Valentina; Isra and Roman,

Lou perched on his wide shoulder. Constantine's blurry gaze flew up to Benningsgate's ragged battlements as torches sprang into sight, held by soldiers whose fealty Constantine could not fathom.

He gasped a breath and looked back to the group of his brothers, his family, spearheaded by the little blond boy staring at Constantine. A boy Theodora somehow already knew, had sent away on a ship bound for Melk?

Adrian bent to one knee and took the torch from the boy's clutching fingers in such a gentle manner that it caused Constantine to shake his head as he tried to protect what little of his sanity remained.

Only Patrice's bones had been found in the ruin of the hall, beneath the single window.

If Lady Patrice had any consciousness in her, she would have tried to escape the hall with Master Christian by any means she could.

No . . .

"Papa," the boy said, clearly, firmly, looking straight at Constantine.

Constantine heard his sword clatter to the road. "Christian?" he wheezed on a sob.

And then, as if in a dream delivered directly from heaven, the boy's feet were pounding down the road as he ran toward Constantine, and once again he was brought to his knees before the ruins of his home.

But this time Christian was in his arms.

Constantine had not wept as he wept then since he was a boy much younger than the one he now held. His ragged sobs echoed and echoed off the stones; he shouted his gut-wrenching joy with his weeping, thanking God through his tears and his trembling for this miracle of all miracles. The greatest gift he'd ever been given, now received twice.

Theodora walked toward the man and the boy in the road, her own face awash with tears, as the group from the ruin came forward and they all met around Constantine and Christian. Dori felt conspicuous in this crowd of people who all seemed to know one another and in which she was the stranger.

Constantine stood, Christian still in his arms, and the boy caught sight of her. He leaned away from Constantine and patted his shoulder. Constantine turned so that both father and son regarded Dori.

"Is that your baby?" Christian asked her.

Dori nodded.

"I'm glad. A boy needs a mother," he said.

Dori smiled. "Even if she's not a good one?"

Christian reached the arm around Constantine's neck toward Dori and she stepped closer, reaching up to grasp his fingers in her own. But the boy tugged on her hand until his arm was around her shoulders, too, and he pressed his hot, damp cheek to hers.

"Thank you," Christian whispered. "For saving my father."

And then Constantine's arm also came around her, embracing all three of them. As Christian pulled himself aright, Constantine stepped back in order to look down into Dori's face.

"You put him on a ship to Melk?"

Dori shook her head. "I just gave him a coin."

The tattooed man, Adrian, spoke. "It was a Chastellet coin, Stan."

Constantine looked back to her. "You saved his life, Dori. You saved my son."

"No," Dori said, unwilling to further usurp the place that needed recognition. She looked at Christian. "Your mother saved your life, didn't she?"

"Glayer Felsteppe hurt Mother, Papa," Christian said, his chin flinching. "He burned the hall. She couldn't get up. But she put me in the window. I had to jump."

"But Christian, how?" Constantine said. "It's so far to the wall . . ."

The little boy looked into Constantine's eyes with a solemnity that was heartbreaking to Dori.

"There were men lying beneath the window. I hurt my leg when I jumped, so I lay there for a long time, waiting for Mother. But she never came. I reckoned later she knew she wouldn't be coming."

Dori closed her eyes for a moment, thinking of how terrified Christian must have been.

Constantine pulled the boy back into his arms, holding his blond head.

"I understand that you have much to catch up on, Stan," said a dark-haired, well-dressed man of swarthy complexion. "But do we no even get a simple hello?"

Constantine turned and set Christian on his feet, although his hand gripped his son's and did not let go as he fell into the embrace of his friends and their wives.

"Forgive me, all of you," Constantine said, looking at this one, gripping the arm of another, touching the red-haired woman's face. He turned to the largest man Dori had ever seen in her life, who claimed white-blond hair and carried a hunting bird on his shoulder. At his side was an exotic-looking woman whose wide-eyed expression gave Dori the idea that she was as anxious about this meeting as Dori herself was.

"Roman," Constantine said. "You, most of all—"

The giant of a man smiled. "It's all right, Stan."

The two men embraced, and then Constantine turned to the woman. "I'm so glad you're both safe."

"As we are you, my lord," the woman said.

Constantine frowned. "Isra, I'm not your lord."

Everyone in the group save Dori laughed, and Dori felt a lump in her throat again at the bond these people shared. She could never compete with them.

"It is good to see you once more, Stan." Isra laughed.

"Do they always call you *Stan*?" Dori blurted out, and everyone turned to look at her. She blinked and quirked her mouth, muttering, "It's dreadful."

The red-haired woman seemed to consider. "'Tis nae worse than Dori now, is it?"

A heartbeat of silence passed, and then the entire group roared with laughter.

Constantine pulled Dori to his side. "Friends, may I present Lady Theodora Rosemont and her son, William Calumet." He introduced each person to Dori, in reverse order to that in which she'd heard them speak, and when he got to the sweet-faced Mary, the woman rushed forward and embraced Dori.

"I'm so happy to meet you," she said, looking into Dori's eyes. "I just know we will become the best of friends. Sisters, you and I. And my home is close, just south at Beckham."

"At least until the king finds out, yes?" her handsome husband cautioned before turning to Constantine. "The soldiers along the wall are the king's. Er . . . *borrowed* from Beckham Hall."

"With a small amount of coin for incentive," Adrian admitted. "My father is coming with the men he can claim, but I don't expect them until after the sun has risen. Your loyal villagers are already inside the walls—they were keeping watch when we arrived."

"They knew a fight was coming," Constantine said grimly.

"Felsteppe left London before us," Theodora offered to the group. "If he has gone to Thurston Hold, he might be warned that Constantine and I are here. He could be upon us at any moment."

As if in an attempt to point to the truth of her words, a shout called down from the wall walk. "Party approaching the village! Perhaps fifty mounted!"

"Papa," Christian said suddenly, grasping at Constantine's tunic. "He's coming! Let's go! Let's just go! We can go away somewhere—all of us—and live. Maybe with Adrian's father and brother. They have cows and pasties," he said, his voice thready with desperation. "And a gate. We can hide!"

Constantine squatted down to eye level with his son. "I know you're frightened, Christian. I would much rather go away with you and Lady Dori and William. Somewhere we could try to forget all this and start over. But the bad man who harmed you and your mother, he has also harmed Lady Dori and William. He's harmed our friends and their families. He is responsible for the deaths of many good men where Papa was away for so long."

Constantine stroked the side of his son's face as he continued. "I made promises when I married your beautiful mother. And when I became a general. And when I swore to help exonerate my brothers' names. And I also made a promise to the man who's done all those terrible things; that I would hold him responsible. I want to make very, very certain that he never harms anyone ever again. It's my duty, son. And Adrian and Valentine and Roman, and the men you see atop our wall there, they are going to help me keep my promise. You understand?"

"You can't go away again," Christian whispered.

Constantine shook his head. "I won't." He leaned forward until his nose touched his son's. "I promise you."

Christian's gaze was dropped to the road and his brow was furrowed. Dori jostled William into one arm and wrapped her other around Christian.

"Come along to the wall with us," she said to the boy. "We'll all wait for your papa there."

Christian turned away from Constantine into Dori's skirt but didn't say anything.

"One thousand yards!" the soldier shouted down from the wall.

Constantine rose and took his sword from Adrian.

"Go into the ward," Constantine said, glancing at Dori as he removed his cloak and tossed it aside. The rest of his friends seemed also to be readying for battle, withdrawing long daggers and swords. The large man, Roman, produced a pair of hammers.

"Five hundred yards!"

Dori seemed rooted to the road, where she could feel the vibration of the riders through the soles of her shoes, and she turned her head, wanting to see with her own eyes. William stirred and began to cry.

"Theodora!" Constantine shouted and she looked to him. "Go!"

Dori looked over her shoulder and saw that Mary Beckham was already retreating with her daughter, albeit reluctantly, also looking back at the road as she walked. Maisie Lindsey and Isra had both failed to heed the orders of their men.

Dori wanted Glayer Felsteppe to see that she was alive. That she was alive and had William. She wanted him to see her face before he died, to know that he had not beaten her.

But she felt the hands in her skirt, the weight of the boy hanging on them. Christian, who had borne too much for his young age. She looked down at his panicked, pale face and felt his fright.

"I don't want to go," he whispered up at her. "I don't want to leave my papa."

It would require little bravery for her to face Felsteppe now, but it would cost her all her will to let her moment of revenge go in order to protect the precious children now in her care.

She withdrew her arm from his shoulder in order to grasp his hand. "Come, Christian," she said firmly. "Let's hurry and do as your father asks. We don't wish to worry him." And she turned and ran with the boys up the road toward the ruin, following in Mary Beckham's wake.

Chapter 26

Constantine stood in the center of the road, facing down the slope toward the deserted village, his head lowered, his gaze trained on the gravel just beginning to lighten in the predawn. He could feel the stones of Benningsgate Castle at his back, bolstering him, anchoring him to this place—this land and people who brought him here, brought him back, called him to stay.

Patrice. Christian. Theodora and William.

Henry, his king.

His villagers, those who had stayed and those he would one day welcome home again.

The three men now standing at his side.

Constantine felt a hand clap his back and looked to his right as Adrian Hailsworth squeezed his shoulder. He looked to his left and saw Roman Berg's grim countenance staring down the road; just past him, Valentine held a slender dagger in his teeth while he shrugged out of his short cape and adjusted his sleeves. He armed himself with a flourish and then glanced at Stan with a roguish smile.

The first of the riders appeared around the bend of the road, their mounts like ghostly dragons in the morning mist, the steam coming from their nostrils like dull, gray smoke. The riders parted in the middle, veering to either side of the road and opening up to expose the rotten heart of the party of king's men and hired mercenaries, and the man who comprised it.

Glayer Felsteppe slowed to a canter and then a walk as he saw the four men stretched across the road before Benningsgate. His face was blank, his eyes black in his face and darting from man to man, to the torches along the battlement. Then he looked at Constantine, and a sudden smirk erupted over his once slender face, now bloated and pocked with excess.

"Glutton for punishment, aren't you, Gerard?" he taunted. "Just had to come back to see for yourself all that I've won. Didn't believe me, did you? That I'd make you pay."

Constantine cocked his head. "What exactly have you won, Felsteppe?"

He held his gauntleted hands from his sides with a laugh, as if indicating all that was around them. "Everything!"

Constantine shook his head. "Nothing."

"Benningsgate is mine, Gerard," Felsteppe needled with a grating chuckle. "What's left of it any matter."

Constantine shook his head again. "No. It's not." He began walking slowly toward Felsteppe.

"I've the decree from the king on my very person," Felsteppe boasted. "It grants me the lands and title of Benningsgate."

"I know exactly what it says. Perhaps you should have read it more carefully. Benningsgate would only ever fall to you if I should die without an heir," Constantine clarified, stopping twenty feet before Felsteppe's horse. "The king gave me my own copy of the decree just last night."

"I hate to be the one to deliver bad news," Felsteppe said in sotto voce over the neck of his mount. "But I'm actually planning on bringing that about in a moment."

"Wrong again," Constantine argued. "My son and heir is alive and well, just behind me at Benningsgate. In fact, Lady Theodora is watching after him. And Reginald Calumet's son, whom your own mother gave over quite willingly once she learned the truth about him. About you."

He saw Felsteppe's first wobble of confidence, then, the draining of blood from his paunchy face in the pearly light. The man adjusted himself in his saddle, his eyes darting to the soldiers, who looked at one another uneasily, around him.

"No matter that," Felsteppe announced loudly, and then he pointed to the battlements. "Take the ruin. Kill anyone you find inside. Especially any women and children."

The mercenaries started forward but then hesitated, turning their horses sideways when they weren't followed.

"Did I stutter?" Felsteppe screamed, his composure clearly threadbare. "Go!"

The outfitted soldier closest to Felsteppe wore a hard expression. "We're to protect the interests of the king, my lord. The men atop the wall are Henry's own—our brothers in arms. We will not attack a fortress being held by them."

"Then what good are you?" Felsteppe shrieked, causing his horse to dance. He growled and then looked at the handful of mercenaries. "Fine. The rest of you, then."

The soldier moved his horse closer. "Nay, Lord Felsteppe. We are sworn to protect the English army. If your hired swords attack, we will defend against the shedding of the soldiers' blood."

Constantine set the tip of his sword in the gravel and rested his hands atop the hilt. "Get down from your horse, Felsteppe. Face me."

"You shut up," Felsteppe said, pointing at Constantine. "You don't command me. You never did. I'll deal with you when I'm ready."

"Hello," a smooth Spanish voice called out from behind Constantine, and Valentine came sauntering down the road toward Felsteppe. "Remember me? I would also like for you to come down from your horse now. We both know my aim is good at this distance, yes? I almost killed you once. This time I will make sure you are dead."

"If the Spaniard comes another step closer, cut him down," Felsteppe said, and Constantine could hear the panic in Felsteppe's voice as Roman and Adrian stepped forward, once more completing the front line. Felsteppe glanced at the English commander, as if waiting for the man to thwart him yet again. "If any of them come closer."

Instead, the soldier looked to Constantine. "As the rightful lord of this hold, do you require the aid of the crown in defending yourself?"

Constantine looked to the men at either side of him and then took measure of the handful of mercenaries surrounding Felsteppe. He looked back to the commander.

"Give my regards to the king."

"Very well." The soldier wheeled around and delivered the command that rallied all the king's troops in Henry's name.

"You can't leave," Felsteppe protested. "The king gave you over to my command!"

Another rumbling shook the road, then, causing Felsteppe to be further startled and turn his horse to face the oncoming sound.

The dawn caught the pieces of steel and weaponry hanging from the army that rushed up the road in an undulating wave, the coarse brown wool of vassals interspersed with bright white mantles, marked in the center with bold red crosses.

Herne Hailsworth, his beard blowing behind him, led the advance, flanked by a man who could only be Adrian's brother. On the other side of Lord Hailsworth, three men more familiar to Constantine sat astride.

The skinny abbot smiled at the four blocking the road to the castle as he drew his mount up just behind the party milling around Felsteppe, trapping the villain on the road. "Good day, Brothers."

"Victor!" Roman announced, the surprise in his voice unmistakable.

"Ugh," Valentine muttered. "No the twins."

The commander of the English forces surveyed the scene with satisfaction on his face. "This is obviously a church matter now. My liege would not be pleased should we interfere. Good day, my lord," he said to Constantine, and then raised his arm in signal and led Henry's soldiers down through the valley of the village, flowing through and around the Templars and men accompanying the Hailsworth father and son.

Felsteppe's mercenaries had been made visibly nervous by the increased forces obviously against them.

"Do you recall the promise I made you the last time we met, Felsteppe?" Constantine said easily, drawing the red-haired man's attention once more.

"I don't remember a word you've ever spoken," Felsteppe hissed with contempt, but his eyes were wild.

"I remember," Adrian offered.

Valentine nodded. "I was no there, but I have heard the story several times now."

"Tell us again, Stan," Roman prompted.

"I promised," Constantine obliged, "that the very next time I saw you, I would kill you."

He saw the man's throat convulse.

"It has been a long time coming, Felsteppe," Constantine said. "And you have done naught but add to your long list of evils. There is much—and many—to which you will be obliged to answer this day."

Then a bloodcurdling howl came from the ruin behind the men as the first true golden rays shot through the tops of the tree branches of the wood. It was not human, and yet it didn't sound like any dog or wolf Constantine had ever heard. Certainly not the amiable Erasmus.

At Constantine's side, Adrian's gaze seemed to search the lightening sky above him, and then his eyes closed and he turned up his face. "My God, Stan, can you hear them? Listen . . ."

The only thing Constantine heard was another terrifying howl, and then a young voice he recognized.

"Garulf! Garulf! No, come back!"

They turned on the road to see Dunny's strange uncle scrambling over the rubble before the barbican, but the man was not standing erect; he was crouched on his haunches, his hair seeming to have grown down his face. Garulf let out another bloodcurdling wail.

"Piece blood duvenet," Adrian whispered, his voice full of awe.

And then the air was filled with a symphony of shouts and howls, the very dawn seemed to vibrate, and to either side of the ruin of Benningsgate, all along the crest of the ridge appeared a line of shadows—beasts on both two and four legs, in the shapes of wolf and bear and man.

"Shite," the leader of the mercenaries whispered in awe. And then he turned to Felsteppe, shaking his head. "No. No. We're finished here."

"You're not finished!" Felsteppe shouted. "I paid you!"

"You didn't pay us enough," the man muttered and wheeled his horse around, leading his small band of comrades away in a run.

"As I said," Constantine began again after Felsteppe was left alone, the wall of warrior monks and stout, laboring men from Clifty Wood behind him, the Brotherhood and all manner of strange, vengeful beasts before him at Benningsgate. "You have much to answer for."

Felsteppe only stared at him.

Constantine's brows lowered. "Dismount your horse."

"You don't command me," he said again, his voice strangled in his throat.

One of the twins spoke up, withdrawing a shockingly large sword from his robes. "I shall assist you in dismounting, dastardly foe of Christendom."

"No," his twin argued, bringing forth his own weapon with a ringing hiss. "*I* shall assist the reprehensible enemy!"

"You killed the last one!"

"Let off, Brother. It was six years ago and my sword thirsts."

"What of *my* sword? Ladislav, I do vow that you're the most self-ish man I've ever had the misfortune of meeting."

"Yes? Well, *you're* vulgar and discourteous!"

Constantine strode forward in the midst of the distraction and reached up and grabbed Felsteppe's leather hauberk, jerking the man from his saddle and onto the packed gravel of the road. The group went silent as Felsteppe skittered backward on his hands and boots, stumbled to his feet, fumbled to withdraw his sword.

The ringing hiss of a hundred weapons answered his.

Constantine only walked toward the man calmly. "You killed my wife. Burned my home. Fouled my name. You separated me from my son—years I can never regain."

Felsteppe was backing slowly away from Constantine, closer to the wood. "I warned you! I warned you to let me be—I told you I would see everything you loved burn! You didn't believe I could, but I did!"

"You caused the slaughter at Chastellet," Roman Berg called from behind. "Destroyed the greatest thing I'd ever built. You are responsible for the deaths of many good men. You tried to kill my friends. My only family."

"Many good men," Adrian emphasized. "And innocents who had done nothing more than try to protect the last bit of hope and goodness in this world. You had hand in the destruction of its holy sanctuary." His voice broke.

Glayer sneered at Adrian's emotion. "Crybaby."

"You are filth," Valentine added with a disgusted curl of his lip. "The worst slime on the earth. You thought to take my wife from me—my Maria. And my brothers." He raised his blade. "I've wished to see you dead for a very, very long time."

Running footfalls sounded on the gravel road, and then Dori's cry.

"Christian, no! Come back!"

"Papa, stop! Don't!" the boy shouted, running into the midst of the group and stopping himself by grabbing great handfuls of his father's tunic. "Don't, Papa. You can't."

"Christian, go back to Lady Dori at once."

"No." Christian gasped and then looked over his shoulder with fearful eyes at Glayer Felsteppe. "You can't kill him."

Constantine shook his head. "Christian, he must pay for what he's done. He's a bad man."

"You can't all kill him!" the boy shouted, turning around to look at the group of battle- and life-hardened men towering over him. "One of you can strike the blow, but how do you decide which when he has wronged you all? Wronged those who aren't here to have their revenge. If killing him brings you justice, what of the others who can't speak for themselves? Where is their justice?"

Christian wheeled around with his fists clenched and glared at Glayer Felsteppe. He stepped forward haltingly and then stopped, sniffing and drawing a deep breath before turning his whole wrath upon Glayer Felsteppe, until Christian's narrow neck was taut with strain.

"I hate you! I hate you! You took my mother away from me! I wish you were dead!" Christian turned back to face his father, and Constantine's stomach clenched at his son's red eyes, the clear snot on his upper lip. "But you can't do it, Papa. It's not your duty."

Constantine didn't know how Felsteppe moved so quickly, but in a blink he had jerked Christian by the arm and dragged him up against his chest.

"Foolish boy," he said with a cackle and a smile. "Lovely, foolish boy! I thank you! Yes, I do!" He kissed Christian's cheek as Constantine rushed forward fruitlessly, Roman Berg's unyielding arms restraining him.

"Ah-ah!" Felsteppe panted, edging closer to the wood. "I'll kill him and you know it. We're going to slip into the trees here and away, Christian and I."

"Let him go!" Constantine screamed, the fabric of his sanity worn down to the last threads as his nightmare bloomed to life before him.

"Yes, let him go, Glayer," a woman's voice echoed.

Eseld stepped from the wood behind Felsteppe, her gray hair hanging from its undone coil, her gray face a mass of creases and sorrow.

"He's my only means of escape, Mother," Felsteppe panted, seeming unsurprised at the old woman's sudden appearance. "I'm taking him with me. Are you coming or nay?"

Eseld smiled at him. "Of course I'm coming with you. But we'll be leaving the boy with his father."

"Are you daft, woman?" Felsteppe demanded. "As soon as I turn him loose, I'll be struck down!"

Eseld turned to Constantine then, and he could see the light in her eyes was gone. The madness had fully claimed her, and she had sunk into its embrace.

"You'll let me take him, won't you, milord?" she asked calmly. "You'll let his own mother take him certainly. It's my place after all. I should have taken him away years ago, when he was born."

"Give me my unharmed son and I won't touch you," Constantine vowed in a low voice, understanding at last. "None here shall. Upon my word."

"See?" Eseld looked back to Felsteppe, a smile on her old, weary, scarred face. "Turn him loose, Glayer."

"Stan," Valentine chastised. "We can no just let him go, after all these years."

"Yes, we can," Constantine said. He met Felsteppe's gaze. "I retract my vow to kill you. Christian is right—it's not my duty."

Felsteppe let Christian slide down his front, but he kept a tight hold on his arm for one moment while the boy struggled to break free. He did at last and bolted to Constantine, throwing himself against his father.

Constantine held Christian's face pressed to his tunic, turned away from the sight of the fiend and his dam.

"Fetch my horse, Mother," Felsteppe commanded, brandishing his sword in a laughable display, as if he would hold off the men before him.

"We don't need your horse where we're going," Eseld said, walking toward him with a smile.

"I'm certainly not walking." Felsteppe sneered at her.

She stood close to him, reaching up with one trembling hand and stroking his face. "I tried my best to love you," she said through quivering lips. "It wasn't your fault in the beginning. But I just couldn't," she said in a coo, raising her eyebrows.

Then Eseld's left hand shot up from her skirts, burying the dagger clenched in her fist beneath Glayer Felsteppe's ribs as he gasped.

"You ruined my life," Eseld said through gritted teeth.

Constantine held Christian's head against his tunic. "Don't look," he whispered.

Felsteppe raised his own blade and drove it into the woman's back. Eseld gave a feeble cry and seemed to gather her strength to withdraw her blade and pierce him a second time.

They collapsed to the dirt together, staring with black malevolence into each other's eyes as first Felsteppe and then Eseld breathed no more.

The road was as silent as the tomb for which it currently acted for the pathetic pair fallen in the weeds. Only the hush of the wind, the creaking of saddle leather, and the scrape of hoof disturbed the silence.

A sobbing breath erupted from Constantine's chest. He picked up Christian and held him high against his body, still keeping his son's face averted from the carnage, and walked up the road toward Benningsgate. He felt more than heard his brothers behind him.

Once he was halfway to the ruin, the line of beings along the ridge of Benningsgate charged down toward the village, setting the road beneath Stan's feet vibrating. The air was filled with howls and the gnashing of teeth, the Latin drone of the Templars, and later, the sound and smell of a crackling blaze.

The odor was sulfurous.

Epilogue

January 1183
Thurston Hold

Adrian stalked into the room, barely managing to swerve around Christian and William, who were lying on the thick rug before the hearth, playing with one of Adrian's own discarded models. He lost his preoccupied frown for a moment to smile down and wink at the older boy before once more shaking the plans in his hand at Constantine.

"A word, Stan," he called.

"Yes," Constantine answered emphatically while holding up his palm, causing Adrian to cock an eyebrow at him as he unceremoniously shoved the cups to the edges of the table and spread the vellum across the top.

"I think he means it, Adrian," Dori said with a smile in her voice, picking up her own cup and moving it out of harm's way. "Constantine has complete faith in your and Roman's expertise."

"Yes, of course he does," Adrian said with a frown, "but we've had an idea that changes the north wall. If we entrench this lower level here"—he drew his long finger down the side of the line of the proposed corridor—"and add a second set of stairs here..." He pointed to the darker-inked square currently outside the wall. "The perfect location for the storage of armaments, accessible to the soldiers should they need them at a moment's notice, in the case of a siege or what have you."

"The oratory," Constantine said and met Dori's eyes, already large and fearful at the thought.

"It's in remarkable condition," Adrian continued, oblivious to

Stan's wife's distress. "Built in the old style. It would greatly add to the structure of the new gatehouse, as well as be of immense practical use. I don't know why we didn't include it in the first place."

"No, Aid," Constantine said quietly.

Adrian raised his eyes. "You really want it filled in?"

Constantine glanced at Dori, who had turned her face away to gaze at the boys still playing on the floor.

"We do," he said to Adrian.

Adrian sighed and stood aright, rerolling his plans. "Fine. It's your keep. By the way, Victor said he will be ready for us after supper."

Constantine laughed. "Supper was two hours ago."

"I was occupied with other things," Adrian said without apology. "You know Valentine will be late any matter. He can barely tear himself away from little Mariette long enough to run through Beckham the stolen cargo Francisco brings in."

"I'd go see them next week," Dori said, ignoring completely the fact that they were discussing piracy on English soil. "Before it snows again."

Constantine rose from his chair and took a leaning step toward Dori to place a kiss on the crown of her head. "If it's too late, we'll stay in the village with Roman and Isra."

"I don't think so," Dori called out in a singsong voice.

He followed Adrian from the room with a smile, reaching down to ruffle Christian's hair and poke at William's ribs as he left, eliciting grins from both boys.

"I'll return in a bit," he said.

Christian nodded. "I know, Papa."

"I don't see why we have to do this tonight," Constantine complained as they rode through the frosty evening toward Benningsgate. "It's dark and cold. The wine was good and warm. So is my wife."

Adrian glanced at Constantine. "You really don't remember?"

"Remember what?"

"It's a year ago today you left Melk."

Constantine looked around himself at the countryside, crisp in the cold, bright moonlight, and took a deep breath, realizing Adrian spoke true. Only one year ago he had been certain his life was over. His chest tightened, and he was glad his friend allowed the silence to ride between them the rest of the way to Benningsgate.

They came into the village past the new barns and the recently graveled section of road leading past the skeletal structure of the manor house where Roman and Isra would eventually live, and on to the little rise where Benningsgate folk had been buried for years.

Where Patrice was buried, now under a finely hewn stone crafted by Roman himself.

Constantine saw the black outlines of the three men waiting for them on the hill, the slender shadows of stakes marking the squared corners of the chapel that would soon be built. He and Dori would bring their sons to that chapel once the keep proper was finished, leaving Adrian and Maisie to oversee Thurston Hold in guardianship for William.

"Good evening, Father," Constantine called to Victor as he swung down from his horse. "Sorry to keep you waiting."

"It's no trouble, Constantine." The old abbot smiled. "Brother Valentine only arrived a quarter hour ago."

"Right again," Adrian murmured smugly.

"Allow me to guess: he only told you about the meeting . . . when? Two hours past supper, I say," Valentine queried. "I had no wish to stand out in this freezing weather for longer than I need."

Roman swung his arms and took a deep breath. "It's not even cold, Val."

Valentine flapped a hand in a rolling motion. "Victor? Can we just get on with it, please?"

Constantine looked down at the large, square stone set near a shallow hole between a pair of tapered stakes. Without word, the men begin rifling through their tunics and satchels, producing small items they kept hidden in their hands.

Victor looked at each man in turn, waiting for their nod. And then the old abbot brought forth a prayer book and opened it in the moonlight, calling down God's blessing upon Fallen Angels Chapel. He looked up at Valentine, who tossed a small round item into the air over the hole. The moonlight glinted off the gold as it spun and then fell into the dark square with a soft plunk.

"May we and all who seek solace here hold close to the family we have found and the families we will create," he said in a tone of rare solemnity. "Knowing that it is the greatest wealth."

Adrian stepped forward and then knelt in the soft, cold loam to place his Chastellet coin deliberately in the bottom of the hole, next to Valentine's. "May we always be wise enough to believe in one another and in miracles." He paused there a moment, his eyes closed in the foggy glow, before rising to his feet.

"My hope is that we remember how strong each of us has had to be on our own," Roman said, leaning forward to drop his own coin in the hole. "And how much stronger we proved to be together."

Constantine felt the weight of his friends' gazes resting on him as he bounced the coin in his palm, looking into the dark hole for a long moment. "May we always remember our duties. And remind one another of them should we forget or become lost." Stan dropped his coin into the hole, hearing its clink as it joined the other three.

Victor recited a final prayer from the book before closing it and placing a reverent kiss on its worn leather cover. He bent and laid it atop the Chastellet gold.

The four men moved at once and without comment to the square stone, each taking a side and straining to slide the heavy rock into place over the hole, covering their pasts, sealing the promise of their futures. Their hands met in the center of the chapel's cornerstone for a brief moment.

Valentine was the first to withdraw. "And now, I bid you all a good night," he said. "I shall see you again when the weather does no threaten to turn my warmest parts to ice."

Constantine laughed. "Expect Dori in a few days."

"That will make Maria very happy," he said with a smile. He clapped Stan's shoulder and moved away into the darkness as the men wished him farewell.

Then Roman looked to Victor. "Do you need me for anything else this night, Father? Nell is teaching Isra to sew, and I'd fetch Lou from Jeremy's lest Erasmus suffer further damage."

"Go, go," the abbot said, waving him away. "I'd have a word with Brother Stan and then make my way to the cottage. Good night."

"Good night." Roman looked briefly to Constantine and Adrian, who returned his casual wave.

Adrian walked past Stan and embraced Victor unabashedly. "I'll look in on the barn. They say the doors are ready to be hung. God bless you, Father."

"God bless you, Brother Adrian."

Constantine and Victor continued to stand together on the rise after Adrian had mounted his horse and ridden down the slope, each of them looking at the fat, round moon in silence. Stan knew it wasn't that night, but he could feel that the priest's time with the brothers was drawing to an end.

"Going back to Melk soon," he said.

Victor sighed. "Yes. Hilbert should have everyone cowering in fear by now. If Wynn hasn't fed him to the tigers."

Constantine chuckled and took hold of his horse's reins, walking with Victor down the slope.

"There are Chastellet coins still unaccounted for, Constantine," the priest said. "Perhaps they are only lost. Or in someone's money chest. Or already melted down. But it is possible others might seek me, begging help for whatever hopeless cause they have been made victims."

Constantine pulled the horse to a gentle stop in order to look directly at his old friend. "Then we will help them, won't we, Victor? Isn't that our duty now? To be the last hope of the hopeless because we ourselves were so long without it?"

Victor nodded. "I thought you'd say as much. I think you know by now that I'm not a prideful man in most things, Constantine. But I find myself believing more and more of late that helping the four of you was the reason God sent me to Melk as a young man all those years ago. And I'm quite proud of you all."

Constantine returned the priest's nod with a thickness in his throat that prevented any reply. Thankfully, Victor had one more piece of information to impart, sparing Stan the burden of conversation for another moment.

"I've found a rector for Fallen Angels Chapel," he said brightly and suddenly as they headed once more down the slope. "A young man, just entered into study, but he should be more than ready to take on duties by the time construction is complete."

"That is good news," Constantine said.

"Yes," Victor nodded. "Ethan Carmichael is his name." Victor was quiet for a heartbeat of time. "I knew his father."

They came to the bottom of the hill where the road split into two paths. Victor continued on toward the village without pause, lifting his hand and glancing over his shoulder at Stan a final time. "Good night."

"Good night, Victor." Constantine watched the priest's outline meld with the shadows and disappear.

Then Constantine turned his gaze up to the black outline of the castle ruin, silhouetted against the infinite, star-pricked heaven above. He stared at it for a long time.

And then, having done his duty, he swung up onto his horse and went home.

Author's Note

I hope you have enjoyed spending time with Valentine, Adrian, Roman, and Constantine as much as I've enjoyed creating them. This was the longest series I've done to date and the most challenging! A couple things before I go:

Chastellet is a real place, and the Battle at Jacob's Ford really happened. I tried to re-create the siege and its aftermath to the best of my ability, but of course I've taken a great deal of creative liberty with the whole thing. The Templar fortress was indeed abandoned after the massacre, buried by years and sand until the last several years, when archaeologists rediscovered and began to excavate the ancient site.

Although Fallen Angels Abbey is fictitious, Melk Abbey on the Danube River is not. The abbey from the Brotherhood of Fallen Angels is based on the historic Melk, before it was completely rebuilt in the Baroque style as it exists today. According to the abbey's own website, "In the order of importance of the rooms in a Benedictine monastery, the library comes second only to the church." And the libraries are indeed magnificent, including one called the "small library room," where a spiral staircase leads up to another area of the library, which is not open to the public.

Perhaps one day someone will figure out how to get the stone door open.

ABOUT THE AUTHOR

Before writing historical romance, **Heather Grothaus** worked as a successful freelance journalist, short story writer, and magazine writer. She lives with her family on a small farm in Kentucky.

Readers can visit her online at www.heathergrothaus.com or connect with her on twitter and Goodreads.